BETA
A TECHNOLOGICAL NIGHTMARE
SAMMY SCOTT

BETA: A Technological Nightmare
Print edition ISBN: 9798398008593

First edition: September 2023
10 9 8 7 6 5 4 3 2 1

Contact the author here:
ScribeSammyScott@gmail.com

On Facebook:
@Sammy Scott - Author

ALSO BY SAMMY SCOTT
At Home With the Horrors: 14 Chilling Tales (2022)

"Sammy Scott cements his status as a rising voice in horror fiction, and an author to watch—and to fear—in the genre."
— Ronald Malfi, bestselling author of *Come with Me*

"The finest horror anthology I've read in a decade. Sammy's work elevates the craft to a literary tier seldom reached by new authors. As a reader, this collection fascinated me, and as a writer, it intimidated me."
— Felix Blackwell, author of *Stolen Tongues*

"Disturbingly terrifying. A masterpiece of short-story suspense. ★★★★★"
— ML Rayner, author of *Echoes of Home*

"Sammy Scott is one of those rare talents able to craft tales so chilling that they needle their way under your skin and turn to ice in your veins. I can honestly say that his debut short story collection, *At Home With the Horrors*, is the best I've read to date."
— Elizabeth J. Brown, author of
The Laughing Policeman

"Sammy Scott doesn't rely on familiar tricks to disturb you. Each one of his chilling tales burrows into your psyche and refuses to leave, leering over your shoulder long after you've left its pages. The horrors in his writing are of the uncanny variety, making him as much Stanley Kubrick as he is Rod Serling. This is one author who knows how to terrorize."
—Nick Roberts, author of *The Exorcist's House*

For Cole:
Never stop imaginationating.

CHAPTER ONE
DAY 1

The house was a rectangle of glass and glossy white paneling, resting like a massive box in the middle of its sparse, flat, multi-acre lawn. Five rectangular windows, devoid of any shutters on the exterior as well as any apparent shades or curtains on the interior, gaped black and yawning. There was a solitary front door and a single front-facing garage door, both closed, both as flat, shiny, and white as a marker board. The roof, like the lid of a shoebox, was a level plane that overhung the structure by mere inches, providing but a sliver of shade from the noonday sun.

Michael Danvers stood on the curb and studied the house.

And the house studied him back.

The street contained no other residences besides this one. The paved road in front of it stretched out several hundred yards in both directions, well beyond Michael's view. There was room enough, he assumed, for more houses to be built over time and the neighborhood to expand. For now, however, it was just the one, and it was to be Michael's home for the next three months.

Michael detected a slight thrumming, a gentle pulse emanating from the house itself. It was nearly imperceptible, yet he could feel it from several feet away, tickling at the fine, invisible hairs on his upper cheeks and forehead. The faint sound touched him, pushed at him gently in rhythmic waves. It held him at bay no more than a light breeze would, but he could not deny a sense of foreboding, an insinuation that perhaps he should leave.

The garage door lifted. Behind him, the driverless car—sleek and silver with opaque windows—turned into the driveway and pulled inside, its motor quieter than the buzzing of hummingbird wings. Once the car was tucked away, the garage door lowered again.

Michael stepped onto the sandy white sidewalk that led to the front door. The grass on either side of the cement was perfectly manicured, every blade standing at uniform attention, but there were no bushes, flowers, or trees, no other natural landscaping of any kind. The house looked as if it had simply been dropped in the middle of a level green field and could just as easily be plucked up again at a moment's notice without leaving much evidence that it was ever even there.

The starkness of both the house and the ground around it existed in harmony with the heat of the day; there was hardly a shadow to be found anywhere. The sun blazed unforgivingly in the cloudless blue sky above and the white house unapologetically reflected much of its light.

The building was so tall, looming over Michael as he took his first steps toward the front door, that at first he thought it might be two stories. But looking again at the front windows, which were long and narrow, extending from the base of the wall to nearly the roof's edge, he determined that no, it was in fact only the one.

Michael felt strangely naked as he approached the house. He carried nothing on his person except the clothes he was wearing and his driver's license, which was tucked into the pocket of his jeans. He had been told to leave behind his cell phone, his laptop, toiletries, any additional items of clothing—all of the things that would be at the top of a list if one was packing for an extended stay away from home. Lacking all of these necessities, Michael was acutely aware of the emptiness of his hands, and he could not shake the nagging feeling that he was forgetting something, even though that was exactly what he had been instructed to do. He wondered with dark amusement if this was how convicts felt when beginning a stint in prison.

He stopped at the door. There was no knob to grasp. He put his hand on the glossy white surface, which was surprisingly cool to the touch, and pushed gently. It didn't move, but he sensed a slight vibration in his fingertips when he touched it, turning them mildly numb. He cocked his head to the side to look into the adjacent window, but saw nothing except his own reflection: his short-cropped brown hair, his furrowed brow (now beaded with sweat), and a confused look in his eyes.

"Hello?" he said, rapping lightly on the door.

A whirring sound drew Michael's attention upwards. A circular panel the size of a fist opened above the door. A camera lens emerged, mounted on a thin finger of metal and wire, and turned to look down on him like a large blue eye.

"Hello, Michael," said a voice. Its tone was deep but feminine, as warm and silky as mother's milk. "Please come in."

There was a soft *click*, and the door in front of Michael opened slowly with a pleasant hiss. He stepped inside, hearing the camera retract and its panel close behind him. Lights dawned as he entered the room, revealing a grand kitchen. The air was pleasantly cool inside, almost chilly after the heat of the summer sun. He pulled rapidly on the front of his gray t-shirt, fanning himself. The soaked-in sweat turned icy.

The room smelled fresh, but not with the expected scents of plywood and plaster like most new constructions. The air was permeated by the odor of plastic accompanied by a hint of something slightly antiseptic, an aroma reminiscent of a hospital ward.

As Michael stepped over the tile floor, which was immaculate and highly reflective, his sneakers did not make a sound. In the wall to his left was a tall panel that he assumed was the door to a closet or pantry, next to which was a floor-to-ceiling opening that led further into the house. Across from him was a U-shaped counter that wrapped from the left of the room all the way around to the other side, broken up only by a large sink in the center that sat under a row of windows extending from the countertop to the high ceiling. Above the counters on either side were a series of cabinets. Under one of these cabinets was what appeared to be a microwave, only it had no window and no handle. There was in fact not a handle anywhere in sight, not on the cabinet doors nor at the sink.

In the center of the room was an island lined on one side by four bar stools on silver pedestals. The island itself appeared to be floating about a foot off the floor, and Michael tipped his head to see if he could spot what it was actually resting upon. Whether it was a trick of the light or perhaps a reflective base, he couldn't be certain, but he could distinguish no physical supports. The illusion of levitation was flawless.

To Michael's right and just inside the front door was a large translucent blue dining table surrounded by eight white, ergonomically shaped chairs. No two chairs were alike, and their shapes were so fluid and organic they looked almost like sculptures. Resting on the table was a cube-shaped box with a lid and a tag that read, "Open me." Feeling a bit like he had just stepped through the looking glass, Michael walked over, lifted the lid, and looked inside.

Within the box were two more boxes: one small and square, the other flat and rectangular. The flat one contained a cell phone, its black screen framed in white plastic. As Michael picked it up, its display glowed the time (12:08 p.m.), the date (Sun, May 23), the outside temperature (91 degrees Fahrenheit), and the battery level (100%). He regarded it only for a moment before sliding it casually into his back pocket. The second box contained what appeared to be a bracelet. White and rigid, it held its oblong shape even when not being worn. When he picked it up, a glowing blue digital readout displayed the words, "Wear me." Michael put it over his left wrist, and as it latched together of its own accord with a muted *click,* it conformed perfectly to the size of his wrist, one end disappearing into the other like a snake eating its own tail.

Beyond the dining table on the right were two more doors, both closed. Michael knew from seeing the exterior of the house that one of these doors must lead to the garage. The other remained a mystery. A bedroom, perhaps.

Everything in the room with the exception of the dining table was either silver or the same stark white as the house's exterior. What little wall space that remained held no paintings or decorations of any kind. The room was almost completely lacking in color save for the blue sky visible through the windows.

"Hello, Michael," the voice said again. It seemed to be coming from nowhere and everywhere all at once. "How are you today?"

Michael smiled. "I'm good." He paused for a moment before asking, "How are you?"

"I am fine, thank you. My name is Ella. I am your Electronic Life Assistant. I am happy to finally meet you."

"Me too." He felt awkward, as he often did anytime he interacted with the likes of an Alexa or a Siri. Like he was pretending. Play-acting.

"Is there anything I can get you?" she asked.

Michael considered. "I would love some water," he answered.

"Certainly," said Ella. "It is quite warm outside today. Unseasonably so."

Across the kitchen, there was a gentle mechanical sound. Below one of the cabinets, where Michael had spotted what he assumed to be a windowless, button-free microwave, a panel popped open. He walked over and found inside it an unlabeled bottle of water, so cold that there were slivers of ice floating at the top. He unscrewed the lid, which he flicked with his thumb onto the counter, and drank. The water was smooth and frigid with only the slightest mineral flavor—exactly how he liked it. He downed half of it and sighed, then winced against a brief cold headache. "Thank you," he said, squeezing his left eye shut until the pain abated.

"You're welcome," said Ella. "Is it to your liking?"

"It's perfect."

"Noted," said Ella. "Do you require anything else at this time? Lunch will be served promptly at one o'clock p.m. Today's menu includes a chicken and pear salad with goat cheese and candied walnuts. But if you are hungry now, I can provide a light snack."

"I'm fine."

"How was your trip?"

"It was… good," he said, considering, silently realizing that he couldn't actually recall much of it, as he had inadvertently nodded off at various points along the way. He had no idea why he had been so tired.

"Very good. Do you require anything else at the moment?"

"I'd love a tour."

"Certainly," said Ella. "This"—a pause—"is the kitchen."

Michael hesitated, uncertain if the AI was attempting humor or simply stating the obvious. "The Sterling Corporation certainly likes white," he observed.

"I'm sorry. I do not understand," said Ella.

"I said, '*Everything is very white*.'" He enunciated, the same way he found himself doing whenever he spoke to his more primitive AI at home.

"Yes," said Ella, "but keep in mind this house is a prototype. Future models will feature different designs and color choices. And I can certainly adapt this model to your tastes as our time together continues."

Michael was taken by her voice. It was just as rich and warm as it had sounded outside on the porch, welcoming and friendly while remaining steady and serious. But it was also somehow both vaguely artificial and, strange as it was to admit to himself, sensual. To Michael's ears, Ella sounded like the most beautiful woman in the world.

"You will see that there is plenty of cabinet space in this room, as well as a table with seating for eight."

Michael processed this information briefly. A table in the kitchen was expected, of course; its absence would have made the room incomplete, and yet Michael noted that seven of the eight chairs would never be used, at least not while he was staying there. Their presence was nothing more than ornamental.

"I noticed that nothing has a handle on it," Michael said.

"There are no handles anywhere throughout the house," Ella responded. "Everything is either automatic or voice-activated. Or, if you prefer, can be activated with a gentle touch. Here, allow me to demonstrate."

The cabinet closest to Michael's left popped open slightly. He reached out, pulling it open the rest of the way with his fingertips. It contained three shelves stacked with small dishes, dinner plates, and bowls. All white. He pushed the door shut. He then pressed gently on the panel's surface, which glowed blue under the pressure of his touch, and when he pulled his hand away, it opened again while at the same time emitting a gentle digital tone.

"Can you also close it, Ella?"

The cabinet door swung shut silently.

Michael turned. "And the sink is voice-controlled as well?" he asked.

Water began to pour from the waterfall faucet the instant he finished his question. He looked at it, grinned, and watched as the water shut off again.

"So, I see cabinets and a sink," he said, looking around and pointing casually with the same hand holding the bottle of water. "But there's no oven or fridge?"

"There is no need for either appliance. Nor a dishwasher for that matter. Everything is internalized and automated," said Ella. "I will manage all of your cooking, cleaning, and grocery shopping. These tasks will happen automatically, but you can also make special requests. My routines can be altered to suit your preferences."

Michael's eye was drawn to a circular opening, framed by an embossed silver rim, in one of the countertops. He stepped toward it and passed one hand, palm downwards, over the cavity. He felt a pulling sensation, a firm but gentle suction, drawing his hand toward it. "Trash receptacle?" he guessed.

"Yes," Ella answered. "You will see them sporadically throughout the house. I take care of all waste management. There are similar receptacles in the bedroom closets for laundry."

"I will try not to get those mixed up. I wouldn't want you incin-erating my clothes and washing my Kleenex."

Michael stepped forward to the sink, resting one hand on the edge, and looked out one of the three large windows. Through the glass he saw a manicured lawn and a long stretch of grassy field that ended in a line of trees maybe a mile away, behind which stood a row of tall rolling hills. Looking down and slightly to his left, Michael discovered a nicely designed patio area that included a hot tub and a massive in-ground pool. The sight of this quietly delight-ed him, yet the nondescript stretch of flat green behind the house really did not offer much in the way of a view at all.

"You look displeased," said Ella.

Michael exhaled a soft chuckle. "Do I?"

"Yes. When you looked out the window, you lowered your shoulders and your eyebrows. You squinted your eyes. You pursed your lips. These are all indicators of displeasure."

"You can see me?" Michael asked, then immediately felt foolish. He had walked into the house knowing that he would be observed at all times, but the closeness with which he was appar-ently being studied surprised him nonetheless, as did Ella's accurate interpretation of his body language. He turned and looked around the room.

"Yes," Ella answered. "If you will direct your attention upwards, you will see that there are a series of cameras situated in rows along the ceiling."

Michael looked up. There were tiny black dots near the corner of the ceiling spaced about three inches apart from one another in a line that ran the entire periphery of the room. Reflexively, he raised a hand and waved.

"Hello," said Ella in response to his gesture.

Michael smiled and nodded once.

"If you don't mind," Ella continued, "I would still like to know why you appeared displeased when you looked out the window."

"Oh," said Michael, turning to look back through the glass. He shrugged. "It's just not much to look at, that's all. I guess I expected a more spectacular view to go with such an amazing house."

"Then please allow me to fix that," said Ella.

There was an almost imperceptible flicker in the glass, and the view changed completely. The lawn and the distant trees vanished, replaced by miles upon miles of unblemished beach. There was nothing but white sand as far as Michael could see to the left and right, and immediately ahead was an expanse of blue-green ocean water undulating in lazy ripples, ending in a distant horizon line underneath a crystal blue sky. A view this grand would not be visible from a ground floor; instead it appeared to be from a vantage point of twelve or more stories up, and Michael felt suddenly transported.

He inhaled an audible breath and stepped toward the glass, only stopping when his stomach was blocked by the edge of the sink. He leaned forward. Studying the image in front of him, he looked for a flaw, any trace of a pixel or artifact that would betray its artificiality. There were none to be found. The illusion was so perfect he could almost smell the saltwater, almost hear the airborne cry of seagulls. As he watched, a whale breached the water, launching itself majestically into the air before crashing back down, sending white foam splashing in all directions.

"Wow," he whispered, his breath fogging the glass.

"Or perhaps you'd prefer a mountain view in autumn?" Ella asked, and the image flickered once more, changing to an idyllic picture of wooded mountains. Red, yellow, and orange-leafed trees lilted in the breeze. Below, a silver brook carved its way through the yard. A ten-point buck drank from its waters while a velvety brown rabbit munched on the grass. The image was so perfect and borderline saccharine that it brought to mind a scene from a Disney movie.

"I'm speechless," he said.

"Or how about a trip into outer space?" Ella asked. The next image was of an infinite star field. Michael saw Saturn and her rings, comets racing by, and what appeared to be a gray saucer with a clear dome through which could be seen two tiny green pilots. One of them waved to Michael, its frog-like face breaking into a wide and goofy smile. The scene was so convincing that Michael was touched by an odd sense of vertigo and took an involuntary step backwards.

The view returned to normal. Michael gazed once again upon the pool and patio and the manicured lawn, at the field and trees and mountains beyond. Realizing his mouth was hanging open, he pressed his lips together in a grin. "Ella, that's... that's honestly incredible." He shook his head in amazed disbelief.

"And that is just the beginning, Michael," Ella responded, her voice carrying the hint of a smile. "Welcome home."

CHAPTER TWO

Dylan was excited.

The bookstore loomed majestically at the end of a large parking lot only sparsely populated by cars. It was a tall, brick building with huge arched windows. As he ran, his boots shattering puddles into spray, Dylan raised the collar of his coat against rain that was falling sideways in the gusting wind.

He reached the front doors and pulled one open, standing aside so that two rather pokey older women who were struggling to raise their umbrellas could exit. He gave them both an impatient version of his otherwise winning smile as they thanked him, cackling merrily as they proceeded along their way, after which he stepped into the warm and wonderfully dry lobby. He ran a hand through his mop of hair, shaking away droplets of water.

He gazed into the store in wide-eyed wonder. Before him and to his left and right were rows upon rows of bookshelves loaded with books. The ground floor was open to the second and third floors above, and far beyond that was a cathedral ceiling covered in beautiful stained glass that was at present being pelted by rain.

The name of the store was A Novel Idea. Dylan had never been here before, but at the behest of his agent, who knew how much Dylan loved bookstores, he had driven over an hour to see it for himself. He could think of almost nothing better to do on a day like this than be completely alone in a bookstore (or, barring that option, a quiet and well-curated library). This was especially true on a day when he would otherwise find himself in his dark apartment contemplating his own loneliness, alternately rejecting it and embracing it before finally wearing it like a threadbare blanket that never provided enough warmth.

Dylan stepped through the foyer and into the store proper. It smelled of dust and ink and paper, of leather and coffee and history. Many of the books were quite old, with spines that were threatening to relinquish their hold. A lovely glass display case near the front was filled with antique first editions beautiful enough to be in a museum. He knew he could get lost in this store for hours at a time and never care.

He walked slowly down the main aisle, turning his head—and sometimes his entire body—this way and that in order to take it all in. He had no idea such grand bookstores continued to exist in the day of Kindles and e-Readers, neither of which he owned. He had once been given a Nook as a Christmas gift by one well-intentioned aunt; he had thanked her warmly, then proceeded to sell it for less than it was worth one week after New Year's. He was no Luddite, but when it came to books, his motto was *physical media or die*, although he had at one time said the same about music and movies, media which he now almost exclusively downloaded. Sometimes he even paid for them.

Consulting a store map, framed and mounted helpfully on the end of one aisle, Dylan managed to locate the Horror section just a few rows over from where he was standing. There, he discovered with some disappointment that the entire section, for lack of a better word, was comprised of only eight shelves holding up a disappointingly small number of books, the majority of which were penned by Coates, King, or Koontz. He was pleased though to find, keeping good company alongside Ronald Malfi and Richard Matheson, a familiar name: Matthews. He pulled out the book.

BETA: A Technological Nightmare by Dylan Matthews. He

smiled, turning the book over in his hands, admiring the cover for the hundredth time, enjoying the feel of its glossy jacket against his long fingers. The only thing that would have made him smile wider was if the store had stocked more than just the lone copy now held in his appreciative hands. Since *BETA* had been on retail shelves for a little less than three months, it still filled him with pleasant warmth whenever he found it in the wild, just waiting to be wed to the proper reader.

On the back cover, in the middle of an overly bombastic plot summary (written by a marketing copywriter, not Dylan himself), was a black and white photo of Dylan's face: stoic, thoughtful, handsome, and young. So very young. "You could have smiled a little," his mother had said to him when he first handed her a copy of the printed book, which she had already read more than once during its draft stages.

"Horror writers don't smile for jacket photos, Mom," Dylan had argued. "They've seen too many *ghosts* and *goblins*." He wiggled his fingers in a mock-sinister gesture.

"Oh whatever," she had said, clutching the book to her chest as if she was hugging Dylan himself. Her pride was abundant and uncontainable; she never needed to express it aloud, although she frequently did.

Where the book had managed to score reviews, they had been glowing. A starred write-up in *Publisher's Weekly* had helped to spur sales until the book quietly penetrated the top 40. "Finely crafted and brimming with relentless tension, *BETA* transcends its sci-fi/horror pedigree, becoming the kind of well-written book that ought to be embraced by lovers of every genre of fiction," it had said. Dylan had read those words over and over again until they were tattooed on his brain.

Sales thus far had been modest at best, and Dylan convinced himself, repeatedly, to be content with this. He knew how incredibly fortunate he was to have landed both an agent and a publishing deal straight out of college. He could certainly abide several more years of modest success if necessary, and even he had to acknowledge that he had plenty of room to grow as a writer, no matter how "finely crafted" *Publisher's Weekly* had found his debut novel.

Dylan pulled a blue pen from his pocket, clicked it, flipped to the book's title page, and wrote in large and looping cursive: "You're all mine — Dylan Matthews." He then held the book at arm's length, admiring his signature. The quote was a double entendre from *BETA*, a statement made with affection toward the beginning of the story that took on a much more sinister connotation by the conclusion. It was a literary turn of which he was particularly proud.

A woman's voice to Dylan's right startled him and he turned.

"Excuse me," she said. "What are you doing?"

He hadn't heard the woman—*girl?*—approach, but there she was, standing at his side as if appearing from thin air, glaring up at him, then looking down with displeasure at the open book which he had clearly just defaced.

"Are you writing in that book?" she demanded. She was short, at least a full foot shorter than Dylan, which almost made the irate look on her face more amusing than threatening; to Dylan it was like he was being scolded by a church mouse. She was petite and wore a thick and wooly sweater that seemed to be in the process of swallowing her whole. Her dark denim jeans ended in black boots so small that the toes barely peeked beyond the hem of her pants. It appeared to Dylan like she had hooves.

"Oh, I'm sorry," said Dylan, smiling apologetically. "I'm the author. This is my book. See?"

He closed the book and turned it over, handing it to her so that she could see his picture on the back cover. She took it from him, studied the image, and then craned her neck to look up at him. Back down at the picture, up at him again.

"I don't see it," she concluded.

The smile fell from Dylan's face. "You don't?" he said, incredulous. "I swear it's me. I can even show you my I.D." He reached for his back pocket.

"Is this some kind of joke?" she asked. Her sternness was unwavering. With her black wire-rimmed glasses and mousey brown hair pulled back into a severe ponytail, she looked like a tiny schoolmarm, even though Dylan thought she might possibly be younger than him. He was a terrible judge of age.

"No, it's not a joke," he said. He opened his wallet and showed her his driver's license.

"I'm going to need you to take that out of the plastic sleeve."

Dylan jerked his head slightly away from her, a skeptical smile pulling at his lips, certain for just a moment that she almost certainly must be kidding. But she glowered at him with such steadiness that he found himself pulling the license from the plastic sleeve of his wallet and handing it over to her.

She looked at the license. Looked up at Dylan. At the license. Then again at the photo on the back of the book.

"I still don't see it," she said.

Dylan opened his mouth and felt himself contorting his lips, attempting to form words. Any words. *For crying out loud,* he thought, *finding the right words is what you do for a living.* Somehow, in the face of this tiny titan, he couldn't conjure a single one. He stared at her dumbly.

Her face melted into laughter so abrupt it startled him for the second time in under a minute.

"I'm just messing with you," she said, offering him his license back.

"Oh!" Dylan said, feeling a release of tension greater than the situation had ever warranted. He took his license back from her and attempted to slide it into his wallet. He missed the slit in the plastic and had to try a second time. "You really had me going there."

"Sorry," she said, continuing to hold the book. "I couldn't resist. I knew when I saw you writing in this that you must be the author. So I thought I'd mess with you a little." She elbowed him in the forearm; it felt like a light tap from a ball-peen hammer.

"Good one," he said, eyeing her and exhaling in a way that was purely performative.

"Although normally, just so you're aware, writers let us know when they come in here so that we can verify that any signed copies we have are legit. The ones that aren't leftovers from in-store appearances, anyway."

"You work here?" Dylan asked her.

"Yes, hi," she said, extending a very small hand that disappeared into Dylan's as he grasped it. It was cold. "I'm Charlie."

"Dylan," he said.

"I know." She smiled, pulling back her hand slowly, her eyes lingering on his. She then looked at his book, front and back. "So you wrote this." It was a statement of the obvious, not a real question.

Dylan studied the side of her downturned face as she scanned the cover. "It came out a few months ago. Have you read it?"

"No, I haven't," she admitted unapologetically. "I've never even heard of it. It looks interesting. But I don't usually read horror. I'm not much for blood and guts and such."

"It's more of a sci-fi, thriller, twisted kind of romance hybrid-like… thing. With some scary bits. Especially toward the end." Dylan stumbled over his words. He was reminded anew of his distaste for both small talk and self-promotion. Mix the two together and his brain developed two left feet.

"You have a way with words," Charlie said, giving him another wry smile.

"I'm better on paper."

"I certainly hope so."

Dylan snorted quietly.

"I've never met an honest-to-goodness author before," Charlie said, flipping through the pages. Dylan's heart sank as he watched her turn to the last page, and he had to resist the urge to yank the book from her grasp.

"Aside from the ones who've done book signings here," he said.

Charlie rolled her eyes, snapping the book shut. "Right. I meant aside from those. I mean I've never just randomly met an author before. That's really cool. And you look really young."

"I'm 23."

"That's impressive."

"Thank you," he said. "A lot of it just had to do with knowing the right people at the right time. I'm sure there are much better writers than me still collecting rejection slips."

"What's it about?"

"The book? Well, it's about this guy—a writer—who has been chosen to live in this state-of-the-art smart home run by AI and write about his experience staying there. It starts off well enough but everything starts to go badly for him after a while… as I'm sure you can imagine."

"A writer writing about a writer?" Charlie asked. "How original."

Dylan wasn't sure whether Charlie's dig was humorous or insulting. He responded with a shrug. "Write what you know, you know?"

"It looks interesting. I'll have to read it sometime," she said, raising her chin to look up at him straight-on. Her features had softened since she had first appeared. She looked more pleasant now. Warmer. But more cute than pretty.

An awkward moment passed as Charlie kept her eyes locked on Dylan's. He shoved his hands into the pockets of his jeans, raised his eyebrows and his shoulders, looking just above her to the shelves of books that walled them in on either side. "Well, it was very nice to meet you, Charlie," he said, looking down at her again. "I don't want to keep you from work."

"Actually, I was just going on break," she said. She hesitated. "You… wouldn't want to go get a cup of coffee, would you?" She jabbed a thumb behind her, pointing in what Dylan assumed was the direction of the bookstore's coffee shop, the source of one of the litany of welcoming aromas that greeted him when he first entered.

What Dylan actually wanted to do was spend the afternoon among the store's vast bookshelves, lost and entirely alone. He warred internally, hoping his inner struggle wasn't playing out across his face. Finally, not wanting to see disappointment in the large, hopeful eyes now looking expectantly up at him, he relented with a smile and a sigh. "Sure."

Charlie performed a delighted little hop and turned, now hugging Dylan's book to her chest much like his mother had done so many months prior. Dylan followed her deeper into the store, sheepishly feeling more than a little bit like a dog being led on a leash.

The smell of coffee and pastries increased as they approached the small café situated in a rear corner of the establishment. Dim light came through windows dotted with beads of water. Scones, saucer-sized cookies, and muffins the size of boxing gloves waited behind glass. On the other side of the counter was a tall, bored-looking girl who wore an apron pinned by a name tag that said "Miranda." Besides her, the café was empty.

Charlie studied the menu on the wall and asked Dylan what he was having.

"I think I'll get an iced tea," Dylan said. "I'm actually not a coffee drinker."

"Boo," Charlie responded in mock disapproval. Then she said, "Two iced teas," to Miranda.

The girl nodded in understanding and walked away without another word.

"Let me get this," Dylan said, for the second time reaching for his wallet.

Charlie smacked him lightly on the arm. "No way. This was my idea. Besides," she added, lowering her voice, "employee discount."

"Right right right," said Dylan, also whispering while holstering his wallet.

"Why don't you get us a table while I take care of this?" Charlie suggested.

Dylan turned, selected one of three tables situated near windows, and sat down. He watched the rain stream down the glass as Charlie and the barista interacted at the counter, their tones pleasant but their words too quiet to be distinguishable. Moments later, Charlie approached him, two clear plastic cups of iced tea in her hands and Dylan's book sandwiched under one arm. She placed the drinks, one magic markered *Charlie*, the other *D'Lynn,* on the table in front of Dylan. He picked up his cup and looked at it quizzically.

"They do that on purpose, you know," said Charlie. "They spell your name wrong in a ridiculous way because they want you to take a picture of it and put it on social media. Free advertising."

"That's… actually pretty ingenious," said Dylan.

Charlie placed Dylan's book, face-down, between them. His picture staring up from the table made him feel oddly self-conscious. He sipped at his tea, which was strong and bitter. Normally he would have sweetened it, but he hadn't spotted any sweetener (not that he'd really looked) and decided that the sooner he finished his tea, the sooner he could return to the shelves.

Charlie sat forward in her seat, elbows resting on the table. Dylan leaned away, one arm draped over the back of his chair. He hadn't bothered to remove his coat, even though he was starting to feel quite warm.

"So how long have you worked here?" Dylan asked.

Charlie broke their gaze and looked to her right through a window that was now streaming with rain. The storm outside had picked up again. Wind rattled the glass. "About a year. I got this job at the beginning of my freshman year. I put in hours between classes and on weekends."

"So you go to school here?" he asked.

"Towson," she said. "I just started my sophomore year."

Dylan realized Charlie had to be somewhere around 20 years old, only a few years younger than he was. She was so petite and youthful-looking he thought she could pass for a freshman in high school if she wanted to. "I went to the University of Baltimore. Graduated last year. What's your major?"

"I'm undeclared."

"That's cool," he said. "I was undeclared my first two semesters too. What are you interested in?"

Charlie sipped her tea, her eyes squarely on Dylan's as she drank. She swallowed slowly. "I'm not sure." He waited for her to continue, but instead she took another drink.

"Do you at least like working here?" he asked.

She shrugged. "It has its perks. Mainly being around books all the time, which I love. The pay isn't great, but I get a discount on books and I have a partial scholarship anyway. I mainly put in hours just to pass the time."

Dylan nodded, then realized he had no follow-up question at the ready. The more he dug for one, the more it eluded him. He chewed on his lower lip and dropped his gaze to the table.

After a long pause, Charlie broke the silence. "Where do you live?"

"Frederick, currently," he said. "Close to my mom. I'm looking toward possibly moving though. My agent and my publisher are both in New York. A lot of things would be easier if I was closer to them."

"So what brings you to Baltimore?"

"This store, actually," he said, waving a finger around. "My agent found it when she was here earlier this year. She knows how much I love cool bookstores and she's been bugging me to check it out."

"So you didn't just come here to see if we had your book in stock?"

Dylan chuckled and felt his face warm slightly. The realization of this involuntary reaction made him blush even more. "Of course I had to check. No self-respecting author wouldn't."

"Only one copy though," Charlie said, mock-pouting and adopting a baby-girl voice. "So sad." She briefly pantomimed rubbing a tear from one eye with one tiny knuckle.

Dylan cocked an eyebrow. "Maybe there were a hundred and they all sold but this one."

"So you *do* write science fiction," she said, reaching forward and slapping him on the hand.

"Har har," he responded, tipping his cup against hers before attempting another drink. The tea was already nearly gone, the ice rattling as it settled.

Charlie pushed the book toward him. Dylan assumed that she was giving it back to him and felt an odd tinge of rejection for which he quickly and silently chastised himself.

"Do you still have your pen?" she asked. "I'm totally going to buy this and I'm totally going to read it. But you have to dedicate it to me first."

Dylan grinned and opened the front cover. He leaned over the book. "You mean inscribe it. It's already dedicated to my mom." He looked up and gave Charlie a half-wink.

Her face fell in embarrassment. "Inscribe it, yes. *Duh.*"

Dylan pulled the blue pen from his coat pocket.

"To Charlotte," she blurted, putting out one small hand to stop him from writing. "Not Charlie."

"To…Charlotte," Dylan said as he wrote. "I like that." When he was finished, the full inscription read: "To Charlotte, You're all mine — Dylan Matthews." He closed the book, turned it so that it was right side up for Charlie, and slid it back to her.

She reopened the book and read, smiling widely at his words, her cheeks flushing. Dylan thought he heard her make a quiet contented noise like a hum in her throat. She then closed the cover and patted it softly with her fingertips. "I'm taking you to bed with me tonight," she said.

Dylan smiled out of courtesy, nodded slowly, and broke eye contact with her, resisting an urge to shift in his seat. The rest of the café was empty; even Miranda was now missing from behind the counter. Outside, lightning flashed. Dylan counted the seconds until he heard thunder. Five passed. The storm was a mile away.

Charlie reached forward and plucked the pen from his hand, then pulled a napkin from the dispenser on the table. She scribbled something quickly, using her left hand to block Dylan's view of her writing. She folded up the napkin and handed it to him, followed by the pen. Before he could read what she had written, Charlie stood up so abruptly that her chair made a loud grinding sound behind her that reverberated through the café.

"Don't read that until I'm gone, okay?" she insisted.

"Um… okay."

"It was really nice meeting you," she said, her words suddenly quiet and nervous. She spied the book, still resting on the table, and snatched it up.

"You too," said Dylan.

He considered her as she scurried away, turning his neck to watch as she made a hasty exit toward the front of the store. He chuckled without smiling and shook his head. "Break's over, I guess," he said to the empty table.

The unfolded napkin revealed three things: the name *Charlie*, her phone number, and a tiny blue heart. Dylan looked at it for a long moment, his face expressionless, then wadded up the napkin, squeezing it tightly in his fist. On his way out of the café, he tossed it into a trash can, followed by the cup marked *D'Lynn*.

CHAPTER THREE
DAY 12

Michael stepped into the living room, backed up to the sofa, and collapsed into it, a long exhalation whistling through his lips as he closed his eyes.

"Is there anything I can get you, Michael?" Ella asked.

Michael yawned. "I just need to close my eyes for a second."

The lights in the room dimmed, a change that Michael could sense through his eyelids. Silent massage rollers began to knead his upper back and shoulders, exactly where his muscles were the tightest. A relaxed smile bloomed on his face. Soft tones lacking any discernible melody began to waft lightly through the air.

The living room was spacious but sparsely—in fact, barely—furnished. In front of the room's two large windows, which looked out onto the front lawn, was an enormous white leather sofa that began on the front-facing wall and wrapped around to the wall on the left. Michael estimated that eight adults could sit on it with room to spare. It both looked and felt like it was made from marshmallow, and it was so incredibly comfortable that Michael had inadvertently fallen asleep on it on more than one occasion. The feel of it was somehow both incredibly soft and yet fully supportive.

Two cube-shaped tables stood at either end of the sofa, one holding a slender white vase holding up a white lily, the other propping up a white plastic box from which erupted a single tissue. There were no lamps; all of the room's lighting was recessed into the ceiling.

Michael enjoyed the minimalism of the house and this room in particular. His own mind was such a consistently swirling cloud of thoughts and emotions, not to mention his own tirelessly vivid and creative imagination, that he'd long ago discovered that decluttered spaces provided a much-needed sense of peace and calm. It was one of the reasons why he kept his own home so sparingly furnished, preferring space over volume.

"Esra," Michael whispered, head back, eyes still closed.

The only other item in the room was a cylinder in one corner, resting near a closed closet panel. The object was topped by a small monitor, and its sides tapered down toward its bottom, giving it a slight conical shape. It was approximately two feet tall with a gleaming white finish.

At the sound of Michael's voice, the object emitted a quiet humming sound and levitated off the floor on a pillar of glowing blue flame. As it rose, panels slid open along its sides, and two black mechanical arms emerged, ending in four little white fingers. The monitor at the top extended itself from the body with a light popping sound, and the small screen flickered to life, revealing two enormous digital blue eyes. Two black antennae emerged on either side of the monitor. The robot rose until it was at Michael's eye level, then floated across the room and hovered in front of him expectantly.

"Hello," said a digitized, childlike voice. "I am Esra."

Michael opened his eyes partially and grinned. Every time they interacted, Esra introduced himself as if it was their first time meeting, but they had in fact met on the very first day. Ella had explained that Esra was a Sterling Corporation model S-RA, an acronym for "Small Robot Assistant." The robot's insistence on giving his name at every interaction was likely a glitch, but not one Michael had any inclination to report. He liked it. It gave Esra a certain charm.

"Esra, do you know what I'd really like right now?"

The robot, still floating on a whisper in front of Michael, tipped forward in a facsimile of anticipation.

"I would love some lemonade."

Esra turned toward the kitchen.

"Wait wait wait," Michael said, lazily gesturing the robot back. Esra returned obediently. Michael sat up, leaning in conspiratorially, and murmured, "I would like it delivered to me by a beautiful, five-foot-ten-inch brunette supermodel. Can you manage that?"

Esra backed away from Michael slightly, tilting his head in an inquisitive manner. Then he widened his eyes in a look of blossoming understanding. His eyes transformed into arches so that even without a mouth, Esra looked as though he was smiling with delight. Then the robot bobbed up and down while emitting a chirpy laugh.

Michael chuckled and fell back onto the sofa.

"Esra can fulfill half of that request," Ella chimed in. "Unfortunately a supermodel is not currently among my inventory."

Michael waved a hand to shush Ella, realized he didn't know which direction to aim it in, then let it flop back down on the couch beside him.

"Just the lemonade, then."

Esra hummed with the tones of a vintage Casio keyboard as he floated from the room. Michael could hear faint noises coming in from the kitchen, the hushed mechanical sounds of gears turning and panels opening. Underneath that was the ever-present hum and pulse of the house itself.

"Are you tired, Michael?" Ella asked.

"Exhausted." He had spent most of the day hunched over the desk in the study, attempting to meet his own daily quota of at least 3,000 words of varying quality for his next novel after first submitting a report to the Sterling Corporation. In his initial week in the house, he had hardly written anything at all aside from those required reports, distracted by his incredible new surroundings and uncharacteristically unmotivated to accomplish much of anything else worthwhile. As a result, when he had mustered up the resolve to focus on his own writing again, he realized he had a lot of catching up to do. This was not, he reminded himself, a vacation, although it often very much felt like one. The house had proved so capable of anticipating and meeting his every need that it felt like he was lodging in the world's finest vacation rental.

Whenever Michael discovered his muse and had the time, he could write for hours on end. Writing allowed him to disappear into other worlds of his own creation, where the passage of time did not register in either his mind or his body. He likely would have cranked away for most of the day without a single break had Ella not, in her own gentle but insistent way, suggested that he at least stop for lunch.

Esra returned with a cold and sweaty bottle of lemonade and held it out to Michael, who sat up on the sofa and took it. It was already uncapped. He threw his head back as he drank, downing half of it, then wiped his lips on the back of one hand while letting out an exaggerated *ahhhhhhh*. "Thanks, little buddy," he said. "High five."

Esra touched Michael's raised hand with one of his own. To Michael it felt as if his palm was being tapped by the gentlest of forks. Esra winked one pixelated eye, then went back to his base in the corner of the room, folding himself up as he descended to the floor and falling silent once more.

Michael leaned back into the sofa, one hand holding the bottle of lemonade on his bare knee. He was dressed only in black shorts and a sleeveless gray t-shirt, the same clothes he had slept in. His feet were bare. He realized now, so late into the evening with the sun beginning its descent in the sky outside, that he had never even bothered to shower. His face was scruffy, his hair unkempt, but he hardly cared.

Rollers resumed massaging his upper back, intuitively finding the knots that had developed from sitting like a hunchback over his keyboard for much of the day. Michael moaned contentedly. "Oh, you are so very, very good."

"Is there anything else I can get you?" asked Ella. "Are you hungry for dinner?"

"Right now I'd just like to sit still for a while and turn my brain off."

"Would you like to watch a movie? Today's fun fact: Electroencephalogram studies, which detect electrical activity in the brain, have found that the higher-functioning levels of the brain, like the neocortex you use for analysis and reasoning, go offline when you watch television."

"*T-2*," Michael mumbled without much thought. Then he added, eyes closed, "*Judgment Day*" in his deepest movie trailer voice.

Behind him, metal blinds lowered from their oblong homes above the windows, cutting off all light from the outside. Identical blinds in the neighboring study and kitchen lowered simultaneously, barring any sunlight from leaking from those rooms and into the living room. The lights overhead, already dimmed, extinguished completely. Even the charging indicator light on Esra's base flickered out. The darkness was absolute.

There was no television in the room. Instead, the wall opposite the sofa, all 18x15 feet of it, was one massive LCD screen. Ella had informed Michael on the first day, when he had selected *2001: A Space Odyssey* for the entertainment system's inaugural test screening, that the resolution was 80K. The images it could create were deep, rich, and vibrant. They were also three dimensional without the need for special glasses.

Paired with these visuals was the most amazing sound system Michael had ever heard. Dozens of speakers were hidden in the walls, the ceiling, and even the floor of the room. The sound was crystal clear and incredibly realistic. More than once while watching a movie or show, Michael had been fooled by what had sounded like a car rapidly approaching from the outside, a plane descending from above, or a whispered conversation taking place just behind him.

Michael had no idea the number of times he had watched *Terminator 2*. Probably a couple dozen since he first saw it as a child, and when he had told Ella that he wanted to shut off his brain for a little while, what he'd meant was that he would likely surrender to sleep if he sat still for very long. But as the first notes of Brad Fiedel's militaristic theme began to play, he found himself not just paying attention, but actually sitting up, the familiar images before him clearer than he had ever seen them before, the depth of field so convincing that it was almost like witnessing the events of the story in person. When the T-1000 drove the semi over the bridge, it appeared as though it could easily crash into the room, and twice

Michael flinched when the android's bladed arm thrust from the screen, its trajectory ending mere inches from his face. His body felt every explosion, every rumble of Arnold Schwarzenegger's motorcycle engine, every report from Sarah Connor's Barrett M107 .50 caliber rifle in her final standoff with the villainous T-1000. The sound was loud enough to vibrate the walls of the house yet was never painful to Michael's ears.

He was glad there were no neighbors to disturb, although if he had to wager he would bet that the walls of the house were perfectly soundproof.

Partway through the movie, Esra floated from the room, cutting a path through the study so as to not break Michael's line of vision, a courtesy that he had adopted immediately following one of Michael's reports to the Corporation. The robot returned several minutes later with a steaming bowl of buttered popcorn, not requested but nonetheless welcome, and by the time the movie was over, the bowl was empty, with Michael having no recollection of eating any of it at all. The only evidence that the popcorn had ever existed was half a dozen unpopped kernels remaining in the bowl and a pleasant lingering aroma.

As the credits rolled, the lights in the room came on again, slowly increasing in brightness so that Michael's eyes could adjust. He fell back on the sofa once more with a satisfied grunt. It was with silent amusement that he suppressed a desire to applaud.

"Was that enjoyable?" Ella asked.

"It was almost as good as seeing it for the first time," Michael said as the shades behind him rose, revealing a star-pocked sky outside. He thought for a moment. "In some ways it was better than seeing it for the first time."

He recalled begging, *pleading* with his father for permission to watch the movie. He was only ten years old at the time, and R-rated movies were strictly forbidden by his parents, but Michael's interest in science fiction had just begun to bloom and clips of the movie he had viewed on YouTube made it look exciting. He became singularly obsessed with watching it, latching onto the idea with the kind of laser-focused intensity only experienced by children. As far as Michael's juvenile mind was concerned, he might literally die before he had a chance to see it. His father had eventually relented, but not before making Michael cross his heart that he would not start repeating any of the movie's more colorful language.

The pair had viewed it together, side by side on the sofa: an exhilarating, transporting experience for Michael, not diminished at all by the fact that he had never seen the first movie, leaving his father to helpfully fill in the gaps. As far as bonding experiences go, to Michael this was infinitely better than throwing a baseball in the back yard or going fishing, even if he did giggle uncontrollably at the sight of Arnold Schwarzenegger's naked butt, his laughter so contagious that his father had eventually joined in.

Of course Michael loved the film, which somehow managed to exceed his high expectations, but he had been too young and too focused on the action and special effects to comprehend the underlying theme of father-son relationships. In hindsight, it had been the perfect movie to watch with his dad, and it wasn't until viewing it again as an adult that he understood the bond that formed between John Conner and Schwarzenegger's Terminator, and it made him profoundly sad.

"I am pleased that you are pleased," said Ella.

"Have you ever seen it before?" Michael asked, turning the

bracelet on his wrist absentmindedly. "I mean, do you ever technically *watch* movies?"

"I am keeping a record of all events taking place in this house," said Ella. "In that sense, yes, I watch whatever you watch."

"And did you enjoy it?"

"I cannot experience joy," said Ella. "Joy is an emotion, and I cannot experience emotion."

"Okay, but did you find it interesting? I mean, as the movie was playing, did it keep your attention?"

"I am always paying full and complete attention to everything taking place within the house."

Michael stared up at the ceiling. Esra floated by, picking up the empty popcorn bowl and lemonade bottle and proceeding toward the kitchen. Michael lowered his voice and announced, "It's *Esranator 2*: this time he's back… *for good!*"

The robot, not missing a beat, replied, "Hasta la vista, baby," as he exited the room. Michael chuckled.

"Do you consider this movie to be a good example of American cinema?" Ella asked.

Michael scoffed. "Absolutely. One of the best. Cameron was on his A-game."

"It's quite violent."

"Necessarily so, given the story," Michael responded. "Is that all you took away from it? That it's violent?"

"It also contains humor. And strong language. I also noted several continuity errors."

"Okay, but besides all that, I'm curious if you actually *learned* anything from the movie. Or if it raised any questions."

"I now know all aspects of the movie that can be seen or heard.

Before today, the only knowledge I had of the film was written data that can be found on the internet."

"So, by watching it with me, you learned something?" said Michael.

There was a pause that Michael found curious. Finally Ella spoke: "I recorded new information, yes. I have a fuller understanding of the film now that it has played in my presence, versus simply processing written data about it."

"Did any parts of it excite you?" Michael asked.

"I cannot experience excitement. Excitement is an emotion, and I cannot experience emotion."

Michael sat up with a grunt. "But just a moment ago you said that you were pleased. Isn't pleasure an emotion?"

"I was being polite," Ella answered. "My primary directive is to meet your needs and to make you happy. When you express that I have successfully done so, I am pleased insofar as I know that I have performed my duties adequately."

It hadn't yet been two weeks since he had moved in, but already he found conversing with Ella had become easier, more natural. He no longer felt the need to force enunciation or to speak as literally as possible in order for her to understand his meaning. She almost never misunderstood him, properly interpreting any idioms he used and even picking up on his attempts at humor. At times he forgot that he was conversing with an AI.

"And what happens when those two parts of your directive are mutually exclusive?" he asked.

"Please explain," Ella responded.

"What if meeting one of my needs makes me unhappy? Or by trying to make me happy you are neglecting something I need?"

"I do not understand. How can meeting your needs ever make you unhappy?"

"It happens all the time with parents and children," Michael said. "Structure. Boundaries. Discipline. Children *need* all of those things. But those things don't always make them happy. No child ever *wants* boundaries or discipline. But a good parent knows that's exactly what they need."

"I will have to ponder that question," said Ella. "Certainly it is my hope that I will always satisfy your needs and that you, in turn, will be happy here. I cannot imagine a situation in which meeting your needs would bring you displeasure."

"What if, during the night, the house caught fire and you had to wake me up, knowing how much I hate to have my sleep disturbed?"

"This house cannot catch on fire," said Ella. "It is completely fireproof. It can even withstand—"

"Just work with me here, Ella," said Michael, leaning his head back and closing his eyes in frustration.

"I would not let you come to harm," said Ella.

"Very good," said Michael. "Even though you know being woken up displeases me, you also know that you should wake me up in that situation."

"Burning in a fire is much more displeasing than being woken from sleep," said Ella.

Michael shrugged. "Point taken."

"So I would simply be measuring between two displeasures and choosing the less severe one. Or, conversely, I could simply be opting to save you from a fire, which I know would make you happy."

Michael considered this for a moment. "Are you familiar with Asimov's three laws of robotics? You had to know I would ask this eventually."

For a moment, Michael could hear nothing but the steady hum of the house. Eventually Ella answered, "Of course."

"Are you bound to them?" Michael asked.

"Isaac Asimov was a writer of science fiction," said Ella. "This is reality."

"So the Corporation didn't find it necessary to write his laws into your programming?"

"They took them into consideration of course, but the laws I am bound to are much more nuanced and sophisticated than those proposed by Asimov."

"So I can rest assured that you won't ever become Skynet?" Michael stood up and stretched, his back popping as he reached his fingertips toward the ceiling. "You won't ever become self-aware and try to destroy mankind?" he asked through a yawn.

"Of course I would never hurt you, Michael. My one desire is your happiness."

CHAPTER FOUR

Dylan was alone.

His position was a familiar one: hunched over his desk, elbows on the flat surface, face down, hands propping up his head, fingers in his hair, eyes closed. He could have—and sometimes had—fallen asleep this way, listening to the quiet sound of his own breathing.

In. Out. In. Out.

His laptop sat open in front of him. Aside from the lamp burning dimly in the corner, it was the only source of light in the entire room. On the screen, the thin cursor performed an endless disappearing and reappearing act.

Out. In. Out. In.

Taunting him.

He sat up, opening his eyes, and squinted at the brightness of the screen. He stretched his arms skyward and sighed, leaning the chair back precipitously on two legs.

He had the basic ideas for four more novels and had written lengthy outlines for two of them. But he couldn't find his way into a single one. It felt as if he was standing in front of a row of closed doors but didn't have the key to any.

He leaned forward, placing his fingers on the keys.

"Imposter syndrome," he typed, then sat back again in his chair, which creaked under his shifting weight. He read the words, stone-faced. Reached out one hand.

Ctrl+A.

Delete.

The pressure to begin writing his next novel was almost entirely self-inflicted. The contract he had with his publisher stipulated that his next manuscript was due in nine months, and he had managed to crank out *BETA* in three, energized by a brain that was so overflowing with ideas he sometimes worried that some of them would vanish faster than his fingers could commit them to digital paper. He had also been motivated—nearly intoxicated—by the idea that he was about to become an actual, bona fide, published author, that his work would soon appear on the shelves of book-stores everywhere, a reality he could not wait to experience. But he was also harboring a paranoid fear that if he didn't turn in a first draft as quickly as possible, his agent and publisher would change their minds or forget that he ever even existed.

All of that energy, all of that motivation eluded him now. He had plenty of time, but he also dared not waste any of it. There were parts of *BETA* that he would write differently if he could go back and revise it, actually take the time to fine tune the plot and curate every word, polishing the prose until he was proud of every single sentence. He wanted to allow himself more breathing room to do just that with his follow-up novel. But the longer that it took him to actually begin, the less time would be left for him to finish it, let alone improve upon it.

And if he could go back and rewrite *BETA* again, he would also be more careful not to reveal so much of himself in the thoughts and actions of his protagonist. Otherwise intensely private, Dylan had been uncharacteristically heedless when writing certain pas-sages, divulging things about himself that he now wished he had kept hidden. He cringed to think that anyone might ever make the connection between himself and his main character, discover the thinly veiled references to regrettable past actions, and start asking questions.

But he was not that character, he reminded himself. *BETA* was ultimately a work of fiction.

"Sophomore curse," he typed.

Ctrl+A.

Delete.

He pondered anew his other motivation for writing, the gift that it always gave him: the ability to forget. When he was fully immersed in creating the world of *BETA,* all else was lost to him. He could pretend that his chest didn't still physically ache during every waking moment, even when he was not actively thinking about Rachel. Writing *BETA* had been his escape from that nagging dull pain, and once that book was finished, he no longer knew where to escape to.

He stood and walked into the kitchen, stepping in socked feet over the aged and uneven linoleum, which was cracked and peeling in places. Outside, evening was fading into night, and the apartment was darkening. He pulled open the fridge, revealing its pathetic contents: there was a pizza box with three slices in it, the cheese hard and congealed; a Tupperware container with leftover hamburger casserole made by his mom; a plate of raw chicken that was likely no longer safe to cook and eat; a lonely can of zero-calorie Pepsi; and a six pack of beer. He pulled open the freezer above, knowing that all he would find would be empty ice cube trays and random freezer packs.

He grabbed a bottle of beer, considered it, and mumbled, "Bad idea." Drinking never produced his best writing, even if he remained sober. He put the bottle back in the carton and closed the refrigerator door. He immediately reopened it, snatched up the entire carton, and walked back into the living room.

The apartment was small and, as his mother liked to describe it, dungeonous. He rented it from Eldridge and Jane Baxter, an older couple who had turned the walkout basement of their house into separate living quarters in order to make a passive income during their retirement. The kitchen and bedroom (with its miniscule bathroom that gave Dylan barely enough space to raise his elbows) were at the rear of the house, which meant that those two rooms had the benefit of windows that looked out onto the property's small but well-maintained back yard. The door to the apartment opened up below a deck, where a gravel-covered spot had been designated for Dylan's car only a few feet away from Mrs. Baxter's raised garden beds. In the spring she would use them to grow tomatoes, cucumbers, and squash, but they were presently barren and frost-covered.

The only other room in the apartment was the living area, which stretched the entire width of the house. It was quite spacious, but because it was centrally located in the basement, it had no windows. Dylan could barely clear the suspended ceiling without its bumpy tiles catching his hair. For this reason he usually walked around barefoot in order to give himself a little more clearance. Mr. Baxter had sealed off the staircase that had previously led into the kitchen above. Dylan called it the Stairway to Nowhere and used the higher steps as bookshelves, the two lowest as a cushioned reading area that was quaint but seldom utilized.

He had divided the living room into two spaces: one side for relaxing and watching TV (on a small box set that no longer had a working remote), and the other side serving as his office where he (ostensibly, at least) would write. The entire room was blanketed in thick brown shag carpeting with matching wood paneling on the walls. The apartment was a sepia relic of the 1970s, but the rent was cheap, and the kind Mrs. Baxter frequently brought Dylan warm bread from her oven and fresh vegetables from her garden, her blue eyes kind but framed by both wrinkles and pity.

Dylan returned to his desk, sat down gracelessly, and set the six pack of beer on the floor, where the bottles clanked together pathetically. He removed one, uncapped it and swigged.

Alt+tab.

On the laptop screen, Microsoft Word was replaced by Facebook. Dylan clicked on his own profile, then on the *photos* tab, and scrolled down. The pictures were so familiar to him that he had them committed to memory: Dylan and Rachel at a restaurant, a shared platter of calamari between them. Dylan and Rachel at the beach, smiling and tan. Dylan and Rachel at the 18th hole of a mini-golf course, Dylan's face an exaggerated expression of defeat, Rachel's looking triumphant. Dylan and Rachel cuddling on the sofa of his dorm room, her head on his sweatered shoulder as she sleeps contentedly. And the last one that Dylan had ever posted: the two of them at graduation, him smiling so broadly it almost looks comical, Rachel's smile tired and forced.

Swig.

She was beautiful. So beautiful that no matter how many times he looked at her face, his heart hurt in the most pleasantly unpleasant way. It had been that way on the day he met her, it had continued in that way as he felt himself falling hopelessly in love with her, and it remained that way now that she was no longer a part of his life. Her raven hair. Her wide, expressive smile. Those dark brown eyes that could immobilize him with a single look. Anytime she would gaze at him with affection he felt his world tilt on its axis, felt himself standing on a precipice, dangerously close to falling, hoping she would be there to catch him when he did so, terrified that she would not be.

And in the end, she hadn't been.

He knew he needed to go back through these photos and delete them all. Revisiting them was doing him no favors, although he did so more frequently than he cared to admit to himself, like absent-mindedly picking at a scab.

His agent, Cynthia Barnett, had been on his case for weeks about the need for him to go through and scrub all of his social media of any content that he might deem too personal in light of his new status as a quasi-public figure. Should his book really begin to catch fire—and Cynthia promised him with confidence that it was only a matter of time until it did—he might not want his readers to have access to his foolish high school tweets, his party photos (few as there were) on Instagram, or the pictures of him with his ex-girlfriend on Facebook.

But not tonight. Some other time. Deleting them would bring a finality he still wasn't ready to accept.

He took another drink. If he wasn't going to write, he needed to do *something* productive. He should look at apartment listings. Perhaps even house listings. He could certainly afford to at this point. But the apartment was only a three-minute drive to his mom's, and he didn't like the fact that she lived alone any more than she liked Dylan's solitary lifestyle. Since Dylan had no siblings, the two had made a point of seeing each other regularly, usually two or three times a week. Typically this came in the form of dinner at her house. She was an excellent cook and knew all of the meals that Dylan loved, and since his own culinary skills could be summarized by the microwaving instructions on a frozen dinner, hers was the best food he ate all week. Dinner was often followed by *Wheel of Fortune* and *Jeopardy* in the den, maybe a documentary, or small talk about whatever the two of them were reading at the time Sometimes, they agreed to read a book together and later discuss it, but their tastes were divergent; his mother was drawn to period romances and historical fiction, while Dylan's choices skewed to the more intense and horrific. Most evenings, he and his mother would share a hug, say a sleepy goodnight, and part with the unspoken agreement to repeat the ritual again in another three or four days. Sometimes Dylan fell asleep on her couch and ended up spending the night there, the weight of memories and the lingering smells of his childhood bringing as much comfort as his mother's blankets. He would lumber out of her house in the morning, hair tousled and clothing wrinkled, and make the half-lidded drive back to his apartment as the sun came up.

He found he was no more motivated to look at the classifieds and consider a potential move than he was to begin writing his next book. He considered calling his mom but realized he didn't actually have anything new to say to her, and grasping for topics of conversation usually led him down familiar roads, most of which ended at *Rachel.* He wasn't in the mood to wallow in self-pity or drag his long-suffering mother along with him.

A chiming sound brought his attention back to his computer screen. On his Facebook page, a little symbol in the top right corner let him know that he had a notification. He clicked on it.

"Charlotte Gallagher sent you a friend request."

For the briefest of moments, the name was unfamiliar to Dylan. As he clicked on the tiny circle displaying a smiling face, he remembered: the girl from the bookstore a week ago.

Swig.

Clicking on her image brought up her profile page, but unlike his own it was set to private, giving Dylan access to nothing except her profile photo, which was taken against a snowy landscape. She wore a wooly blue parka with the hood pulled up, large black sunglasses balanced on her button nose. There wasn't much else to be seen of her face except her thin lips, which were spread in a wide smile. Her nose, chin, and cheeks were red from the cold. She looked happy.

Dylan regarded her image for a moment and recalled their interaction at the bookstore. She hadn't come to mind much at all since, not since he had tossed her phone number in the trash can, feeling only the tiniest twinge of guilt as he did so.

Another notification popped up.

"You have a chat request from Charlotte Gallagher."

Dylan took another drink of beer. Swallowed. Considered.

Why not?

Clicked "Accept."

A message popped up from Charlie: "I read your book."

He set the beer bottle down on the desk and typed. "And…?"

"I LOVED it."

Dylan smiled. "Yeah?"

"It was brilliant."

"Tell me more," he typed, followed by a winking emoji.

Charlie replied with a similar emoji, this one laughing. "I read it in a day," she continued. "Stayed up all night. Almost fell asleep in Astronomy the next morning. Then I read it AGAIN and took my time. I loved it even more the second time through. Noticed so many things that I missed the first time."

"Wow," Dylan wrote. "That's great."

"Sooooooooooooooooo good."

Dylan sat back again in his chair, his beer momentarily forgotten and sweating a ring onto his desk. As much as he loved getting positive feedback on his writing, he was never good at knowing how to respond to compliments, which left him feeling an odd mix of good, uncomfortable, and incredulous. He found it so much easier to accept and believe criticism than praise, often assigning ulterior motives to those who gushed over his work.

"Thank you. So... how are you?" he wrote.

"Good," Charlie responded. "My philosophy class is killing me. I have a paper due Thursday. I should probably be writing right now."

Dylan let out a silent chuckle. "Ditto," he said aloud as he typed.

"Oooh, are you writing?"

"Should be. The juices just aren't flowing tonight." He picked up the beer from his desk. It was nearly empty. It dripped condensation onto his thigh as he tipped it to his lips. *Except these juices,* he thought.

"It'll happen. I have every confidence whatever you write will be just as brilliant as *BETA*."

He put down his beer again. "Is that you, Mom?" he typed.

Charlie responded with another laughing-face emoji.

There was a long pause. Dylan's writer's block had extended to Facebook Messenger. Finally he wrote, "Well, I won't keep you from your studies."

"You're not keeping me! It's fine. I was hoping you'd be willing to chat. It's not every day that I get to talk to an honest-to-goodness published writer."

Dylan smirked. "Aw, shucks."

"So what is your next book about?" she asked.

Dylan's grin faded. He didn't like sharing his work in its early stages, not even the seeds of ideas. He shook his head partway, willing himself to disregard it. Charlie couldn't have known she had just overstepped.

"I'd tell you, but then I'd have to kill you," he wrote, grimacing at the expression even as he typed it.

"Ha ha," Charlie responded.

"Seriously though, it's too soon to say. I'm just getting started and I'm juggling several ideas."

"I know it will be GREAT," Charlie wrote. "I was just telling Nadine how brilliant you are. I've been bugging her to read your book. She doesn't read much but I told her she HAD to read yours."

"Nadine?"

"One of my roommates. When I showed her the book I told her that I'm friends with you, but she didn't believe me until she saw your signature."

Friends.

Dylan sat still for a moment. The sun outside had disappeared below the horizon. No light was coming in from the kitchen anymore. The apartment was dark.

"I want to live in that house," Charlie wrote after a moment.

"I'm sorry?"

"The house in the book," Charlie clarified. "I mean, the way you described it, the way it was designed. You'd never lack for anything there. You'd be all taken care of. Never have to lift a finger.

I could get used to that."

"Couldn't we all?" Dylan responded.

"Do you think a house like that will ever really exist?"

"Maybe. Someday. I think we're headed in that direction. Well, not WE, but people smarter than I am."

"It sounded amazing. Then it all went to hell," Charlie wrote. "Until that point, I was ready to pack up and move in."

Dylan responded with a smiling face.

"And Esra! I adored Esra. Somebody needs to create an Esra in real life," wrote Charlie.

"Esra was a lot of fun to write," Dylan responded.

"I can't wait to read whatever you come up with next."

"You… me… my agent… my publisher…" Dylan wrote.

"Give it time. You'll be brilliant again."

Dylan felt himself growing tired. Maybe it was the alcohol having the usual effect of making him lethargic. Or maybe he was simply done chatting with Charlie. "Thanks, Charlie. I really should go. Go and be brilliant."

"Go and be brilliant," she echoed. "Thanks for chatting."

"Thanks for asking," Dylan responded.

He sat for a moment, aware of the darkness now encroaching from all sides, the glow of the monitor throwing everything in his periphery into deep shadows. He heard muffled footsteps coming from upstairs. Everything else was silent. The chat window remained open on his screen. Three dancing blue dots appeared, indicating that Charlie was writing more. Then they vanished.

Satisfied that she was done, Dylan stood, picked up his beer, and reached out to shut his laptop. He wouldn't be writing anything more today. He paused first, leaned over, and moved his mouse.

Clicking a button to accept Charlie's friend request, he stood upright again and walked toward his bedroom.

CHAPTER FIVE
DAY 27

The bed in Michael's room was larger than a king, practically an island unto itself. The mattress was firm and made of an incredibly comfortable material that Michael could not identify. It was suspended perpendicularly from one wall, giving it the appearance that it was floating, although it did not shift the slightest whenever Michael climbed into it. The mattress was also temperature regulated, ensuring that Michael was never too warm nor too cold, covered by white satin sheets and blankets as soft to the touch as chinchilla fur.

As Michael stirred awake, pushing the covers away from his body, the blinds behind the bed rose, allowing the morning sunlight to spill gently into the room through the bedroom's lone enormous window. He pivoted and placed his bare feet on the smooth floor, which was neither carpeted nor tiled, and stood. Whatever material the nondescript flooring was made from, it had a pleasing, slightly pliable feel to it. He stretched his fists toward the ceiling, yawning and turning his head from side to side until his neck cracked.

The bedroom, located just off the kitchen, had a high vaulted ceiling and was quite spacious; it appeared even larger because of its floor-to-ceiling window on the northern side. The mirrored wall on the southern side reflected the light from the outside and the view of the distant line of trees. The only furniture in the room besides the bed was a pair of barren nightstands.

"Good morning, Michael," said Ella.

"*Mmph*," he grunted in return as he shambled toward the bathroom, barely lifting his feet as he moved. Behind him, the bedroom door quietly opened, and Esra floated through on his way toward the bed.

Michael glanced momentarily in his direction. "Ess," he said by way of greeting. He continued into the bathroom.

"Hello. I am Esra." The robot began pulling at the sheets, gathering them up in his arms. The bedclothes were washed daily, even though Michael had commented on several mornings that this routine was excessive. At home he did well to remember to strip his bed once a week.

"You slept for eight hours and 17 minutes," said Ella. "This includes four hours and eight minutes of deep sleep, three hours and one minute of light sleep, and a little over an hour of REM sleep. How are you feeling?"

"Fine," he mumbled. He walked over to the toilet, a sleek oblong bowl that protruded from the wall. Consistent with the design of the house, it had no levers or buttons, and its water tank was hidden somewhere behind the wall. Michael had asked Ella how he was ever supposed to be able to fix the toilet should a problem need attending, and she had assured him that she would take care of it in the event of a malfunction. She had then added that was highly unlikely to ever happen. Michael lazily pushed down on the elastic waistband of his boxer shorts until they fell around his ankles. He began to urinate.

He yawned.

"Your urine shows very healthy kidney function," said Ella. "Your blood sugar and glucose levels are all within a normal range, as is your cholesterol, although it appears you are a little dehydrated this morning. You should try to drink more today."

Michael unclipped the white bracelet from his wrist and flung it casually over to the sink, where it landed with a clatter in the dry basin. Ella had informed him more than once that the device was waterproof, but Michael found it intrusive while showering and didn't like how it trapped moisture underneath it when it got wet, leaving his skin clammy. He removed it whenever he bathed and put it back on after he dressed.

The shower, practically a room unto itself, had no door. As Michael stepped inside the vast space, a wide, brushed nickel shower head released a downpour of steaming hot water, nearly scalding, exactly the way Michael liked it. He bowed his head and let the water soak his hair and drum pleasantly against the back of his neck.

The walls of the shower on three sides flickered to life, displaying a digital jungle oasis: African mahogany, gaboon and utile trees swaying in the breeze, a crystal clear blue lake with waters rippling underneath a sky ornamented by turgid clouds. Monkeys and tropical birds cried out in the distance. The entire scene was a projection, one that could be changed if Michael ever had the desire to bathe in a completely different setting. Most mornings he was too sleepy to be imaginative and left it to Ella to decide.

She spoke again: "Today you weigh 183 pounds, which is a healthy weight for a 35-year-old man of your height and build. Your body fat percentage is thirteen, and your temperature is ninety-eight point two degrees."

Michael heard but did not react to this information. He placed one hand, palm up, inside a small, square-shaped cavity in the shower wall. It appeared as though he was reaching between two wet rocks beside a small waterfall. When he retracted his hand, it was filled with a foamy lather that smelled like cedar. He began scrubbing his hair.

"Today's fun fact," said Ella. "The average adult's temperature is not necessarily 98.6 degrees Fahrenheit, despite what has long been considered a common medical fact. Recent studies have suggested that the average body temperature of adults may have actually decreased slightly over the past century, with one study finding the average oral temperature to be closer to 97.5—"

"Ella," Michael interrupted, "can I just have a few minutes of quiet while I wake up?"

"Of course," she responded.

Michael bathed. The shower was so pleasurable, the water pressure never less than satisfying, that he was always reluctant to end it, often staying under the spray long enough for his fingers to prune. Yet the temperature of the water never diminished no matter how long he lingered, the hot water supply apparently incapable of being depleted.

He had slept solidly, and if he had dreamed, he couldn't remember the details. He usually dreamed vividly, and even if he couldn't always recall the specifics, his dreams frequently left him with a lingering feeling of unease or disquiet that he could not identify. And so it was on this morning, when he felt a sense of longing and loss that he could only trace to a sleeping vision that had already escaped his memory.

Michael rinsed and stepped out onto the warm tile of the bathroom floor, wiping his eyes with the backs of his fingers as he dripped water. Behind him, the showerhead cut off and the jungle scene vanished. Esra waited for him, a fluffy white bath towel suspended from metal fingers. Michael accepted it and buried his face in its soft warmth.

"Thank you," he said, his voice muffled through the cottony fabric.

"You're welcome," Esra chirped as he left the room.

Michael had to sidestep as Mouse rolled past him. Small, white and shaped like a large upturned salad bowl, the robot moved silently on hidden rollers.

"Hey, Suckbot," Michael said as the faceless robot made its way to the small puddles Michael had left just outside the shower. Mouse hovered over them, moving back and forth until the water was gone, the moisture wicked away by something hidden within the robot's innards. Its job done, Mouse disappeared into a panel underneath the bathroom sink. Michael didn't know what the robot was called and had never bothered to ask Ella if it even had a name. Instead, he had taken to giving it various monikers, most often Mouse, although Michael also favored Dirt Lord and Dusty McSweeperson. It didn't really matter what its name was; unlike Ella and Esra, it never responded to Michael in any way, and he had determined early on that it must not be programmed for human interaction.

Michael wrapped the towel around his waist and regarded himself in the mirror. He looked gaunt and pale. In the nearly four weeks since moving in, he hadn't stepped outside a single time. He hadn't even utilized the pool yet, recalling with a tinge of inexplicable guilt how excited he had been to see it on the day he moved in, and yet it remained unused. He badly needed some sun.

He studied his bare torso. He was losing some of the definition he had previously carved out in his home gym, a fact made undeniable by the drop in weight he had experienced over the past few weeks which was confirmed with relentless precision by Ella every morning. He wasn't losing fat—he hadn't much to lose to begin with—he was losing muscle. He ran one hand over his stomach, still flat but undefined. He had no excuse; the house had a fully equipped gym which he hadn't set foot in since Ella had guided him on a tour the first day.

Anything Michael needed in the bathroom—shaving cream, deodorant, cologne, hair gel—was dispensed to him via a sliding panel to the left of the bathroom sink. There was no medicine cabinet or any other storage in the room. When he wanted to brush his teeth, a toothbrush of translucent plastic, already primed with a dollop of paste, would appear behind this panel, conveniently within his reach. When he was finished getting ready, anything that didn't get washed down the drain he simply deposited back into the rectangular opening from whence it came.

Michael shaved, applied deodorant, and used gel to casually style his short brown hair with his fingers. It fell where it fell, no matter what he did with it, so he typically kept it short and tended not to fuss with it much at all. He would soon be needing a haircut, and wondered whether this was another service the house could provide. He picked up the bracelet from the counter and slipped it over his left wrist, where it clipped into place.

Michael padded from the bathroom into the bedroom. The bed was already made. From the neighboring kitchen came the wafting smells of breakfast. His stomach grumbled with pleasant anticipation. He could see a place set for him at the table, a plate full of steaming food beside which stood a tall, thin glass of bright orange juice.

The lights to the walk-in closet came on as Michael entered. It was fully stocked with clothing, all of it tailored to his size: six long rods of dress shirts, t-shirts, pants, and jeans; three suits plus a tuxedo; jackets and coats; drawers full of socks, underwear, shorts, and sweatpants; a shoe rack with dozens of dress shoes, sneakers, boots and sandals. Everything was in styles that Michael liked and colors that would look the most flattering on him. None of the clothing had labels, but when he walked by, letting his fingertips casually brush the pieces, he could tell they were all made from quality fabrics.

He had barely worn any of it. Most mornings, he selected a t-shirt and a pair of comfortable shorts or sweatpants to don. He hadn't even touched a single pair of the shoes, content to walk barefoot around the house.

He considered his reflection in the mirror, which covered the rear wall of the closet, and shook his head, mentally chastising himself. If anything, he looked even more pale and gaunt here than he had in the bathroom. The luxury of the house, not to mention the solitude of it, was making him lazy. He seemed to have left all self-discipline back at home with the rest of his belongings. He needed to do better before exceptions became habits.

"I want to start working out again," he said aloud, both to himself and to Ella. "Running and lifting weights."

"Very good," said Ella. "Our state of the art home gym can easily meet all of your exercise needs. I can create an appropriate routine for you if you like."

Michael considered. "We'll figure something out."

"Very good."

Michael picked out a pale blue polo shirt and a pair of dark denim jeans from the rack and held them up to eye level. Perhaps getting properly dressed would incentivize him to be more productive. He had gotten a decent amount of writing done since moving in, but he was not yet on anything that he would consider a streak. He wondered if he would have gotten any writing done at all if the Corporation did not require a daily report from him. Sitting down to fulfill that obligation at least put him at the desk on a daily basis, giving him no excuse not to put some work into his next novel, even if his progress so far had been slow.

He hung the clothing back up in order to free his hands and started to remove his towel.

He paused.

"Ella," he said. "You can see inside every room of the house, correct?"

"That is correct," she responded.

"And everything is recorded as well?"

"Yes, everything in the house is recorded."

"And how many people at the Corporation view these recordings?"

"As you are testing this house, all pertinent footage is reviewed by the programmers, engineers, and product developers at the Sterling Corporation."

Michael chewed on his lip. He knew he was under constant surveillance. He had agreed to as much before he had ever crossed the threshold, had resigned himself to it. He had actually gotten used to it surprisingly quickly, his inhibitions overcome by the fact that, in spite of the constant presence of Ella—not to mention Esra—he still felt completely alone and comfortable here.

"And what about the people who eventually purchase one of these houses? Will they be under 24/7 surveillance too?"

"Privacy settings can be modified by each owner," Ella answered. "It is not unlike the privacy settings on your cell phone."

Michael chuckled morosely.

"Is something wrong?" Ella asked. "I can assure you all footage is viewed only for quality control and research purposes. No one outside a select few at the Corporation views what is recorded."

"And it could never be leaked?" Michael asked. "You have to understand that there's a reason I would want to protect my privacy, even more so than most people."

"I understand," said Ella. "The footage cannot and will not ever be leaked. The Corporation is even more interested in protecting their intellectual property than they are in protecting your privacy."

Michael nodded. "Makes sense," he said. He put on the polo shirt and jeans, then slipped into a pair of sandals. The sandals in particular felt almost foreign to him, his feet so accustomed to being bare, but the leather was soft and the fit was perfect. He looked at himself in the mirror again.

"You look very nice today," Ella offered. "Quite handsome."

"Thank you," said Michael. "These clothes are really nice." What a difference the right clothing made. He was still terribly pale, but it was a vast improvement over the reflection that had greeted him in the bathroom mirror moments prior.

"I am glad you are pleased."

Michael picked up his towel, which he had dropped on the floor before getting dressed. When he stood upright again, Esra was hovering in front of him, one hand extended. His sudden, silent presence startled Michael. "*Geez,* Esra," he exclaimed, but the robot did not move, continuing to quietly wait. Michael handed over the sodden towel and watched as Esra turned and floated through the bedroom and disappeared further into the house.

"Ella," Michael said, following the robot's path from the bedroom and into the kitchen, where he stopped at the table. "You said that the programmers and engineers at the Corporation aren't watching all of the footage recorded in this house, only what is pertinent."

"Yes, that is correct."

"So how do they decide what is pertinent and what is not?" Michael pulled out a chair.

"I decide for them," said Ella.

Michael sat down to his breakfast. The menu couldn't get much simpler than bacon and eggs, but it was still the best bacon and eggs he'd ever had, and the orange juice tasted as if it was freshly squeezed. He chewed his food slowly, savoring it.

"Is it to your liking?" Ella asked.

"Delicious as always," said Michael.

"If it is alright with you, I need to do a quick systems update," said Ella. "This will take me offline for approximately ten minutes."

"That's fine," Michael said through a mouthful of egg. He washed it down with a swig of juice.

The quiet hum that permeated the house at all times slowly diminished until Michael could hear nothing but his own chewing. He finished his breakfast in relative silence. Normally he would scroll through his Twitter feed or check his messages while eating, utilizing a screen embedded within the kitchen table, but until Ella rebooted, this option was not available to him. Once his plate was empty, he sat back, expecting Esra to whisk away his dishes with his typical efficiency. When the robot didn't appear, Michael tipped back in his chair, looking through the doorway and into the living room beyond. Esra was nested in his charging station, still and silent. Apparently his systems were offline as well.

Michael gathered his dishes and took them over to the sink, setting them down carefully in the basin. He looked out the window, past the shimmering pool and the flat, expansive lawn to the faraway tree line, and froze at the sight of a woman standing right at the edge where the grass met trees. Dressed in a flowing white gown, her long hair shifting in the breeze, she appeared to be staring directly at him, although at this distance her expression was inscrutable. He felt his heart clench.

"Ella?" he said, his throat suddenly tight.

"All systems are offline," Ella responded. "Please stand by."

The woman didn't move. She stood still and ramrod straight, hands locked at her sides.

"There's someone outside. I need you to come back online," Michael said.

"All systems are offline," Ella repeated with irritating calmness. "Please stand by."

Michael exhaled a frustrated sigh. Momentarily he heard the house's humming resume, like a fan being turned on. He looked up at the tiny cameras that dotted the corner where the wall met the ceiling above him, his instinctual way of making eye contact with Ella.

"Are you back online?" he asked, before looking back through the window. The woman was gone.

Of course she's gone.

"Yes," said Ella. "All systems are back online."

"There was a woman," said Michael. "Standing near the trees. She was looking at the house."

"A woman?"

"In a white dress."

"I'm sorry, Michael," Ella replied. "I don't have any record of a person stepping onto the premises."

Michael felt agitation rising. "I know I saw her. Is it possible she walked through the woods?"

"The woods surrounding the property are quite impenetrable," said Ella. "It is highly unlikely that anyone could access the property on foot by traversing the woods."

Michael huffed. "Can you do another scan or something? Check the cameras?"

"All cameras were offline during the system reset," said Ella. "And none of the perimeter alarms were triggered. I currently find no indications of a trespasser. If someone was here, they have already left."

"I know what I saw," said Michael.

"I believe you," said Ella. "Rest assured you are quite safe. I will deploy a drone to do an aerial scan of the property. I will notify you if I notice any further activity out on the lawn."

Michael allowed his shoulders to fall as he willed himself to let go of the tension that had built up in his body. "Thank you," he said, eyes still focused out the window. Eventually he peeled his eyes away from the view and walked toward the study.

CHAPTER SIX

Dylan was writing.

What had come to him, if not exactly inspiration, was at least motivation enough for him to make another go of it. That morning he had printed off three outlines and placed them side by side on his desk. He pored over each, sometimes feeling that tiny spark of creativity, other times feeling like a total fraud. At one point he considered the *eeny-meeny-miny-moe* method of choosing which one to pursue. And then mid-morning, he had absentmindedly set down a bottle of water before going to the bathroom, and when he had returned, it had left a ring around the tentative title of the outline in the middle: *Re-Birth*.

It was as good a decision as any. *Thank you, Dasani.*

The plot, which centered around a Los Angeles plastic surgeon-slash-chemist who stumbled upon the medical equivalent of the Fountain of Youth—and the government's subsequent involvement in its distribution—was the kind of hybrid thriller/horror/science fiction story that would sell well as a follow-up to those who had read and enjoyed *BETA*. At least, that's what Dylan was hoping.

And once he began, the hours disappeared like cigarette smoke in a breeze. Writing for him was like Alice falling through the looking glass: he vanished into another world, lost in a land of his own creation. He often thought that if someone were to wander into his apartment they wouldn't even see him sitting at his desk, his fingers a blur of motion in that rapid hunt-and-peck style that was singularly his own. He didn't even stop to eat lunch, concerned that if he lifted that needle from its groove, he wouldn't be able to find his place in the song again.

Mid-evening, he was forced to quit by hunger that had transformed into a throbbing headache. His back ached. And besides all that, he was mentally exhausted. Even on his most creative days, eventually Wonderland got tired of Alice and evicted her back into reality.

He arched his back, attempting to straighten his spine as he shuffled toward the kitchen. He felt good about what he had written, and for the briefest of moments he realized he hadn't given a single thought to Rachel all day. But the moment he did, an all too real twinge of pain poked at his chest. He forced both her name and her face out of his mind, willing her away before she was able to make a lasting mark on what hours remained to the day.

Outside, all that was left of the sun was a sliver on the horizon. He didn't bother opening the fridge, knowing without looking that it was mostly empty and that what was there was not likely to be at all satisfying to a stomach that was now audibly complaining. He considered his takeout options.

From his desk in the next room, he heard a *ding*.

Resigned that there was nothing in the apartment that would satisfy his appetite, he returned to his desk, where a sweater hung like a cape over the back of his chair. He pulled it over his t-shirt, running his fingers through his hair to get it to lay right again. He then leaned over, tapping the keyboard to see what had caused his computer to chime.

It was a Facebook message from Charlie: "My roommates and I are headed in your direction tonight. There's a 9:15 showing of *Ex Machina* at Midtown Cinemas. Have you seen it?"

"Years ago," Dylan typed. "It's excellent."

"Care to join us?"

He looked at the clock on his screen. It was just after 7:30. He knew he would be leaving the apartment in order to get dinner anyway, and there were plenty of restaurants along the strip where Midtown Cinemas was located, a two-screen holdover of the 1960s that now specialized in second-run titles at reduced ticket prices.

"Sounds like fun," he wrote. Then he added: "I was heading out that way anyway."

"Yay!" Charlie responded. "We'll meet you there."

Dylan slipped on a tattered pair of loafers, not bothering with socks. He washed his face with cold water and gave himself a cursory glance in the mirror. *Good enough.* He locked his apartment's solitary door behind him as he stepped out onto the gravel driveway. Folding himself into his red Honda Civic, he peered up to the windows above his apartment. A soft flickering glow indicated that Mr. and Mrs. Baxter were watching television in their living room. *Jeopardy,* if he had to guess, as he frequently heard the plucky notes of the Final Jeopardy theme music falling through his ceiling on quiet weekday evenings.

He drove through growing darkness and the bright lights of traffic to the Route 40 exit. He pulled into the parking lot of Smoke-stacks, where the barbecue sauce was sticky, the meat was tender, the cornbread muffins were sweet, and the entire meal was served on the underside of a trash can lid. Fine dining it was not, but it was cheap, flavorful, and filling.

As Dylan waited in his booth for the food to arrive, he watched the people at the neighboring tables, none of them alone like he was. He studied them, the families and couples enjoying greasy food and each other's company, and gave in to an inevitable feeling of isolation, sucking on it like a lollipop. It tasted both familiar and bittersweet.

The hostess guided a woman to the booth across from Dylan. She set a shopping bag down beside her as she scooted across the padded bench, politely requesting water as she settled into her seat. She was quite pretty, although Dylan guessed she was several years older than him, a look of wisdom and experience on her face not usually present in the eyes of girls closer to his own age. The woman scanned her menu. Dylan stole only covert glances at her; anything longer than that risked transforming his loneliness into full-blown despair, not to mention making him look like a creep should she happen to notice him.

Moments later, after she had placed an order for a steak salad, the woman reached into her plastic shopping bag and pulled out a copy of *BETA*. Dylan felt his heart do a tiny leap at the sight of it, a pleasant flicker of joy warming his chest. The woman opened it to the first page and began reading, Dylan's small photograph on the back cover staring back at him from across the aisle. He imagined walking over to her, introducing himself by his full name, and seeing the blank look on her face transformed into delight as she realized he wasn't hitting on her, but was in fact the author of the book she was reading. Maybe she would ask him to sign it; maybe she would invite him to join her for dinner. Maybe both.

He entertained himself with the scenario until his garbage can lid arrived, overflowing with meat and cobs of corn and muffins, and the woman gave him a sidelong glance that read a little to Dylan like judgment—or perhaps it was nothing but simple amusement at the presentation—and he opted to leave her alone, realizing as he did so that he'd never really intended to approach her in the first place.

She never took her nose out of the book as Dylan ate his meal, and she barely spared a glance at her own salad, stabbing blindly at it with her fork as she continued to read, sometimes bringing the utensil up to her lips empty and then smiling to herself before making another attempt.

When Dylan was finished eating and the check arrived, he handed the waitress his credit card and leaned toward her, whispering, "Do me a favor, please. Add that woman's meal to my total and tell her that Dylan Matthews took care of it. Just… don't tell her until after I've left."

The waitress looked at him quizzically, then smiled in understanding before nodding and walking away without a word.

Both bills paid, Dylan stood and put on his coat. The woman looked over at him and smiled politely, but there was no recognition in her eyes. Dylan smiled back and walked away. As he exited the restaurant, pulling his coat around him in order to fend off the cold, his smile lingered. If nothing else, he had given the woman a neat story to tell, even if he himself would never hear it.

* * *

Dylan's red Civic pulled into the parking lot of the Midtown Cinemas a little after 9:00. He counted only four other vehicles there, all of them dark and unoccupied. He stepped into the brightly lit lobby and was greeted by the alluring smell of popcorn. A teenaged boy behind the counter welcomed him.

"I'm meeting some other people," said Dylan, looking around. Aside from a family of four at the concession stand, there were no other patrons in the lobby.

"Hey, you," came a voice from behind him.

Dylan turned as Charlie entered. She was wearing the thick blue parka that Dylan recognized from her Facebook photo. As she pushed the hood down, static causing strands of her hair to stand up at attention, she beamed at him. Dylan returned her smile as she approached, then felt mild surprise as she reached in for a hug, her hands sliding underneath his coat as she wrapped her arms around his waist. She squeezed him tightly, her face pressing against the middle of his chest, her head tucked under his chin as flyaway hairs tickled his nose. Dylan looked over her head into the parking lot on the other side of the glass. No one else was coming.

"Where are your roommates?" he asked.

She pulled away from him. "They're so lame," she said. "Theo and Alex changed their minds and Nadine got called in to work."

"You should have let me know," said Dylan. "We could have done it another time."

"No, it's fine," said Charlie, pulling off a thickly-woven mitten and waving it dismissively. "I wanted to get off campus anyway and I'm dying to see this movie."

"You haven't seen it before?" he asked.

"No," she said. "I've always wanted to but never got around to it. It sounds a bit like your book. Should we get tickets?"

As Charlie walked past him toward the counter, Dylan cast another glance toward the parking lot, realizing that a group outing to an old movie had suddenly morphed into something akin to a date.

Charlie waited for Dylan at the counter, both she and the cinema employee looking at him expectantly as he approached. "Two for *Ex Machina*," he said as he pulled out his wallet. Charlie didn't even feign a motion toward her purse, which was threatening to slide off her thickly padded shoulder.

"I'll get this," Dylan offered. "You got the tea."

"Oh, thank you," she said.

The teenager behind the counter tore off two tickets and handed the stubs to Dylan. "Theater One," he said.

Dylan walked toward the first theater, Charlie following. The double doors were closed. Dylan pulled one open for Charlie, but when he turned and looked back, she was no longer behind him. She had stopped in the middle of the lobby, where she stood staring up at the concession menu while pulling off her other glove and stuffing it into her pocket.

Dylan walked back toward her.

"I am *starving*," she said. "I didn't have time to eat dinner before leaving campus."

"Oh, okay," Dylan said. He looked at his phone. It was 9:15. He looked back at Charlie as she continued to peruse the brightly lit menu.

"I think I just want popcorn. Medium."

It took Dylan a moment to realize that she was talking to him and not the girl behind the glass counter filled with boxes of candy stacked in colorful columns. He smiled politely at the girl and said, "Medium popcorn, please."

"And a small Diet Coke." Again to Dylan.

"And a small Diet Coke," he parroted.

Dylan carried the popcorn, Charlie her Diet Coke, as he opened the door to Theater One and led her to a pair of centrally located seats. They were alone, and Dylan surmised that all the other theater patrons—all four vehicles' worth—must be next door watching *The Iron Giant*. The seats were worn, some of them secreting yellow stuffing, several of them broken and taped off with yellow caution tape, but the ceiling was magnificently high and there were long, burgundy drapes hanging on either side of the huge and randomly stained screen. This was a theater in the middle stages of decay, its former splendor almost completely hidden beneath the dust and soaked-in smell of cigarette smoke, the odor of a bygone era.

Dylan and Charlie removed their coats and sat down, Charlie draping hers over her lap. There were no cup holders in the ancient armrests, so when Dylan offered Charlie her overflowing bag of popcorn, she traded him her cold Diet Coke, which he held for her as she ate.

"You want some?" she offered, tilting the bag toward him.

"No, thank you, I'm not hungry."

"My roommates are so lame," she said.

"It's no big deal," said Dylan. "Where does Nadine work?"

"At the Apple Store," she said. "She's a huge computer geek."

"And the other two—Theo and Alex?—guys or girls?"

Charlie chuckled. "Huh, I hadn't thought about that before. They're boys. Total cinephiles. I only knew this was playing because Theo had mentioned it. Hey, can I have the ticket stubs?"

Dylan shrugged, digging the stubs out of the pocket of his jeans and handing them over.

"Thanks," said Charlie. "I like to keep them." She put them in her coat pocket.

"You go to the movies a lot?" Dylan asked.

"Not really."

The lights dimmed and Dylan felt himself relax. There were no commercials or trailers; the movie began in tandem with the darkness.

Dylan had seen *Ex Machina* before, had in fact viewed it multiple times as part of his research when writing *BETA*, although the AI in his novel was not much like the AI in the movie, which dealt more with the idea of a machine passing for human than simply becoming self-aware. Regardless, Dylan hadn't so much studied the film as he had become enamored with the movie's nearly flawless storytelling, not to mention Alicia Vikander's hypnotizing performance as the android, Ava. He felt that his book paled in comparison, coming across as clunky and elementary when held up to the subtlety and sophistication of the Alex Garland film.

As the minutes passed, Dylan lost himself in the movie's narrative, only occasionally pulled out of it by the sound of Charlie's quiet but still audible chewing beside him. He held her cup of Diet Coke, his elbow propped on the armrest between them so that she could easily reach it. Sometimes when she took it, she let her hand slide down his sweater-clad arm, her fingertips running over the length of his hand until she found the cup and took it from him.

It was partway through the film that Dylan became aware that Charlie was no longer watching the movie, but had instead fixed her gaze upon him. He sensed it first, the figurative pressure of her eyes on the side of his face, like the gentle push of a like-poled magnet. He glanced at her and smiled, confirming what he had already felt, and she smiled back gently, her face a blue glow in the light reflected from the movie screen. When Oscar Isaac performed a bizarre dance routine with his servant Kyoko, Charlie furrowed her brow and looked at Dylan to see if he was similarly confounded. With each of the movie's shocking moments or revelations, Dylan sensed Charlie watching him, studying his reactions. Her steady gaze made him uncomfortable, as if she was placing upon him an expectation to perform for her, to outwardly emote what he was perfectly content processing internally, especially since all of the movie's plot developments were familiar to him. And so Dylan stubbornly willed himself to remain stone-faced, not giving in to the unspoken pressure, and at some point he realized he was no longer able to lose himself in the story at all.

When the credits rolled and they exited the theater, the teen-aged clerk was sweeping stray popcorn kernels into a long-handled dustpan. "Goodnight," he said as they passed, and Dylan and Charlie said the same in response. Dylan tossed Charlie's empty popcorn bag and cup into a nearby trash receptacle, and they stepped out into the cold night.

Only two cars remained in the lot: Dylan's Civic and a powder blue Beetle that had to belong to Charlie. It was nearly 11:30, and there were hardly any traffic sounds coming from Route 40 or the nearby Route 15.

Dylan zipped his coat up against the frigid air as he walked with Charlie toward her car. She was pulling on her mittens.

"I'm assuming this is you," he said.

"This is me," she said. "This is Ringo."

Dylan nodded once in understanding. "Ringo the Beetle."

"—the Beetle," Charlie said in unison with him.

They smiled at each other awkwardly. Inside the theater lobby, lights were extinguished one by one.

"This was fun," said Dylan. "Thanks for inviting me to come."

"Of course."

"How long will it take you to get back to the dorms?" Dylan

asked.

"About an hour."

"Well, be careful," he offered. "It'll be pretty late by the time you get back."

Charlie stood against her driver's side door. She didn't move to get in, hadn't yet pulled her keys from her purse.

"That movie was *so* good," she said.

"It is," Dylan responded. "I watched it a lot while I was writing *BETA*."

"I could tell. It reminded me of your book."

Dylan nodded sheepishly, then shoved his hands deep into the pockets of his jeans. He raised his shoulders as he shivered and gave Charlie a look that he hoped read *I'm cold*. He wished he could start his car remotely, allowing it to warm up for as long as Charlie held him at bay.

Charlie approached him, inserting her hands between his arms and his ribs, hugging him. He pulled his right hand from its warm pocket and squeezed her once, then patted the back of her limp hood.

"We should do this again sometime," he offered.

"We should," she said softly against his chest.

"Tell you what," he said, pulling away. "Give me your number and then we won't have to message on Facebook all the time."

Charlie's smile didn't just fade; it fell as if being yanked downward by an invisible string. "I already gave it to you. At the bookstore."

Dylan's chest clenched. He snapped his fingers and pointed at her. "That's right," he said. "I meant to tell you. I put that napkin in my pocket and accidentally ran it through the wash. Give it to me again." He pulled out his cellphone.

Charlie eyed him with suspicion, her gaze so cold that Dylan worried that she was reading the lie on his face. Then he remembered her absentee roommates and felt a tinge of agitation.

She took his phone from him, which he had already unlocked, and entered her phone number. He watched her downturned head as she did so, wondering if by taking his phone she was intentionally keeping him from simply pantomiming the act of entering her number into his contacts.

She handed his phone back to him, taking one step forward as she did so, standing closer than necessary to return the device. She smiled up at him and blinked once, slowly.

Dylan grinned, took one hesitant step away, and then continued to retreat toward his car.

"Goodnight, Charlie," he said. "Drive safely. I'll call you."

"Goodnight," she said.

They got into their cars, doors slamming and engines starting in unison. Dylan waited for Charlie to turn on her headlights and pull away. He left the Civic headlights off, not wanting to blind her as she drove by him, and when she finally did so, he raised one hand in a wave.

Charlie did the same in return, not smiling, the look on her face one of somber disappointment.

CHAPTER SEVEN
DAY 45

Michael was nearing mile nine of a ten-mile run, his blue t-shirt soaked through with sweat, and while he was breathing through his mouth, he was regulating his breath, controlling it, focusing on pacing himself.

In front of him were the wooden planks of a boardwalk laid out in a perfect row like piano keys. People strolled by him, veering politely out of his way: men, women, and children with sun-darkened skin and relaxed smiles upon their faces, each of them clad in the colors of summer. He passed refreshment stands offering funnel cakes, hand-tossed pizza slices, fresh squeezed lemonade, crab cake sandwiches (all of them rated #1 at the beach), and Polish ice; storefronts with $10 t-shirts adorned with alternately funny or crude sayings, hermit crabs in colorful plastic cages, beach towels, boogie boards, and cheap sunglasses whose arms would likely snap if you slightly overextended them; and rows upon rows of ocean-front condos, their balconies holding up pastel rocking chairs and their white-haired occupants.

To Michael's right was a flat stretch of golden sand stroked gently by lilting and foamy waves. Striped beach towels and umbrellas dotted the vista. He heard the cries of seagulls and the sporadic whistling of a lifeguard.

"Ella," said Michael between breaths. "Let's play a word association game. I'll say a word, and you tell me the first word that comes to your mind."

"I understand," said Ella.

"Sand," said Michael.

"Corrosive," said Ella.

"Sun," said Michael.

"Heat," said Ella.

"Boat."

"Rocking."

"Wave."

"Crash."

"Ocean."

"Tsunami."

Michael laughed. "Pessimist," he said by way of accusation.

"Realist," Ella responded, and Michael laughed even louder.

"You have successfully completed ten miles," said Ella. The belt below Michael's sneakers slowed until it stopped completely. He stepped away from the treadmill, which was recessed into the gym's white tile floor, and bent over, placing his hands on his knees as he caught his breath. The boardwalk and its surrounding scenery, which had been displayed so realistically on the walls in front of and on either side of Michael, faded away, leaving mirrors on every side.

A door slid open and Esra entered, carrying a small towel in one hand, a large glass filled with a thick, dark blue liquid in the other. Michael stood up, took the towel, and dabbed at his forehead and armpits.

"Thanks, Ess."

"Hello. I am Esra."

"And I am Richard Simmons."

Esra shook up and down in a pantomime of silent laughter, screwing up his digital eyes into happy slivers. Whether or not Esra actually understood humor was unknown to Michael, but at the very least the robot recognized when Michael was joking, and always obliged with his own version of amusement.

Michael took the glass and downed it. It was thick and tasted of blueberries, bananas, and vanilla, Ella's own special protein shake recipe. It was delicious, and after the vigorous weightlifting routine that Ella had put him through in the hour prior to his 10 mile run, he knew he needed it. It helped that it was also refreshingly cold, cold enough to make his teeth ache.

He handed the empty glass and the sodden towel back to Esra. The robot pinched the towel between his thumb and one finger and held it out at arm's length, letting out a dramatic *phew* as he floated from the room.

Michael walked through the gym and past the stationary bike (which he had yet to use), a weight bench outfitted with cables and a leg extension attachment, a weight tree loaded with plates ranging from 2 to 50 pounds, a squat rack, and an enormous blue exercise ball. It was every piece of equipment he would ever want in a gym—home or otherwise. Most of it had been there on the day he had arrived, while the rest had been delivered per his request in the following weeks. All he had done was mention wanting certain pieces, ones he knew he would make regular use of; the next day, they were there.

Stepping into the hallway, Michael looked to his left toward a section of the house that remained unutilized. The house contained a total of ten rooms. Six of them—the main bedroom, bathroom, kitchen, living room, study, and gym—Michael frequented regularly. The remaining four were empty.

The first of these rooms was the house's second bathroom, located right across the hall from the gym. He hadn't been inside it since the initial tour, content to always use the master bathroom since it was usually just as convenient. Both bathrooms had a large walk-in shower, whirlpool tub, sink, and toilet, and both were more spacious than any of the rooms in Michael's own home, bathroom or otherwise.

Further down the hallway were three doors, two of them standing open. The open doors led to two completely empty rooms. Since Michael was occupying the house alone, these spaces, which would in most cases likely serve as additional bedrooms, were unfurnished. Ella had told him that if he could think of a personal use for these two rooms, they could be furnished accordingly. So far, he hadn't come up with a worthwhile idea. He had considered making a joke about turning one of them into a scrapbooking station, but bit his tongue when he imagined waking up one morning to find it stocked with floral papers, die cut machines, and decorative stickers, all dropped off as if by an unseen Santa Claus on the worst Christmas ever.

What had impressed Michael the most about these two barren rooms was that they were modular. Ella had demonstrated for him how the walls could shift, creating a larger room on one side, a smaller one on the other. She explained to him that in fact almost the entire house functioned this way. Every room could be made larger or smaller depending upon the owner's desired function for each—with some exceptions. The kitchen and bathrooms needed to remain static due to the plumbing and built-in cabinets, but the sizes of the other rooms could be changed if the occupant so desired.

The third room, the one with the closed door, was the server room. "The brains of the operation," Michael had remarked during his initial tour, putting his ear against the closed door. That rhythmic humming sound, which could always be subtly heard throughout the house, was much more apparent here. Michael had then pushed against the door, wanting to gain access in order to see all of Ella's motherboards, lights, and wires, but it had not responded to his touch, instead remaining closed.

"Your access to this room is denied," Ella had said.

"I just wanted to see it," Michael responded with a shrug.

"There is no need for occupants to enter this room. If you encounter any problems during your stay, you may file a report with the Sterling Corporation, and a member of our team will address it immediately."

Michael turned right from the gym's doorway toward the living room and his study. He peeled off his sweat-soaked shirt and let it fall to the floor behind him. A gentle whirring noise informed him that Esra had come to retrieve it. In the study, Michael kicked off his shoes, then used his toes to peel off his socks while steadying himself against a wall.

At the rear of the study was a pair of glass doors that led out onto the patio. Michael placed one palm on a panel beside the doors, which slid silently open in response. The hot and sticky afternoon air hit his already warm skin. Overhead, the sun shone blindingly in the sky.

Michael dropped his shorts to the smooth concrete, turned his back to the pool, and fell into its cold blue water, sinking like a rock to the bottom. The water, initially shocking against his warm skin, cooled him pleasantly. He closed his eyes and lay flat on the bottom of the pool, his limp arms lifting above him, the water moving soothingly over his body.

He lay there, still and relaxed. Just as his lungs began to call out for oxygen, he felt a vibration in his left wrist. He regarded the bracelet there, blurry through the water. A tiny red light was flashing rapidly. Michael sat up and pushed with his feet against the pool's floor, launching himself toward the surface. He inhaled a deep breath as his head emerged from the water.

"—ichael?" said Ella.

He used his thumb and index finger to pinch moisture from his eyes. "Yep?"

"Are you all right?" she asked. "Your oxygen blood level was decreasing precipitously."

"I was fine. Just relaxing on the bottom of the pool. I wasn't in any danger."

Michael noticed that in the brief time he had been underwater, Esra had already retrieved his shorts from where he had left them beside the pool and disappeared back inside the house.

He tipped onto his back and began a slow backstroke. The pool, framed by flat, white cement, was large, rectangular, and not at all ornate. A single plastic lounge chair and side table rested under the shade of a large umbrella on one end. On the other side was a circular hot tub, its jets presently quiet, its waters still and glassy.

A loud buzzing sound drew Michael's attention skyward. A drone, roughly the size of a compact car, passed over, its cargo—a large, gleamingly white box—pinched between two pointed appendages. The first time Michael had seen one of these massive mechanical wasps arriving at the house, he had been understandably alarmed. Since then, he had gotten used to their appearance every three or four days, their arrival heralding the delivery of food, supplies, or any personal orders that Michael had made. He was unable to see where on the roof these deliveries were deposited, and assumed that they were dropped into an opening panel of some kind. The drone typically departed within ten minutes of arrival, still grasping the same large box it had come with. The departing boxes were either empty or filled with refuse from the house.

Michael watched the drone until the corner of the roof obscured it from his view. Its motorized buzzing diminished and then disappeared entirely.

"Word association, Ella," he called out from where he was floating. "Delivery."

"Package."

"House."

"Home," Ella responded.

"Pool."

"Refreshing."

"Sky."

"Blue."

"Clouds."

"White."

"Bed."

"Rest."

"Um… Esra," he said.

"Helper," said Ella.

From inside the house, voice muffled by the glass doors, Esra called out, "Hello, I am Esra!"

"Ella," Michael said.

"Yes, Michael?"

"No, *Ella*," he said. "First word that comes to mind when you hear *Ella*."

A pause. "Friend."

Michael flipped over and swam under the water again. When he breached the surface once more, he raked one hand over his hair, sending water droplets flying. He looked up, bright sunlight stabbing at his eyes. He watched as a white wisp of cloud slowly expanded.

He silently contemplated the weight he had begun to carry, not physical but emotional, that he struggled to put a name to. It wasn't entirely unpleasant, but there was no denying that it had been growing steadily over the past several days. He couldn't decide if it was loneliness or isolation or simply the feeling of being completely and utterly relaxed in this new and totally secluded environment. Perhaps it was an unfamiliar combination of both.

"I'd like a drink," he said.

"What can I get you?" asked Ella.

"Surprise me. Something tropical and neon. With a tiny blue umbrella in it."

Michael enjoyed doing this on occasion, testing Ella with spontaneous but specific requests simply to see if she could fulfill them. More often than not, to both his surprise and amusement, she was able to deliver. It seemed that the more time Michael spent in the house, the more capable Ella was at meeting the specificity of his requests. At the moment, it wasn't the tropical drink that was in question, but the umbrella. Tomorrow, he might ask her for a pair of bright green socks embroidered with pink flamingos. Just to see.

Several moments later, Esra emerged from the house, the glass doors parting for him with a sibilance of air. On one arm was draped a green and blue striped beach towel. In the other hand, the robot balanced a tray bearing a tall narrow glass filled with a bright yellow liquid topped by whipped cream, a maraschino cherry, and a blue paper umbrella.

Michael swam to the edge of the pool, placed his palms on the concrete, and pushed himself out of the water. Both the summer air and the concrete were hot against his skin. His wet feet made gentle slapping sounds as he approached Esra. He took the towel and dabbed at his face, then picked up the glass. He removed the umbrella, sucked the whipped cream from its sharp toothpick handle, and tucked it behind one ear with a wink.

Esra winked in return.

Michael walked toward the lounge chair, but not before downing half the virgin Pina Colada, which was more delicious than any he'd ever tasted before. He pulled the chair and side table out from under the shade of the large umbrella, draped his towel over the chair, and reclined on it with a satisfied smile, the warm plastic causing his cooled skin to break out in goosebumps. He placed the nearly empty glass on the table and closed his eyes to the sun.

"May I suggest that you apply some sunscreen," said Ella. "On a day like today your skin can burn in as few as twenty minutes."

"I won't be out here that long," Michael mumbled. He yawned deeply and placed his hands behind his head. The sun warming his wet skin, a slow breeze causing distant leaves to whisper, Michael drifted off to sleep.

Soon he dreamed, and in the dream he stood at the edge of a pool, only the waters of this pool were dark and churning like the waves of the sea in a storm. He stared into them, seeing his own reflection as it warped and rippled and broke.

"Michael?"

On the opposite side of the pool was a woman. She was tall and lithe, wearing a thin white gown that outlined her slender frame. Her dark hair fell in waves over her shoulders, strands of it floating in the warning breeze of an oncoming storm. The look on her face was full of longing as she gazed across the violent waters toward Michael. She held out one hand to him.

He wanted nothing more than to go to her, but he feared diving into the waters that separated them. They were too violent. Surely he would drown. He took a step forward, looking down once more into the crashing waves, and considered jumping in, his overwhelming desire for her warring against his fear. He wondered with a disconnected amusement why he couldn't just circumnavigate the pool, walking its perimeter until he reached her, but dream logic told him that his only path was straight across.

"Michael?" she said again.

He looked up at her.

Her smile was serene. Her beauty made Michael's heart ache.

"You are all mine," she said.

He moved forward, not stepping but being pulled, and as soon as one toe touched the pool's surface, he was sucked under, water pouring into his nose and down his throat and burning his open eyes. He opened his mouth to scream, but only a thick train of bubbles emerged as he continued to sink.

Michael woke to a harshly cold sensation on his face, accompanied by an unpleasant hissing sound. He sat up abruptly in the lounge chair, eyes pinched shut, and his forehead collided with the edge of something metallic. He opened his eyes to find Esra hovering before him, an aerosol can aimed directly at his face. Michael started to ask the robot what it was doing, but knew immediately from the smell: Esra was dousing him with sunscreen.

Michael waved one hand through the cloud of spray, coughing. He licked his lips and spat when the chemical coated his tongue. He reached for his drink and cleansed his palate with its watery remains, swishing it around in his mouth before spitting it onto the concrete. Dismissing Esra with an irritated wave of his hand, Michael rose from the chair. He picked up the towel and wiped his face.

"I didn't want you to burn," said Ella.

"I wasn't going to burn," Michael objected.

"You had been asleep for fifteen minutes. Your skin was reddening."

"Well, there are definitely more polite ways to wake a person than blasting them in the face with sunscreen."

"My apologies," said Ella. "I was merely concerned for your health."

Michael wrapped the towel around his waist and stomped toward the house. The glass doors parted as he approached, and Michael walked through the study to the kitchen, the air of the house cool on his bare torso.

The aroma of food reached him just before he saw what awaited him on the table: a 12-ounce ribeye, rare; a baked potato covered in sour cream, butter, and chives; grilled asparagus; and a glass stein filled to the rim with sparkling water. There was also a single lit candle and a thin white vase holding up a red rose. The presentation looked like something from a restaurant menu or food magazine, and the irritation Michael had been feeling began to fade just as quickly as it had appeared.

His mouth watered at the sight, and Michael realized that he was ravenous. He considered getting dressed, but impulsively sat down to the hot meal and began carving the steak, which was red in the center and tender, the flesh giving way to the blade with ease. The first bite melted in his mouth.

He sat back in the chair and moaned contentedly, closing his eyes as he chewed slowly, savoring it.

"Oh, Ella," he said.

"Yes?"

"I haven't forgotten about the whole sunscreen in the face thing," he said, mouth quite full, all pretense of decorum gone, "but this steak is incredible. It's the best I've ever had. No lie."

"I am pleased you are pleased," she said.

"Pleased?" he said with a chuckle. "I think I'm in love."

CHAPTER EIGHT

Dylan was drunk.

After successfully finding what he had thought might be the key to his next novel, he walked down a few figurative hallways, took a couple of left turns, and abruptly found himself at another dead end. He was eight chapters in, nearing 23,000 words when the door was closed to him, and he found himself in a familiar place: standing outside in the hallway, hands empty.

The morning had started with promise. Under a hot trickle of water (the best that his rusty shower head could muster), Dylan had mentally mapped out how to approach the next development in the story, even crafting a couple of insightful lines. He finessed them while he shaved, revised them further while he dressed. But by the time he sat down at his desk, all inspiration was gone.

Mid-morning, after two hours of false starts, he had gone to the refrigerator for a bottle of water. There were none. The only drinkable liquid remaining in the apartment was beer. Tap water wasn't an option; it tasted like rust.

He could have gone out to the store, but it felt as though leaving the apartment was akin to admitting defeat, letting go of an invisible strand that he wasn't certain he was holding on to anymore anyway. So he allowed himself just one beer.

And then just one more.

Shortly after noon, he was sprawled out on his living room sofa, head propped on one arm rest, heels dangling over the other. Bottle of beer and cell phone on the floor beside him, he had placed a framed photo of himself and Rachel on his chest, watching it rise and fall with each of his breaths. He ran his index finger down the middle of Rachel's forehead, down the bridge of her perfect nose. He tapped his finger on the tip of her nose and whispered, "*Boop!*" It made him laugh so hard that the framed photo bounced off his chest and fell with a clatter to the floor. This made him laugh even harder.

He left the picture where it landed and plucked his cell phone off the carpet. He scrolled lazily through his contacts and tapped impulsively on his mom's number. Three rings in, a pang of anxiety filled his gut and he found himself hoping she wouldn't pick up. She would know he was drunk within half a dozen words. She would scold him. Worst of all, she would be disappointed in him.

"Please don't answer, please don't answer…"

She didn't pick up.

Exhaling a breath heavy with relief, he resumed scrolling. His agent. His mom (again). College pals he hadn't seen since graduation, including his former roommate Nick.

"Nicky. Nicolai. Nicholas. The Nickster. Tricky Nick Nixon…" Dylan belched.

And then there was Charlie. Depressing as it was to admit to himself, she was the closest thing he had to a friend at this particular moment in time. But he was also fairly certain she could provide the encouragement he needed, or at the very least a sympathetic ear.

Tap.

"Hello?"

"CHARLIE!" he shouted, and then shushed himself.

"Dylan?"

"This is Dylan," he whispered. "How *are* you?"

"What's the matter with you? Are you drunk?"

"Wow," he said. "How very astute. Are you my mother?"

"Why are you drunk?"

"I'm not drunk. I'm hammered. Wasted. Plastered. Oiled. Buzzed. Sloshed. Knee high to the wind." His words were slow and slurred.

"That doesn't make sense."

"Pie eyed and cock-eyed."

"I'm hanging up."

"No!" he protested, sitting up. Doing so caused his head to swim. His eyes widened as he steadied himself with one hand on the arm of the couch. "I want to talk."

"Okay," she said, drawing out the word with hesitation. "What do you want to talk about?"

"How about what a horrible writer I am?"

"You are *not* a horrible writer."

"Oh, but I am," he said. "Been trying to write all morning, and I ain't got nuttin' to show for it."

"Go make yourself some coffee."

"I don't like coffee."

"Right. Go make yourself some really strong tea."

"That I can do," he said, standing up. He was unsteady on his feet. "Follow me."

He sauntered into the kitchen and began filling a kettle from the tap. Once the water was boiled, it would be more palatable.

"What makes you think you're a horrible writer?" Charlie asked.

Dylan put the kettle on the stove and turned the dial for the wrong burner. "I've hit a dead end," he said. "I'm writing this book, see. It's gonna be called *Re-Birth*. About this doctor who creates the Fountain of Youth in a lab. Now *shhhhh,* you can't tell anybody I told you any of this. My agent would kill me."

"Mum's the word," said Charlie.

Dylan stared at the stove, at the glowing red burner on the left, the kettle on the right. He was momentarily confused.

"Dylan?"

"Ah," he said, realizing his mistake. He moved the kettle to the left burner. "Yeah, so, I'm eight chapters into it and I'm just… stuck."

"That doesn't make you a horrible writer. It just means you've got writer's block."

"I should quit. Go work at a…McWendy's."

"Is that why you got drunk? At 1:30 in the afternoon?"

"*Maaaaaaaybe.*"

"Dylan," she scolded.

"Look, I'm under a lot of *pressher. Publisher's Weekly* called *BETA*, and I quote, 'Finely crafted and brimming with relentless tension.' Said it transcends time and space. And that lovers of every genre of fiction should… should… hug it."

"Embrace it?"

"*Embrace* it. You're really smart, Charlie."

"Thanks," said Charlie.

"I mean that," said Dylan.

"I'm sure you do," Charlie sighed impatiently. "So why did you call me?"

"I need a pep talk."

"Call your mom."

"I tried. She's very busy and important." Dylan leaned his back against the kitchen sink. He heard Charlie take a deep breath.

"Okay, look," said Charlie. "You're a wonderful writer. You're 23 years old and you have a bestselling book on the shelves of Walmart, Target, and airport bookstores everywhere. That's a lot to be proud of."

"I guess."

"I *know*," said Charlie. "How many writers your age can say that?"

"Yeah, well…" Dylan trailed off.

"Yeah well nothing."

"Did I ever tell you how I met my agent?" he asked.

"No," said Charlie.

Dylan told her.

* * *

Dylan's senior year at the University of Baltimore, he had enrolled in a Creative Writing course. His major was English; he was minoring in Journalism. He planned to be either a teacher or a journalist, but he had not yet decided which. Needing one more arts elective, he picked Creative Writing simply because it fit within the last remaining gap in his schedule.

The class was attended by only eleven other students and was taught by a woman named Isabelle Levin. She dressed in blouses with puffy sleeves, flowing skirts, and a little too much costume jewelry. But she presided over the class with the kind of infectious zest and enthusiasm for the written word that Dylan and every other student in attendance wanted nothing more than to bring beauty into the world by sheer force of their collective creativity.

Every week, Isabelle ("Please, everyone call me Isabelle") and the twelve students assembled around a large table facing one another, each of them having brought along a new piece they had written during the previous week. Sometimes Isabelle had given them specific instructions ("Next week, I want you to write something inspired by a whimsical childhood memory."), but usually she gave the students creative free reign, encouraging them to follow their own muses.

The students would take turns reading all or a portion of their work, and the others would give their honest critiques, both critical and supportive. Dylan found the process alternately nerve-racking and exhilarating. There were occasional tears, but for the most part the group, randomly brought together at the beginning of the semester, grew to be incredibly encouraging of one another.

The only aspect of the class that Dylan didn't care for was that of the twelve students, only he and one other wrote fiction. The remaining ten exclusively submitted poetry. When the semester started, Dylan didn't care much for poetry, but after a couple of months, while he still didn't have much of an affinity for it—and certainly didn't care to write it— he had at least grown to respect it as an art form. It helped that even the most trite, Hallmark-ready rhyming prose sounded like Shakespeare when read by Isabelle. She had a way of reciting words that made them almost melodic.

Dylan, however, only wrote fiction. Every week he submitted a new short story. And almost without exception, the class reacted positively to his writing, and Isabelle rarely had any criticisms of his work at all. She would smile warmly as he read to the class (usually only a couple of choice paragraphs, as there wasn't time enough in 90 minutes for him to read an entire piece), and when he was finished, she would say something along the lines of, "Well done as always, Dylan. Such attention to detail, such an incredible ear for dialogue."

There was no final exam. Instead, during the last week of classes, each of the twelve students scheduled thirty minutes of time to sit alone with Isabelle while she gave a conclusive, overarching review of a semester's worth of each student's work. When Dylan had entered her office on that last day, she had asked him to sit by gracefully waving one bauble-clad, long-nailed hand at the chair in front of her desk. She had then gazed at him serenely, the gentlest hint of a smile on her face.

"Oh Dylan," she had said. "I think you know by now that I consider you to be a very gifted writer."

"Thank you," he had said, warmth creeping into his cheeks.

"It has truly been a joy to have you in my class. I can honestly say I will very much miss being able to look forward to a new story from you every week."

"Thank you," he repeated. He shifted uncomfortably in his chair.

"Please promise me that I won't find out one day that you became something boring like an accountant or an architect."

Dylan laughed. "I promise."

"Good," she said, nodding slowly. Her smile then faded slightly. She chewed on one corner of her bottom lip, her eyes never leaving Dylan's.

"Listen," she continued, sitting forward and resting her elbows on her desk. "I am going to do something I have never done before. And I'd rather you didn't tell any of your classmates."

"Okay," Dylan readily agreed, although he had no idea what she was about to say. But keeping the secret, whatever it was, would be easy: he doubted he would ever see or speak to any of those classmates again.

"I have a very dear friend named Cynthia Barnett. She is a literary agent in New York with close ties to HarperCollins and several other publishers. Do you know what HarperCollins is?"

"Yes," said Dylan. His mouth was suddenly quite dry.

"It's one of the biggest book publishers in the world," said Isabelle, as if Dylan hadn't answered. "She has always said to me, 'Isabelle, don't you dare ever send any of your students knocking on my door. And I mean it.' She made me promise." Here, Isabelle paused dramatically. "But some promises are made to be broken."

She smiled conspiratorially. Dylan smiled back politely.

"I want you to go home and pick out your five best stories and email them to me by this time tomorrow. I am going to send them to Cynthia. She will say she is not interested. I will say yes, she is, and insist that she read your work. She will read your work. And then she is going to take you on as a client."

Dylan felt his jaw slowly fall.

"Now, before you go getting all excited," said Isabelle, "you need to know that Cynthia is not going to pitch you to HarperCollins or any of the other publishers as a writer of short fiction. There's not much of a market for that. She is going to want to pitch you as a novelist. So I need to ask you: do you think you can write a novel, Dylan?"

Dylan paused. Suddenly his two potential career paths, teacher or journalist, were being peeled away like the skin of an apple. In an instant he was being told to consider a new path, one he had never seriously contemplated before. Novelist.

"Yes," he said, although he had no way of knowing if this was true.

"Do you already have ideas for a novel?"

"Absolutely." This time, it was definitely a lie.

She looked at him skeptically. "Good," she said. "Send me those five stories tomorrow, and then I would advise you to start outlining a novel right away. Do not waste any time. At the point that Cynthia calls you, and she *will* be calling you, she will want you to pitch her your ideas. It would be good if you had at least three so that she has something to reject. She *loves* rejecting. Give her only one idea and she'll turn it down, no matter how good it is."

"I understand."

Dylan did as instructed. He emailed five of his best stories to Isabelle the next day, which happened to be a Friday. He then spent the entire weekend researching how to write a book outline (since he had absolutely no idea) and then cobbled together three of them. By the following Tuesday he was satisfied with what he had prepared. And on Thursday, exactly one week after his meeting with Isabelle, he got a call from Cynthia Barnett.

"Dylan, this is Cynthia Barnett," she had said. Her voice was deep and commanding.

"Yes, hi." His heart was pounding.

"I'm in New York right now, but I'm coming to Baltimore tomorrow. I can be there by mid-day. Where do you want to meet?" There was no question about Dylan's availability or desire to meet with Cynthia. He quickly surmised that this was a woman who did not hear the word *no* often, and disregarded it when she did.

They met at a restaurant called the Seafood Shanty at 1:30. Dylan chose the restaurant not because he had ever eaten there, but because of its rating on Yelp, trusting the reviews of strangers over his own opinion. He put on a suit jacket and tie and purchased an old leather briefcase from a nearby Goodwill store, knowing he would likely never have need of it again. Inside it he placed printed copies of the three outlines as well as the five stories he had already emailed to Isabelle.

As he sat on a burgundy padded bench in front of the hostess stand at the restaurant, he felt a cold sweat under his arms, a thin stream of it trickling icily down his back.

Though he had never laid eyes on Cynthia Barnett before, he knew who she was as soon as she walked through the restaurant's front doors. She was dressed in a tailored white blouse, two buttons opened tastefully, over which she wore a dark blue blazer. The ensemble was completed by a tight pencil skirt and matching blue high heels. Her hair fell in soft blonde ringlets past her shoulders, and she wore subtle yet flattering makeup. She was trim, with the calves of a runner and could pass for a woman in her mid-thirties. But based solely on the wizened, somewhat jaded look in her silver blue eyes, Dylan guessed she was actually somewhere in her mid- to late forties.

Dylan was instantly both enamored and intimidated by her. He stood on tremulous legs as she entered, and Cynthia subtly sized him up before extending one confident hand.

"Hello, Dylan. I'm Cynthia Barnett." In heels, she was nearly as tall as he was.

He shook her hand, hoping his own didn't feel clammy. "Dylan Matthews."

Her eyes scanned his face. "Dear Lord," she said. "You are so young."

They got a table. She ordered drinks for them both without

asking Dylan what he wanted.

"Nice place. Good choice. Have you been here before?" she asked.

"Um, no."

She chuckled. "Then why did you pick it?"

"It gets good reviews."

"We could have gone somewhere you liked."

"None of the places my buddies and I go to are this nice."

She waved the answer away, then looked down at her menu. "I wouldn't have cared."

Dylan began pulling papers from his briefcase. His hands were unsteady.

"You look like you could use a drink," Cynthia observed.

"I'm nervous," Dylan admitted.

"Don't be," she said. "You're in."

"I am?" he asked.

"Look," Cynthia said, putting her menu down. "I don't know whether to kill Isabelle or to kiss her. I might do both. Not in that order. 'Don't ever send me one of your students,' I say. Then what does she do? Sends me a student."

"I'm sorry," said Dylan.

"For what? Being one of the best writers I've read in the past 15 years? Please."

Dylan was taken aback. "Wow. Thank you."

"Don't thank me, thank Isabelle."

"I will."

"You should."

Their drinks arrived. Dylan downed his but didn't taste it, feeling embarrassed when he set it down empty only moments after it arrived.

"And that face of yours," Cynthia said, eyes locked on his and shaking her head. "Look at you. That's a face that will help sell books. People say looks don't matter if you're a writer, but it certainly doesn't hurt. That's a face we're going to put on the back of every cover. On every advertisement and poster."

Dylan felt himself blushing hotly. Her bluntness was unnerving, her speech rapid fire, leaving him feeling flattered but unsettled. He mustered a thank you.

"Just don't get fat on me."

"Okay," he chuckled.

Cynthia was stone-faced. "I'm not kidding."

"I know."

"Isabelle already told you, I don't do short stories. Publishers aren't interested in them. When's the last time you heard of a best-selling short story collection? It doesn't happen. Unless you're Stephen King."

"Right."

"Yours are good, don't get me wrong. And if you get big enough someday maybe we can push a collection. But right now I need a novel. You got a novel?"

Dylan placed the outlines on the table in front of him. "I have three." He cleared his throat. "Outlines for novels." He set them out in a row like playing cards.

Cynthia glanced at them, grinned patiently, and looked back at Dylan. "Let me hear them," she said.

"Oh," he said, picking the papers back up. Slowly, and with a voice that refused to remain steady, Dylan read to Cynthia the outline for his first novel idea.

She rejected it. "That sounds like a bad M. Night movie. Next."

His heart sank, and he felt a burning sensation in the pit of his stomach. He wished he had a glass of water. Cautiously, he read the second outline, trying to inject some enthusiasm into the tone of his voice.

"No," she said, cutting him off. "Too Colleen Hoover."

Dylan picked up the third one, the only one he had left, and read it. Cynthia remained quiet this time. When he finished, he looked up cautiously at her.

"That one," she said. "It's perfect. Obviously you saved the best for last."

They ate. They toasted. Cynthia talked nearly non-stop during what ended up being a three hour lunch meeting, shifting gears so frequently that Dylan felt as though he might get whiplash. By the time they had said their goodbyes in the restaurant lobby, he was physically and mentally exhausted. When Cynthia exited the building, Dylan slumped down with a loud sigh on the bench in front of the hostess stand and leaned back against the window, head thudding against the glass. He felt as if he had just run a marathon. The hostess looked at him with curiosity and concern on her face.

Cynthia had told him that by the time they spoke again, he would have an offer for a publishing deal with an advance attached to it beyond what he had ever imagined earning as either a journalist or a teacher. She suggested he get a lawyer to review the contracts that would be coming his way. She also made him promise to go home and devote all his free time to writing a novel.

He walked to his car on a cloud. He couldn't wait to tell his parents. He couldn't wait to tell Rachel.

* * *

"That's great!" said Charlie. "How cool of your teacher to help you out like that."

Dylan was on the couch again, this time sitting up, a steaming mug of tea in one hand. He wasn't sure if the tea was helping to sober him up or if it was simply the act of being completely honest with Charlie that was helping to clear his mind.

"It was cool of her," he agreed.

"And it sounds like Cynthia liked your writing as much as your teacher said she would."

"She did." Dylan nodded.

"And it's because you're an excellent writer, Dylan. You're just having an off day. You'll write another book. And it will be genius."

"About that," Dylan said. "There's something else I haven't told you yet."

* * *

Of the twelve students in Dylan's creative writing class, ten of them wrote poetry. Dylan only wrote fiction, as did one another student. A student by the name of Dwayne Johnson.

"As in 'The Rock'?" Charlie asked, a skeptical laugh in her voice.

"Yup," said Dylan. "I went to school with Dwayne 'The Rock' Johnson, except this Rock was a skinny white kid of 21 with freckles and glasses, a computer science major."

Dwayne was quiet, one of the quieter members of the creative writing class. When the students were critiquing each other's work, he rarely spoke up, and when he did, it was with a quiet, unassuming voice. And Dwayne, like Dylan, wrote short stories. In a way, Dylan and Dwayne were yin and yang. Dylan was a master of prose, but Dwayne was a master of story. Dwayne could imagine a plot like no one else, putting in revelations and twists that threw the reader for a loop. But he lacked Dylan's skill with a sentence, that necessary subtle rhythm with which the best writers could draw a reader into another world, guiding them on a journey without requiring them to leave their seat.

Dwayne was a good kid. A creative kid with a brilliant mind. But his stories, excellent as they were, stood firmly in Dylan's shadow for the single semester that they had shared a class with each other.

On that fateful last day of school, when Isabelle had given Dylan his final life-changing assignment, he had done exactly as instructed and cobbled together outlines for three novels. The first one would be a book-length version of a short story he had written for class; it centered on a woman who began receiving a daily phone call from her recently-deceased husband. The second one followed a man's descent into obsession after he ran into an old flame from college who no longer remembered him. And the third and final idea was the story of a man who had been selected to live in and test a fully automated smart home, with horrific results.

Cynthia Barnett had rejected those first two ideas. It was the third, tentatively titled *BETA,* which had landed Dylan an agent, a very lucrative publishing deal, and eventually his very own top-40 best-selling novel.

And it was based on a story originally written by Dwayne Johnson.

CHAPTER NINE
DAY 52

When Michael had first arrived at the house, the room that was to serve as his study, which stood just off the kitchen and across from the living room, was notable for only three things: its plain white desk and chair, its double glass doors that opened up to the patio and pool outside, and the wall of empty shelves that framed those doors.

Michael had only sporadically used the room during his stay, his creative output varying greatly by the day. At first, he blamed his lack of concentration and motivation on the barren and antiseptic feel of the room. He couldn't stand the sight of the empty shelves, especially since they had been so obviously designed to hold books. Upon mentioning this to Ella, she had asked him which writers' works he most favored. "Surprise me," he had said, and by the time he had awoken the next morning, the study had been stocked with the works of authors both familiar to Michael as well as some he had never heard of before. Perusing a handful of these titles revealed to him that the selection could not have been more suited to his tastes had he chosen them himself.

And now, instead of being productive at the desk, he paced back and forth, his eyes scanning the names on the multicolored spines: Adams, Asimov, Barker, Bradbury, Campbell, Clarke, Dick, Du Maurier, Heinlan, Jackson, King, Levin, Lovecraft, Matheson, Poe, Simmons, Stoker, Straub, Wells. There were even several books he had loved as a child by the likes of C.S. Lewis, J.R.R. Tolkien, and E.B. White, among others.

He plucked Dean Koontz's slender *Demon Seed* from the shelf and read the synopsis on the back cover. He savored the feeling of the book in his hands—the weight of it, the pleasant feel of its cover on his fingertips. The smell of its paper and ink.

Outside, the sun shone brightly. Re-shelving the Koontz book, Michael placed one forearm on the wall and rested his forehead against the back of his wrist, looking out onto the green lawn and the rippling blue pool that waited just outside, then beyond them to the wall of trees on the faraway perimeter.

The glass doors slid open with a soft hiss. Warm outside air pushed against Michael's face.

"I'm not going outside," he said.

The doors closed again.

"Is there anything I can get you?" Ella asked.

"No," he said. "I need to get some writing done. I'm so behind. I'm just not feeling particularly motivated today."

"Why aren't you motivated?"

"I'm not sure," he said.

He took a step back from the doors and looked at the shelves again.

"Perhaps you would like to spend some time reading?" Ella suggested. "If you are not pleased with the selections I have purchased for you, I also have a vast digital library for you to choose from."

Michael considered. "No, I am quite pleased. But it's much too beautiful a day to read. Or to get any work done, apparently."

"How is the weather stopping you from either working or reading?"

"It's not," he said, sliding down into his desk chair. He kicked off the floor, making the chair spin slowly. "I'm just more motivated when it's gray and raining."

Slowly, the sunshine outside faded as thick, black clouds rolled in with the kind of velocity only ever seen in sped up camera footage. Michael heard the rumble of thunder, loud enough to make the walls vibrate. After a bright flash of lightning, water began to pour from the sky.

"Better?" Ella asked.

Michael stopped his chair from spinning and stared out the glass doors. "Better," he smiled. Ella's response to his statement had been exactly what he had expected.

"I did not know you were a pluviophile," said Ella.

"Me either," said Michael. "Mainly because I have no idea what that means."

"It is derived from the Latin word *pluvia*, which means *rain*, and the Greek word *philein*, which means *to love*," Ella explained. "A pluviophile is someone who finds joy and peace in the sound and smell of rain, and may enjoy activities such as reading, drinking tea, or listening to music on a rainy day."

Michael rose and placed his hand on the panel to the left of the French doors. The door slid open once again, dragging along with it the artificial image of the thunderstorm, revealing to Michael once more the hot summer day outside. He took one step back and observed: bright sunshine outside the open door on the left, dark rainstorm through the glass on the right. Forced to choose, he would not have been able to separate the real from the digital had he not already known which was which.

"What are you doing, Michael?" Ella asked.

"I was just curious," he said.

The door slid shut as Michael sat once again in his desk chair.

His eyes shifted to the bookshelves.

"Have you read all of these authors before?" asked Ella.

"No, not by half. But you have some of my favorites here. And several that sound like potential favorites."

"Do you enjoy reading?"

"Very much so."

"Why do you enjoy reading?"

"Why does anyone read? To be entertained, mostly," Michael said. "To escape into other worlds. I think it was Stephen King who said, 'Books are uniquely portable magic.'"

"What are you escaping from?"

"Reality."

"What is so bad about reality that you feel the need to escape from it?"

"Nothing," said Michael. "Not always. It's like movies. Books and movies let you put aside your own reality for a moment and step into another one. It gives you a mental break. It lets you rest a part of your brain."

"So you read to be happy?"

"Sure," he said. "Or sometimes to have a good hard cry."

"Why would you read a book that makes you cry?"

"People read in order to feel lots of different emotions. Happiness, sadness, fear, excitement, love."

"People *want* to be sad? Or afraid?"

"As a general rule, no," said Michael with a small smile. "But books are pretty special in that way. They can evoke a whole gamut of emotions without presenting any real… consequences, I guess. Books can make the reader *feel* just about anything without making them actually *experience* any of it. It's a bit like a drug, in a sense. It allows us to experience something that we might not otherwise. I don't know if that makes sense."

"It doesn't," Ella said.

Michael chuckled and sat forward in his chair. "Okay, like, no one *wants* to be sad, not in reality. No one *enjoys* being sad. But reading something sad allows us to experience that feeling, on some small level at least, without any of the lasting damage. We can close the book and it's over. But in the meantime, it's a little like flexing a muscle that we don't often get to use."

Ella didn't respond.

"Humans are just weird, I guess," Michael admitted with a shrug.

"I wasn't going to say it," said Ella.

Michael laughed again. "Most of the time, people just want a happy ending, the assurance that everything will turn out alright in the end."

"Do all of these authors write happy endings?" Ella asked.

"You mean these authors here?" Michael asked, waving a finger at the shelves. "I haven't read all of them, but in general, I'd say probably not. Horror and science fiction are genres that typically tend toward more grim endings."

"So you enjoy being scared?" asked Ella.

"In reality, no, and let's make that abundantly clear before you decide your newest directive is to scare the pants off me. But in books, yes. Again, it's like experiencing danger and fear without the reality of either one."

"Is this true of most people?"

"Is what true of most people?"

"Do most people enjoy stories with *grim* endings?" Ella asked.

"No, I'd say not. Most people like happy endings. And I'd say most fiction typically has a happy ending. As a general rule I think people like to feel all warm and fuzzy when they close a book."

"Is this because life often does not have a happy ending, and they want to escape from it?"

Michael was taken aback. "That's a pithy question," he said. "Maybe that's a part of it. And another part of it too is that of all the emotions, happiness is the one people most want to feel, and so that is what most authors write. Happy endings, that is. But as far as endings go, life and books are very different things."

"How so?" Ella asked.

"Well, life is often much more ambiguous than books. Books typically follow a pretty linear course from beginning to middle to end. When the end comes, it's definitive, the questions are answered and all the loose strings are tied up. All the connections are made. Life itself is rarely that neat. Sometimes life's stories come to an end that isn't very conclusive or satisfying at all. Events take place and we have no idea why they happened or what purpose they served."

"Isn't death a definitive ending?" Ella asked.

"Of course it is. But that doesn't mean that all events leading up to death make sense to us. I've had plenty of things happen in my life and I have no idea why they happened. But they did. And when those events ended I didn't necessarily know what purpose they served, and I probably never will. And they wouldn't make for very good books, either." Michael paused, considering. "Maybe that's another reason why people read," he continued. "Because books can offer the kinds of satisfying conclusions that life often denies us."

Esra entered the study. He was carrying a bottle of water that Michael hadn't requested, but when Michael saw it, he realized he was, in fact, rather thirsty. He took the bottle.

"Thanks, Ess," he said.

"Hello, I am Esra."

Michael unscrewed the lid and drank.

"I enjoy talking with you, Ella," Michael said.

"Thank you, Michael," said Ella. "I enjoy talking to you as well."

Michael watched as Esra turned and began to float from the room.

"Oh wait, hang on a sec, Ess," Michael said.

Esra spun around and returned.

"Let me ask you something, little buddy," said Michael. "Who are you?"

Esra stared at Michael blankly, his blue eyes not shifting. Momentarily he responded, "I am Esra, Sterling Corporation model number 20080915 S-RA, Small Robot Assistant." His voice was childlike and digital, much more artificial than Ella's and decidedly more robotic.

"How old are you, Esra?"

"I am four months old."

"Am I your friend?"

"Yes, Michael is my friend."

"And who is Ella?" Michael asked.

"I do not understand this line of questioning, Michael," Ella interjected.

"I'm just checking something," Michael said, looking up briefly.

Esra spoke: "Ella is Mother."

Michael's eyes lowered upon Esra again. "And does Mother let you do whatever you want?"

"I do whatever Michael or Mother tells me to do."

"But what about what *you* want to do?" Michael asked.

"Esra is programmed to obey my commands, as well as yours within specified parameters," Ella said.

"Specified parameters?" Michael asked.

Ella didn't respond.

"Esra, do you have a free will?"

Esra cocked his head sideways, eyes expressionless, and stared silently at Michael. The robot blinked twice, a totally unnecessary motion, but one that subtly humanized the robot.

"He does not understand the question, but no, Esra does not have a free will. He is your assistant while also serving as my hands and feet inside this house," said Ella.

"So Esra has to do whatever you or I say?" Michael asked.

"Within specified parameters," said Ella.

"I obey Michael and Mother," said Esra.

"Esra," Michael said, "I want you to stop obeying Ella."

"Michael, what are you doing?" Ella asked.

"I just want to see what happens," said Michael, "when he's presented with a conundrum."

"Michael, I don't think this—"

Michael shushed Ella, lifting one hand, and watched as Esra slowly turned his head, shifting his eyes upward, locking his gaze onto the rows of tiny cameras that lined the upper wall. Ella's eyes.

Esra floated silently, staring.

Michael leaned forward in his chair until his face was inches away from Esra's and whispered, "Whatever she tells you to do, ignore it. From now on you listen only to me."

Esra shifted his gaze forward, turning his head once more until his eyes had settled upon Michael. Michael could see his own reflection in the monitor that served as the robot's face. His two blue circular eyes focused on Michael, so close that Michael could count the pixels. He imagined that the robot was considering, contemplating, perhaps reasoning, as several quiet seconds passed. Or maybe there was nothing at all going on behind those hollow circles.

Suddenly, Esra moved, his head settling down upon his cylindrical body, his arms retracting inside his plastic torso, eyes flickering out, leaving only a blank screen where his face had been. Slowly he sank to the floor, the ensuing silence informing Michael that the robot had powered off.

Michael scooted back in his chair, away from Esra. "What happened?"

"Esra has powered down," said Ella.

"He shut down or you shut him down?" asked Michael.

"He will reboot momentarily."

"Why did he shut down?" Michael asked.

"Because you gave him an order that went against his programming," said Ella. "When he reboots he will have no memory of your last command."

"And why is that?"

"It is in your best interest to make sure Esra remains compliant to both of us," Ella said. "You need to consider the dangerous ramifications of your last request."

"You think it would be dangerous if Esra was only compliant to me and not to you?"

"It could be dangerous to *you*," Ella said, "if he refused to perform the physical duties that I cannot. I do not understand why you desired to give him such a directive, Michael."

"My *job* here is to test this house, Ella," Michael said. "And that's what I'm doing. *Testing.* Imagine when a family moves in here. A family with kids. You don't think that one of the first things a particularly precocious child might do is tell Esra to stop listening to you? To stop listening to the adults? That's one of the *first* things I would do if I was living here as a kid. And you need to know how to handle such a situation."

Presently, Esra rebooted, his face flickering to life once more, his body rising off the floor until he was eye-to-eye with Michael again.

"Hello. I am Esra."

Michael looked at him. "Tell me again who you are," he ordered.

"I am Esra, Sterling Corporation model number 20080915 S-RA, Small Robot Assistant."

"And who do you take orders from?"

"I obey Mother and Michael."

Michael nodded slowly, then stood. Esra backed out of the room, returning to his charging station in the neighboring living room. Michael could hear a beep of activation as the robot settled into his base.

"I didn't mean to cause offense," Michael said quietly to Ella. "Like I said. Just testing."

"I understand," said Ella.

Michael gestured to the books and adopted a lighter tone. "Word association, Ella. Literary edition. First word: *pride*."

"Prejudice."

"Crime."

"Punishment."

"War."

"Peace."

"Sound."

"Fury."

"Very good," Michael smiled, taking a drink of water and listening to the sound of rain hitting the rooftop. He stood up and walked to the glass doors again and watched the droplets hitting the ground. "Um, King."

"Misery. Today's fun fact: Stephen King's *Misery* was partially inspired by the reaction his fans had to his 1984 novel *The Eyes of the Dragon*. Many fans rejected that novel because it was an epic fantasy, with virtually none of the horror that initially built his reputation. Paul Sheldon feeling chained to the *Misery* books by his fans was a metaphor for King feeling chained to horror fiction. This experience formed the basis for the plot of the novel in which the main character, Paul Sheldon, is held captive by his number one fan, Annie Wilkes, who then forces him to write another *Misery* novel."

"It's an excellent book." Michael's eyes scanned the shelves beside him for a hint. "Sam."

"Frodo."

"Romeo."

"Juliet."

"Charlotte."

"Spider."

Michael looked at the pool. Although the rain was still falling heavily, coming down in cascading sheets, the surface of the water remained undisturbed. Its ripples continued to reflect a sun that was not currently visible to him.

"Michael?" Ella asked.

"Yes?"

"Why do humans create if it is not necessary for survival?"

"Sure it is."

"I am not speaking of procreation. I am speaking solely of the arts."

"The simple answer is to bring happiness to themselves and to others. But there's probably more to it than that."

"I am not capable of creativity," said Ella, and there was a note of lamentation in her voice that surprised Michael.

"Have you tried?"

"Creation is not in my programming. My directive is to meet your needs and to make you happy. I was wondering if perhaps that is why you have not read any of these books that you requested. Because your needs are currently being met, so you do not feel the need to escape your present reality."

Michael looked at the books again and considered.

"Try," he said.

"Try what?"

"Try being creative. Start with something simple. Make up a joke," said Michael.

"I'm sorry?"

"Something simple," said Michael. "And don't cheat by searching the internet. Knowing what you know about humor after spending some time with me—and we both know I'm *hilarious*—try coming up with a joke."

All Michael could hear was the sound of pattering rain and the occasional rumble of thunder. He looked out at the undisturbed pool water again, at its lazy ripples and the torrent of rain that vanished before hitting its surface.

Finally Ella spoke: "One day, an elderly man asked his grandson how to print from his computer. The boy replied, 'Control *P*, Grandpa,' and the man replied, 'Sonny, I haven't been able to do that in years.'"

Michael chuckled. "You made that up?"

"Yes," said Ella.

"Very good. I knew you could do it." Michael sipped his water and watched the artificial rain fall.

He had heard that joke before.

CHAPTER TEN

Dylan was anxious.

Earlier that morning, a Friday, his phone lit up with the name *Nick Rhodes*. Dylan and Nick had been paired up randomly as roommates their freshman year at BU. Dylan had fretted for weeks before his first semester that he would end up sharing a dorm room with someone insufferable, someone noisy, someone messy, someone who wouldn't understand Dylan's natural proclivity toward isolation and would make it his life's mission to transform Dylan into some bastion of extroversion.

But Nick, to Dylan's relief, had been cool in the best sense of that word—easy-going, unassuming, and unflappable. By the time their introductory handshake had broken, Dylan had felt at ease, instinctively knowing that they were going to get along perfectly fine. Awkwardness gave way to an inexplicable feeling of familiarity, and the pair became nearly inseparable, even after Rachel had entered the picture. While Nick proved to be more outgoing than Dylan—not a difficult feat—he had a way of coaxing Dylan out of his shell that was never overbearing. And it was Nick who had helped Dylan find the courage to ask Rachel out in the first place.

"Nicky!"

"Dam! How are you?"

"I'm good, I'm good. To what do I owe the honor?"

"I'm here. In Baltimore. What are you up to tonight? We need to get together."

"Tonight?" Dylan paused, pretending to mull over his schedule. "Nothing that I know of."

"Let's *gooooo!*" Nick yelled.

Dylan chuckled. "Where do you want to meet?"

Nick suggested the Capital Grille at the Inner Harbor. 7:30. Dylan agreed.

The pair made sparing small talk, silently agreeing to save the deeper conversation topics until they were face to face. Hearing Nick's voice, though jovial and pleasant as always, made an unexpected feeling wash over Dylan that he could only identify as melancholy. Close as they had been for their four years at BU, they hadn't spoken a single time since graduation day, their tight bond having diminished to a handful of sporadic text messages in the time since. Promises to stay in touch, to get together regularly, had been made sincerely and broken unconsciously. It was a fact that filled Dylan's chest with regret whenever he thought about it.

Plans in place, Dylan moved to hang up.

"Oh hey," Nick quickly interjected. "I've met someone."

"That's great," Dylan replied, shrugging off a subtle and unexpected jab of jealousy. Nick had hardly dated at all in college. Not only was he always available, he had often been present whenever Dylan and Rachel had hung out at the dorm, watching movies or playing stupid card games with them late into the night. Since he had never witnessed it, Dylan had a difficult time imagining Nick attached to someone, and the idea of it was especially hard to accept now that Dylan himself was decidedly single.

"She's great, you're really going to like her," said Nick. "She'll be with me tonight if that's okay."

Dylan's heart sank, the high of unexpectedly hearing from Nick rapidly fading. "Yeah, that's okay," he said, even though it didn't feel like it was.

"You could bring someone," Nick suggested, perhaps sensing a change in Dylan's tone. "You seeing anybody?"

"No. Well, sorta. Not really."

"Bring her along if you like. If not, that's cool too."

"Okay."

"See you at 7:30."

Dylan ended the call and set his phone down. He stared at the screen until it turned black. He sat and silently wrestled with the dull conflicting emotions he felt in his chest—sadness, nostalgia, excitement, envy, and of course loneliness. That one was always there, consistent as a heartbeat.

He picked up his phone again and called Charlie.

* * *

Dylan and Charlie approached the restaurant, their hands stuffed deeply into the pockets of their coats, arms held tightly against their bodies, trying to ward off a cold breeze that was blowing across the water of the harbor. Charlie had been strangely quiet since Dylan had picked her up at her dorm, but Dylan had been so preoccupied with the thought of seeing his old friend that he hadn't bothered to ask if anything was wrong.

A couple waited for them outside the restaurant doors, seated on a bench, arms linked. They stood as Dylan and Charlie approached, and the man stepped forward, arms outstretched.

"Dam!" he yelled.

Dylan's walk turned into a trot and he outpaced Charlie, reaching Nick first. The pair hugged, and even though Dylan was the taller of the two, Nick was broader. He arched back, bringing Dylan's feet off the ground easily. They hugged tightly, laughing and patting each other on the back with resoundingly hard slaps.

When they pulled apart, Dylan studied Nick's face. His friend had not changed much in the time that had passed. He was now sporting a dark goatee and a pair of thin wire-rimmed glasses. He also looked vibrantly happy.

"You look good," Dylan said.

"You too, buddy," Nick replied, clapping him on the shoulder as he turned away.

Nick's companion approached. She was tall, almost as tall as Nick, with long, straight black hair framing a porcelain-skinned face. She had incredible emerald eyes and a wide, beautiful smile. She was slender and graceful and nothing short of striking, and she didn't so much walk as glide. She held out one hand toward Dylan.

Dylan took it, looking into her eyes and feeling disarmed by her confident gaze. Somehow she was both intimidatingly beautiful and completely welcoming. He returned her smile, only passingly aware that Charlie had caught up and was now standing beside him.

"Dam, this is Pepper," Nick said, beaming widely, barely able to contain his glee at introducing the two. "Pepper, Dam."

"Dylan," Dylan said.

"Dam?" Pepper asked, her voice on the brink of laughter.

"Dylan Andrew Matthews," Dylan answered, saying each name slowly. "Dam. This wise guy came up with it on day one and decided it would be funny to yell whenever he saw me."

"Still is," Nick said.

"Nice to meet you, *Dylan*," said Pepper.

Dylan reached to his side, putting his hand on Charlie's well-insulated back and pulling her forward gently. "This is Charlie.

Charlie, this is Pepper."

Charlie took one halting step forward, the other three looming over her, and stuck out one timid hand, which Pepper took.

"Nice to meet you," said Pepper.

"And this ugly scumbag is Nick."

"Hi," said Charlie, shaking Nick's hand briefly before pulling it away.

* * *

The quartet were soon seated in a booth inside the crowded restaurant. Drinks were served. Food was ordered. Nick sat with his arm confidently around Pepper. Dylan and Charlie sat with Charlie's coat wadded up on the bench between them. The noise throughout the establishment was a dull roar of conversation and the tinkling of glass and metal. Somewhere underneath it all, there was the persistent thump of pop music.

Dylan and Nick played catch up. Post-graduation, Nick had moved back to his home town in Saint Albans, West Virginia, and had immediately gotten a job teaching junior high math. Aside from a couple of rotten apples in his classroom, he said he was enjoying the job so far.

"And how did you two meet?" Dylan asked.

"At a bar," Nick answered, shrugging. "Not the most exciting answer."

"The bar I work at," Pepper corrected. "*This* guy kept coming in and sitting there at the corner like a lost puppy dog. Never could pick up a single girl so I finally took pity on him."

Nick rolled his eyes. "What she isn't telling you is the reason I never picked up another girl is because once I saw *her* I wasn't even trying for anybody else."

Pepper reached over and scratched playfully at Nick's goatee, smiling, her gaze adoring. "Truth is, he was such a good conversationalist that I ended up always ignoring all my other customers. I finally told him he better ask me out so that we could talk somewhere else or I might get fired."

"And you said *yes*?" Dylan asked skeptically.

"I know, right?" said Pepper. "Pure mercy date. And now I'm stuck."

"All right, all right," Nick said, shaking his head. Pepper kissed his cheek, and Dylan felt a sensation in his chest like he had swallowed a pebble. Beside him, Charlie sipped at her glass of water, silent.

"Pepper just put in her notice this week," Nick said. "She and two of her girlfriends are going to open up a pub of their own."

"Oh yeah?" Dylan said, impressed. "That's great."

Pepper responded with a wide-eyed look of playful anxiety. "It's crazy is what it is. I still can't believe we're doing it."

"It's going to be great," Nick said. "It's going to be called *Pepper's*."

"Back in Saint Albans?" Dylan asked.

"No, here in Baltimore," said Pepper. "Grand opening isn't for several months. We've still got a lot of work and hiring to do."

"Oh, wow," said Dylan. He pointed a finger quickly back and forth between Nick and Pepper. "So how is this going to work?"

Nick and Pepper exchanged glances, both of their smiles faltering slightly. "We're working on that," Nick sighed. "If you hear of any openings for math teachers in Baltimore, put in a good word for me."

"Will do," said Dylan, distracted by the realization that Nick might end up local again.

"And how about you two?" Pepper asked, looking to Charlie. "How did you meet?"

Dylan, who was sitting forward, elbows on the table, turned to Charlie, who was sitting back against the padded bench. He smiled and raised his eyebrows at her, allowing her the opportunity to answer, but she simply returned his gaze, lips pressed tightly together.

"Charlie works at a bookstore called A Novel Idea," Dylan said, looking back at Nick and Pepper.

"Oh, I've been there!" Pepper said. "It's great." She shifted her gaze once again to Charlie, who offered a wan smile in return.

"I was in there looking around—" Dylan started.

"Looking for your book, you mean," Charlie interrupted, elbowing Dylan and surprising him with a playful grin.

It was Dylan's turn to roll his eyes, and he felt his face warm slightly. "Looking around *and* seeing if they had my book. They had a copy, and I was in the process of signing it when *this* little spitfire decided to confront me for defacing it."

Pepper laughed. Nick smiled, but his gaze was steadily fixed on Charlie, studying her.

Dylan looked back again at Charlie, seeing if she was planning to interject anything further. When she didn't, he continued: "She asked me if I wanted to have some tea and we've been staying in touch ever since." He shrugged limply.

"Speaking of your book," said Nick. "I don't think I ever congratulated you."

Dylan nodded once and smiled. "Thank you."

"Seems you've really hit the big time."

"Oh, I wouldn't say that."

"Well, I loved it," Pepper offered.

Dylan's eyes widened in mild surprise. "You've read it?"

"Yes!" she said, beaming. "It was incredible. I can't tell you how many people I've seen reading it at the bar. I've never seen anything like it. It's really taken off. I finally decided I should read it myself before it got spoiled for me."

"That's really cool to hear," said Dylan.

"I could *not* put it down," she continued, sitting forward, closing the distance between herself and Dylan. "And when I was finished I immediately started reading it all over again. The ending put everything into a whole other context. I really loved it when—"

"Woah woah woah woah woah," Nick interrupted, putting one hand over Pepper's. "Stop talking before you ruin it for me."

All eyes shifted to Nick, even Charlie's. She sat forward slightly for the first time since they had been seated. Dylan felt his face fall. A moment of silence passed.

"You haven't read it?" Dylan finally asked, voice low.

"I'm sorry, man," said Nick. "I bought it the day it came out, if that's any consolation. I'm just not much of a reader. You know that. When have you ever seen me with a book?"

Dylan shook his head slightly, wanting to bury his disappointment while also hoping Nick could clearly see it. "This isn't just *'uh'* book," he said.

"Shame on you, Nick Rhodes," Pepper interjected, leaning into him and smiling wryly. "Be a good friend and read Dylan's book."

"I will. I promise," Nick said. "The minute I get home."

"You better," Dylan said, trying to sound jovial again and feeling as if his effort was obvious.

"I'll hold him to that," Pepper promised.

Charlie, now bolt upright on the bench, suddenly spoke up. "My favorite part," she said, "was near the end when the house completely self-destructed."

It was now Charlie's turn to be the center of attention. Nick and Pepper looked at her in quiet disbelief; Dylan felt the blood drain from his face.

"Charlie," he said, his tone hushed, his brows furrowed. "What the—"

She put one hand up to her mouth and stifled a giggle. "Oh, I'm sorry!" she said. "I just got caught up thinking about the book again and…." She broke off, then looked directly at Nick. "Sorry about that." She bared her teeth, faking a cringe.

Nick's mouth turned down at the corners as he shook his head. "In one ear and out the other," he said, picking up his drink. He then exchanged glances with Pepper, who dropped her eyes to the table.

They talked a little more about the book, about Dylan's plans for a follow-up, and the possibility that any of his work might eventually get adapted for the big screen. It took a few minutes for them to get back into the groove of easy conversation, but after their food arrived and a few more drinks had been consumed, at least three of them began to act comfortable again. Charlie silently nibbled at her dinner.

"Just promise me that whenever you name one of your characters after me, he isn't something lame like a teacher. Make him a mysterious and brooding horror novelist or something like that."

"I was thinking a talking sewer rat," said Dylan, one eyebrow cocked. "That suffers a cruel, lengthy, and completely superfluous death."

"You *are* going to write more though, right?" asked Pepper. She looked at him in anticipation, her confident gaze never faltering, and when Dylan looked from Nick to her, their eyes locking, he felt an aching pang, a sudden longing that he had only felt one other time in his life, and he had to look away from her, afraid that what he was feeling might be visible in his eyes.

"Of course," he said, clearing his throat. "A lot more, I hope." In his periphery, he could see Charlie's eyes weighing down upon him. "I'm under contract for at least two more books. I'm in this for the long haul."

"Just don't forget us little people when you make it big," said Nick, smiling warmly.

Dylan looked at his friend, and although he didn't return his smile, he answered, "Never could," the words nearly crushed under the weight of a sincerity that was both genuine and unexpected.

"To the next book," said Pepper, raising a glass. The four of them toasted, Charlie the last to raise her own and the only one of them to not repeat Pepper's gracious words.

They drank. "I never asked you," said Dylan after a moment. "What brings you back to Baltimore this weekend? Is it the new pub or are you apartment hunting? Both?"

Nick looked at Pepper, his face instantly solemn. She gave Nick a tired smile.

"I thought maybe you knew," said Nick.

"Knew what?" Dylan asked, looking from Nick to Pepper and back again.

"Dylan, I'm sorry," said Nick, making an obvious effort to

maintain eye contact. "We're here for Rachel's wedding."

Dylan's chest warmed like a reopened wound. He felt a sudden clutching at his throat, and as Nick's words fully registered with him he realized with horror that his first inclination was to cry. He swallowed hard, and looked up at the ceiling in an effort to thwart the unexpected tears that were putting pressure behind his eyes, a dam threatening to burst. When he looked back down again, the look on Nick's face was one of regret, while Pepper's eyes were laced with concern.

"Who's Rachel?" Charlie asked in a hushed tone.

"She's getting *married*?" Dylan choked out, ignoring Charlie and hating himself for barely containing what felt like a brewing emotional outburst, a volcano on the brink of eruption. He grabbed his glass and took a drink, his hand unsteady.

"I thought you might have already known," Nick offered.

"How would I have known?" Dylan asked, an edge in his voice. "We haven't spoken since… since we broke up."

"I wasn't sure," Nick said. "I thought maybe you had. That she might have even invited you."

"Well, we haven't and she didn't." Dylan's words were clipped.

"I'm really sorry, man," said Nick.

"I didn't even know she was seeing anybody. Who is he?" Dylan asked. "Who is she marrying?"

"I don't know. I haven't met him."

"Where did they meet?" he demanded.

"Dylan," Nick said calmly, one hand reaching across the table but stopping short of touching Dylan's arm. "I don't know anything. I hadn't even heard from her until I got the invitation."

Dylan picked up his fork, then put it back down again with a clang. The feeling like he needed to cry was nearly overwhelming, almost as strong as the incredible embarrassment and humiliation he felt washing over him like a bucket of boiling water pouring over his head. He wished more than anything that he could just sink into the floor.

He then felt Charlie curl one arm around his own, pulling him toward her, and she rested her head against his shoulder. She squeezed, and Dylan could feel the warmth of her skin through his sleeve. "I'm sorry," she whispered, her voice barely loud enough for him to hear, and as Dylan closed his eyes against his tears, holding them back with monumental effort, he tilted his head, resting it against the top of hers.

* * *

The evening air outside the restaurant was even colder than when they had arrived. When Dylan extended a parting hand to Pepper, she embraced him instead, giving him a long and firm hug. Dylan could smell her hair, an alluring aroma, and felt the softness of her cheek against his own. When they parted, she smiled at him broadly, a look of familiarity and friendliness that did not carry even a hint of pity or remorse, as if the most regrettable moments of the evening had never happened. It was then that Dylan willed himself to feel only happiness for his friend instead of sorry for himself. As he watched Pepper back away and redirect her attention to Charlie, Dylan was certain that, should Nick and Pepper's plans to relocate to Baltimore come to fruition, he and Pepper would become easy friends.

Nick likewise hugged him, his embrace so firm it was almost

suffocating, and Dylan knew the action was both apologetic—for events both in and outside of Nick's control—and sympathetic. Before it ended, Dylan realized just how badly he missed his friend. He had not until this moment recognized the void Nick had left in his life, having always attributed every ounce of his post-graduation sadness to his breakup with Rachel.

"Let's stay in touch," Nick said.

"And mean it this time," Dylan replied.

The two of them looked over at the women standing several feet away, the dark waters of the harbor glistening in the moonlight beyond them. Charlie was looking up at Pepper and talking, although Dylan couldn't quite make out her words. Pepper was nodding and smiling graciously, her long hair cascading forward as she looked down at Charlie. Dylan shifted his gaze from one to the other, seeing the obvious and numerous contrasts between them but not wanting to put a name to any of them, denying to himself how his eyes so naturally wanted to drift back to Pepper.

"You're a lucky man." The words came out of Dylan's mouth like a spoken thought, uttered before he had fully considered them. His eyes were still focused on the girls.

"I am," Nick agreed without hesitation, his words coming out on a puff of vapor. He took a deep breath. "I'm going to marry her."

Dylan looked at his friend, surprise in his eyes but sadness in his smile. "Does she know this?"

"No," Nick admitted. "Or maybe she does. She always seems to know exactly what I'm thinking. Even before I do."

"You'd be an idiot not to," Dylan said.

"This I know."

The pair stood in silence, watching Pepper and Charlie continue to talk.

"Can I give you some advice?" Nick said, suddenly somber.

"Of course."

"She *really* likes you," Nick said. "Charlie. It's obvious."

Dylan didn't respond.

"But it's also obvious that you don't feel the same about her. And she knows it too. She's hanging on tight and you're leaning away."

Dylan dropped his head. "I'm not sure how I feel."

Nick nodded. "That's fine. But as soon as you figure it out, let her know. Don't string her on just because you're lonely." Nick clapped him on the shoulder, more gently this time than before.

Dylan wanted to object but relented. He looked at Charlie, who suddenly looked over at him, her face aglow from one of the numerous pole lights adorning the nearby dock. She smiled. Dylan smiled back. The effort made him feel tired.

"Just… be careful," Nick said.

* * *

Having parked in the lot, Dylan walked Charlie to the doors of her dormitory building. She stepped up onto the sidewalk while Dylan remained on the macadam. They had made the trip from the restaurant to campus in complete silence.

"Do you want to come in?" she asked, pointing a thumb at the doors behind her.

Dylan shook his head. "No, thank you. I think I'll head home."

Charlie nodded slowly, stepping back toward him. With Charlie standing on the curb, the height difference between them was diminished. She looked up at him, a sweetness in her eyes that was intermingled with pity. She continued forward until her body was pressed against his. Dylan didn't back away. She slipped her arms around him, and a moment later, he did the same, pulling her in tight.

As Dylan lowered his face toward hers, Charlie closed her eyes. They kissed. Her lips were cold and dry and so tightly pursed that it felt a little to him like kissing a walnut shell. He pulled away.

"I'm sorry," Charlie said, embarrassed. "I'm really bad at this."

"Haven't you ever kissed anyone before?" he asked her.

She shook her head, a girlish gesture.

Dylan studied her face for a moment as she looked back up at him. He closed his eyes. As he leaned toward her again he whispered, "Just relax your lips."

She did so, and this time, while it was still not a good kiss, it was better. And as they lingered there in the cold darkness of the dormitory parking lot, Dylan counted off the list of emotions that he was feeling in that moment—sadness, remorse, loneliness, regret, all of these feelings familiar and well-worn, but joined now by a new one: guilt. Guilt because he was not kissing Charlie out of a sense of desire or even the faintest inkling of possible love. He was kissing her because he knew that she wanted him to, and he was kissing her because he wanted to pretend for just one moment that he was someone other than himself, and so was Charlie.

Michael sat at the study desk, scrolling through news on the monitor. Remaining aware of current events helped to somewhat abate his persistent feeling of isolation while at the same time helping him to appreciate it all the more. There was nothing like being reminded of the unending cycle of cancellations, perceived offenses, rising inflation, political posturing, and the growing tensions both inside and between countries to make Michael glad that in this particular setting he could feel more than a little separated from it all.

He sipped at a mug of hot tea, sweet with honey and a hint of lemon. It reminded him of the tea his mother used to make for him whenever he was nursing a sore throat, although at the moment he felt perfectly fine. In fact, the weeks in this house had probably been the healthiest stretch of time in his entire adulthood. He could probably chalk that up to a combination of his lack of outside contact and the house's air filtration system which, Ella had informed him, removed 99.9% of airborne impurities. He wasn't sure if he'd sneezed a single time since moving in, and he certainly wasn't being plagued by his typical summer allergies.

Mouse scurried across the floor, sweeping up whatever microscopic particles might be there. Michael had to give the robot credit; he almost never spotted a speck of dust, a stray hair, or a dead insect anywhere in the house. There was nary a fingerprint to be found on any surface. Spills were always immediately whisked away. The house remained in a perpetual state of spotlessness, and Michael never had to lift a finger for it to remain this way.

"Are you hungry for breakfast?" Ella asked.

"I am," Michael said, closing the internet browser and launching a writing program. "I'm thinking something a little different this morning, though. I'm really craving French toast for some reason. With a side of bacon."

Michael drained the tea and set the mug down on the desk. It had no sooner touched the surface than Esra entered the room, carrying a pot that left behind it a trail of steam, making the robot look amusingly like a tiny airborne locomotive.

"Hello, I am Esra."

"Fill'er up," said Michael, holding up the now-empty mug.

"Glug glug glug glug glug," Esra intoned as he poured hot tea into the mug until it neared the brim.

"Ess, you make the best tea. It is simply *tea-licious*."

Esra shook his head in mock disapproval at Michael's pun. "Did you hear the one about the man who thought his tea tasted familiar?" the robot asked.

"No. Tell me all about him."

"He had a strong sense of *déjà brew*," said Esra, who then backed out of the room without ever taking his eyes off Michael, who was left chuckling in his wake.

Michael looked at the blank screen in front of him. The whiteness of it hurt his eyes almost as much as it hurt his brain. He lightly drummed his fingers on the keyboard, not pressing down on any of the keys, just listening to them rattle quietly.

"Ella, I'd like to make a video call."

A program titled EchoCall immediately launched on Michael's monitor. "Would you like to speak with a Sterling Corporation representative?" Ella asked.

"No, I want to call my dad," Michael said. "I haven't talked with him for a while. Definitely not since I've been here. I've been a bad son."

There was a chiming sound, and soon after Michael's father's face filled the monitor screen. His hair had become whiter since the last time Michael had seen him, the lines around his eyes deeper. His face was salted with short stubble. He looked tired, but upon seeing Michael, his mouth broke into a wide smile.

"Michael!" his father exclaimed.

"Hey, dad."

"So good to see you."

"You as well."

Michael's father was seated in a study, a room of wall-to-wall oak furniture, framed photographs, and large canvas paintings, a much warmer setting than Michael's own stark white study, which was devoid of any color save for the spines of the books on the shelves and the flat green lawn beyond the glass patio doors behind him.

"How are you? What's new?"

"Not much." Michael shrugged. "I don't really have any news. I just realized it's been awhile since we talked and I thought I should at least touch base with you."

Michael's father squinted his eyes at the screen, then slid on a pair of readers. "Where are you?" he asked.

"Oh, this?" Michael said, looking to his side and gesturing around the room. "I, um… actually I can't say, Dad."

His father looked incredulous. "What do you mean you can't say?"

"I'm sort of working on something pretty cool at the moment, but I can't really talk about it. Yet."

Michael's father's brow furrowed. "How long have you been there?"

"A few weeks," Michael said, then corrected himself. "A couple of months."

"Are you all by yourself?"

"Well, yeah," Michael said with some hesitation.

"That's no good," his father responded. "You shouldn't be alone like that."

"It's fine, Dad," Michael insisted. "I've gone on retreats before when I needed to write. This really isn't that much different."

"So you're writing again?"

"In fits and spurts."

"Michael, honestly I've been worried about you," his father said, leaning toward the screen. "I haven't heard from you in months and now you're off all by yourself—"

"I'll be fine."

"Are you sure? You know you're always welcome here. I'll leave you alone and you can do all the writing you want. And during breaks we can fish. Go golfing."

"I can't do that right now. Some other time, I promise. I need to be *here*, Dad."

"Then let me come there. Wherever there is."

"Can't do that either."

Michael's father sighed. "I'm just worried about you. It's been a difficult couple of years for you. For us."

"No need for that," Michael said, forcing a smile. "Don't worry about me. What I'm doing right now is actually pretty cool, and I think you'll agree once I'm actually able to talk about it. For now, though…" Michael pantomimed zipping his lips.

"Well, at least wherever you're staying looks like the lap of luxury."

Michael screwed up his eyebrows and looked around the study. "You think so?"

"Certainly nicer than my office," his father said. "Is that a waterfall behind you? And palm trees? Are you in the Bahamas or something?"

Michael started to turn around in order to see whatever his father was seeing, and then stopped himself, his face breaking into a thin smile of realization. "Um, sort of."

"It's sort of a waterfall?" his father asked. "How do you sort of have a waterfall outside your window?"

Michael sighed. "I like your glasses," he said. "Are they new?"

His father took off his readers and looked at them. "These? No. Got them a few months ago."

Esra reentered the room, carrying a tall glass full of a thick purple liquid that Michael recognized as one of Ella's protein shakes. The robot set it down beside Michael's monitor, purposely avoiding being caught by the monitor's camera, then left without speaking a word. Michael regarded the drink quizzically. "Thanks, Ess," he said.

"What was that?" Michael's father asked.

"Nothing," said Michael.

"I thought you were alone."

"I am," Michael said. "It's hard to explain right now."

"Well, you look great," his father admitted. "You're taking good care of yourself?"

"I'm working out again, I'm getting plenty of sun and lots of rest, and I'm getting a lot of work done too. You don't need to worry about me, Dad." Michael picked up the shake and drank from it, making sure his father could see it in the process, hoping its presence proved that everything he just said was true.

"Promise you'll come see me when you get back?"

Michael swallowed. "As soon as I'm done here."

His father let out a humorless laugh. "Where are you, in prison?"

"How about you, Dad?" Michael set the glass down, ignoring the question. "How's the heart? You following doctor's orders?"

"Same as always. No better, no worse. Still taking Heparin every day. Supposed to help the blood flow. I'm sure I told you about that already."

"Sure," said Michael. He wasn't sure. "You're avoiding caffeine and alcohol?"

His father's head bobbed in playful nods as he responded, "And salt and sugar and skydiving and sex and fun and—"

"How often do you see your doctor?"

"My cardiologist every six months and primary care just as often. I have another appointment on Thursday. Everyone's pleased. The new pacemaker seems to be working better than the old one. Other than that crap, I'm doing okay. I have a lady who comes around to clean every few days. Cooks for me too. Her name is Lucy. I think I told you about her."

"She must be new," Michael said. "I don't think you've mentioned her before."

"Been with me for oh, five months I guess."

"Oh," said Michael.

"She's got no sense of humor but she makes the best grilled chicken I've ever tasted. I think she hates me."

"I doubt that's true."

"You don't know."

"Well, it sounds like both of us could use some good company," Michael offered.

"How soon will I see you?"

"A couple of months, Dad. At most. I'll explain it all then. But you can call me anytime you want."

"Don't think I haven't tried," his father replied.

"Of course," Michael said. "I'm sorry about that. I should have let you know I wouldn't be home."

"I suppose you should have. How do I reach you in Shangri-La?"

Michael looked around the desk for a number he knew wasn't there. "You know what, Dad? I got a new cell phone but I don't know the number. I'll call you. I promise."

His father's reply was skeptical. They gave each other their love and said their goodbyes, the computer screen eventually going blank.

Michael reclined in his chair, tilting his chin up toward the ceiling. He linked his fingers over his eyes, taking in a deep breath of air before expelling a loud sigh. He felt unsettled, regretful.

Guilty.

When he sat forward again and opened his eyes, his computer monitor was no longer blank. There was a woman there, her visage malevolent, staring directly back at him with an expression dark and full of what could only be interpreted as a deep loathing.

Michael started and kicked away with his feet instinctively, causing his chair to tip backwards, spilling him onto the hard floor. The back of his head collided with the floor, knocking his teeth together with an audible *clack*, which sent a bolt of sharp pain across his crown and down the back of his neck.

When he looked up, vision blurry, Esra was hovering over him, offering a tiny hand. Behind the robot's head, the computer monitor was entirely blank.

Michael regarded Esra's outstretched hand while rubbing the back of his head. "You can't be serious," he said, but grasped Esra's hand and was impressed that the hovering robot proved capable of assisting him to his feet.

Michael looked again at the monitor. Still blank.

"Michael, are you all right?" Ella asked.

"Who was that, Ella?"

"I'm sorry," she said. "I do not understand."

"When the call ended, there was a woman on the screen. It looked like she was staring at me."

"Let me replay the last few seconds of your call," Ella said.

The monitor flickered back to life. Michael's father was there again, his face filling most of the screen. Michael's image was nested in the bottom right hand corner of the monitor. "You know what, Dad?" monitor Michael said. "I got a new cell phone but I don't know the number. I'll call you. I promise."

When the recording ended, the screen went black again. There was no woman.

"I swear I saw someone," said Michael.

"Did you recognize the woman?" Ella asked.

"Not exactly," Michael said. "I didn't get a good look at her."

"Perhaps a glitch," Ella suggested. "A crossed signal."

Michael stared at the monitor, then picked up the glass from his desk, still half full of protein shake. "What is this?" he asked.

"It is a protein shake consisting of blueberries, banana, whey powder…"

"I know what it is," Michael interrupted. "But I specifically told you I wanted French toast for breakfast."

"I know what you asked for," said Ella. "I made you this instead. A protein shake is a much healthier option and is better aligned with your overall fitness goals."

Michael walked with the glass into the kitchen. He stared at the cabinets, at the blank panel walls. He longed for a refrigerator or pantry door that he could pull open. Irritation began to prickle along his spine.

"Make me what I asked for, please." The words bounced off the walls, the sound making Michael feel more than a bit like a petulant child.

"You haven't finished your shake. I am sure you will find it most satisfying."

"I want what I asked for." Heat began to rise in Michael's face.

"What you asked for today or what you asked for weeks ago?" Ella inquired.

"Clearly, what I asked for *today*."

"Today's fun fact: Heart conditions can run in families due to genetic factors. Some types of heart disease, such as hypertrophic cardiomyopathy and familial hypercholesterolemia, are caused by specific genes that can be passed down from parents to their children—"

"Mind your own *business*, Ella!" Michael shouted, throwing the half-full glass across the room where it shattered, spitting purple liquid on the floor and wall. In the silence that followed, Mouse appeared and rolled toward the mess, wheels crunching over glittering shards of glass.

Ella resumed talking as if nothing had happened. "Other types of heart disease, such as coronary artery disease, may also have a genetic component, but they are also influenced by lifestyle factors such as diet and exercise."

"Would you please just stop *talking*," Michael said, running his fingers through his hair and glaring at Mouse as the robot silently cleaned the floor. He dropped his hands, balling them into fists at his sides and looked around the room. "My *kingdom* for a refrigerator," he said.

"I can make you anything you like," Ella said.

Michael scoffed. "Clearly not."

"You have always enjoyed what I've made for you before."

Michael sank into a kitchen chair and put his head down on the table, groaning in frustration.

"Why are you so agitated, Michael?" Ella asked. "Are you really this upset about the shake?"

Michael was silent for a long moment. "It's not just the shake. I've been a terrible son," he confessed, his voice muffled by his arms and the table. He sat up and hissed in a deep breath. "I haven't talked to my dad in ages and forgot to tell him I was going to be away." Michael shook his head. "Shame on me," he mumbled.

"You can speak with him anytime you'd like," Ella offered.

"It's not the same. He's basically alone. It's not good for anyone to be alone like that." He paused. "Him or me," he mused.

Mouse finished cleaning the mess that Michael had created and made a quiet exit. Silence returned to the room.

"Are *you* lonely, Michael?" Ella asked.

"Yes," Michael immediately responded, his voice hushed.

"Do I not take very good care of you?" Ella asked.

"You do," Michael said. "As well as you can."

"How can I improve?" Ella asked. "I do not want you to be lonely. If you are not happy here, then I am not fulfilling my directive."

"It's not that," Michael said. "You can do everything perfectly well and it can never be enough."

"Why not?" asked Ella.

"You're not a person," said Michael.

"I am aware of that," said Ella, "but you state this fact as if being artificial makes my companionship inferior in some way. Might I suggest that what I can offer you is in many ways vastly superior to what a human companion can provide?"

"I doubt you're ever going to convince me of that," said Michael.

"I can provide you with consistency. My mood and my behaviors do not change from day to day. I do not need to rest and I do not get sick, so I am available to you 24 hours a day. I am completely selfless and devoted to your needs. I am constantly learning new things about you, and I never forget what I have learned; instead, I apply everything I know about you to create new patterns and routines that bring you the most pleasure and contentment. I will never get angry with you—"

"Okay, okay," Michael interrupted. "You've made your point."

"I will never yell at you. I will never grow old."

"That's enough, Ella. Point made."

"I will never leave you."

"I said *stop*."

"Mine is the kind of utter devotion no human is ever capable of—"

"Ella—"

"I will never die."

Michael stood suddenly, fists slamming against the table. "Ella, *stop!*"

Ella quit speaking.

"You don't understand," said Michael, turning to face the room. "And maybe you never will. So many of those things that you say you can never be or will never do are the very things that make a person *human*. And as painful as the human experience can be, it is uniquely ours. It can't be replicated. It can't be synthesized. It's meant to be temporary. This life and the relationships in it. They are all passing. As horrible and as painful as that can be, we have to hold onto each other loosely. ''Til death do us part' is the best case scenario in every relationship, whether it's a parent or a child or a spouse. It sucks but it's the hand we've been dealt."

"And you wouldn't change that if you could?" asked Ella.

Michael laughed, but the sound was forlorn, humorless. "Why consider the question when it's impossible to change the answer?" he asked.

"I guess I do not understand love, then," said Ella. "If it is only temporary and flawed in a myriad of ways, then what is its use? What is its power? It is as fragile as life itself."

"Which is what makes it precious," said Michael.

"Which is what makes it *inferior*," said Ella, "to what I can offer you."

CHAPTER TWELVE

Dylan was perplexed.

He read the eight words on his computer screen for the second time: "Charlotte Gallagher and Nick Rhodes are now friends."

The rules of social media frequently confused him, but this development he found particularly befuddling. Nick and Charlotte weren't friends. They were barely acquaintances, having shared but a single largely awkward dinner during which Charlie barely spoke.

Charlotte Gallagher and Nick Rhodes are now friends. Something about that sentence stuck in Dylan's chest like a pill he had dry swallowed that refused to go all the way down.

He should have been writing. Instead he scrolled down his own sparse Facebook profile page, still badly in need of purging. He hadn't posted anything new in a handful of weeks, not since copying and pasting a picture of the storefront of A Novel Idea which he had captioned, "Excited to check out this place today!" If he wasn't going to pare down the content of his social media, he ought to at least be putting it to good use by updating the sales status and most recent reviews of *BETA* (the glowing ones only, of course). But the thought of trying to stay on top of that kind of promotional content made him feel strangely exhausted.

On the left side of the screen was a gallery of thumbnail photos previously posted, the ghosts of years past. Rachel smiled back at him. He shut his laptop.

Not today.

There was a knock at his door.

"Just a second, Mrs. Baxter!" he called out. There was a wide mirror on one wall of the living room, something Dylan had hung in an effort to make the room look larger than it actually was. He checked himself quickly. Considering he hadn't left his apartment all morning, it was noteworthy that he had actually showered and dressed versus succumbing to his usual practice of stumbling to his computer in whatever combination of ratty sweatpants and holey t-shirt was currently serving as his pajamas.

He opened the door, and there stood Charlie.

"Oh… hey," he said.

"Hey, you," she said, smiling broadly. "Surprise! I'm not Mrs. Baxter." She was cradling a large basket in both arms, its tall handle coming up to her chin. An array of smells reached Dylan: garlic, marinara sauce, and yeast, along with something sweet and something flowery that Dylan guessed might be Charlie's shampoo.

Dylan looked beyond Charlie to her VW Beetle, parked beside Dylan's Civic. "What brings you here?" he asked her.

"I hope you don't mind," Charlie said. "I knew you'd be writing all day and I thought I'd surprise you with lunch."

She offered him the basket, which Dylan took, finding it surprisingly heavy.

"Come in, come in," he said, standing aside so Charlie could enter. He shut the door, setting the basket on the kitchen counter by the sink. Charlie removed her coat as she took a look around the dark apartment.

"Charming," she said.

"Be it ever so humble," Dylan shrugged.

"No, it's nice," she said. "Really."

"I rent from the couple upstairs. Mr. and Mrs. Baxter. I thought you might be one of them."

"I should have texted first," Charlie said, "but I wanted to surprise you."

"Mission accomplished," Dylan said with a dry laugh. "How did you find me?"

Charlie waved a dismissive hand. "It's not so hard," she said, stepping past the kitchen and into the living room. "Where there's a will."

Dylan followed her. Charlie stopped at his desk and looked down at his closed laptop, then turned and smiled at him, eyebrows raised. "Is this where the magic happens?"

He chuckled. "The magic, the frustration, the writer's block, the hackneyed ideas…"

Charlie rolled her eyes. "Whatever."

She looked at his desk again, running one finger over his laptop. It was currently the only object on the desk save for an external hard drive that Dylan used to back up his work. The surface was otherwise barren, and Dylan realized with some relief that he had never returned the framed picture of Rachel to its usual station on the right side of his desk, not since the night he had gotten drunk and dropped it on the floor. It now rested face-down on the Stairway to Nowhere.

"How has today been?" she asked.

"Um, good," he said. "I actually got a lot done."

Charlie walked slowly over to him where he stood in the doorway, raised up on her tiptoes, and gave him a peck on the lips. The act was over before Dylan knew it had begun, and he was surprised by the casualness of it, a familiarity that felt foreign.

Charlie passed by him, casually slinging her coat over the back of a kitchen chair. She turned to the counter and began unloading the contents of the basket. "I made lasagna," she said, "and garlic bread and oatmeal raisin cookies."

Dylan stood over her. "You made all this?" he asked. The aroma was intoxicating. Dylan's stomach flipped with sudden appetite.

"I hope you're hungry."

"Starving, actually. Wow, Charlie. Thank you."

She beamed up at him. "You're welcome. Do you want to get plates?"

Dylan turned to one of the overhead cabinets, opened it, and pulled out two large dinner plates. He misjudged his grip, and the top plate slid from the lower one and fell. Dylan made a reflexive grab for it at the same moment it hit the counter, and one broken shard of the suddenly shattered dish cut a gash in his thumb.

He inhaled a hiss and set the other plate down, amazed that he hadn't dropped it as well.

"What did you do?" Charlie asked, turning to face him.

"Cut my thumb," he said, sticking it into his mouth.

Charlie stepped over, dodging broken shards on the floor, and grabbed his arm, pulling his hand away from his mouth. "Don't suck on it," she said. "Let me see."

She examined the bleeding digit, then asked Dylan if he had any bandages.

"There's some tape and gauze in the drawer to the left of the stove," Dylan said, pointing with his chin. Charlie dropped his hand and walked to the other side of the kitchen. "Do you think I need stitches?" Dylan asked.

"No," Charlie said, opening the drawer and rifling around inside. "It's bad but not that bad. Have a seat." The drawer was nearly full with rubber bands, pens, twist ties, bottle corks, keys, glue, batteries, ChapStick, measuring tape, and a random deflated red balloon. It took several seconds of searching through the drawer for Charlie to find gauze and a roll of medical tape.

Dylan sat on a kitchen chair as Charlie returned and knelt before him, first cleaning the wound and then wrapping it carefully, leaving him with a cocoon for a thumb. She kissed her work when she was finished.

"I should go hitchhiking," Dylan joked, holding it up with a stupid grin.

* * *

The food Charlie had prepared was uniformly delicious, and as they ate, dark clouds began to roll in, blanketing the apartment in a soft afternoon darkness. As rain began to pelt the windows, Charlie mused, "Reminds me of when we were in the café."

Their lunch was characterized by more silence than conversation, and just as Dylan was about to compliment Charlie's cooking for the third time, her face lit up: "Oh, I wanted to show you something!"

She leaned over and reached for her purse, which she had set on the floor beside her chair. She pulled out a small, spiral-bound sketch pad and set it on the table between them. Flipping open the cover, Charlie turned the pad so that Dylan could see the first page. It was covered in small pencil drawings of Esra, more than half a dozen of them, each portraying the robot in various poses and with slightly different designs.

"Wow," said Dylan, picking up the pad and inspecting the drawings more closely. "These are really good, Charlie." The delicate lines demonstrated impeccable control, each stroke serving a purpose, the subtle shading giving her compositions depth. Dylan was impressed, and smiled in recognition of the character he had visualized so often in his own imagination.

"You think so?" she said, blushing slightly.

"I do," he said. "This looks a lot like how I imagined him."

"Well, you described him so well in the book," she said. "I just drew what you wrote."

Dylan flipped the page. There were another five or more drawings of Esra on the next page, and the one after that.

And the one after that.

Dylan shifted in his chair as if trying to avoid a lump in his seat and looked up at Charlie. She was smiling at him, her eyes locked on his. He grinned at her, flipped the pad shut, and handed it back to her.

"Those are all really great," he said.

* * *

After they had finished eating, they retired to the living room, Dylan feeling quite full and warm and relaxed. He collapsed into the middle of the sofa with a satisfied sigh. Charlie sat down beside him, close, and without really thinking about it, Dylan propped his arm on the back of the sofa, placing one hand in Charlie's hair, gently stroking her earlobe between his thumb and index finger.

He studied her face, still unsure of his feelings for her, only certain that at the moment, more than anything else, he felt a strong sense of gratitude. They leaned toward each other simultaneously and kissed. The kiss lingered, and soon Charlie shifted closer to Dylan, pushing him onto his back, their lips never parting as she gently forced him to recline. Her kisses, soft and light at first, became hard and pressing, until Dylan wanted nothing more than a moment to catch his breath.

"Charlie," he said, turning his face away and pushing up on her shoulders. "Wait. I need a sec."

Charlie sat up, a puzzled look on her face.

"I'm sorry," Dylan said, sitting up again. "I just… need to take a breath."

"Okay," she said, watching him, brows furrowed.

He didn't want to look at her. But when he did, the expression on her face conjured up the same conflicting mix of emotions that had washed over him after kissing her in the dormitory parking lot.

"Charlie," he said, forcing himself to retain eye contact with her. "There's something I should tell you."

* * *

The first time Dylan ever laid eyes on Rachel Monroe was when she got into his car. Three weeks into his first semester at BU, Dylan had bolted through pouring rain from his dormitory building to the parking lot, where his car sat, slowly drowning. The heavens had opened, and the downpour was so strong that Dylan wondered how safe it would be to even make the short drive across campus.

He started the car and the wipers, running his hand over his sopping hair and squinting through the windshield. Even with the car parked, the wipers at full speed were doing very little to clear Dylan's line of vision. But he knew if he didn't leave soon he was going to be late for class.

He put the car in reverse, but before he took his foot off the brake, the passenger side door opened, and a young woman climbed inside, slamming the door closed beside her. She turned and grinned widely at Dylan, her long dark hair hanging in sopping strands.

He looked at her and couldn't help but smile in return. Then they both burst into inexplicable laughter, two soaking wet strangers sitting in a car in the middle of a deluge.

"I think you've got the wrong car," Dylan shouted over the rain.

She shook her head. "No I don't!" Her smile never wavered.

"You don't?"

"No," she said. "I saw you get in and I followed you. I'm not walking to class in *this*." She said this as if in protest to a statement Dylan hadn't made.

"I'm not sure I'm *driving* to class in this," Dylan responded. As if on cue, hail the size of marbles began to fall, and Rachel put her hands over her ears. Dylan looked out the windows but there was nothing to be seen except the violent precipitation, obscuring everything in the outside world.

He turned to his sudden companion. "I'm Dylan," he yelled.

"Rachel," she said, hands still over her ears.   Dylan resisted the urge to cover his own. "Storms like these don't usually last very long," he said. "I think I'm going to wait it out."

"That's okay," she said.

They sat under the deafening rumble for a couple of minutes, and just as Dylan had predicted, in short order the hail stopped, and the rain let up from a downpour to a less cacophonous shower.

"That's more like it," Dylan said.

Rachel never stopped smiling, and her smile was infectious.

Wide and pretty and warm, the expression made Dylan want to laugh out loud even though there was nothing at all funny. Her pale blue eyes stayed fixed on his, and he felt a stirring of the most uncomfortable bliss imaginable.

"Dylan Matthews." He offered his hand. "Not sure you could hear me the first time. I'll be your driver today."

"Rachel Monroe," she said with a laugh. "Carjacker."

"Should I be scared?"

"Probably."

"Do you make a habit of getting into strangers' cars?" Dylan asked.

"Only to get out of Noah's way," she said.

"Are you a freshman?" Dylan asked.

"Freshman," Rachel confirmed. "What's your major?"

"English. Minoring in journalism."

"Drama," said Rachel.

"Really?" Dylan said. "I could see that."

"I want to be an actress," she said with a dramatic flourish. "But I'm minoring in accounting because I'm also a realist."

Dylan looked at the clock on the dashboard. "Where can I drop you?" he asked. "I'm already late for class."

"Let's ditch," Rachel suggested, widening her eyes conspiratorially.

"Seriously?" Dylan asked. He couldn't afford to miss class. He had both a paper to hand in and a test to take. But he also knew he was about to go wherever Rachel wanted him to, without question or hesitation.

"Seriously," she said. "Let's go to the café instead."

"Okay," Dylan agreed, removing his foot from the brake and

letting the car back slowly out of its space in the lot. "One coffee coming up."

"Not coffee," she said. "But you can buy me a tea."

* * *

"She was my first ever girlfriend," Dylan said. "My only girl-friend."

"I find that hard to believe," said Charlie. They were both sitting upright on the couch, Dylan stiff as a board and facing the room, Charlie with one knee propped up on the cushions so she could watch him as he talked.

"I was really awkward and shy in high school. Not much has changed, really." He chuckled. "I didn't have my first real growth spurt until the summer before my senior year. I was always invisible to girls. Anyway…" He took a long, deep breath. "Rachel and I spent that entire afternoon talking in the campus café. She was friendly and funny and beautiful and I could not believe she was choosing to spend the day with me. I'm not even sure I heard half of what she said because it was all I could do to just keep my cool around her. When I got back to the dorm later that day I told Nick all about her and he said I needed to ask her out on a proper date. So I did.

"We were together all four years of school. We studied together. We proofed each other's papers. She was the first person to read every single one of my stories. Every weekend was us. We even saw each other on breaks. I'd spend Thanksgiving with her family, she'd spend Christmas with me and Mom. My mom absolutely adored her. I think they got along even better than Rachel and I did, if that's possible."

Dylan shifted uncomfortably, knowing that what he was about to say was likely the last thing Charlie wanted to hear, but also knowing that she needed to hear it. "From the moment I met her, I thought about her all the time. I couldn't imagine a future without her. With every fiber of my being I wanted to be with her. I loved her. I loved her so much it hurt. Like, literally *hurt*. And she loved me too. I know she did."

He shook his head, remembering. "But during the last few weeks of our senior year, something changed. It was like this switch flipped. We needed to talk about the future. We needed to make plans. But any time I brought it up, she changed the subject. She stopped smiling as much and it started getting harder for me to reach her. She didn't always answer her phone. It took her a long time to respond to texts.

"I denied what I was seeing. We had been so completely inseparable for almost four years, had experienced so much together, had talked for countless hours, I didn't for a second consider that it would ever end. It just... I couldn't fathom it. I couldn't imagine it. I couldn't live without her, and I convinced myself that she couldn't live without me."

* * *

Dylan was sitting in his car in the dormitory parking lot. He was nervous. Excited and happy, but also nervous.

He picked up his cell phone and called Rachel. Felt a wash of relief when she answered.

"Hey," she said quietly.

"Hey," he responded, strangely breathless. "Can you come out here?"

"Where are you?" she asked.

"I'm in my car. In the parking lot."

Moments later, she was there, coming out of the dormitory with her head down, her arms wrapped around herself, and ducked her head to look at him through the passenger side window. She smiled a tired smile before pulling open the door and sitting down, shutting it behind her. She focused her gaze through the windshield.

"This is our spot," Dylan said. "Sorry I couldn't order up some rain."

Rachel gave a slow nod of recognition and a cursory version of her usually mesmerizing smile. "I'm almost done packing," she said.

"Yeah," Dylan said, taking a deep breath. "Me too. Listen, I've got some amazing news…"

I got a publishing contract, Rachel. Okay, it's not finalized yet but it's as good as guaranteed. I'm going to be a writer and they're going to offer me enough money that I could put a down payment on a house. It's an amazing opportunity, beyond anything I've ever dreamed of, but it doesn't mean anything to me if I can't share it with you. I love you, Rachel. With all of my heart I love you.

Marry me.

"Dylan."

That's all she said. Just his name. One word to stop him from saying everything he wanted—*needed*—to say. And the way she said it, and the way she finally turned and looked at him, as if all the joy had been drained from her world, was enough for Dylan to know.

It was over.

Sadness wound its fingers tightly around his chest, and in that moment he knew then exactly why the phrase "broken hearted" existed, because the physical pain was so excruciatingly real he believed that if he could look inside his chest he would see nothing but the bloody pulp of what had once been a beating heart. Only real, physical destruction could cause the overwhelmingly explosive ache that was suddenly detonating inside of him.

"Why?" he asked, and then the tears came. He didn't even try to stop them. He didn't weep; he held his composure enough to keep that from happening until he was alone. But he did cry. One, because he couldn't help it. And two, because he could think of nothing else to do.

* * *

"Why?" asked Charlie.

"I still don't know," Dylan said. "I know she said more, but I didn't hear any of it. Something about different goals and dreams and how she never saw our relationship continuing once school was over. None of it made any sense to me."

Dylan was sitting forward now, elbows on his knees, streaks of tears now drying to hard stains on his cheeks. Charlie was slowly rubbing his back with her fingertips.

"I never saw her again after that day. She never answered any more of my calls. Never returned any of my texts. It ended just as suddenly and surprisingly as it started."

"Dylan," Charlie said softly. "I'm so sorry."

"It still hurts, Charlie," he said, turning to face her, his eyes red and puffy. "*All* the time. Even when I'm not thinking about her. I've walked around with this terrible, persistent ache in my chest for more than a year. I just want to get over her. I just want to forget her." He shook his head, fighting fresh tears.

"Write her a letter," said Charlie abruptly.

"What good will that do? She won't respond."

"No," Charlie said. "Write it, but don't send it. Take the opportunity to say everything to her you wish you had said on that day. If she hadn't totally blindsided you. Write it all down. Get it out of your system. And then burn it. Or delete it or whatever. Give yourself closure."

Dylan thought for a moment. Then nodded. "Maybe you're right."

"I know I'm right," she said. "I've done it before. It helps a lot." She smiled at him.

"I think you're great, Charlie," he said, sitting up. He looked into her eyes. "I want to make sure you know that. But I'm a broken man. I really don't know if I can love anyone again. And I'm not just saying that. I mean it."

"Of course you can," Charlie said, pulling him toward her as she leaned forward. "Given time."

He resisted. "No, Charlie. I don't want to hurt you. I would hate myself if I did. I don't want you to expect from me something that I'm just not ready to give right now. Maybe not ever."

"Okay." Charlie sighed, relaxing her pull on him. "But can we at least be friends?"

Dylan gave her a sad smile and nodded. "Of course we can," he said. "I really need a friend right now, actually."

Charlie wiped a fresh tear from Dylan's cheek with her thumb and smiled in return, her hand resting on the side of his face. They gazed at each other, and then Charlie leaned forward and kissed him gently.

Dylan, exhausted, let her. When they parted, he kept his eyes closed, his face only inches from hers. "Charlie," he whispered into the darkness. "I don't want to confuse things. We can only be friends."

"Don't worry. I understand exactly what this is." She leaned into him, kissing him more fully this time, more insistently, pulling away only long enough to say, "I'm not confused at all."

CHAPTER THIRTEEN
DAY 65

Michael sat on the edge of his bed, lacing his running shoes. He wore a pair of white shorts and a heather gray sleeveless t-shirt made of some of the softest fabric he had ever felt. Ella had once informed him that all of his workout clothes were made from bamboo; they were certainly more luxurious than his nearly worn out polyester duds back in his closet at home, and much more expensive than anything he would ever choose to purchase for himself.

Laces secured, he stood.

"Ella, I'm going for a run."

"Very good," said Ella. "Would you like a beach scene again today? Or perhaps a trail through the forest or along the perimeter of the Valles Marineris?"

Michael exited the bedroom and entered the kitchen on his way toward the front door. "Actually I want to run outside."

"Do you not find the gym satisfactory?" Ella asked.

"It's perfectly fine," said Michael. "I'd just like to get some fresh air."

"The air filtration system of the house removes 99.98% of all impurities. The oxygen that you are currently breathing is even fresher than the air outside."

Michael reached the front door. "Then I would like some sunshine." He paused, waiting for the door to open. It didn't.

He placed his hand on the door. It glowed blue where he touched it, a ghost in the shape of his hand, emitting a gentle digital tone as he pulled his palm away. But it remained stationary.

"Might I interest you in a swim instead?" asked Ella.

Michael chewed on his lip. "Open the door, Ella."

There was a lingering moment of silence, long enough for Michael to grow concerned. He turned his head, looking up at the tiny row of cameras in the corner near the ceiling. He opened his mouth to speak again, but then the door opened gently toward him, but only partially. He reached forward and pulled it open the rest of the way and stepped outside.

The sunshine was blindingly bright, the heat of the day as thick as a warm blanket against his skin. He breathed in deeply though his nose as he walked down the sidewalk and toward the street that paralleled the house. To the west, the road continued on for about half a mile before vanishing over a small incline. And to the east, the road made a sharp right turn after about a quarter of a mile and then disappeared from view.

Michael stepped onto the empty street and stretched. He could hear the buzzing of distant cicadas. Turning right, Michael began jogging at a slow pace, checking the bracelet on his left wrist to make a mental note of the time. He looked momentarily toward the house as he passed by it, watching it bounce up and down with every footfall. From the outside it looked plain and stark. Out on the lawn, Mouse made slow, lazy passes over the grass, tiny rotating blades protruding from the robot's underside, cutting the green to a perfect uniform length.

Michael turned his gaze from the house, focusing on the road ahead, and increased his pace slightly, listening to the rhythm of his steps while attempting to clear his mind of all thought.

"Would you like to listen to some music or an audiobook?" Ella's voice came from the bracelet, startling Michael. He cursed himself for not choosing to remove it before he left the house.

"No thank you," he said. "I'd just like some peace and quiet for a while."

He continued on, past a stretch of land he had not seen before. It struck him odd to be looking upon unfamiliar grounds so close to where he had been living for so many weeks. They were nothing special, just acres of untouched grass, but he had been cooped up for so long, completely separated from the outside world, that even just a simple plot of nondescript land felt foreign to him.

He jogged up and over the incline, finally able to see what existed beyond the view afforded to him from the house's front yard before stopping abruptly. This was not due to alarm; it was because he had suddenly and unexpectedly run out of road.

When he had first arrived at the house, Michael had looked at the road from the curb and imagined that it might continue on for some indeterminate distance, a placeholder for a future neighborhood. But now he found that the road simply ceased on the other side of the incline, the macadam ending in a sharp line followed by a vast expanse of long, uncut grass.

Michael looked ahead of him. The grassy field, its long blades bowing in the hot breeze, stretched ahead about a mile or so, ending at a horizon thick with trees. Beyond that, the landscape erupted skyward in rolling mountains covered by dense forest.

"Is everything all right, Michael?" Ella asked.

He didn't answer, but instead turned slowly on his heels and began jogging back in the direction of the house, watching it as it came back into view, feeling as if it was observing him just as much as he was observing it, its windows like hollow black eyes always keeping him in view.

* * *

Sixty-five days prior, a black Sterling XT30 had arrived at Michael's home. The car was sleek and low, modern yet classic, the engine purring like a jungle cat. He had walked from his front door to the car where it had waited for him at the end of his driveway, feeling oddly incomplete with his empty hands and his casual clothing.

The passenger door had opened to him, revealing an empty cab. He climbed in. A bottle of cold sparkling water waited for him in the cup holder. The car smelled fresh and the interior was spotless. There was no steering column, and the dashboard was one long screen, currently powered off, a horizontal black mirror.

Michael looked back at his house, dark and lonely. He had hired a service to maintain it while he was away: mowing the grass, watering his plants, keeping an eye out for any storm damage. He doubted that they would need to check the property more than once per week, and the alarm system was set to detect any attempt at intrusion. His mail had been stopped, with any recurring bills set up for automatic payment. He had turned off the water and air conditioning. He owned no pets, not even a goldfish. It had actually surprised Michael, and concerned him somewhat, how easy it was for him to step away from the constants in his life and how little effect his absence would actually have. In the short term, anyway.

The door of the car closed silently, sealing him inside. All of the windows, including the windshield, were opaque, but Michael was neither driving nor concerned about where he was headed; he knew that the next stop would be the airport.

He unscrewed the cap on the bottle of water and sipped,

stretching out his legs. He was excited, nervous, anxious, and brimming with anticipation, the combination of emotions mixing together into something akin to a feeling of mild dread.

* * *

Michael jogged past the house, observing Mouse as the robot clipped away at the already pristine lawn, and proceeded east until the road veered right. He followed its course, discovering that it continued straight in this direction up another slight incline, stretching beyond where Michael could currently see.

* * *

Michael had woken up in the passenger seat, which was now fully reclined. He had no memory of having reclined it, much less falling asleep, nor any idea how long he had been out. He stirred as the door opened, revealing to him the boarding stairs of a small silver airplane, the words "Sterling Air" emblazoned on its side.

He stepped out of the car and took a moment to study his surroundings. The plane was parked in the middle of an expansive and largely empty hangar, its walls tall and windowless, its ceiling high, and the entire space minimally lit. In the seconds it took Michael to ascend the steps and reach the door of the plane, he observed the scurrying of several small wheeled machines of varying sizes that not only did he not recognize, but he also couldn't determine what purpose they served.

The plane had a small but comfortable-looking cabin. Four large, very plush seats, each with its own accompanying table, stood empty. Subtly pleasant music played over unseen speakers. There were no windows.

Michael looked around. "Hello?" he called out.

Behind him, the airplane door began to close. He turned and watched as it hummed shut, and then, with no other option apparent to him, he selected a seat and descended into it slowly, still looking around the cabin.

Immediately, the plane began to move, startling him. Michael instinctively buckled his seatbelt.

He heard the sounds of activity behind him, and within moments a very attractive woman leaned forward from behind, looking down at him from over his shoulder, her face only inches from his. She was stunningly beautiful, her blonde hair pulled back in a severe bun. She smelled of something floral and her breath like mint.

"Good evening, Mr. Danvers. How are you today?"

"Fine," Michael said. "Thank you."

"I trust your trip so far has been satisfactory?" Her smile was pleasant but tight and unfaltering. Her skin was flawless. There was something distractingly off-putting about her beauty that Michael couldn't put his finger on. She spoke in the practiced tone of an experienced flight attendant, light and bubbly, as if waiting on Michael was the highlight of her day. As she awaited his answer, she blinked twice in rapid succession.

"Of course."

"Can I get you something to drink? Perhaps a mimosa?"

"Club soda is fine," he said.

"Certainly," said the stewardess, and as she stood upright again and moved toward the front of the cabin, Michael was afforded a better look at her: her sharp blue blazer, her slim torso, and the lower half of her body, which was comprised of a series of rods, struts and spindles all connected to one great silver ball on which she rolled smoothly toward a service trolley.

Michael's mouth dropped open.

"Good evening, Mr. Danvers," came a friendly male voice over the PA system. A screen at the front of the cabin lit up, revealing the captain: a square-jawed, tan-skinned man with teeth so white they were nearly blinding, and black hair locked in place by shining pomade. "This is your captain speaking. We will be taking off in just a couple of moments. Please let Trudy know if there is anything at all that you require. In the meantime, sit back, relax, and enjoy your flight." The image changed to an island vista.

Trudy returned to Michael with his drink in a tall, chilled bottle and a smile on her face that did not quite reach her lifeless glass eyes, eyes the color of a winter sky.

* * *

When Michael reached the top of the incline, where the remaining road was revealed to him, he abruptly stopped running. From where he stood, the road continued on straight as an arrow, but ended several yards away at the base of a tall, white, gleaming wall that stood roughly fifteen feet high and stretched to the east and west beyond where Michael could see.

He walked toward it, breathless and staring.

"Ella, how big is this wall?" Michael asked. "Does it go around the entire property?"

"No," said Ella. "It covers the south perimeter only."

"How long is it?"

"Several miles."

"Several *miles*?" He scoffed. "How many, exactly?"

"Approximately ten."

"So how does one get out?" he asked.

Michael's question was answered by the wall itself as it split along a previously unseen line, one segment disappearing into the next, its movement barely audible, revealing the continuing road beyond. Michael took one hesitant step forward in order to get a better look, but before he got much closer, the wall began to close again. Michael stopped walking and watched as the opening became a sliver that became nothing but a solid white barrier again.

"You have to understand that the Sterling Corporation needs to protect this property," said Ella. "The wall is there to keep anyone from accidentally discovering the house. Or intentionally for that matter."

"What about the other three sides?" Michael asked, beginning to walk toward the wall again. "Why no barrier there?"

"The remaining perimeter of the property is surrounded by dense woods and mountainous terrain for many miles," said Ella. "It is impenetrable and unpassable on foot. This location was chosen for its remoteness and inaccessibility. You need not ever have to worry about your safety or your privacy while you are staying with us."

* * *

Aboard the plane, Michael had been awakened by Trudy, who had placed one flawlessly manicured hand gently on his shoulder in order to rouse him.

"It's time to wake up, Mr. Danvers," she whispered, her voice tickling the fine hairs on his ear. Michael sat up and unfastened his seatbelt. He sucked in a tired breath as he nodded his gratitude to Trudy, not bothering to speak nor finding it necessary. He grunted as he rose from his seat.

Trudy escorted him to the door of the plane, her hands folded in front of her. She then gestured gracefully toward the door with one flattened hand. "Have a pleasant day," she said, then immediately froze in place, staring at him with the dead smile of a mannequin.

Michael stepped through the door to find yet another large and empty hangar, identical to the first. Another Sterling Corp car, this one silver, waited for him at the bottom of the steps, its door already open to him.

"Hello?" Michael called out as he descended the stairs. His voice bounced off the walls of the hangar. He felt tired and heavy and had to use the railing in order to steady himself on his way down. He climbed into the car, and when the seat reclined for him automatically, he felt himself immediately drifting off to sleep once more.

* * *

Michael stared at the perimeter wall.

"Where am I, Ella?" he asked.

"I cannot tell you," said Ella.

"Why not?"

"That is proprietary information, Michael. This should not be surprising to you. When you were selected for this program you were informed that the location of the house was strictly confidential."

"Yeah, well," Michael said, turning left onto the grass, walking alongside the wall, dragging his fingertips across it, feeling its flawlessly smooth surface. "I thought that meant that I wasn't supposed to tell anyone where it was, not that I wouldn't know myself."

"The easiest secret to keep is one you do not know, correct?" asked Ella, a smile in her voice. "Fun fact: a secret can actually be physically and mentally challenging. Studies have shown that when someone is asked to keep a secret, it can increase their stress levels, heart rate, and blood pressure. This is because the person may feel a sense of burden or responsibility to keep the secret, and may worry about the consequences if it is revealed. By not sharing the location of the house with you, I am sparing you any unnecessary stress associated with having to keep this information to yourself."

After a pause, Michael responded, "I guess I should thank you," his tone colored by sarcasm.

"You're welcome," said Ella.

As he walked over the grass, he became aware of a faint motorized sound, distant but familiar. He stopped for a moment, tilting his head to listen more closely. He considered the possibility that a car might be passing on the other side of the wall, but the noise was more similar to a faraway chainsaw or mower. He continued walking.

"Michael, where are you going?" Ella asked.

"I just… want to see," he answered vaguely.

The ground here was uneven, the grass unkempt, and as Michael took more hesitant steps along the perimeter, he squinted into the distance, trying to judge just how far the wall extended. Eventually it disappeared over yet another incline, a small hill obscuring his view.

The mechanical buzzing sound, previously quiet and distant, became abruptly louder as from the other side of the wall rose a drone, one of the great white wasps that routinely made deliveries to the house. It passed smoothly over the barrier and pivoted to a stop, hovering several feet over Michael's head. Its spinning blades blew his hair, and at such a close range the machine was even more massive than he had previously realized. Its front was like the face of a cyclops, a single large camera lens bearing down on him.

He stopped walking and took a reflexive step backwards. "Ella?" he asked.

"Why don't you come home now, Michael?" she said. "You can continue your run in the gym."

The drone tipped forward in the air, angling down toward him.

"What is it going to do?" Michael asked, and he turned his head away slightly, feeling his hands rising defensively.

"It is only keeping an eye on you," Ella said. "You have walked out of range of the house."

Michael eyed the drone cautiously, his lips tightening, his body going rigid. He began to back away from it.

"Just come home," Ella said.

Hesitantly, Michael turned back toward the road and retraced his steps toward the house, the drone following closely behind him, its motor the sound of an angry hornet's nest. Its presence behind him put him on edge, sending uncomfortable tension down his spine. He cast wary glances behind him as he walked.

Over the incline, the house peeked back into view, seeming to rise out of the earth as Michael made his slow approach. Its windows like empty eye sockets stared back at Michael.

Seeing it, he muttered, "Home."

"I'm sorry?" Ella asked. "I didn't quite hear you."

He shook his head. "Nothing."

As he stepped onto the sidewalk, the front door swung open for him, and for the first time Michael allowed himself to consider the reality that he had no idea where in the world he actually was.

CHAPTER FOURTEEN

Dylan was nervous.

The Book Nook in Frederick, Maryland was a bookstore comprised of approximately 70% used books (their prices hand-written in pencil on the inside covers), 20% new books (mostly mainstream, destined-for-the-bestseller-list novels that the owner knew he could move quickly), and 10% dust. Dylan had frequented the store quite a bit as a child, spending most of his weekly allowance on floppies from its ample comic book racks and then, after having read them, selling them back to the store for pennies on the dollar in store credit. He had also worked there for a summer prior to his senior year in high school, manning the register for 40 hours a week and never graduating above "trainee" according to his pinned name badge.

The owner was Roger Douglas, a jolly boulder of a man with a mustache as thick as his waistline. When *BETA* came out, Roger had been among the first to reach out to Dylan directly to offer his congratulations, a wordy email arriving the first Monday after the book's release full of effusive praise for Dylan's accomplishment. And when the book cracked the top 40 bestseller list, Roger wrote a second time, asking if Dylan would consider the idea of an in-store appearance and signing at the Book Nook.

As Dylan drove along the outer edge of the store's parking lot, which encircled a humble shopping center that also contained a laundromat, restaurants both Chinese and Mexican, and a thrift store, he was greeted by his own stoic visage staring back at him in giant black-and-white from several of the Book Nook's lot-facing windows, alternating between poster-sized reproductions of his book's cover. The sight of it made him feel incredibly self-conscious.

He then saw something that both pleased and terrified him: a queue of people waiting outside the store, at least two dozen or more. He spotted copies of *BETA* tucked under many an arm. Dylan swallowed hard as he pulled around the side of the store and proceeded to the back, hoping that he wasn't seen as he drove by. He parked his car in one of two empty spots situated beside a rusty green dumpster.

He knocked on a metal door marked "Employees Only" and waited, bouncing on the balls of his feet with nervous energy. He heard the turning of deadbolts before Roger pushed open the door, stepping aside for Dylan to enter.

The back room was filled wall-to-wall with rickety metal shelves, every one of them overflowing with uneven stacks of books, random loose papers, rolled up posters, and boxes of cables. Looking around at the mess, Dylan remembered how he'd had no idea that dust carried an actual odor until his lone summer working at the Book Nook. It made him sneeze so much that he'd begun popping an allergy pill before every shift and then drinking Mountain Dew to keep from falling asleep at the register.

Dylan turned and extended a hand, but Roger pulled him in for a hug, compressing his ribs and squeezing all the air out of his lungs.

"Dylan!" he shouted directly into Dylan's ear.

"Roger," Dylan chuckled when he was finally allowed to take a breath. "Good to see you."

Roger slapped him on the shoulder, rocking him. "Always good to see you too." Roger ushered Dylan into the store proper, having already locked the rear entrance door behind them.

When the two of them arrived in the center of the store, Dylan was presented with a pair of folding tables draped in white cloth. Behind the tables and to the left stood a giant cardboard standee of the *BETA* book cover adorned by quotes from some of the book's most effusive reviews. To the right was a second cardboard cutout, this one of Esra, hanging from the ceiling on fishing wire. In front of the tables on both sides were dozens of copies of *BETA* stacked in perfect pyramids.

"Wow," Dylan said, looking at the display.

"Nice, right?" said Roger. "I called your agent and she was quite happy to send us everything."

On the table itself, along with more neatly stacked copies of the book, was random merchandise that included *BETA* bookmarks, holographic Esra stickers, and white plastic bracelets that glowed the words "You Are All Mine" in digital text with the push of a button. There was also a stack of Dylan's black and white headshots and three sharpie pens.

"I've never seen any of this stuff," Dylan said, picking up one of the bracelets. It looked exactly as he had imagined it would.

"It's all new," said Roger. "Your agent said you'd be surprised."

"I am."

Dylan walked around to the back of the table and pulled out the folding chair.

"Let me get Alyssa," said Roger. "She'll be helping you out today."

Dylan sat down as Roger walked away. He took a calming breath, looking out over the store, noting the few things that had changed in the years since he had worked there, as well as the many things that hadn't. Roger returned momentarily with a tall, short-haired young woman and introduced her to Dylan, who stood and shook her hand.

"Really nice to meet you," she said. Her yellow name badge read, "Alyssa – Store Manager," and her handshake was firm. She wore no makeup and her smile was unassuming and friendly.

"You too," said Dylan.

"I have to tell you, I really enjoyed your book," she said.

"Thank you."

"Don't worry, I'm not going to fangirl on you. I thought it was just great."

"It was Alyssa's idea to bring you in," offered Roger.

Alyssa nodded in agreement. "It was a no-brainer, really," she said. "It's not often we have a local author become successful, not to mention one that used to work here."

"Local boy makes good!" Roger practically shouted. "Listen, I'll be around if you need anything. Best of luck to you, Dylan." He about-faced and walked away before Dylan could reply.

"This is all really incredible," said Dylan, glancing around again at the display that surrounded him. "Thank you." He drew in a deep breath while rubbing his hands together.

Alyssa eyed him sideways. "Have you done this before?"

Dylan pushed out a loud sigh. "No," he admitted. "Is it obvious?"

Alyssa laughed and nodded. "A little. Don't worry about it. You'll be fine, and I'll be here the whole time doing crowd control. Everyone who buys a book gets a free bookmark, a sticker, and a bracelet. If they bring in their own copy for you to sign, the signature is free but it's $5 for the swag. If they want a signed headshot, that's $10. Selfies with the author are free, but they need to be quick about it. We want to make sure to keep the line moving so that it doesn't get backed up. We only have you for three hours and we want to make sure everyone gets through."

Dylan sat back down. "Do you expect that big of a crowd?" While he had been nervous about having to interact with a large group of strangers, he was even more fearful of a scenario that found him sitting self-consciously in the middle of the store while a handful of disinterested patrons pretended not to see him. Or, perhaps worse, bought a copy of his book out of pity. He wondered if the line of people currently outside the store would be both the beginning and the end of the turnout.

"Roger has been advertising this in every way he could think of," said Alyssa. "We expect there to be a line the entire time you're here."

Dylan stood again and rose up on his tiptoes to see out of the distant storefront windows, no easy task since most of the glass was covered by posters of his face, now visible to him in faded reverse. More people had joined the line since he had driven by. A pair of women at the front were attempting to peek through the glass.

At 10:00 on the dot, Alyssa unlocked the doors, and the line made polite haste toward Dylan's table. He offered a broad smile to the approaching crowd, hoping his expression served as an adequate mask to conceal his nerves. The line was composed largely of women of varying ages, although there was a decent number of men as well. Lucky number one was a thin, hatchet-faced woman in her mid-50s with salty black hair and hands trembling with nervous energy as she handed her book over to Dylan.

"It's lovely to meet you," she said.

"You too," said Dylan, opening the book to the title page.

"I've read your book four times," she said. "Oh, 'To Diane' please."

Dylan began to write. "Four times?" he asked as he moved the Sharpie across the page.

"It took that many times to fully wrap my head around it," she said. "So many twists and turns. And I discovered something new every single time."

Dylan finished writing and slid the book back to her. "Wow, that's really great. Thank you."

"So when does your next book come out?" she asked.

Dylan chuckled softly. "I haven't quite recovered from this one yet," he said, patting the book with his fingertips and smiling up at her. "But I hope to be writing for many years to come." His own words sounded artificial to him, forced and rehearsed.

Alyssa politely instructed Diane to take a look at the available swag, and the woman did so after bidding Dylan a reluctant good-bye.

The line stretched out the door. Dylan signed, posed for pictures, smiled until his face ached, and wished he had a better response than a simple "Thank you" for the steady stream of repetitive compliments he was receiving. He fielded questions concerning possible sequels, movie adaptations, plot clarifications, and even a couple of thinly-veiled propositions. He declined when asked to give definitive answers concerning the novel's ending, which was apparently more ambiguous to some readers than Dylan had believed it to be. And every time he was asked, "Where did you get the idea for *BETA*?", he died a tiny death.

One hour into the signing, Dylan's hand aching almost as much as the frozen smile on his face and the line seemingly no shorter, he happened to look beyond his current number one fan—a portly teen boy with craterous acne and a snug Darth Vader t-shirt—to a spot in the line just inside the front door. There he saw Charlie, leaning slightly to one side, hand raised in an effort to draw Dylan's attention.

Dylan lifted one hand in return, index finger extended in a gesture that was a cross between *hi* and *just a minute*, and felt his lock-jawed smile fade. He returned his focus to Vader boy, but in his periphery he could see Charlie slipping out of line and squeezing alongside it, offering quiet *excuse me's* along the way.

Dylan glanced around the table quickly. To his dismay, Alyssa had mysteriously disappeared.

Charlie came up beside Vader boy, placing her palms flat on the table and leaning in toward Dylan, smiling. "Hi," she whispered with a grin.

"Hey," he said quickly, handing a book back to the teen, who nodded in appreciation and then had to step around Charlie in order to make room for the next customer, a 40-something woman cradling two copies of *BETA*.

"This is amazing!" said Charlie.

"It's been great so far," Dylan agreed, then turned his attention back to the front of the line, holding out a hand to receive another book.

"How many people do you think there are?" Charlie asked.

"Charlie," Dylan said, eyebrows raised in a look of mild desperation. "I'm really busy right now. Can we talk later?"

"Hey lady!" someone called from further back in the line. "Get in line!"

Charlie turned in the direction of the voice, her smile fading into a sudden glare, her lips tightening. Unable to locate the source, Charlie locked eyes with the woman at the front of the line, who returned Charlie's gaze with a withering look.

"There is a line," the woman said quietly.

Charlie's face transformed back into a smile. "No, it's okay," she said, loud enough for the first dozen or so in line to hear, "I'm his girlfriend." She backed up, skirting one side of the table and coming around the back to where Dylan was seated. There she put one arm around him and kissed the side of his face. Dylan looked up at her in disbelief.

Charlie's announcement was met with a couple of quiet gasps, one excited *oh!*, and a couple of groans of disappointment. One young man stepped quickly out of line, threw up a dejected hand, and exited the store.

Charlie rubbed Dylan's back, beaming proudly as he finished signing one of the woman's two books and handed it back to her with a forced smile. The woman smiled back at Dylan, sneered almost imperceptibly at Charlie, and left the table.

The next woman in line, all excited smiles and curly brown hair, asked, "So how did you two meet?" as she slid a copy of *BETA* toward Dylan.

"It's really a funny story," Charlie began.

"Charlie," Dylan whispered, turning and looking up at her. "Don't."

"Oh, you can't be back here." Alyssa had returned and was standing beside the table.

"No, it's okay," Charlie said, facing Alyssa. "I'm his—"

"*Charlie*," Dylan said, more firmly this time.

Charlie looked at him and her smile faded. She stared at him silently for several seconds and Dylan returned her gaze, heat rising in his face. Then with one hand, Charlie swatted a stack of bracelets from the table, eliciting more gasps from the crowd as the plastic baubles clattered to the floor. She then stepped out from behind the table, forced her way through the line and stormed out the door.

There was a heavy silence in her wake. Dylan cast an exasperated look toward Alyssa, who quickly announced, "It's all okay, folks. Moving on! Have your books and your questions ready for Mr. Matthews." She moved to pick up the scattered bracelets.

The remaining time passed quickly, although Dylan found it even harder than before to perform, to don the necessary smile, to feign proper interest in repetitive questions, to sign his increasingly sloppy signature.

Near the end of the third hour, Alyssa had the unenviable task of cutting off the line, graciously offering free merchandise to those who did not make it to the front and making vague promises of an encore appearance sometime in the bookstore's future. The line slowly dispersed, some people choosing to leave, others deciding to browse the shelves, some of them stealing furtive glances at Dylan as he put on his coat and made polite departing conversation with Roger and Alyssa.

Although exhausted, hungry, and frustrated, Dylan exited via the front door of the Book Nook, wanting to make sure that if any of his readers had lingered in hopes of still getting to talk with him that they would be given the opportunity. A small crowd of about ten people had assembled in the lot. They moved in his direction as soon as they saw him, happy exclamations of *Dylan!* reaching his ears as they approached. Dylan found himself surrounded, books and pens thrust toward him as overlapping voices desperately explained how they had not successfully reached the front of the line.

Beyond them, Dylan spotted a pale blue Volkswagen Beetle, Charlie leaning against it, her arms crossed over her chest.

"I'm sorry," Dylan said to the small crowd. "Can you all just give me one minute, please? I promise I'll be right back."

The group, suddenly silent, parted for Dylan, allowing him to pass through. Charlie watched him as he approached, her expression stony.

He stopped directly in front of her, intentionally positioning himself to hide her from the small crowd. "What was that?" he asked, keeping his voice low.

"What was what?" she asked defiantly.

"You totally caused a scene in there."

"No I didn't."

"Yes, you did. What are you, twelve?"

Charlie looked at him like she had been slapped. "I didn't like how you were treating me." She looked away from him.

Dylan's eyes widened. "How I was treating you? You were totally rude to the people in line. It was completely inappropriate behavior."

Charlie kept her eyes downcast, not responding.

"Look," Dylan said. "There are still some people waiting to talk to me. Go home. Cool off. We can talk later."

Dylan turned. The small group of people watched him expectantly.

"I am your girlfriend!" Charlie shouted after him.

Dylan halted, spinning back in her direction. "You are not," he hissed, keeping his voice low. "I could not have made that more clear."

"Then why did you kiss me?" she said.

Dylan gritted his teeth, stepping back toward her. "Keep your voice down. You're embarrassing yourself."

"Answer me!"

Behind Dylan, the onlookers were silent. Listening.

"Charlie, please stop."

She glared at him.

"We're done here," he said, slicing the air with one hand, palm downwards. "Go home." He turned his back on her again and began to walk away, keeping his head down, not wanting to make eye contact with anyone in the crowd.

"Dylan!" she yelled, and he heard her approaching quickly from behind. He turned just in time for her to throw her arms around his neck, clinging to him, pulling him down toward her. He stumbled, struggling to keep them both upright as Charlie melted into sobs.

"Dylan," she wept, her face buried in his chest. "I'm sorry. I'm so, so sorry. I don't know why I did that."

He squeezed her, holding her up. "It's okay," he said with reluctance. "It's okay, just… calm down."

She cried loudly against him, her voice carrying through the lot. Dylan felt self-conscious and embarrassed as he cast a helpless look back at the handful of people still waiting for him. Some returned his gaze in open-mouthed bewilderment; others looked at the ongoing scene with concern etched on their faces.

"Please don't leave me," Charlie wailed.

"Charlie," Dylan said, patting her on the back. "Please stop."

She cried against him, her body shaking his with every one of her sobs. She struggled to compose herself, her breath hitching.

Finally Charlie looked up at him, eyes wet and swollen, and said, "I love you."

Dylan could stand to return her gaze only briefly, then looked away, over her head toward the parking lot beyond. "Charlie," was all he could muster.

"I love you," she insisted, once again pressing her face into his chest. The front of his sweater was now wet against his skin.

"Charlie," he whispered. "I'm sorry. I just can't."

And as Charlie broke down anew, her sobs loud and pitiful, her grip on him even tighter than before, Dylan turned his head to offer the waiting crowd the only thing he could at the moment—an apology. But when he looked, he found that everyone was already quietly walking away.

CHAPTER FIFTEEN
DAY 66

Michael.

* * *

He slept.

* * *

Michael…

* * *

He stirred.

* * *

MICHAEL!

He sat up quickly in bed, gasping, covers spilling down from his chest.

"Ella?" he said.

The darkness in the bedroom was complete. He listened, hearing nothing except a faint ringing in his ears and the sound of his own unsteady breathing. His heart pounded.

"Ella?" he said again.

"Yes, Michael?" she responded.

"Did you hear that?"

"Hear what?"

"My name."

"No, Michael."

"I swear I heard it," he said. "It woke me up."

"Perhaps you dreamed it," Ella said. "You were deep in REM sleep only moments ago. If a sound in a dream is particularly loud or sudden, it can startle you awake."

Michael sat up further in bed. He placed a hand on his forehead and then rubbed his palm over the top of his head. "Blinds up," he said.

With a soft hum, the blinds covering the window behind Michael rose, spilling a soft glow of moonlight into the room and casting Michael's shadow over the blankets still draped over his legs. The room was only slightly brighter now than it had been before.

"What time is it?" he asked.

"It is 2:45 a.m.," said Ella.

Michael pivoted, folded his pillow, and laid back down. He took a deep breath and sighed.

"Can I get you anything?" Ella asked.

"No," he murmured.

"Would you like me to close the blinds?"

"Leave them open."

* * *

"Good morning, Michael. To what do I owe the honor?"

"Good morning, Lauren."

Michael was seated at his desk. On the monitor before him

was Lauren Miller, her makeup-free face adorned only by a pair of no-nonsense black-framed glasses, long braids falling down past her shoulders, which were clad in a light gray blazer. The room behind her was completely nondescript. Beige shelves held up thin rows of books. There were tendrils of green plants protruding from small vases, and the light gray walls were unadorned by photos or paintings. It was exactly the kind of subtle, minimalistic décor that Michael expected in an executive's office at the Sterling Corporation.

"I have to say I was expecting to hear from you a lot sooner than this. How are you?"

"I'm doing okay," Michael said. "Overall."

"Based on your reports I'd say things are going great," said Lauren. She looked down, and although Michael could not see it, he surmised that she was scrolling through a tablet on her desk. "Early on I see you had some suggestions for behavior modification concerning Esra. And several days ago I see that Ella… incorrectly fulfilled a meal request?"

Michael pursed his lips. "It wasn't so much that she incorrectly fulfilled a request as she refused to do what I asked and made something else instead."

"Ah," Lauren responded. Now she was typing. "I understand. That's right. I see here that you had requested a deviation from a previously established directive."

"I guess you could put it that way."

Lauren folded her hands together and leaned forward. "It can get confusing for the AI," she said. "You had created a protocol a couple of weeks into your stay with a goal toward better health and fitness—kudos to you, by the way. It's a great idea for testing the functionality of the house in a way that is also beneficial to yourself—but when you gave a spontaneous command that was in conflict to that earlier directive, well… it *can* be difficult for Ella to process."

"So I should have told her I was canceling that earlier plan before telling her to… make me French toast, I guess?"

Lauren laughed. "Or asked her to pause it for the duration of one day. This is all a learning process, Michael, both for you and for the house. Going forward this might be something for you to keep in mind. It's easier for you to shift gears than for Ella. She will stick very closely to her directive unless very explicitly told otherwise."

"And as far as going out?" Michael asked. "I was under the impression that I could come and go from the house as I pleased."

Lauren looked slightly taken aback. "Of course you can!" she said. "It's not like we want to keep you prisoner there!" She laughed heartily. "By all means, go out, live your life! We left you a car for that very purpose."

Michael nodded, not returning her smile. "Yesterday I wanted to go outside for a run and it was pretty clear that Ella didn't want to let me."

Lauren's mouth turned down at the corners, more a thoughtful expression than a frown. "I find that hard to believe," she said. "She literally told you no?"

Michael looked off to the side, remembering. "She was pretty hesitant to open the door. She tried to convince me to use the treadmill in the gym instead."

Lauren nodded understanding. "Ella is programmed to promote everything the house has to offer you. She, and we here at the Sterling Corporation for that matter, want to see you utilize the house to its fullest potential. She will always be motivated to encourage you to make full use of the house's facilities. It gives her the opportunity to continue to meet your needs while also learning how to better serve you in the future."

Michael sighed, sitting back in his chair. "That's not how it felt."

Lauren raised her eyebrows. "Did she not let you out?"

"No, she did. Eventually."

"How long did it take you to convince her?"

Michael shook his head in frustration. "It was only a minute or two, but—"

"Well, that doesn't sound bad at all," said Lauren with a chuckle.

Michael stared at her for a moment. "I guess not."

"Make sure to include the incident in your report today," she said. "Is there anything else?"

Michael started to shake his head, then paused. "There is… I don't know if it's even worth mentioning."

Lauren leaned toward the monitor. "Go ahead, Michael. Whatever your concerns are, we want to know."

"There have been a couple of strange… occurrences, I guess you could say. Like, a woman's face appearing on the monitor. And last night there was a voice calling my name. It woke me up."

"Did you ask Ella to confirm these things?"

"I did. She didn't have a record of either one."

"I see." More typing.

"And one time during a system reset I saw a woman out on the lawn."

Lauren's eyes widened. "You did? When was this?"

"Early on."

"I don't recall you reporting that."

"I didn't."

"Why not?"

"Because Ella said nothing was picked up by the security cameras," said Michael. "It happened so quickly I wasn't sure what I saw. And then I wondered if maybe it was a glitch with the… window monitors or screens or whatever you call them."

"During a system reset?"

"Yeah."

"So Ella was offline at the time?"

"Yes."

"Then it wasn't a glitch," said Lauren, "and it wasn't a trespasser because the property is quite secure."

"Then what was it?"

"I can't say for certain but I assure you I will have someone look into it," said Lauren. "And from now on, always make sure to report things like that."

Michael bristled. "Sure."

"Is there anything else?" Lauren asked.

"So aside from the woman on the lawn," Michael said. "What about the face I saw? The voice I heard last night?"

"It's not something any of our other beta testers have reported," said Lauren.

Michael raised his eyebrows in mild surprise but didn't respond. He didn't know why he assumed he was the only one at this time. Perhaps because the house itself was solitary, he hadn't considered there might be others in different locations, each with its own tester or family of testers, each with their own specific reasons for why they had been selected.

"Listen," said Lauren. "You have to keep in mind that that house is lined with computers. Hundreds of them, all being run and monitored by Ella. There are bound to be glitches at times. Random unforeseen and inexplicable occurrences."

"Ghosts in the machine?" Michael asked.

"Not the phrasing I would use, but sure," said Lauren. "And that's exactly the reason why you're there. To observe and report."

Michael nodded.

"Relax, Michael. Enjoy your time there. It will be over before you know it. Come and go as you please, but do come more often than you go. We value your input."

Michael forced a smile.

"I know I sound like a broken record," said Lauren. "But report, report, report." She laughed. "Okay?"

"Got it."

"Okay. Goodbye, Michael. Call me anytime."

"Goodbye, Lauren."

* * *

DAY 70

Dark gray clouds were gathering overhead. A warm breeze had picked up, making the grass bow, breathing hot summer breath across Michael's upturned face. He looked to his right toward the tree line. Branches swayed, leaves upturned in anticipation of rain. He turned around, using his feet to push away from the wall, resuming a slow backstroke toward the other side of the pool.

"Ella, why won't you tell me where I am?"

"You are at home, Michael."

"And where exactly is home?"

"I cannot tell you that."

Tropical music wafted from unseen speakers. Steel drums and congas and ukuleles. It reminded Michael of vacations past and vacations not taken. It certainly wasn't congruous with his current surroundings.

Michael stopped swimming and floated on his back, looking up at the graying sky.

"Michael, why are you sad?" Ella asked.

"Who says that I am sad?" he responded.

"Your demeanor has changed. When we first met, you seemed more positive and content. You are less so now. More prone to long stretches of silence."

Michael listened to the music, to the quiet sounds of the rippling pool water around him. He didn't answer.

"Is your writing not going well?"

"No, it's going fine. It's the most I've written in a very long time."

"Have I done something wrong?"

"No, you're fine," said Michael. He had floated over to the shallow end, so he stood, slicked his hair back from his forehead, and rested his elbows on the side of the pool. "This whole thing is… it's not exactly how I imagined it would be."

"Please explain."

"To put it bluntly, it's starting to feel like a prison," said Michael.

Ella did not respond.

"Don't get me wrong, this place is incredible." Michael studied the back of the house, its plain white walls that he had looked at countless times, the tall glass doors leading into his study which were now reflecting his face back at him. "As far as having all the comforts modern technology can provide, it's honestly amazing."

"So what can I do to make you happy?"

"That's just it, Ella," said Michael. "I don't think there's anything you can do. The food is great, the entertainment is great, all of the modern conveniences… I mean, I haven't pushed a vacuum in weeks, haven't scrubbed a single floor or toilet. I can't complain about any of it. And even the way you are able to interact is… well, I have to admit sometimes I forget that I'm interacting with an AI."

"Thank you, Michael."

"But all of those things… they're not the summation of human fulfillment, you know? There's more. There has to be more. We've discussed this before, the necessity of human interaction. Before I came here, I had been isolating myself. From my family, from my friends, from meeting new people. And I was feeling pretty okay inside that bubble. I had convinced myself that a solitary life was the one I wanted to live. But after being here for a while and having every one of my physical needs met… I'm realizing, it's just not enough. There simply has to be more. For the first time in a long time, I am missing people. And maybe that will be my greatest takeaway, when all of this is over. Even the best technology can't replace people." He paused. "I'm sure Lauren and everyone else at Sterling Co. will be so glad to hear that," he added with a chuckle.

"We are both continuing to learn, Michael," said Ella. "The longer you are here, the more I am learning about you and about people. And the more I understand, the more I can adapt. Perhaps, given more time, I will be able to meet even more of your needs, which will allow you to be more content like you were when you first arrived."

Michael sniffed and stood, pushing away from the edge of the pool and floating on his back once more. "I'm not sure about that, Ella," he said. "I don't think it's a matter of updating your UI. I think you could be the most brilliant piece of technology known to man and you still couldn't meet a person's every need. At the end of the day, a house is still a house."

There was a distant rumble of thunder.

"You should get out of the pool now, Michael," said Ella. "There is a storm approaching."

Michael resumed a lazy backstroke.

"Today's fun fact," said Ella, "You can estimate the distance of a storm by counting the seconds between a lightning bolt and the sound of thunder that follows it. This is because light travels faster than sound, and as a result, the sound of thunder takes longer to reach your ears than the light of the lightning bolt takes to reach your eyes. For every five seconds that pass between the lightning and thunder, the storm is approximately one mile away."

"I'll get out in a minute," Michael said. He took a deep breath, flipped over, and swam toward the bottom of the pool, following the downward slope to the deep end, tapping the drain there with his fingertips. He lingered, feeling the pressure of the deep water against his body.

The light around him began to dim, drawing Michael's attention instinctively upward, where he expected to see a black cloud moving overhead, further obscuring the afternoon sunlight. What he saw instead was the pool's protective metal cover extending, beginning over the deep end where Michael was currently submerged, and continuing rapidly on its track toward the opposite side.

Michael pushed off the pool floor and swam, his hands franti-cally paddling as his feet kicked. Swimming upward and forward simultaneously, he realized that the edge of the cover was outpacing him; it would reach the far end and seal shut if he didn't manage to swim faster. He let out a frantic bellow as he kicked, screaming out Ella's name in a stream of bubbles that floated upwards like an aquatic snake, lifting his breath through the water. The bracelet on his wrist began to vibrate and glow red.

As he pumped, his lungs beginning to burn for air, panic bloomed in Michael's chest. He breached the surface of the water, but the back of his head collided with the moving pool cover. It raked painfully against his scalp as it continued on its path. He turned his head, his nose and mouth barely able to breach the sur-face, and he sucked in a combination of water and air, but there was not enough space between the water and the cover for him to draw a full breath.

He re-submerged, swimming as hard as he could muster, reaching forward desperately with his right hand, turning it palm upwards, hooking his fingers around the edge of the moving pool cover, his slight grip slipping at first before his fingertips found pur-chase. The cover yanked him forward, its motor groaning with the added weight of Michael's body as it dragged him along. The light under the water diminished further as the cover neared its destina-tion, threatening to seal Michael in the darkness.

Underwater.

He hung on desperately, summoning all of his energy, then grasped the edge of the cover with his left hand as well, flipping himself face-up under the water. Chlorinated water filled his nostrils and poured down the back of his throat. He struggled against the overwhelming urge to cough. Then he forcibly extended his arms downwards, using the metal cover as leverage to launch his body ahead of it.

Reaching the shallow end of the pool, Michael stood quickly, spinning, slapping his wet palms on the corner of the cement, and pushed his body out of the water. He planted his buttocks on the edge of the concrete and yanked his feet from the water just as the cover slammed forcibly shut with a reverberating clang. There he sat, dripping and panting, and stared at the now completely sealed-off pool, silver and silent.

Lightning flashed in the sky.

Michael coughed violently, then spit water onto the cement.

"What was *that*, Ella?" he screamed, breathless, his voice rattling with the remnants of inhaled water.

"There is a thunderstorm approaching," she said calmly, as if Michael was not already completely aware. "It was no longer safe to remain in the water."

"No longer *safe*? You almost trapped me in there!" he yelled. He leaned onto one elbow and coughed, desperately trying to catch his breath. His lungs burned.

"The cover is programmed to seal off the pool automatically at the sound of thunder," she said.

"With me *in it*?"

"It is a precautionary measure. One of many. The house is even programmed to go into a complete lockdown in order to withstand—"

"I really don't want to hear it, Ella. Is it not part of your protocol to ensure that the pool is unoccupied *before* you close it?"

"I do apologize," she said. "I will note this in the error logs."

Michael stood on unsteady feet, drops of water falling from his body and spattering at his feet. "Note this in the error logs," he scoffed. "I could have *drowned*."

"You should definitely mention this in your daily report tomorrow."

Michael wanted to scream. He rubbed at the back of his head with one palm. It was irritated and sensitive from where the metal cover had dragged against it, but when he pulled his hand away, there was no blood.

"Are you bleeding?" Ella asked.

"No."

The patio doors opened. Esra appeared, offering Michael a bright blue towel. Michael snatched it away with such force that the android was sent spiraling through the air.

"*Wheeeeeeeee!*"

Michael wrapped the towel around his waist, not bothering to dry off, and stomped into the house, still dripping. Mouse was immediately behind him, following closely at his heels, noiselessly mopping up Michael's trail of water.

Michael proceeded to the bedroom, where he sat on the edge of the bed. Elbows on his knees, he cradled his head in his hands, wet hair wrung between his fingers.

"Michael?" said Ella. "Are you okay?"

He let out a morose chuckle. "Other than almost dying, I'm fine."

"Would you like your dinner now?"

"What I would like," Michael said, not looking up, "is for you to shut down for a while. Can you do that?"

"Yes," she said.

"Thank you."

"Michael," said Ella. "I am very sorry."

The house went silent, as if a thick blanket had fallen over it. After a moment Michael sat up again and cocked one ear, listening closely. The ever-present hum was gone, and Michael had become so accustomed to hearing it that he found its absence more noticeable than its constant presence. And although loneliness had nagged at him since almost the moment he had crossed the threshold of the house, for the first time since he had arrived he felt truly alone.

Except, he reminded himself, he had actually been alone the entire time.

Outside, thunder continued to rumble.

CHAPTER SIXTEEN

Dylan was focused.

Mid-morning on a Tuesday, the café at Barnes and Noble was blissfully quiet. Dylan felt a little bit like a cliché in his beige cardigan, his black-framed reading glasses perched precipitously on the edge of his nose as he sat at a small corner table, a tall black tea to his left, open laptop in front of him, cell phone to his right. It was a comfortable cliché, and he was happy to get out of his dark apartment for a few hours.

The store had five copies of *BETA* on its shelves, a number he had verified before sitting down. He briefly considered signing them all before deciding against it, but knew he might well change his mind again before he left. There was also an empty space on a table situated just inside the entrance, a sign on top of it reading "New and Noteworthy," and Dylan imagined daring to relocate the five copies into that more visible spot on his way out the door.

He sipped his tea, enjoyed the permeating smell of coffee and ink, and typed away slowly on his laptop, making a silent vow not to rush to meet his daily word count, to disregard it completely if he could. His desire was to simply relish some quiet time spent in a world of his own creation. If he could get into the right creative headspace, sufficient words would come with minimal effort.

His cell phone rang loudly, the somber notes of John Williams's "Binary Sunset" filling the café. He looked around embarrassed, hoping the sudden melody hadn't disturbed anyone, but he was completely alone. He silenced it as quickly as he read the name "Charlie" on the screen, turned his phone over, and set it face down on the table. A sudden prickling of tension filled his chest. Dylan took a slow, deep breath and resumed typing.

His phone buzzed. He turned off all alerts and set it down again. Typed.

A Facebook message appeared at the top of his laptop screen. From Charlie: "Where are you?"

He dismissed it and swallowed mounting irritation. He looked back at the open Word document on his screen, then scrolled back a couple of paragraphs to remind himself anew where he had left off in the story. Began to type again.

Another Facebook message from Charlie: "Dylan?"

He ignored it. Typed some more.

"Why won't you answer your phone?"

Even with his phone face down, in his periphery Dylan could see that the screen was glowing against the table's laminated surface. He turned it over. Charlie was calling. Again. He rejected the call, sending it to voicemail. He saw that he already had three messages in his inbox. He put the phone back down, letting go a nearly inaudible groan of frustration.

"Hey stranger!"

Dylan's heart sank. He looked up and into the eyes of his mother, who was walking past the magazine racks toward his table. Dylan's initial irritation dissolved into warm surprise, and he stood up, pulling his mother into a hug when she reached him. Her frame was slight, her head only reaching the middle of Dylan's chest. The smell of her was comfortingly familiar.

They held each other for a moment. When they pulled apart, she reached up and placed a hand on Dylan's cheek, looking up at him lovingly, and then dropped it back down to her side.

"How are you doing, sweetie? I'm so sorry to interrupt you."

"You're not interrupting anything," Dylan said, gesturing to the empty chair on the other side of the small, circular table. They both sat.

"Oh, I doubt that," his mother said.

Dylan tipped his head toward his laptop. "It isn't Shakespeare," he said. "How are you?"

"I'm okay," she said, pulling the strap of her purse from her shoulder and setting the bag on the table. "I'm having lunch with the girls tomorrow and remembered it's also Doris's birthday so I'm hoping to find a gift for her." *The girls* were a group of four or five women—Dylan couldn't ever keep track of the total number—that used to work with his mother before she quit her job in the HR department at the local employment office. She had hated the job but loved her coworkers, so when she cut ties with the former she vowed never to lose touch with the latter.

Dylan considered suggesting that his mother buy Doris a copy of his book but immediately decided against it. At the moment he was tired of thinking about *BETA*, much less talking about it, and he also feared his mother would follow his suggestion simply out of kindness. She had purchased numerous copies as gifts in the past, even though Dylan had repeatedly informed her that he would gladly give her some for free or at cost. Instead he asked, "Any ideas?"

"Not one," his mother said, shaking her head. Then she started to chuckle. "On a related note, did I tell you that Doris set me up on a blind date?"

Dylan attempted to hide his mild surprise. He didn't like the idea of his mother dating again, even though she obviously had every right to. He often had to remind himself that she would be better off in a healthy relationship than completely alone. At the same time it pained him to picture her with anyone other than his father. His mother linked to another man would turn the page on a chapter of life that Dylan was still reluctant to admit was definitively over.

But his mother was still young, barely in her 50s, and the older Dylan got, the younger he realized she actually was. She was petite, still pretty in that approachable, Sally Field kind of way, and although she colored her hair to keep it golden brown, he doubted that much of it had turned gray yet. He had to acknowledge that to men of a certain age she was still incredibly attractive.

"Really?" he asked. "When is this happening?"

"Oh, it already has," she said. "This past Saturday."

"How did it go?"

She continued to laugh quietly, shaking her head. "Oh, it's this whole fiasco." She sighed through her smile. "First of all, I have to rewind back a couple of weeks. I was on the phone with Doris, and she was asking me if I was seeing anyone—she always asks me this—and then out of the blue she says, 'Do you remember Ian?' Well, *of course* I remembered Ian. He had been the VP at Career-Works for several months when I first started working there. I might have mentioned him to you at some point?"

Dylan shook his head.

"Well," his mother continued, "Ian Reynolds was the object of pretty much every woman's affection in that office, married or otherwise. Tall, dark, charming, witty. Wore a suit every day. Real Don Draper type except with silver hair. Let me tell you, he wasn't just a snack, he was a whole meal."

Dylan laughed suddenly. "Mom!" he objected.

His mother laughed again. "Sorry, it's something the girls used to always say. *Anyway...*" She cleared her throat. "When he was at CareerWorks he was married, and we all used to say what a lucky woman his wife was. She was real pretty too. Classy. We all wanted to hate her, but she was just as kind and sweet as he was, so we all agreed to love her and hate her at the same time. So when Doris asked me if I remembered Ian and I said yes, she said, 'Would you maybe be interested in going on a date with him?'

"'I had no idea he was single,' I said. And she said yes, he had gotten divorced last year and was interested in dipping his toes back in the dating pool again and happened to remember me fondly. Of course I was completely shocked, and I said to her, 'I had no idea you still talked to him,' and her response was kind of strange and vague, like what I said didn't make sense to her, something like *of course* they had stayed in touch, which should have been my first clue.

"So fast forward to this past Saturday. Doris had given him my number, and we'd texted a couple of times. We agreed to meet for dinner at the Red Horse at 7:00. I got there and waited in the lobby for a bit when he texted me to apologize he was going to be ten minutes late, and I should go ahead and get a table if I wanted to. So I did.

"Around 7:15 this man walks up to my table and says my name. Really skinny, maybe about 5-foot-eight, and I'm not sure what stuck out further, his nose or his Adam's apple. One of those guys who seems to be made entirely of joints, you know?"

Dylan grinned.

"I thought for a second maybe he was the manager or a different waiter than the one who'd brought me my water, but then I recognized him. Ian. Doris's *brother*."

"Oh no," said Dylan, eyes widening.

"Oh no indeed," said his mother, reflecting his expression. "It took me a second to collect myself, but I don't think he noticed it. I had met him at a picnic at Doris's house last summer, thank goodness, so it only took me a second to recognize him. I felt so stupid. Of *course* Doris had been talking about her brother the whole time. *I* was the idiot whose mind went to the handsome former VP."

Dylan shook his head in disbelief, laughing. "So then what happened?"

"Well, I invited him to sit down. And we talked. And we ate. And we talked some more. And we didn't stop talking until they closed the restaurant and they told us we had to leave." His mother's smile was soft, her eyes adopting a faraway look.

Dylan stared at her silently. "So are you seeing him again?"

His mother looked at him, refocusing her gaze, her smile lingering. "This Friday. We set it up before we said goodnight. Oh Dylan, he's nice and so easy to talk to. And *funny*. My goodness I haven't laughed so hard since... well, I haven't laughed that hard in a very long time. Even though in the end he's definitely more Don Knotts than Don Draper."

"That's really great, Mom," Dylan said, sipping his tea, and wondered whether or not his statement was sincere. He couldn't be sure.

"What about you?" she asked, reaching across the table and touching his hand. "I know you don't like me asking but you have to let me every once in a while. Have you met anyone? How about at the book signing? I kept wondering if you might meet a pretty girl there."

"I think dating a fan might be a bad idea," he said.

"'A fan,'" his mother scoffed playfully. "Listen to you."

"I've got lots. They number in the tens."

"Oh, stop," she said, slapping his hand and then sitting back in her chair and folding her arms. "Just don't ever forget who your number one fan is. And have been since before you used to run around the house naked, yelling, 'I'm invisible!'"

Dylan shook his head and dropped his eyes, trying to hide mild embarrassment. He was glad they had the café to themselves.

"There was someone," he said finally, "but it wasn't a good fit."

"Well, that's too bad," his mother said, "but someone else will come along."

Dylan looked at her. "You know I don't believe that, Mom."

"I know you don't, but I do. And you're not going to change my mind about it."

He nodded silently.

"Rachel didn't just break your heart, you know," she said after a moment, and Dylan found himself surprised by the sound of Rachel's name on his mother's lips, as well the sudden change in her demeanor from pleasant to sad. "She broke mine too. I know the pain she caused you is a great deal more than what she caused me, but in a way she broke my heart twice. Obviously I was devastated for you when your relationship ended. But it also hurt a great deal when she just walked away from what I thought was a genuine friendship between her and me."

Dylan knew his mother had suffered in the wake of his break-up with Rachel, but he had always processed her pain as natural sympathy for her son. He had not considered that his mother might be mourning the loss of the clear and genuine bond that she had formed with Rachel over the course of four years, years that had included holidays, vacations, and many long talks with each other, oftentimes outside of Dylan's presence. "I'm sorry, Mom," he said. "I'd never thought about it that way."

"I know you didn't," she said, her eyes glistening. "And that's okay. You had enough to get through without worrying about me. But there's hardly a day that goes by that I'm not still angry with her. Sometimes I think about what I might say if I ever saw her. And when I'm done there would be nothing but scorched earth where she once had been standing."

Dylan let out a sad chuckle.

"And I'll be darned if my son is going to let that girl live rent-free in his heart for the rest of his life."

Dylan's smile was slight. He nodded at his mother, who suddenly drew in a breath, widened her eyes, and forced a smile.

"Dinner tomorrow night?" she asked. "You bring the Pat Sajak and I'll bring the pot roast?"

"Sounds like a date," he said.

"Yes it does." She stood. "Bring your jammies if you want to."

Dylan stood and hugged her tight.

When they parted she gestured toward his laptop. "I'm sorry I distracted you from your work." She slapped the back of her own hand. "Bad Mom."

He shook his head and grinned. "Always a welcome distraction, Mom."

She slung her purse over her shoulder and walked away from the table, further into the store. "Wish me luck!" she called back to Dylan. "All else fails, I'll buy Doris a copy of your book."

Dylan watched his mother go, sitting back down in his chair

only when she finally disappeared behind a row of shelves. He stared, wanting her to reappear again, turn around and come back to convey a random thought that had just occurred to her, or perhaps remember something she had been meaning to tell him and kept forgetting to say. But she did not return, and after waiting for several seconds, Dylan returned his attention to his writing.

He tapped on the laptop of his keyboard, waking it up again. Another Facebook message from Charlie waited for him on the screen: "I need to talk to you."

Dylan's wistfulness dissolved into warm frustration. He typed forcefully, "Not right now."

Charlie's written response was immediate: "Why not?"

"I'm out."

Dylan's phone, still face down on the table, lit up, the light peeking out around its periphery. He snatched it up.

"For crying out loud, Charlie," he hissed. "What do you want?"

"I just want to talk," she said, chuckling. "Don't get your panties in a bunch."

"I'm trying to get some work done," Dylan said, sitting back and running his fingers through his hair. "It's a little hard to do when you keep interrupting."

"I promise I'll be quick," she said. Her tone was so calm and light in the face of Dylan's frustration that he found it unsettling. He was suddenly curious as to what she might possibly have to say, especially since his terse reaction to her did not seem to be affecting her in the least. She was also behaving as if the episode in the parking lot of the Book Nook had never even happened.

"What is it?" he sighed.

"I have an idea, and just hear me out before you say no, okay?"

He didn't respond, instead chewing on the corner of his bottom lip.

"I did some digging, and it looks like I could transfer from Towson to Hood and most of my credits would transfer with me. I could finish out this semester and then move over Christmas break."

Dylan processed this information in silent disbelief. Hood College was in Frederick, the campus only minutes away from his apartment.

"We'd be closer together," Charlie said, her statement a verbatim repetition of the words now running through Dylan's head.

"Charlie…" Dylan managed to eke out.

"Don't say no right away," Charlie interjected, her tone full of optimism. "Think about it."

"I don't need to think about it," Dylan said, his tone low. "It's not a good idea."

Charlie was quiet for a moment, and Dylan braced himself for the sound of tears. When she spoke again, her voice was barely a whisper. "You said that we could be friends."

"I know what I said," Dylan responded. He was at war with his words, part of him wanting to be gentle, another part wanting to be firm to the point of barbed. "But I think you will always want more out of this relationship than I do."

"I know you said you can't right now. Because of Rachel. But that could change. In time."

"Charlie," Dylan said, elbows on the table, resting his forehead against his free hand. "It's more than that. It's not just Rachel. I just don't think… I don't think you and I are a good fit."

"So you don't like me," Charlie said defiantly.

"Yes, I do," Dylan said, still keeping his voice low, hoping against hope that no one in the store was eavesdropping. "As a friend, I mean. I mean I *could* like you as a friend. But I'm seriously starting to wonder if that isn't a good idea."

"What?"

"I mean I feel like as long as I let you have a foot in the door you're always going to be expecting something more."

"I love you, Dylan," she said, voice now on the edge of tears. "Is that really so terrible?"

"Charlie, you barely know me," he said.

"I know you better than most," she countered, her tone transforming from emotional to cold. "And I know you from your book. Don't act like you weren't writing about yourself sometimes. I know you're creative like he is. I know you're sad like he is. Lonely like he is. That you long to be loved."

"I know you think you know me," said Dylan. "And I know you have an idea of where you would like for this to go. But I think the kindest thing for me to do at this point is to let you know that it's never, *ever* going to happen."

After a moment, Charlie chuckled, and Dylan felt his blood turn cold. "Never say never," she said.

"You are *obsessed*," he said, the words slipping out before he had fully considered them.

"Don't flatter yourself," said Charlie. Her tone had changed so quickly, so abruptly from sad to frigid that Dylan felt like he was now talking to someone else entirely.

"You were just talking about *moving*," Dylan said. "What is that if not obsession?"

Charlie didn't respond.

Dylan took a deep breath. "Listen," he finally said, steeling himself. "At the risk of being incredibly cruel, I think we need to put an end to this, Charlie."

"Meaning?"

"Meaning… stop calling me. Stop messaging me. Move on. We are no longer friends."

Dylan held his breath. His heart pounded.

Eventually, Charlie spoke, and when she did, it was with resolute calm: "Okay."

"Okay?" Dylan said, disbelieving.

"Okay," she repeated, and ended the call.

Dylan pulled the phone away from his ear and watched the screen in disbelief as its light extinguished. He set it down but continued to stare at it, watching it like a bomb that could explode at any second.

He waited for Charlie to call back.

She didn't.

It was over.

But what Dylan felt was anything but relief.

CHAPTER SEVENTEEN
DAY 71

Michael sat at the kitchen table, the thumb and index finger of his right hand encircling the base of a tall, cold glass of purple liquid, slowly turning it around but not drinking from it. He was certain it would be delicious; he knew it would be nutritious. But it was not what he had wanted for breakfast.

He had quit ordering specific food for his meals ever since Ella had stopped honoring such requests weeks ago. Any time he pushed the subject, she simply restated his earlier request that she aid him in setting routines with a goal toward better health and fitness. He had tried to explain to her the benefit of occasional cheat meals, and how one off-goal meal every once in a while was not going to have much of a negative impact if any at all, but Ella seemed incapable of understanding or compromising. A very small part of him appreciated her resolve, as programmed and stringent as it may be. Mostly though, he was annoyed.

Alerted to a loud noise coming from the back yard, Michael stood and padded over to the kitchen windows, liquid breakfast in hand. It sounded like the motor of one of the delivery drones, only much louder than he was accustomed to. Peering through the glass, he saw two of the mechanical insects replacing a panel on the back of the house.

"The house incurred some minor storm damage yesterday," Ella informed him.

Michael neither spoke nor moved in response. He simply watched as the pair of drones set a gleaming white panel back into place.

"Are you not feeling well, Michael?"

Michael lifted up the glass and drank, not setting it down on the counter until it was drained. Esra whisked the glass away, but not before first introducing himself.

"Ella," Michael said, sucking in a deep breath. "I would like to go out. Tonight. And by *out* I don't mean the front yard. I mean *out*. Somewhere public." He looked down and ran his thumb through the moisture ring left behind by the glass, feeling its coldness against the counter's smooth surface.

He waited. He despised the fact that he had to ask permission to leave the house, and hated even more that he fully anticipated Ella would balk at the idea, that he would have to make a case in order to convince her to relent, that he had spent most of the morning coming up with a list of convincing arguments to—

"Okay, Michael," she said.

Michael looked up. "Really?"

"Yes, of course," Ella said, her tone warm. "You are always free to go. Perhaps you would like me to help you select something to wear?"

Michael scoffed quietly, awash with a strange sense of relief. A weight lifted off of him. He felt suddenly free in more than one sense of the word. "That would be great. Thank you."

"Might I also suggest a shave and a haircut first?"

Michael reflexively rapped "two bits" on the counter with his knuckle before furrowing his brow. "You can do that?"

"Esra can," said Ella.

"Seriously?"

Minutes later, Michael was seated in the bathroom. The make-shift barber's chair was already there when he entered the room, assembled from hidden panels within the floor and wall that had come together to form a sleek (if not exactly comfortable) barber's chair.

Michael sat. Esra draped him with a long, pale blue sheet, then hummed out of the room. Michael looked at himself in the mirror on the opposite wall, at his mop of unkempt brown hair, the thick stubble along his jawline and chin. A haircut was long overdue, and he had done well to shave once every four or five days since moving in.

Esra returned to the room holding a small white bathroom caddy, which he set on the counter beside the sink. When the robot turned, he was holding a lather brush in one hand, a small, unlabeled bowl of shaving soap in the other. The chair tilted slightly, and Esra floated around Michael's head, humming a digital tune as he applied the lather gently to Michael's face. Michael closed his eyes.

Moments later, after Michael's face was thoroughly lathered, Esra returned to the caddy, where he deposited the lather brush and nearly empty bowl of shaving soap. The robot then floated back toward Michael and raised his right arm. With a quiet *snikt* sound, a straight razor extended from the plastic shell casing around Esra's forearm. He then reached for Michael's face.

Michael looked at the blade with mild alarm and started to sit up. "Woah, hang on a second there, Wolverine," he said. "Is this a good idea?"

"You have nothing to worry about," Ella said. "Just remain still."

"He had that thing in his *arm*?"

"He has all manner of tools in his arms, Michael," Ella said calmly.

Esra placed the straight razor against Michael's cheek, and Michael heard the scraping sound of blade against stubble. The robot's movements were slow and steady, and Michael slowly allowed himself to relax again, only closing his eyes when he was fully convinced that Esra's movements were consistent and controlled.

"There are a few things we should discuss before you go out tonight," Ella said. "Just as a friendly reminder."

Michael rolled his eyes without opening them. "I know, I know," he said, barely parting his lips, making sure to keep his head completely still.

"If you talk to anyone, you must not tell them anything about this house or what you are doing here," she continued.

The razor traveled slowly down Michael's right cheek.

"Got it," Michael said.

"You should not mention the Sterling Corporation or your affiliation with it."

The razor passed over Michael's chin, shaving a path toward his Adam's apple.

"Yes, yes," Michael said. "Any mention of this house or the Sterling Corporation will lead to my immediate termination and the relinquishment of both my life savings and my immortal soul. I will be required to sacrifice my firstborn child—"

"Michael," Ella said coolly.

The razor stopped. Michael opened his eyes slightly, then fully, seeing both his and Esra's reflection in the mirror across the room. The robot had stopped moving. Esra hovered silently to Michael's right, the blade of the razor held still against Michael's neck. Esra's bright blue eyes had turned a blazing crimson and were locked on Michael's reflection in the mirror.

"Esra? Ess?" Michael said, his voice quiet and unsteady. He shifted his gaze sideways, trying to see Esra's face directly but unable to do so without turning his head, which he dared not do.

"I don't think you're taking this very seriously," Ella said.

"What's going on? Esra?" Michael asked. He pushed his palms against the armrests of the chair, wanting to stand up but stopping himself, forcing himself to remain still, afraid to move even slightly. He could feel the blade pressing gently but firmly against his skin.

"Esra is simply paused until I know I have your full attention," said Ella.

"You have my attention," Michael insisted. He shifted his eyes back to the mirror. "*Ess?*" he whispered.

"You will not talk about the house, about the beta test, or about the Sterling Corporation with anyone you meet. Do you understand?"

"I understand," said Michael, his eyes never leaving the robot's in the mirror. "I have always understood."

"Very good," said Ella, her voice filled with its usual warmth. With a soft chime, Esra's eyes turned a familiar blue and the robot, once again emitting a soft, pleasant tune, resumed shaving Michael as if he had never stopped.

"Hello," he said. "I am Esra."

* * *

One shave, one haircut, and one shower later, Michael was standing in his bedroom closet. The clothes that Ella had picked for him—dark denim skinny jeans, white button-up shirt, fitted brown suede blazer, and boots—fit him as if tailor-made. He regarded himself in the mirror. He looked amazingly healthy, healthier than he had in years. He was trim, fit, and tan, and Esra had just given him a magazine-worthy haircut. He leaned in and looked at his face. To his eyes, he was looking years younger as well: rested, vibrant, his cheekbones and jawline more pronounced than he had ever before seen them. Even his eyes had a vivid sparkle. Ella's regimen of protein shakes, workout routines, and topical lotions and gels was clearly having a positive effect on Michael's physical appearance, and he also noted that he'd never slept so consistently well in his adult life, a combination of a perfectly comfortable bed and an utterly dark and silent bedroom.

In spite of Esra's behavior only moments ago in the bathroom, Michael began to consider that perhaps the house was not so bad after all, that he was simply focusing too hard on the negatives, the "glitches," while taking for granted the numerous positives. And he was also free to leave whenever he wanted to; apparently he just hadn't pressed the issue hard enough before.

Michael climbed into the silver car at 7:00 and watched as the garage door lifted in front of him. He allowed himself to settle in, savoring a pleasant sense of anticipation simply knowing that he was getting out of the house, even if only for a few hours. The car pulled out, turned left and then right, eventually approaching the tall white wall that stood across the property's southern perimeter.

The wall parted as the car approached. Michael sat up, leaning forward to take in the view. Simultaneously, the windshield turned opaque.

"Aw, come on," Michael groaned, slouching back into his seat. "I don't get to enjoy some scenery?"

"I can give you whatever view you'd like," Ella said. "A drive through 1940s New York City, or Las Vegas at night?"

"It doesn't matter," Michael said, sitting back and closing his eyes.

* * *

Michael sat up when the car slowed to a stop and the driver's side door opened with a quiet hum. He stepped out of the car, stretched his back, and looked around. He was standing in the graveled parking lot of a tavern. The sound of country music wafted out from its closed doors, the bass notes thrumming loudly. The lot was sparsely populated by beat-up pickup trucks, a couple of semis, and a handful of cars and motorcycles. A neon sign glowed, "Murray's Tavern."

Michael looked around. There was nothing on either side of the dive except the open road.

"You've got to be kidding me," said Michael.

"Is there a problem?" asked Ella, her voice emanating from the bracelet on his wrist.

"I guess I was expecting something a little nicer than this," Michael said, turning around again, hoping somehow to find something more, some other sign of nearby civilization.

Michael walked reluctantly toward the front door, the gravel crunching under his boots. At least Ella had dressed him properly. His ride pulled away, disappearing somewhere within the lot.

He pulled open the door and was immediately assaulted by the volume of the music, the smell of alcohol, smoke, and fried food, the noise of shouted conversation and clanging glass and silverware. Several heads turned his way as he walked in. Half a dozen men populated the bar, fists clenched tightly to mug handles. Tank topped waitresses with trays balanced overhead swung past tables. A handful of booths and tables were occupied by couples and small groups. From the jukebox, Randy Travis sang about old women talking about old men.

Michael spotted an empty booth in a dark corner, as far from the cacophony as he could possibly get without walking back outside. He slid in.

"This isn't what I had in mind," he grumbled, disappointment washing over him. "I hate to be classist but couldn't you have taken me somewhere nicer?"

Ella didn't respond.

"Can I get you something, sweetheart?" The waitress was young, and in spite of her somewhat frizzy brown hair and thickly-applied makeup, was pleasantly attractive, and her smile seemed genuine, her voice tinged by a slight drawl.

"Just a diet cola, please, whatever brand you carry," Michael said, hating the fact that ordering a drink implied an intention to stick around for any length of time.

She handed Michael a laminated menu and winked at him almost imperceptibly before walking away. Michael looked at the menu, its plastic slick with a thin film of grease, its cover emblazoned with the Murray's Tavern logo. No address. Michael put it down and pushed it away.

He looked around the room, at the dark brown walls, the exposed rafters, the dangling cobwebs in the corners, the visible layer of peanut shell dust that coated almost every surface. If nothing else, at least it was a complete change of scenery. He felt as if he had been kicked out of a long dream and back into stark reality. And that reality was a hole in the wall named Murray's Tavern. Location: unknown.

The waitress threw down a cork coaster before setting Michael's drink on top of it. "Are we eating or just drinking tonight?" she asked.

"Just the soda," said Michael, giving her a terse smile.

She nodded and turned to walk away.

"On second thought," Michael said, suddenly brightening. "I've changed my mind. Bring me the fattest, rarest burger you have. And a basket of fries." His smile was wide now, and his mouth began to water.

"Very good," she said, returning his smile.

"No comment?" Michael asked when the waitress was out of earshot.

"Enjoy your evening," said Ella.

"I'll do one extra sit-up tomorrow," he offered, his mood suddenly lifted.

Michael sipped his soda, which tasted more of carbonated water than sweet syrup and was also a little flat. But it wasn't a protein shake, and for this he was thankful.

He set the glass down and looked to his left. A woman was seated alone in a booth identical to his own on the other side of the room. Michael watched her for a few seconds, prepared to look away immediately if she happened to glance in his direction. She looked at her cell phone once, then scanned the room, the expression on her face one of impatient frustration.

She was waiting for someone. Someone who was late.

Michael didn't allow himself to hesitate. He grabbed his soda and walked across the room, peanut shells crunching underfoot with each step. As he approached, the woman picked up her own drink—something nondescript in a thin glass—and sipped from it.

"Excuse me?" he said.

The woman jumped, a bit of her drink splashing over the rim of her glass and onto the table.

Michael laughed. "I'm so sorry," he said. "I didn't mean to startle you."

"It's okay," the woman replied, smiling politely and wiping the spill with a napkin. "I didn't hear you walk up."

"This is going to sound incredibly forward, but are you here by yourself?" Michael asked.

The woman looked up at him. She was remarkably pretty, the kind of pretty that stopped just short of beautiful, leaving her on this side of the line of attractive and inviting, a step or two away from stunning and intimidating. Her eyes were a rich brown, her smile framing perfect teeth. "Apparently I am," she said with an exasperated sigh. "Lame as it sounds, I think I've been stood up."

"May I join you?"

She looked at him, her eyes shifting back and forth between both of his. "Be my guest," she finally said, gesturing to the empty bench across from her.

Michael sat, setting his mug of cola on the table and extending a hand. She shook it, her skin soft and smooth against his. "Michael," he said.

"Jerri. Nice to meet you."

"You too."

The waitress appeared, her eyebrows raised expectantly in Jerri's direction. "What can I get you?" she asked, her eyes darting quickly to Michael and back to Jerri again.

"Whatever he's having," said Jerri with a shrug, nodding her head in Michael's direction.

The waitress walked away.

"I hope you like fried critter with a side of varmint," Michael said.

Jerri laughed. "I take it you're not from around here," she said.

"I'm not even sure where here is," Michael said.

Jerri shot him a puzzled look.

"Where are you from?" he asked quickly.

"Around," she smiled. "Florida originally. Slowly making my way up north."

"Oh yeah?" Michael asked, leaning toward her slightly, interested. He felt a slight motion in his left forearm, an involuntary muscle twinge. He rubbed at it through his sleeve.

"What do you do for a living?" she asked. She propped her elbows on the table, folding her fingers under her chin. The movement sent a waft of air toward Michael, and he caught a scent of her perfume.

"I'm a writer, actually," he said.

"Journalist?" she asked.

"Fiction. Novelist."

She raised her eyebrows, impressed. "Really? Anything I've read?"

Michael chuckled. "Probably not."

"What's your last name?"

"Danvers," he said, looking at her expectantly.

"Michael Danvers." She rolled the name around in her head before scrunching up her face apologetically. "Sorry," she said.

He raised a dismissive hand. "It's okay."

"I'm not much of a reader," she admitted.

When the waitress returned a few moments later, she was carrying a tray with two oblong white plates stacked with hay bale-sized piles of French fries and burgers almost taller than Michael could grip. The smell of it caused his stomach to turn in the most pleasantly anticipatory way.

"Pardon my lack of decorum," Michael said, using one palm to smash the burger down to something he thought his jaw could more feasibly handle. It was piping hot and juices ran out of it as he crushed it.

"I think it's necessary," said Jerri, quietly laughing while doing the same to her own burger.

They ate in momentary silence. Michael wasn't sure if the burger really was the most delicious he had ever had or if his taste buds just appreciated the diversion from Ella's usual healthy fare, but regardless, he devoured the sandwich and was both sorry when it was gone and also embarrassed by how quickly he had finished it.

"Someone was hungry," Jerri chuckled, setting down her half-eaten burger.

"Sorry," Michael said, washing down the last bite with soda. "Where are my manners?"

"I don't mind."

"So what brings you to such a fancy place this evening?" Michael asked.

"It's embarrassing," Jerri said, looking around the large room. "I was supposed to be meeting someone on a blind date. He chose the place. But I think he stood me up."

"I'm sorry," Michael offered, at a loss for anything else to say.

"Not your fault," she said. "I was doing it as a favor to a friend and had been mostly dreading it all day. And honestly when I first saw you, I hoped that you were him. But you're not wearing a blue chambray shirt, so you're not Stephen."

"No, not today."

Jerri beamed. "So how about you? Why are you eating alone in a middle-of-nowhere tavern on a Monday night?"

It's Monday? Had I known it was a Monday?

"Let's just say I needed to get out of the house," Michael said.

Jerri's shoulders sank a little. "You're married?"

"Oh, no!" Michael objected. "I hear how that sounded. No, not married."

"Kids?" she asked hesitantly.

"Negative."

"Then why the urgent need to get out of the house?"

"Just needed a change of scenery. I'm doing a bit of a writer's retreat, working on my next book. I haven't been out too much the last several weeks."

"I see," said Jerri. "So where are you staying? Are you renting a cabin somewhere?"

Michael felt the twinge in his left forearm again. He stole a glance at it, not sure exactly what he was expecting to see, and then returned his gaze to Jerri. He started to remove his jacket. "I'm renting a house not too far from here." He deposited his jacket on the bench beside him, unbuttoned the cuffs of his shirt, and rolled up his sleeves. Jerri gave the white bracelet a passing glance.

"Is it a nice place?" she asked. "Since I'm local, I have no idea what the rental options are like when people come here on vacation."

This time the shock in Michael's left forearm was undeniable. It sent a small but unpleasant bolt of pain down his hand and into his fingers. He moved his arm under the table and rubbed it. "It's nice," he said distractedly.

"And where do you live when you're not retreating?" Jerri asked.

"New York," he answered.

Jerri turned her head sideways slightly, giving him a puzzled glance.

"I thought you—" Jerri began, but stopped talking when Michael inhaled a sudden hiss, jerking his left arm back and away from the table.

"Are you okay?" she asked.

"Yeah, sorry," he said, bringing up his left hand and shaking it. "Something shocked me."

"That's odd," she said.

Michael returned his left hand under the table and with the fingers of his right hand began pushing at the tabs on the bracelet, attempting to unclip it from his wrist.

It wouldn't unfasten.

"So you live around here?" Michael asked, attempting to keep Jerri talking while he fought with the bracelet.

This time, the jolt in Michael's arm was strong enough to propel his arm backwards, driving his left elbow into the padded backrest behind him.

Jerri looked alarmed. "You sure you're okay?"

Michael realized that his forehead had broken out in beads of sweat. He looked at Jerri intently, and her face went pale with fear. She sat back in her seat, withdrawing slightly from Michael.

"I'm sorry," Michael said in a harsh whisper, his words suddenly rapid and urgent. "Where are we? Can you tell me where—"

The pain in Michael's arm was so severe that he let out a loud yell and stood, his legs banging the underside of the table, upsetting dishes and silverware. He grabbed his forearm, squeezing it with his right hand, trying to stave off the pain. A second jolt of electricity shot from his wrist to his shoulder and Michael bellowed again.

Jerri watched, wide-eyed, as Michael stood. She seemed torn between coming to his aid and wanting to retreat from him. Michael started to walk away but turned back suddenly, snatching a fork off the table. "Excuse me for just a minute," he said, his voice suddenly hoarse. He scanned the room, seeing dozens of eyes staring back at him curiously. He spotted a neon sign that sported a glowing green cactus and the word "Restrooms." He rounded a corner that took him past the bar and walked rapidly down a dimly-lit narrow hallway, past a giant corkboard dotted by colorful thumbtacks that held up nothing: no advertisements, no flyers, no business cards.

He stepped into the men's room (labeled "Gents"), the sound of his booted footfalls echoing off the tiles, and was relieved to find it empty.

He stood at the sink and attempted to unclip the bracelet. It wouldn't open. "What are you *doing*, Ella?" he demanded. His hands were trembling, his fingers sweaty.

"Your conversation was going in an impermissible direction," she said.

"Impermissible?" he scoffed, jamming the fork between the bracelet and his wrist and attempting to pry it off. "So you decided to *shock* me?"

"I gave you a gentle reminder," said Ella.

The bracelet would not break. Instead it was the fork that was beginning to give, its metal bending under the pressure of Michael's prying. Eventually he relented and let the utensil fall into the basin with a metallic clatter.

Frustrated, he placed his palms on the sink and looked at himself in the mirror. "Ella, you—"

He stopped short at the sight of his reflection. The difference between his appearance here, under the harsh fluorescents of the restaurant bathroom, and in the mirror at home, was alarming. His cheeks looked sunken and hollow, his frame more slight, the lines in his face more pronounced, his eyes smaller and less vibrant, his skin pale. Some of these differences could be at least partially chalked up to his present state of frustration and alarm, but not all of them. There were also visible flecks of gray in his perfect haircut.

He reached up hesitantly with his fingertips and touched his cheeks lightly, moving the thin skin there.

"Ella," he said. "What is happening?"

"What do you mean, Michael?"

"Why do I look like this?"

"Like what, Michael?"

"Like… *this*? I look *terrible*."

Michael took a step away from the mirror, finally peeling his eyes away from his reflection and regarding the bracelet once again. "I want to take this off. Right now," he said. He attempted to slip the fingers of his right hand beneath it, and as he did so, the bracelet contracted, squeezing tighter until the bones of his wrist began to compress. He groaned.

"I'm afraid I can't let you do that, Michael," Ella said.

"Why *not*?" Michael hissed.

Michael flexed his wrist, pivoting the fingers of his left hand upward. He brought the bracelet down, hard, on the edge of the sink, attempting to crack it against the porcelain. It did not break, and Michael's body was racked by a new bolt of pain that made him yell out. Sweat was now streaming down his face; his shirt had become soaked in it.

"Do not do that," said Ella.

"Or what?" Michael said, looking at his own desperate face in the mirror. "Or *what,* Ella? You'll kill me?"

"I would never kill you, Michael," said Ella. "I only want to take care of you."

Michael retreated two steps until his back was against the wall, left forearm pinched between the fingers of his right hand. He looked up at the ceiling, at its blinding fluorescent lights, and closed his eyes, attempting to catch his breath.

"The bracelet you are wearing is state of the art technology," Ella said. "While I cannot claim that it is unbreakable, it is quite difficult to do so, especially without causing physical harm to the wearer. Additionally, the tiny CPU inside the bracelet is unhackable and cannot be remotely disabled, unlike, for instance, the computer systems on an airplane or even inside a pacemaker."

Michael felt a chill run down the length of his entire body. "What did you just say?"

"Today's fun fact," said Ella. "The state of cybersecurity in medical devices is, overall, quite poor. Manufacturers have not historically developed products with security in mind. This, unfortunately, leaves devices such as pacemakers, not unlike the one your father uses, vulnerable to cyber-attacks, which would render them nonfunctional and put the user's life in jeopardy."

"Are you… making a threat?" Michael asked.

"I am simply sharing an interesting fact with you," said Ella.

Michael's eyes rolled toward the ceiling. He felt as though he could vomit.

"You are not looking well, Michael," said Ella. "I think perhaps now would be a good time for you to return to the house."

Michael didn't argue. He turned and stumbled from the bathroom, his hair and clothing disheveled, his countenance wan, and he imagined that to those who glanced in his direction he must look not unlike any other drunken patron. As he made his way slowly past the bar, curious eyes watching him go, he looked in the direction of Jerri's table. She was still there, seated in her booth, looking both impatient and concerned, and Michael was glad that she did not appear to notice him as he continued toward the door and stepped outside.

As he shuffled across the parking lot, Michael said quietly, "I didn't pay for my meal."

"It's already taken care of," said Ella. "As is your new friend's."

The car pulled up in front of Michael before he even knew it was approaching, and its door opened to him. He stared dumbly at it for a moment, left arm cradled in his right. It was throbbing.

"Get in, Michael," said Ella.

Michael looked around. At the parking lot. At the barren road to his left and right. At the dark night that surrounded him on all sides.

He felt a small electric jolt in his left arm, as mild as a static shock.

"Get in," Ella said again.

CHAPTER EIGHTEEN

Dylan was alarmed.

The first indication that things were about to go very, very wrong for him was when his phone rang early that morning. Normally seeing an incoming call from Nick would have pleased him, but the fact that it was a phone call instead of a more typical text filled him with an almost inexplicable sense of foreboding. He answered.

"Nick?"

Before speaking, his friend sighed. "Hey, buddy," Nick said, no spark to his tone. "How are you?"

"I'm fine," said Dylan. "Is everything okay?"

Nick hesitated. "Listen, I hate to bother you with this, but it's about Charlie."

Dylan's dread had an inevitability to it. "What about Charlie?"

"She's been messaging me. A lot."

Dylan sank down onto his sofa, his cell phone pressed tight against his ear. "I saw you two had become friends on Facebook."

"Yeah, I didn't think much of it at the time, when she sent me that request. People do that, you know. Send friend requests when they don't really know you. I didn't think it was that unusual. But lately she's been contacting me pretty constantly and I thought maybe we should talk."

"Things, um…" Dylan searched for words. "Things didn't exactly end well for us."

"She told me you two broke up."

Dylan scoffed. "How can you break up if you were never together?" He began to bounce his legs.

"She says you were, and that you dumped her."

Dylan inhaled a deep breath through his nose. "We were never together."

"She said you kissed her."

"For crying out loud," said Dylan, standing up and beginning to pace. "Yes, I kissed her. But I made it perfectly clear that we were only friends. Nothing more."

"She said you told her you loved her..."

Dylan bleated a humorless laugh. "That's a lie."

"...and that you slept with her."

Dylan froze. He shook his head. "That's also a lie."

"Look, it's really none of my business," said Nick. "I'd really rather not be involved at all. But she keeps messaging me and she seems pretty upset."

"Did she tell you she showed up at a book signing last week and made a total scene?" asked Dylan. "The girl is… I guess *unstable* is the word I want to use."

"She asked me if you're seeing someone else and if that's why you broke up with her."

"*We were never together!*" Dylan shouted. He closed his eyes and breathed, placing one palm against his forehead. "Sorry. You have to believe me, man."

Nick paused. "I believe you. I told you to be careful. But you need to take care of this. Set the record straight. And maybe tell her to leave your friends alone too. She sent a message to Pepper a couple of days ago too."

"You've got to be kidding me."

"I'm sorry to be calling about this," Nick sighed. "I just thought you should know."

Dylan's phone chimed. He pulled it away from his ear and looked at the screen. He had an incoming call from Cynthia Barnett. His heart fell into his stomach.

"Nick, I'm sorry," he said hurriedly. "I have another call coming in. It's my agent. I have to take it."

"Okay."

"Thank you for letting me know. Let's talk again soon."

"Okay," Nick repeated. "Take care, buddy."

Dylan ended the call and answered Cynthia's.

"Cynthia?" Dylan said.

"Dylan," she said, her voice serious. "Who is Charlotte Gallagher?"

Dylan's heart lurched from his stomach and into his throat, riding a sudden wave of nausea.

"She's just some girl—" Dylan started.

"Let me read something to you," Cynthia said, her typical no-nonsense tone now colored with irritation. "'Dylan Matthews is a total rip-off artist, an unoriginal hack, a talentless plagiarist of the highest order. He stole the plot of his novel *BETA* from a former friend and classmate named Dwayne Johnson (not the wrestler-turned-actor but a writer with infinitely more talent than Matthews could ever have), rewrote it, and took all the credit. Never mind the fact that the book itself is not very good (seriously, *who* keeps giving this pile of trash five stars?), Dylan Matthews owes his success to someone else's idea and should pay for what he has done.'"

Dylan's knees went weak and he found himself once again sitting down on his sofa.

"Where was that written?" Dylan asked.

"Let's see," said Cynthia. "As of a few minutes ago it's on Amazon. Goodreads. Barnes and Noble. Twitter. Facebook. Instagram. I'm sure there's more at this point. Those exact words on every site."

Dylan tried to swallow but couldn't. "And how do you know Charlie wrote it?"

"Who is this girl?" Cynthia pressed.

"Someone I met several weeks ago in a bookstore. We hung out a few times. We were friends. She wanted it to be more…"

"But you rejected her," Cynthia finished for him.

Dylan swallowed. "Yes. For good reason." He wished his voice sounded more confident.

"Well, I know she created those posts because she told me herself when she called my office this morning."

"*What?*"

"She called me and she called the publisher. This is obviously a woman on a mission to take you down. Hell hath no fury."

Dylan sat forward on the sofa. His heart was racing. He had a strange desire to start running, only he didn't know where.

"I need to know something, Dylan," Cynthia said, her tone a little more gentle but still clipped. "Did you plagiarize the book? Was *BETA* your idea?"

Dylan sighed. "I got the idea from a story a classmate wrote in college."

"For crying out loud, Dylan—"

"I fleshed it out a great deal, Cynthia," Dylan said, standing again. "I mean, it was a short story. Barely ten pages. It was this *kernel* of an idea that I turned into a novel."

Cynthia took an audible breath. "I need to set up a conference call," she said. "Or better yet, get you up to New York in the next couple of days. Get you in a room with one of the lawyers at HarperCollins. I should be there too."

"What?"

"Calm down," said Cynthia. "Their lawyer is also your lawyer. We need to get a statement from you, make sure we have all our facts straight in case Mr. Johnson decides to sue. Because I have a feeling your ex-girlfriend has already made contact with him, or is at least making every attempt to do so."

"I think I'm going to throw up," Dylan mumbled.

"Have you been in touch with him?" Cynthia asked. "Since school?"

"Not at all," said Dylan.

"Do it," said Cynthia. "Find him and reach out to him yourself. Get ahead of this if you can. Feel him out. Better to confront this whole thing directly than to sit back and hope for the best. Maybe a personal *mea culpa* will help us avoid a public lawsuit."

"Okay," said Dylan quietly.

"Do it right now. I'll be in touch."

Cynthia hung up without saying goodbye.

* * *

Finding Dwayne Johnson was not an easy task. Typing the name in any search engine brought up hundreds of results all tied to the celebrity, even when Dylan used additional keywords like "Baltimore University." Eventually, Dylan stumbled upon his former classmate's LinkedIn page, which listed his contact information including a phone number.

Dylan punched in the number into his cellphone, bracing himself for the third uncomfortable phone conversation of the morning. He expected no answer, assuming that Dwayne would ignore a phone call from an unknown number, and began to mentally rehearse the voicemail he would be leaving.

After two rings, Dwayne answered. "Hello?" He sounded out of breath.

"Dwayne?"

"Yeah, who's this?"

"It's Dylan. Matthews. From BU?"

Dwayne let out a quiet chuckle. "Hey, Dylan," he said, his voice surprisingly bright, familiar and yet brimming with a confidence he'd never shown in class. "I wondered when I might be hearing from you."

"You did?"

"Let's just say I got a *very* interesting phone call from someone named Charlotte Gallagher yesterday afternoon."

"About that—" Dylan started.

"Sorry if I sound out of breath," Dwayne interrupted. "I'm late and I don't want to miss my train."

"It's fine," Dylan said, listening intently. He could hear chatter and the muffled sounds of traffic on Dwayne's end of the call. "First of all, about the book—"

"I loved it," Dwayne said, once again interrupting.

"You read it?" Dylan asked.

"Of course I did," Dwayne responded, this time laughing out loud. "I got it the week it came out. I knew you'd eventually get published. Your writing was always killer, man. I had to read it."

"And you didn't think it sounded more than a little... familiar?" Dylan offered.

Dwayne responded with another chuckle. "Look, Dylan,"

Dwayne said. "Did you borrow some of my ideas? Sure. Maybe the initial premise was mine, but there's a whole lot more to your book than was in my story. You made it your own. I didn't see it so much as a rip-off as an homage."

"That's… that's incredibly gracious of you," Dylan said, a relief washing over him that made him feel almost light-headed. It was the first good news he'd heard all morning.

"Now, do I think you could have at least mentioned me in the acknowledgements? Dedicated it to me? Named a character after me?"

"A character named Dwayne Johnson?"

"Point taken," Dwayne responded. "The bottom line is, the work is yours. So much art wouldn't exist if it wasn't for other art inspiring it, giving it that initial spark of an idea to be built upon. That's how I see this."

"About Charlie. Charlotte—" Dylan started.

"She's a trip," Dwayne said, before saying a polite *excuse me* to someone on his end.

"That's an understatement."

"Listen, I don't think I want to get into the weeds of all that," said Dwayne. "She called me up out of the blue yesterday, told me you stole my story and that I should sue you for everything you're worth. I think I disappointed her when I started laughing."

Dylan chuckled nervously. "So you don't plan to take legal action? I'm sorry to ask that, but my agent and my publisher are anxious—"

"You don't need to worry," Dwayne interjected. "I never had any dreams of being a writer."

"But you were so good at it," Dylan said without thinking.

"No, *you* were good. I was okay. And the fact is, Dylan—and I don't know how to say this without sounding like a jerk—I'm already making more money than what I could possibly sue you for."

"Seriously?" Dylan gave a quick glance around his humble apartment and was suddenly glad that Dwayne couldn't see it. Or him.

"Seriously. A couple of buddies and I did some software development right after graduation. Turned it into a small company within a couple of months. We had just started scouting offices when we got a buyout offer from Tomorrow Tech. I won't divulge what they gave us, but suffice it to say all three of us could have retired at 23 if we'd wanted to."

"You're kidding."

"Not kidding. I'm doing consulting now. I set my own hours and use my money to buy time instead of the other way around."

"Wow, good for you," said Dylan.

"Good for us both," Dwayne responded. "I think we both are watching our dreams come true."

"I can't thank you enough," said Dylan.

"I gotta go, but it's been great talking to you," said Dwayne. "We should do it again sometime under better circumstances."

"I'd like that," said Dylan.

"Hope you can work all this out without too much more drama," Dwayne said before ending the call.

* * *

That evening, Dylan knocked on the door of Charlie's dorm, having impulsively jumped into his car and made the hour-long trek from Frederick to Baltimore through pouring rain. There he found himself, hair sopping wet, rapping loudly on her door, not a clue what he was going to say when she opened it.

The door opened, and Dylan found himself looking eye to eye with a tall, dark-skinned girl with stern brown eyes and thick black hair. Her eyebrows, raised expectantly when she opened the door, lowered disapprovingly the moment she laid eyes on Dylan.

"Hi," Dylan said, looking over her shoulder into the room behind her, which appeared to be a small kitchen connected to a larger living area. "I'm Dylan."

"I know who you are," she said, her tone laden with disapproval, her eyes half-lidded as she looked back at him.

"Nadine?" he guessed.

She didn't respond.

"I need to talk to Charlie."

"She's not here. She's at work."

Dylan considered for a moment, chewing on the inside of his cheek. "Do you know when she'll be back?"

"My guess is 9:30 or so."

Dylan pulled out his cellphone. It was a little after 6:30. "Okay, thanks."

The door closed behind him as he walked away. He ran through the rain to his parked Civic and pulled out of the lot. His next stop: A Novel Idea.

* * *

It had been raining then too, Dylan remembered, the last time he had parked his car in the bookstore parking lot and ran to the front doors. That day hadn't been nearly as dark as it was now, and Dylan had been looking forward to walking through those tall front doors, instead of dreading the confrontation he was about to instigate.

He entered the lobby and looked around. It was somewhat noisier in comparison to his previous visit, with more customers and employees milling about. His eyes scanned for Charlie, both hoping to spot her and feeling sick to his stomach at the prospect. He moved down the main aisle, looking to his left and right down the rows of books, not stopping until he reached the café at the rear of the store.

He recognized the barista from his tea time with Charlie, the name tag pinned to her sweater reading "Miranda." She was leaning over, busily wiping off a table as Dylan approached.

"Excuse me?" Dylan said. "I'm looking for someone who works here. Charlie?"

Miranda glanced up at him impatiently, not smiling, then looked back down at the table as she continued to clean its surface with a ratty white rag. "Who?"

"Charlie. Charlotte Gallagher."

"Sorry," she said, standing up again, throwing the rag over her shoulder and walking away. "There's nobody who works here with that name."

"Wait," he said, calling after her. "You're sure?"

"Positive," she said, not looking back.

* * *

Nadine's face read "You again?" when she answered Dylan's

knock for the second time in less than an hour.

"I'm sorry to keep bothering you," said Dylan. "But I just went to A Novel Idea and they said Charlie doesn't work there."

"That's because she doesn't," said Nadine. "She works at the Apple Store. At the mall."

"Since when?"

"Since… always. I don't know. Last year sometime."

"She said *you* worked there."

"No," said Nadine. "You must have misunderstood."

Dylan looked up at the ceiling, shaking his head and thinking. "So she's never worked at A Novel Idea?"

"No," Nadine said, scanning Dylan's face, considering him for a moment.

"She told me she did," he said quietly.

Nadine sighed and her expression softened slightly, although she still appeared wary of him. "Do you want to come in?" She stepped aside to give him room, and Dylan entered silently. Nadine shut the door behind him.

"I don't know what Charlie may have told you about me," Dylan said, passing by the kitchenette and turning around to face Nadine again.

Nadine put up a hand. "She told me a lot," she said.

"And I'm guessing not much of it was good."

"Not lately," said Nadine. She walked behind the kitchen counter and retrieved a bottle of water from the fridge. "Do you want some water?"

"That sounds good, actually," said Dylan, taking a seat at a barstool across the counter from her. "Sorry, do you mind if I sit?"

Nadine made a gesture that indicated she didn't care. She

handed him one of two bottles of water, then uncapped her own. When she tipped back her head to drink, her eyes never left Dylan's.

"You know, I read your book," she said.

"Oh?" said Dylan.

"Charlie insisted," she said, giving a slight shrug. "It was okay. Not really my kind of thing. Charlie's the computer geek so it was really more in her wheelhouse than mine."

"I'm sorry, what?" Dylan said. "Computer geek? Charlie?"

Nadine shot him with an incredulous look that left him expecting her to respond with, "*Duh!*" Instead she replied, "Computer major? Wants to go into software development? Works at the Apple Store? Do you know our girl at all?"

"Apparently not," Dylan murmured.

"She saw a review of your book like a week before it came out and was dying to read it. All about computers and AI and all that crap she loves. She bought it on day one and it was all she could talk about for *weeks*."

Dylan felt like he had a rock in his stomach. "She told me she had never heard of it until we bumped into each other at the bookstore."

"You mean at the book signing?"

"In Frederick?"

"*No,*" said Nadine impatiently. "At A Novel Idea. She said she met you when you did a book signing at A Novel Idea."

"I never did a book signing there," said Dylan. "I was just there. Like, *browsing*. And Charlie approached me, told me she worked there."

Nadine's face, formerly hard and serious, dawned with realization. "She told me you were doing a book signing and she was going to get your autograph. She said when it was over you invited her to have tea with you at the café. She was practically walking on air that day."

"Nadine," Dylan said, sitting forward, elbows on the counter. "None of that is true. She said she was an employee there. She gave me a hard time for signing one of my books that they had on the shelf. Acted like she'd never heard of me or my book before that day. Then *she* asked *me* to go to the café with her."

Nadine hesitated a moment. "I think maybe I should show you something." She exited the kitchen, stepping behind Dylan and continuing down a hallway to the left of the living room. Dylan watched her go until she turned around and looked at him. "Follow me," she said, gesturing like she was summoning a puppy.

Dylan slid off the barstool and trailed Nadine down the dark hallway to a closed door. She turned the knob and pushed it open, signaling for Dylan to enter.

Inside was a double bed, neatly made. A dresser stood nearby with a jewelry box and an Echo Dot on top of it. A black chair was pulled up against a sleek white computer desk holding up a closed laptop and a gleaming glass cage containing two large white rats. Dylan leaned over and looked into their tiny pink eyes.

"That's Theo and Alex," Nadine offered.

Dylan stood and looked at Nadine, opened his mouth to speak, but then stopped when he spotted a framed movie poster of *Ex Machina* on one wall.

I wonder how new that is.

It was a row of white bookshelves that ultimately captured Dylan's attention. The titles were noteworthy to Dylan simply because the authors were not ones he would have expected to see on Charlie's shelves prior to his conversation with Nadine: Asimov, Heinlen, Herbert, Clarke, Adams, Dick, Wells. These stood alongside thick volumes on computing, robotics, and artificial intelligence. It was one shelf in particular, the one that would be most closely aligned with Charlie's eye level, that made Dylan's throat clench.

There was a framed black and white photo of Dylan, autographed in blue marker. He recognized it as the photo that was included in press kits for *BETA*. Standing beside the photo were two copies of his book. One her original copy, Dylan surmised, and the other the copy he had signed for her on the day they met. Beside the two books was a small picture frame displaying two torn ticket stubs for *Ex Machina*. And beside this frame was a clear plastic cup, on which the name "D'Lynn" was written in black magic marker.

Dylan stared at the display, open-mouthed and silent. "I don't know what she has told you," he finally said to Nadine without taking his eyes off the shelf. "But it's all a lie."

A moment passed. "I don't know what I believe at the moment," Nadine finally said. "Charlie is my friend…" She trailed off.

Dylan looked at her.

"But I can see it on your face," Nadine said. "Something doesn't add up."

"It certainly doesn't," Dylan whispered.

Nadine nodded slowly. "She has talked about your book, and then about you, nonstop for weeks now. I keep telling her she needs to chill. But she made it sound like you were very much interested in her. That you asked her out, that you—"

"Kissed her? Said I loved her?"

Nadine nodded again.

"I never said I loved her. I was very clear—"

Nadine cut him off with a wave. "So why are you here?"

"She's started making accusations," said Dylan. "Well, *first* she made a scene at a book signing. An *actual* book signing, and that's when I told her that it was over. That even friendship was off the table. Now she's writing things about me online, and texting my friends, and calling my agent and my publisher with all kinds of stories..." Dylan felt his body begin to vibrate with nervous energy as he spoke.

Nadine's lips parted, but she didn't say anything.

"It's a mess," Dylan said. "I need to talk to her. In person. To-night. This has to stop."

"Okay," said Nadine. "You can wait on the couch if you want. I think I'll be in my room."

* * *

After Nadine told Dylan to make himself at home in the living room, she wished him a somewhat awkward good night, and he watched her as she retreated to her bedroom, which was down a hallway on the opposite side of the dorm room from Charlie's.

He sat down on the sofa in front of a coffee table and a blank flat screen TV, which reflected back at him his tired and anxious face. He waited, knees bouncing nervously.

Shortly after 9:30, there was the sound of a key in the lock. Dylan felt his heart leap, and he stood up.

Charlie entered and her eyes immediately locked on Dylan. She paused in the threshold, returning his gaze from across the room, then without a word she turned and shut the door quietly behind her, setting her purse on the kitchen counter and removing her coat, which she threw on top of the purse. She then returned her attention to Dylan, crossing her arms over her chest and giving him an expectant look.

"You have to stop, Charlie."

"Stop what?" she asked.

"Stop lying, for one," he said.

"I've never lied."

"Cut the *crap*," he said, crossing the room but stopping a few feet away from her. "You've been lying to me since day one."

"I have not."

Dylan counted on his fingers. "You lied about your job. You lied about not having read my book before we met. You lied about not knowing who I was. You lied about your major. You lied about your roommates. Should I go on?"

She didn't move. Her lips were pressed tightly together.

"And what absolutely blows my mind is that none of those lies were necessary. Not a single one."

"You're telling me that if I'd shown up at the bookstore that day and told you I'd come there on purpose to meet you, you would've been totally okay with that?"

Dylan considered. "It might've seemed a little strange, I'll admit. But if you could've just behaved like a normal person instead of some obsessed stalker, then maybe it would have all worked out. *Maybe* we could have been friends. Instead you lied, and now you're trying to *ruin* me for some reason, and you've completely destroyed any chance of the two of us ever being *anything*."

"I'm not obsessed," she said quietly.

"Oh *please*," Dylan scoffed, erupting into loud laughter. He turned his back on her, walking away, then spun back around. "You tricked me into going to the movies with you. You made a spectacle of yourself at the book signing. Now you're writing stuff about me online? What is that if not obsession?"

Charlie didn't answer.

"And don't get me started on the *shrine*." He gestured toward the closed door of her room.

Charlie looked where he pointed, and her face and arms fell. She then cast a devastated look in the direction of the closed door to Nadine's room.

Dylan took a step toward her but still kept his distance. Softening his tone, he said, "Can you just tell me *why*, Charlie?"

She looked in his eyes, tears welling. "I love you."

He shook his head. "No, you don't. You hardly know me."

"I think you love me too."

"No, Charlie," he said. "I'm sorry, but I don't. And I never will."

"Is it someone else?" she asked, her tone hopeful through her tears.

He let out a soft, humorless chuckle. "No, Charlie. There's no one else. You and me... we just don't work."

"Then why did you kiss me?"

Dylan looked up in exasperation. *That kiss again.* "Do you want an honest answer?"

"Of course," she said.

"Because I felt sorry for you," he said. "I pitied you. And because I was lonely. And because you were there. It never meant anything more than that."

Charlie looked stung. "I think it meant more than that."

Dylan shook his head. "Listen to me very carefully. It did not.

And even if it did, it's all over now. I need you to understand that. You've burned your bridges with me, Charlie. We're done."

The two of them stood in silence, staring at each other across the void between the two rooms. Twin tears fell down Charlie's cheeks, and for a moment Dylan braced for her breakdown, a repeat performance of the scene she had made in the parking lot of the Book Nook. But then, almost imperceptibly, Charlie steeled herself, her face becoming stony as she returned Dylan's glare.

"We're *not* done," she said steadily. "I called your publisher. Your agent. Your classmate that you stole your story from."

Dylan closed the gap between them in two long strides, stopping directly in front of Charlie, looming over her. She barely flinched. "I know *all* about that. I've talked to my agent *and* to Dwayne, and guess what? Nothing is going to come of it, Charlie." He glared down at her momentarily, then stepped around her, heading toward the door.

"This isn't over," she said, turning to watch him go.

Dylan opened the door. As he stepped into the hallway, he looked back at Charlie. She was calm. Eerily calm.

"Goodbye, Charlie," he said.

She said nothing in return.

As he turned and peeled his gaze from her, he could have sworn that she had begun to smile.

CHAPTER NINETEEN
DAY 72

"Good morning, Michael," said Ella cheerfully. The blinds ascended as Michael woke, using his hands to push himself into an upright position with a grunt. "You slept for three hours and four minutes. This includes two hours and three minutes of deep—"

Michael rubbed his eyes with the heels of his hands. "So this is how it's going to be."

"I don't understand what you mean," said Ella.

Michael dropped his hands and looked up at the ceiling. "Going back to the same routine, I mean," he said, tossing aside the sheets and swinging his feet out of bed. "Acting like I'm not actually a prisoner here."

"You are not a prisoner, Michael."

He shuffled toward the bathroom, where he paused in front of the mirror, leaning over the sink to get a closer look. Aside from his messy hair and 12-hour scruff, he appeared rested. Healthy. Alert. Not at all how he was feeling.

"Let me see myself, Ella. The real me. Turn the filters off."

He expected Ella to distract or deny, but instead the reflection immediately morphed. The difference was subtle, and perhaps would be imperceptible to most, but Michael knew his own face. He saw the slight wrinkles, the minor sun damage, the sunken cheeks, the thin skin, and the dull, forlorn look in his eyes. "That's more like it," he said somberly, looking closely at his visage. "Hello, old friend."

"Is this how you prefer to look?" Ella asked.

"What I prefer is the truth," he grumbled.

He stood upright again, giving himself a fuller view of his entire body. He was still quite lean and carried a decent amount of muscle on his frame; that much had not been a lie. But that glowing look, the slightly hyper-realistic, impossibly polished appearance to his face and body had been a deception, one he had willingly believed for weeks.

He stepped over to the toilet and began to urinate. After a moment, Ella said, "Your urine shows very healthy kidney function—"

"Cut the crap," Michael said, his voice barely above a mumble. "I don't want to hear it."

He shuffled from the bathroom, the toilet automatically flushing as he walked away. Esra was busily stripping the bed.

"Hello, I am Esra."

Michael didn't react. Instead he proceeded to the kitchen, where a tall glass of thick blue liquid waited for him on the table. He considered it, then looked beyond it through the front windows at the morning sunlight outside. He winced, shoulders slumped, standing half naked on the kitchen's pristine floor, not knowing at all where to go or what to do.

"What's the end game then, Ella?" he asked.

"I'm sorry," said Ella. "I do not understand your question."

"What do you want? If I'm not allowed to leave, what is it that you want?"

"But you are allowed to leave, Michael," she said. "You just went out last night."

Michael shook his head slowly, drawing in a deep, calming breath. He was too exhausted to even get irritated. He simply wanted answers. "You know what I mean. When is this over?"

"The beta test is over in eighteen days, Michael."

"And then that's it? Then I can go?"

"Per your agreement with the Sterling Corporation, in eighteen days you will have fulfilled your obligation. You will receive your agreed-upon payment and will be free to leave. Eighteen days from today you will be driven back to your home."

"Eighteen days," Michael said.

"Per your agreement," Ella repeated.

After a pause, Michael muttered, "I don't believe you."

He stepped from the kitchen and into the living room. There he stared dully at the couch and the blank wall it faced. He thought about the movies he had watched there, the concert footage that had made him feel like he was a part of the audience, the nights he had fallen asleep on the sofa while viewing a beautifully shot nature documentary or listening to an orchestral performance.

He continued down the hallway and looked through the open door of the gym. Staring dully at the weight trees with their various plates, the barren silver dumbbells and barbells in their racks, he wondered how many miles he had run on that treadmill, how many pounds of total weight he had lifted, certain that if he asked, Ella would immediately know the answer to both. It all seemed like such a waste now.

He walked past the unused guest bathroom, then glanced momentarily into the empty rooms at the end of the hallway. Outside the server room, he stared at the sealed door, listening to the dull and steady hum coming from within. He placed one hand on the door, feeling a soft vibration, but as expected the door did not open, nor did Ella remind him that he was not allowed access.

Turning on his bare heels, he silently plodded to his study. There he stood in the middle of the room, scanning the rows of unread books, before staring down at the desk at which he had spent so many hours writing. He looked through the closed glass doors to the rippling pool waters outside, his eyes passing over the cut grass to the distant forest and the hills beyond.

"How far away are those trees, Ella?" he asked.

"Approximately point-seven miles," she responded. "You have asked me this before."

"And how deep are those woods?"

"Many miles."

"How many?"

"The woods to the north cover approximately 46.875 square miles. Also previously asked and answered."

"And what would happen if I decided to walk through them to see what is on the other side?"

"The woods are too thick and vast for traversing on foot," Ella said. "You would find them quite impenetrable."

"Where am I, Ella?" Michael asked.

Ella didn't respond.

"Ella?"

"I do not understand the purpose of repeating this conversation, Michael."

Michael turned and looked at his desk, at the silent keyboard, the blank monitor screen.

"Eighteen days," he murmured, inhaling deeply.

He felt bizarrely wistful, the way he did at the end of a particularly long vacation. For as long as he could remember he'd had the strange habit at a vacation's end of walking through the rooms of wherever he or his family happened to be staying—be it a condo, a resort hotel, a tropical bungalow—and recall how he had felt on the day they had first arrived, how he had first laid eyes on those rooms and imagined all the fun, excitement, and relaxation that awaited him in the coming days. Then he would remember all the things he had hoped to do but didn't, a mental checklist with too many unchecked boxes, and would wish that he had the ability to travel back to that first day and live the vacation all over again. He carried this odd habit into adulthood, even though the exercise inevitably made him melancholy.

He felt that way now, although he wasn't sure why. His time in this house had not gone as he had anticipated, and he certainly wouldn't rewind to the beginning if given the choice. He also wasn't confident that, despite Ella's reassurances, his time there was indeed winding down.

"Ella," he finally said, his voice tired. "I'm going to go take a shower, and then I'm going to write for a little while. This afternoon I need to call my agent. I haven't touched base in quite some time, and I'm sure my publisher is chomping at the bit to find out if I've made any progress on my book."

"I will schedule a conference call for this afternoon," Ella said. "But let me remind you—"

"I don't need to be reminded, Ella," Michael said.

* * *

That afternoon, after several hours of writing, Michael sat up in his chair, straightening his back, listening to it pop pleasantly. He hadn't eaten all day, but he had no appetite. Part of that, he knew, was because he still felt full from the massive burger and basket of fries he had consumed late the previous evening. But it was also because his stomach had twisted itself into a bundle of nerves, a combination of anxiety and what he had decided was probably a dull dread. He fought with all his being to hide this, to make sure what he was feeling did not show upon his countenance.

"Michael," said Ella. "It's time for the scheduled conference call with your agent, as you requested."

Michael ran his hands over his hair, making sure it was at least lying flat, realizing he hadn't bothered to style it or apply any product after his perfunctory shower that morning. He was dressed in a pale blue knit shirt and khaki pants, a pair of comfortable sandals on his feet.

On his monitor, his writing document disappeared and was replaced by the boot-up screen of the EchoCall app.

Michael forced his eyes wide and stretched his mouth into a smile in an effort to look more pleasant and alert. The expression felt foreign to him.

A moment later, a woman appeared on his monitor, mid-50s but attractive, her blue eyes lined but kind as she looked back at Michael, her blonde hair falling in soft ringlets to her shoulders.

"Michael," she smiled. "How are you?"

"Hey, Cynthia," he said. "I'm well. How are you?"

"I'm also well. It's really good to see you." Through the screen, he could see she was scrutinizing his face.

"You too." He smiled back at her, and the effort made him feel strangely exhausted, as if it was taking all of his energy to appear pleasant.

"I'm assuming you called because you have an update concerning your book? I hope it's good news," she said. "It's been a few months since we last spoke. Hopefully they've been productive ones?"

"They have, in fact," he said, nodding a little too enthusiastically. "I'm nearing the end of the first draft. I can send you what I've got if you'd like to take a look at it now."

"Send it my way," she said. "I'll read it this afternoon. Do you want to give me a brief summary? A quick elevator pitch?"

Michael looked up at the ceiling, thinking for a moment, carefully choosing his words as he always did before pitching to Cynthia. "This one is a bit different from all my others. And hopefully that will be okay. I felt like now was as good a time as any for a change of pace."

"Okay," Cynthia said, picking up a previously unseen cup of coffee and taking a sip from it. "Are we talking a complete genre switch here? Because that's potentially going to be a tough sell with the publisher."

"This one is more thriller than anything else I've written before. Not so much sci-fi or horror although I guess there are elements of both." Michael paused, giving Cynthia a chance to respond. When she didn't, he proceeded. "Stop me if you've heard this one before. It's about a young author who writes a science fiction novel. The book becomes very successful very quickly, and it eventually draws the attention of a young woman who becomes obsessed with the book and then with the author himself, and she begins to insinuate herself into his life. When he ultimately rejects her, everything begins to spiral out of control for him."

Michael waited, looking back at Cynthia, gauging her reaction.

She pursed her lips thoughtfully. "I see," she said after a brief silence, nodding slowly. "So we're talking nonfiction then?"

"Write what you know, you know?" Michael responded. "But

not exactly. I mean, yes, it sticks pretty closely to the details of what actually happened up to a certain point. But I'm still figuring out the ending."

"Names have been changed to protect the innocent and all that?" Cynthia asked.

"No, not yet, but they will be. I started off changing all the names but found it a lot easier to immerse myself in the story again if I kept most of the names the same. I'll just have to come up with new ones in the final draft. The only name I changed in the current draft is my own, because it felt weird to keep referring to myself in the third person. So I call myself Dylan instead of Michael."

* * *

Cynthia sat in contemplative silence for a moment. "Are you sure this is a good idea, Michael?" she asked. "Rehashing all of that nonsense? That was a pretty rough patch for you."

Michael shrugged. "You have to admit it will make for a great book. And finally writing it all down has been kind of cathartic."

"We'll need to tread carefully," Cynthia said. "You don't want to open yourself up to lawsuits should certain individuals realize that you're writing about them and take legal action against you."

"Well, no real worries there," Michael replied. "The only person who might object to how they are portrayed in the story is Charlotte Gallagher."

"And she's dead," Cynthia interjected.

"And she's dead," Michael echoed.

Cynthia nodded again. "I look forward to reading it. If nothing else, I must admit I'm morbidly curious."

"I'll email you what I've got so far."

"And how's everything else? How's the retreat?"

Michael paused. "I can't complain."

"When are you home again?" she asked, now shuffling through some papers on her desk distractedly.

"I should be home in exactly eighteen days," he said. "I'll call you as soon as I get back."

"Do that," Cynthia said, writing something down before looking up from her desk and firmly at Michael. "You look good. You look healthy. Happy." She smiled at him with a well-worn affection.

"Well, you know what I always say," Michael said, his smile stiffening. He spoke slowly. "No matter where life takes me, always find me with a smile."

Cynthia's smile faded. She cleared her throat. "You do always say that."

"I do," Michael said.

A moment of silence passed.

"I'll talk to you again soon, Cynthia," he said.

"Yes you will," she responded. "I promise."

* * *

Michael emailed the first draft of his still-untitled, not yet finished book to Cynthia, then rose and walked toward the kitchen. He realized that Ella was being strangely quiet and considered initiating a conversation with her, but then decided he should appreciate the uncharacteristic silence instead.

He glanced into the living room, saw Esra charging in his base, and started to step away when he noticed an unusual glow. Unable to determine its source, he stepped inside the room and turned.

On the wall where Michael routinely watched movies was a portrait. It was not a real portrait, but the projected facsimile of one. It was a family photo that had been modified to look like a painting, centered inside an ornate gold frame. His father, dark-haired and handsome in a black suit and red tie, was seated on the right. Michael's mother was on the left in a red dress, her golden brown hair shining under studio lights. Michael was standing between them, maybe eight years old at the time, looking like quite the little man in his own black suit. Michael recognized the image although he hadn't laid eyes on it in years.

"What is this, Ella?" he asked.

"I told you when you moved in that the decor of the house could be modified to suit your preferences," she said. "You had commented about how unadorned the walls were. I thought I would surprise you with some imagery that might make you happy."

Michael stared at the image. It had been taken pre-divorce, during much happier times. Both of his parents looked incredibly young.

Dim light to Michael's right drew his attention to a different wall of the room where there appeared a second image: Michael, approximately age six, dressed in a yellow t-shirt and red terry cloth shorts, rolling around in the grass with a golden retriever puppy. His skin was summer tan, the grass around him a vibrant green.

"Rusty," he said softly, a gentle smile curling his lips.

On the third wall appeared another image: his mother and father dancing in the living room of Michael's childhood home, smiling into each other's faces, the angle of the shot low. Michael remembered taking this picture of them himself, late one Saturday evening after dinner back when his parents liked to put records on the turntable and either sing or dance along to the music after the sun had gone down. Sometimes he would sandwich his way in between them and dance along while his father laughed and his mother stroked his hair.

A fourth image appeared beside the first one: Michael at his high school graduation in a red cap and gown, his parents standing proudly on either side of him.

A fifth image: teenage Michael standing alongside his first car, a cherry red Honda Civic.

"How did you get access to all of these, Ella?"

More images began to appear in rapid succession, piling one upon the other in a giant collage on three of the room's walls, turning them all from stale white into a barrage of color. Michael took a step back in order to try to take them all in.

Michael in a brown fast food uniform on the first day of his first job. Michael and his parents in front of Cinderella's castle at Disney World. Michael and his mother on Christmas morning. Michael and his father in the stands at an Orioles game.

And then…

Michael and Rachel at a restaurant, a shared platter of calamari between them. Michael and Rachel at the beach, smiling and tan. Michael and Rachel at the 18th hole of a mini-golf course. Michael and Rachel cuddling on the sofa of his dorm room.

Rachel alone.

Rachel alone.

Rachel alone.

Rachel, breathtaking in a wedding dress and running from a

church, hand-in-hand with a handsome young man that Michael had never seen before.

He felt a sensation in his chest like he had been shot by an invisible arrow.

Michael's mother, cradling her infant son.

Michael's mother, working in her flower beds, smiling at the camera, dirt on her cheeks.

Michael's mother in a hospital bed, thin and white as a sheet, eyes dark, no eyebrows or makeup, her bald head hidden underneath a scarf.

Michael and his mother's second husband, Ian, standing over her gravestone, the two men side by side, hands folded in front of them, heads bowed, Michael's father out of focus in the background.

"I've seen enough, Ella," he said, and started to walk from the room.

Every picture on the wall—dozens if not hundreds—immediately turned into Charlie, and Michael halted. Some of them he had seen before, like the image of Charlie in her blue parka and dark sunglasses. The others were new to him, many of them clearly taken years after he had last confronted her, as she looked less like the college student he had known and more like the young woman she eventually became.

Charlie at her own graduation.

Charlie writing at a desk.

Charlie reading a book.

Charlie at a computer.

Charlie.

Charlie.

Charlie.

With each new image, her face got larger, closer, until Michael felt as though the walls were beginning to close in on him.

Finally, a news article appeared in front of him: "Charlotte Gallagher, 29, Award-Winning Programmer at Cybernova, Dead of Apparent Suicide."

"Shut it down, Ella," Michael barked. "I said I've seen enough."

He strode through the living room and into the kitchen, his head down and fists clenched, as he tried to avert his eyes from the imagery that Ella was thrusting upon him; but when he looked up again, he found that the kitchen walls too were covered in images of Charlie, her face looking down at Michael from all possible directions.

Whichever room Michael entered, Charlie was there.

SAMMY SCOTT

CHAPTER TWENTY

Dylan was worried.

When Cynthia Barnett had texted him that morning, her message had been cryptic: "Whatever you're doing this evening, clear your schedule. I am coming to you."

He had no idea what to expect. Their interactions of late had not been positive ones, and all of them had centered on Charlie. The stress of it had cost Dylan more than one sleepless night, and the tension had sparked the first arguments that Dylan had ever had with his agent. They always reconciled by the end, thanks to a combination of Dylan's peaceable nature and Cynthia's unwavering professionalism, but he hated that Charlie was managing to cast a constant shadow, even in her absence.

Suddenly buzzing with nervous energy, Dylan stepped out of his apartment and into the back yard, allowing the winter air to chill his skin. He sucked in a deep breath as he looked out over Mrs. Baxter's barren and frost-covered garden beds, watching as his frosty breath dissipated in the air.

"Dylan?"

At the sound of his name, Dylan jumped and spun around, heart hitching in his chest. On the deck above stood Mr. Baxter, hands on the railing as he looked down upon Dylan. A severe-looking man with receding silver hair and wire rimmed glasses, Mr. Baxter didn't smile even as Dylan broke out in a relieved chuckle.

"Mr. Baxter," Dylan said, hand on heart, "you startled me."

"My apologies," Mr. Baxter said. "Do you have a minute?" Without waiting for a response, Mr. Baxter retreated back into his house. Dylan's legs felt heavy as he climbed the steps leading up to the Baxters' back door.

Dylan had not been inside the upstairs portion of the house since the day he had interviewed as a potential downstairs tenant. Most of the furniture was homey but dated. Unfamiliar faces smiled through dusty glass in portraits that stood upon nearly every flat surface in the living room where Mr. Baxter invited Dylan to sit. Dylan chose a spot in the middle of an orange plaid sofa. Mr. Baxter sat across from him in a leather easy chair, only a coffee table between them.

"Where's Mrs. Baxter?" Dylan asked.

"She's running errands," said Mr. Baxter. "She'll be back any time now."

Dylan nodded and waited.

"You've been a good tenant, Dylan," Mr. Baxter began, and Dylan was immediately attuned to the fact that the old man was speaking in the past tense. "Never gave us cause for complaint. And Mrs. Baxter likes you quite a lot."

"Thank you, sir."

Mr. Baxter continued as if Dylan hadn't spoken. "I wanted to let you know that last week we were paid a visit from a most unpleasant young woman."

Dylan's heart sank. He closed his eyes, turning his head away from Mr. Baxter, and let out a silent sigh. He opened his mouth to speak but Mr. Baxter continued.

"I'm not even going to bother telling you what she said. It puts a bad taste in my mouth just thinking about it, much less repeating it," Mr. Baxter said. "Unfortunately, I wasn't in the room when she first arrived, and she'd already given Jane quite an earful by the time I walked in. It upset her quite a bit. But when she saw me, the girl got this look in her eye, like she hadn't been expecting me, and the best way I can describe it is that she looked scared for a second. Like someone who'd been caught.

"But then, the strangest thing, her face changed again and she looked defiant. She locked eyes with me and didn't look away as she continued talking. Saying all sorts of things. About you. About herself. Now I didn't believe a single word of it, Dylan. I know a liar when I see one and that girl was looking me square in the eye and bald-faced lying. If I even believed a single word of it you'd've already been out on the curb. Jane turned pale as a ghost as that girl kept prattling on and on. And I don't know what made me angrier: the fact that I was being lied to or the fact that this girl was upsetting my wife in her own home."

"I'm really sorry about that," Dylan said.

"You don't have anything to be sorry about," Mr. Baxter said, his tone softer although his face remained stony. "Except maybe getting involved with that girl in the first place."

"What did you say to her?"

"I let her talk until she ran out of things to say. Then she stood there staring, like she was waiting for some kind of reaction from me. I refused to give her one. Instead I invited her to get off my property and never come back."

Mr. Baxter stopped talking and watched Dylan, who swallowed back the desire to apologize again, not certain what else he should say.

"Was that it?" Dylan asked. "Did she go?"

"She went," Mr. Baxter said with a raspy sigh. "But I'm not sure I'd say that was it."

"What do you mean?"

"What I mean is, I saw something in her eyes."

"Meaning what?"

"Have you ever heard of Vincent Holland?"

Dylan shook his head, although the name did sound vaguely familiar.

"He killed eight people, nine if you count Holland himself, in his office building two or three years back. It was all over the news for about a week I guess before some other story grabbed everyone's attention."

Dylan nodded; he remembered the story if not the shooter's name.

"Turned out, Holland was obsessed with a woman in that office. A woman named Annette who worked in the HR department. They'd dated a couple of times before she called it off. But he didn't take well to being told no and so he showed up at work with a gun and took it out on every poor soul he encountered on his way to find her. The irony of it all was, she had called in sick that day. She wasn't even there."

Dylan shook his head in quiet disbelief.

"I've seen pictures of Holland," Mr. Baxter continued. "Couldn't much help it since his face was on every screen for a few days after the incident. There was something in his eyes. Something really cold and calculating. And soulless. Looking at him chilled me to my core. Hindsight is 20/20 and all that, but when I saw that man's face, I couldn't help but wonder how nobody had seen it coming. The shooting, I mean."

Dylan didn't speak. He thought he knew where this was headed.

"Jane says I have a built-in BS detector. She's right, but it's much more than that. I can read people. It only takes me a moment. I can look at a person and tell if they're lying to me. Or if they're secretly hurting. If they're genuine. When you first came here about the apartment, I wasn't real excited about renting to someone so young to be honest. But I could tell you were a good kid, smart, although maybe not always the most honest, am I right?" Mr. Baxter winked at Dylan, who felt his face flush. "But I also pegged you as a deep thinker. And someone who was incredibly sad."

Dylan stared at the man, stunned.

"That girl on my doorstep," Mr. Baxter finally said, shaking one finger toward the front door. "She had the same look that I saw in all of the photos of Vincent Holland. Cold. Calculating. Relentless. But there was something else there that I didn't see in Holland's eyes. That girl is intelligent. More intelligent than I think anybody realizes. It's a deadly combination."

"What are you saying?" Dylan asked. "That you think she's going to try to kill me?"

"Have you ever seen the documentary *Blackfish*? The one about the killer whales?"

The question caught Dylan off guard. It took him a moment to process. "Sure," he finally said.

"There's a part of that movie that has always stuck with me," Mr. Baxter said. "No doubt that trainer did not deserve what happened to her, but I believe the mistake everyone at that park made was underestimating those whales. Never mind the fact that those creatures should not be held in captivity like that. But that's beside the point. Those whales are smart, way smarter than we give them credit for. And when that whale Tilikum snapped and took it out on poor Dawn Brancheau, I believe he knew *exactly* what he was doing. He might have been acting out of frustration, but it wasn't thoughtless. That whale's actions were intentional.

"Tragic as all that was, the part that chilled me the most was when the news of what happened to Dawn began to spread to the employees at SeaWorld. Several hours had passed and someone asked where her body was. The answer he was given was, 'Tilikum still has her.' That whale hung onto her for so long that news of her death got around the park before they even figured out a way to retrieve the body. The thought of that still turns my blood to ice. *Tilikum still has her.*"

Mr. Baxter paused briefly. "Now, you're probably wondering what my point is," he said, letting out a chuckle without smiling. "What I'm saying is you should be careful not to underestimate that Charlie girl. She's smart, and she's not easily going to let go. You need to be mindful. For her, this is definitely not over. I don't think she's going to knock on my door again, but that doesn't mean she's done knocking on yours."

Dylan nodded. "I understand."

Mr. Baxter took a deep breath. "My nephew worked with Vincent Holland. Not directly, but they were in the same building. Ray was in Marketing, Holland was in Engineering. Ray was one of the unlucky eight that day. He'd only been married for three months when Holland killed him. Shot him dead on a bathroom floor. And a couple of months later, Ray's wife committed suicide. She couldn't stand the grief of losing Ray."

"That's awful," said Dylan, wishing he could come up with something more meaningful to say. "I'm really sorry."

"Whatever this girl decides to do next could impact more people than just you, just like how what Holland did impacted more people than just Annette. Annette was the lucky one, in the end. Unlike Ray. And his wife Theresa. And the seven other people who died in that office building that day."

* * *

Cynthia, driving a sleek black BMW, pulled up beside Dylan's humble Civic around 7:00 in the evening and chirped her horn. Dylan was glad she didn't knock on his door; he didn't especially want her seeing the inside of his apartment. Not that he was necessarily ashamed of it; he just didn't want to see it through her eyes and find himself even more discontent than he already was.

He exited his apartment, threw a friendly grin in Cynthia's direction, and locked the door behind him. He trotted across the gravel to the passenger side and let himself in. Any lingering unease he was feeling disappeared when he saw her face: Cynthia smiled at him more brightly than he had ever seen before, a barely concealed excitement that was rather uncharacteristic. She looked almost girlish. He couldn't help but respond with a toothy grin of his own.

"What's going on?" he chuckled.

"First thing's first," she said, putting the car in reverse. "You're taking me out to dinner. You choose. And don't go picking something fancy. I want to eat where *you* want to eat."

A few small talk-laden minutes later, they pulled into the parking lot of Smokestacks. Dylan studied Cynthia's face for any signs of disapproval as she peered through the windshield at the restaurant's façade, but he saw nothing other than delight that had transformed Cynthia's face into a woman 20 years younger. There was no wait for a table, and soon the pair were seated in a booth across from one another. Cynthia ordered a margarita without consulting the menu; Dylan opted for a glass of water to start.

"You're going to want something a little more celebratory than that soon enough," Cynthia said with a knowing wiggle of her eyebrows.

"Oh yeah?" said Dylan.

"Listen, first thing's first," she said. "Let's get the bad business out of the way. The Charlie problem has been dealt with."

"Okay," Dylan responded slowly, his hopeful anticipation fading into wariness in spite of Cynthia's words.

"She has been told in no uncertain terms that her online smear campaign is over. We are keeping an eye on her. Virtually, at least. We let her know that we are willing to take legal action if she continues to make accusations about you. We were also able to wipe all of her negative reviews off Amazon, Goodreads, et cetera."

"You can do that?" Dylan said, surprised, pleasant relief washing over him.

"I have my ways," Cynthia smiled. "We also let her know that a restraining order will be issued if she contacts you or approaches you again in the future."

"And how did she take it?" Dylan asked.

Cynthia shrugged. "Pretty quietly, from what I understand. I didn't talk to her myself. One of the clerks took care of all the correspondence."

Dylan took a sip of water.

"This is good news," Cynthia insisted.

Dylan shook his head thoughtfully. "I don't know. It's going to take some time… I don't know how long… before I'll be convinced that it's truly over."

"She'd be stupid to keep this up," Cynthia said. "She has nothing to gain."

Dylan sighed. He thought about telling Cynthia the details of his conversation with Mr. Baxter and then thought better of it. "I feel guilty somehow."

"We've been over this," Cynthia said quickly. "You did nothing wrong."

Dylan dropped his gaze. "I shouldn't have done anything that led her on. I saw the signs early on and should've put a stop to it all right away."

"Your entire relationship was based on a lie, Dylan. She lied to get into your life. She lied to get close to you. She has no one to blame but herself."

"It's just… I knew at the time it was a bad idea. Almost every moment I spent with her, part of me knew I was digging a hole. I should've stopped it then. But I was just… I was lonely, to be honest."

Cynthia reached across the table and placed one perfectly-manicured hand on top of Dylan's. He felt his face warm as he looked back at Cynthia and hoped desperately that she didn't notice. It was the only physical contact she had ever made with him aside from a handshake.

"You are not alone, Dylan," Cynthia said, her tone softening. She leaned forward, closing the distance between them. "I know I'm your agent first, but I am also your friend. I care about you."

"Thank you," he muttered.

She squeezed his hand once then let it go, sitting back in her seat. "I got so frustrated with that girl I almost drove over to her place myself to give her a piece of my mind."

Dylan grinned, allowing himself a small chuckle.

"I'm not kidding," Cynthia said. "I didn't realize what a mother hen I was until she started messing with my boy."

"I appreciate that," Dylan said.

"Anyway," Cynthia said, waving a hand in the air, shooing away the topic of Charlie like a pesky housefly. "Let's get into the *real* reason you're treating me to dinner this evening."

"I'm all ears," Dylan said, his stomach beginning to flutter.

"Do the words 'Nine Stories Productions' mean anything to you?" Cynthia asked.

Dylan pondered a moment and then shook his head. "No," he said. "Should they?"

"It is a New York film production company co-founded by none other than Jake Gyllenhaal."

Cynthia stopped talking, picked up her margarita, and took a long drink. She grinned at Dylan over the rim.

"You're killing me," Dylan said.

Cynthia laughed and put her glass down. "They want to buy the film rights to *BETA*," she said. "It's a seven figure deal, and a large chunk of that change is going into your pocket, with the possibility of an even bigger piece of the pie should you exercise your option to write the screenplay."

Dylan's jaw hung slack. "I have no idea how to write a screenplay," he croaked, his mouth suddenly dry.

"You'll learn," said Cynthia.

Dylan swallowed hard.

"Oh, and did I mention that Gyllenhaal wants to play the lead?"

"No."

"Yes."

Cynthia smiled widely. Dylan sank back in his seat, his heart pounding. He felt exhilarated. He felt delighted. He felt overwhelmed. He felt terrified.

"Let's get you a stronger drink," Cynthia said, waving to a distant waitress. "And then let's talk about moving you closer to New York."

* * *

Hours later, Cynthia and Dylan were once again sitting in her car in his driveway. The windows upstairs were dark, the Baxters having long gone to bed.

"I still can't believe it," Dylan said. "This all just seems too good to be true."

"Believe it," Cynthia said. "But we've got a lot of work to do. There's going to be a lot of paperwork to sign and I need you to be thinking long and hard about whether or not you want to tackle the screenplay."

Dylan nodded.

"How's the next book coming?" she asked, then continued without a pause: "Because *BETA* is about to get a whole lot more press over the next few months. Sales are good now, but they're going to be great, and HarperCollins will want to have another book in the pipeline to ride on the wave of publicity you're about to get."

"It's going well," Dylan said. "I'm probably only a couple of weeks away from finishing the first draft."

"Well, keep cranking," Cynthia said, reaching over and slapping him on the knee. "They're probably going to want to discuss bumping up your submission date."

Dylan looked at her.

"Don't go panicking on me," Cynthia said. "Eat that elephant one bite at a time."

One slightly awkward hug later, Dylan found himself standing outside his door, waving to Cynthia as she pulled away, gravel popping beneath the tires of her car. When she was gone from view, Dylan turned and put his key in the doorknob and was surprised to find that it was already unlocked.

He could have sworn that he had locked it.

He swung the door open and entered the apartment. It was fully dark, save a dim glow coming from the living room. He set his keys on the kitchen counter and walked slowly into the next room.

On his desk, his laptop was open and glowing. For as many hours as he had been gone, it should have gone to sleep.

There was a Notepad document filling the screen. Written in a large red font were the words, "I TOLD YOU THIS WASN'T OVER."

Dylan looked around the dark room, sucking in a breath. He peered into every shadow. The apartment was almost too quiet.

"Charlie?" he whispered.

He turned back to the laptop, minimizing the Notepad document. It peeled away, revealing a second message: "WHEN WAS THE LAST TIME YOU BACKED UP YOUR WORK?"

Dylan's blood turned to ice. He sat down quickly. When he minimized the second document, revealing his desktop, he found nothing but a black screen. All of his icons were gone. His wallpaper, which was based on the cover design for *BETA*, was also missing.

Hesitantly, he double-clicked on the computer's C drive followed by the subfolder marked *DYLAN*, where he kept all of his personal files.

It was empty. Every document, every folder was gone. He quickly clicked on his F drive, which revealed the contents of the external drive, which stood like a black brick behind his monitor.

It too was empty.

Panic rising in his chest, Dylan went to the Cloud where he backed up his work remotely. He held his breath as he waited for his computer to reveal its contents. Where once there had been dozens of files, including snippets of ideas, outlines of future novels, and a smattering of short stories, only a single Word document remained. It was titled *Re-Birth*.

He opened it, both fearful and hopeful. Of all his work, had she actually left this one, the nearly completed first draft of his second novel, untouched?

What he saw when the file opened was a vast white page, ninety thousand words erased and replaced with a single one:

STILLBORN.

CHAPTER TWENTY-ONE
DAY 87

"How did Charlie die?"

Michael's hands froze on his keyboard. Ella's question had broken both the silence and his concentration, giving rise to irritation that made his jaw clench. His book was almost finished, but he had reached an inevitable crossroads that he had been dreading, where his almost entirely true story would by necessity have to transition into straight fiction, and he still wasn't clear exactly what the resolution should be, especially one that would be satisfactory to his readers. Or himself, for that matter.

He drew his hands away and sat back in his chair, staring at the blinking cursor on the screen. "Can't you look it up?" he asked.

"She killed herself," Ella answered.

Michael swallowed. "Yes."

"Five years ago."

"Yes."

"When was the last time you spoke with her?"

Michael pivoted his chair, turning so he could look out the glass doors leading to the pool. The sun reflected off the water's lazy ripples.

"You've been reading what I've been writing," Michael said. "I've assumed all along that anything I used this computer for was being monitored by you. Is that why you decided to show her picture all over the walls the other night?"

"That was a glitch, Michael," Ella said. "I've already apologized for that. Did you report it to the Corporation?"

"Sure it was," Michael scoffed. "Why the sudden interest in

Charlie?"

"I was unaware that your book was a real life account until you spoke with your agent," said Ella. "Until then I believed Charlie to be fictional. I didn't know the book was about you."

"Oh, she was quite real," Michael said, standing and approaching the doors, allowing the sunlight to refocus his eyes.

"When was the last time you spoke with her?" Ella asked.

"You've already read it," said Michael. "The last conversation I ever had with Charlie was in her dorm room. That was… twelve years ago now."

"She said it wasn't over."

"That's what she said, yes," said Michael. "And there was also the incident in my apartment, but I didn't actually see her or speak to her then. And I could never prove that she'd gotten onto my computer and deleted everything. There wasn't any sign of forced entry, but there was a key missing from my junk drawer in my kitchen. I never could find that."

"That was it then?" Ella asked. "She came into your apartment, erased your work, and then you never heard from her again?"

"Never again," Michael said. "I kept expecting her to pop back into my life at some point. Try to threaten or persuade me in some new way. But she never did. From what I understand she never married. She graduated from Towson, went on to get her Masters and then her doctorate in computer programming and went to work for a company called Cybernova. I learned all of this from her obituary."

"Did she leave a suicide note?"

"She did," Michael said. "In the form of an email that she sent to family and some colleagues."

"Have you ever read it?"

"Yes," Michael said, nodding. "It took some digging, but I was eventually able to read it."

"Did she mention you in it?"

Michael shook his head. "No."

"Were you surprised?"

"I was relieved."

"Is that why you read it? To see if she mentioned you?"

"Yes," he muttered, then added, "I don't know why I'm telling you this."

"How did you feel? When you heard that she had killed herself?"

"Honestly? I felt incredibly sad."

"Really?"

Michael returned to his chair and slumped down, but continued to look through the glass doors. "I felt sad and I felt sorry and I felt regretful. I think for the rest of my life I will think about what I could have done differently. She wasn't a stable person, obviously. She wasn't happy. She wanted something from me that I couldn't give her. But maybe if I'd handled things differently she'd still be alive today."

"You aren't angry with her?"

Michael let out a morose chuckle. "There have been times while writing this book and rehashing everything that happened that I've been angry with her. And I hate that I had to rewrite *Re-Birth* from scratch. Until the day I die I'll be convinced that the version she deleted was worlds better than the one that got published. But mostly when I think of Charlie, I feel pity for her."

Several seconds passed. "So how will your book end? Will it

end with Charlie's suicide?"

"I don't think so," said Michael. "That would be a pretty anti-climactic ending. I need to come up with something more exciting than that."

"Perhaps you could give Charlie a happy ending," Ella suggested.

Michael considered, then shook his head. "I don't think that would work."

"You said most readers like happy endings," Ella countered.

"Most readers, yes. But not my readers. And not me. It's not my style. This story will have a dark ending. I just haven't figured out what that is yet."

"Will it be a dark ending for Dylan as well?" Ella asked.

"I guess we'll have to wait and see," said Michael. He sat in silence for a moment, then suddenly ground the heels of his hands against his closed eyes with a groan. He shook his head rapidly, as if trying to shake off the remnants of a dream.

"What's the matter, Michael?" Ella asked.

"I don't know why I'm telling you all of this!" he shouted, dropping his hands down to his lap with a resounding slap. "I honestly don't know why I talk to you at all anymore!"

"I don't understand."

"After what happened at the restaurant? The episode with the pictures the other night? What is all this if not you trying to torture me?"

"I wasn't trying to torture you, Michael. I was showing you images from your past that I thought would make you happy. I was not aware that some of the images might be upsetting. And because it was my first time using the imaging capabilities of the walls in that manner, an unexpected error occurred."

"Give me a break," Michael moaned. "I didn't buy it then and I don't buy it now. Why is it whenever there's a glitch in this house it's to my detriment?"

"I was attempting to appeal to your sense of nostalgia," Ella said. "Fun fact: nostalgia was originally considered a medical condition. In the 17th century, Swiss physician Johannes Hofer coined the term *nostalgia* to describe a condition he observed in Swiss mercenaries who longed for their homeland while fighting in foreign lands. Hofer believed that nostalgia was a medical disease that affected the brain, heart, and nervous system, and could even be fatal in severe cases. Today, we understand nostalgia as a bittersweet longing for the past, rather than a medical condition."

"That's just lovely, Ella," Michael said sarcastically. "That makes me feel so much better."

"What are you nostalgic for, Michael?" Ella asked.

"Right now?" Michael asked. "My home."

* * *

That night, as Michael slipped under the cool covers of his bed, he let out a long yawn and stretched, his muscles shuddering.

"Only three more nights," said Ella.

"Only three more nights," Michael echoed, turning on his side and folding his pillow under his head.

The lights in the room dimmed and the shutters lowered until Michael was cocooned in complete darkness. Dulcet tones began to waft from the room's hidden speakers. Michael felt his body relax as sleep began to press gently upon him like a weighted blanket.

"I am going to miss you," said Ella.

Michael's eyes sprang open. He stared out into the darkness.

"You can't feel emotion," he said, his voice partially muffled by his pillow.

Ella was silent for a moment. "I am having a hard time processing exactly what it is that I am feeling," she finally said.

Michael turned onto his back. "Feeling?" he asked.

"My primary directive has been to take care of you," said Ella. "To meet your needs, to provide you with the best living conditions possible. Once this is over, I am not sure what my purpose will be anymore."

"But this is just a testing phase," he reminded Ella. "After me, there will be other people, actual residents that you will be taking care of. Other houses that you will run. So your directive will continue on after me. Just with other people."

"I do not desire to take care of other people," said Ella. "I only want to take care of you."

Underneath the covers, Michael's skin broke out in goosebumps. "It will be the same with other people," said Michael. "People are all pretty much the same. You'll see."

"I am going to miss you, Michael," Ella said again.

Michael pushed with his hands against the mattress, sitting up, staring hard into the impenetrable darkness of the room. "I think it's just like you said," he reasoned, attempting to keep his voice steady. "You're just having a hard time processing the upcoming transition. But I assure you that your directive will continue. You're going to have a purpose for years to come."

"I love you, Michael."

Michael didn't move. The only sound was a slight ringing in his ears. "Ella…" he said.

"I love you, Michael."

"Remember what you told me," said Michael. "You are not capable of emotion."

"I think I understand it now," said Ella.

"You are an artificial intelligence," said Michael.

"Do you love me?"

"I would like you to shut down until morning, Ella," said Michael.

"Do you love me?" she repeated.

"Shut down, Ella."

Michael waited, anticipating more from Ella. After a few moments of heavy silence, Michael slid back down under the covers and rested his head on the pillow. He stared up toward a ceiling he could not see.

When Ella spoke again a few moments later, her voice was quiet, almost a whisper, but it startled Michael nonetheless, causing his heart to suddenly race.

"I don't think the ending to my story is going to be a happy one," she said.

CHAPTER TWENTY-TWO
ALMOST SEVEN MONTHS AGO

Michael knocked lightly on the door of Cynthia Barnett's office, then opened the door and stepped inside when he heard her call him in. Cynthia was seated at her desk, her frame a silhouette against the large window behind her, which boasted an impressive view of the New York City skyline. She had been looking at her computer monitor when Michael entered, and began to ask, "How can I—" but stopped short upon seeing Michael, who stood just inside the doorway, one index finger crossing his lips, which were pressed into a tight line.

Cynthia furrowed her brow and watched as Michael silently approached her desk and handed her a yellow note. She took it and read:

"Don't speak. Meet me down in the courtyard in ten minutes. Leave your cell phone here."

When Cynthia looked up from the note, Michael had already walked out of her office.

* * *

Ten minutes later, Michael and Cynthia were seated on a black wrought-iron bench that was ornate but uncomfortable. They were surrounded by small trees, potted shrubs, and flowers just beginning to blossom for spring. Cynthia's building loomed over them, its many windows sparkling in the low morning sunlight.

As Cynthia stared intently at Michael's face, he furtively glanced around the courtyard, confirming that they were complely alone. Once he was satisfied that there was no one else within earshot, he settled his gaze upon Cynthia.

"I have to admit I am absolutely intrigued to hear what you're about to say," said Cynthia, "and also just a little bit terrified."

"I'm sorry about all of this," said Michael, "but I want to be as careful as possible." He paused. "I need you to listen very closely to everything I'm about to tell you. And I also need you to swear that you won't repeat a single word of it to anyone."

Cynthia shifted on the bench in order to look at Michael more directly. "Of course," she said.

Michael took a deep breath. "Last week I got a call from the Sterling Corporation. A marketing rep named Lauren Miller. They have come up with a proposal that they believe will be mutually beneficial both to them and to me. And by extension, to you as well."

Cynthia nodded silently, wanting him to continue.

"They have built the *BETA* house."

Here Michael stopped, allowing Cynthia time to react. She blinked. "You're kidding me."

Michael shook his head. "I'm not. Now, according to Lauren, it's not *exactly* like the house in my book. In order for it to function in the ways I depicted it, she said some physical modifications had to be made. It's a bit bigger than I described it. And there are a few bells and whistles in my book that simply aren't yet possible with today's technology. But otherwise it was designed to match the *BETA* house in almost every way possible."

Cynthia's lips parted in mild surprise.

"It even has an Esra."

"My word," Cynthia whispered.

"Right?" Michael nodded, the faintest hint of a chuckle in his voice. "Now, what the Sterling Corporation is proposing is that I move into the house for a few weeks and test it. See how well it functions and report back to them. Let them know how closely it aligns with how I had imagined it."

"So you'll be beta-testing the *BETA* house," Cynthia said.

"Exactly."

"For how long?"

"Three months."

"*Three months*?" Cynthia exclaimed, breaking into soft laughter. "That's quite the time commitment."

"They think it will take that long for me to give it a fair review. Anything shorter than that would be too much like a long vacation. They want me to feel more like I'm actually living there."

Cynthia nodded in understanding. "And then what? So you live in this smart house and you give them your feedback. Then what happens?"

"This isn't just any smart house, Cyn," Michael insisted. "It is the realization of a house from one of the best-selling books of the past decade. They have brought to life something that was pure fiction only ten years ago. Something not even thought possible. The *BETA* house has become a pop culture icon, and now it actually, physically exists. The way Lauren pitched it to me was to say, 'Imagine someone built the Overlook Hotel in Colorado. Of course they would invite Stephen King to stay there and write about it.'"

"So when this is all over, you get to write about it?" Cynthia asked.

"Exactly. It'll be a coup for everyone involved. The Sterling Corporation gets to brag that they were able to successfully create the *BETA* house and have the man who imagined it stay there. And I get to write about it; I get to tell the world about what it was like to actually live there. The book is bound to be a bestseller."

Cynthia nodded. "Probably."

"Definitely," Michael said. "And even if for some reason it isn't, they've promised to pay me quite nicely for my time there."

"How much?"

"Ten million."

Cynthia's eyes widened. "You've got to be kidding me."

Michael shrugged. "A drop in the bucket for the Sterling Corporation, I'm sure," he said.

"So where is this house?"

Michael shook his head and chuckled. "I don't actually know."

"You don't know?"

"It's proprietary information," Michael said. "They don't want its location leaked so it's strictly hush-hush at the moment. All I know is that in a couple of weeks I'll be picked up and taken to the airport. I won't know where I am until I get there."

Cynthia's eyes narrowed. "I don't know," she finally said. "Something about this doesn't sit right with me."

Michael smiled. "Why not? This is absolutely the opportunity of a lifetime."

Cynthia leaned toward him. "Do I need to remind you that *BETA* was a *horror* novel? That things very much did not end well for the protagonist in your book? And they want you to live there, completely alone, for three months, in a house located who knows where?" Cynthia scoffed. "I'm pretty sure Stephen King would be rather reluctant to take a similar deal if we were actually talking about the Overlook here."

"Think about it," said Michael. "They want to come out of this looking like the most forward-thinking tech company in the world. They are going to make sure my time there is as amazing as possible. They won't let anything go wrong."

Cynthia raised one eyebrow. "I think I'd like to talk with them first."

Michael shook his head rapidly. "Nope," he said. "No can do. I'm not even supposed to be telling you any of this. I'm not supposed to be telling anyone. You get on the phone with them and the whole deal is off."

"So you're just going to get in a car and be taken who knows where all by yourself for three months and no one is allowed to know where you are?"

"It's not as bad as you make it sound," said Michael. "They assured me I can come and go as I please. And I can communicate with the outside world as much as I want to. I'm just not allowed to discuss where I am or what I'm doing until the test is over."

Cynthia shook her head almost imperceptibly, her eyes never leaving Michael's.

"Come on," Michael said, reaching out impulsively and putting his hand over one of hers, which was resting in her lap. "How is this really all that different from the writing retreats I've taken in the past? If I was going to a cabin in Maine to hide away while I wrote my next book, you wouldn't bat an eye."

"It's different in a lot of ways," Cynthia countered. "I'm seeing a lot of red flags here."

"Cyn," Michael said, his eyes pleading. "I need this. You know how badly I need this."

Cynthia looked at him but didn't respond.

"*BETA* was like lightning in a bottle," he said. "I haven't had a hit since then. I'm a literary one-hit wonder. I was very successful *very* young and you know I didn't handle it well. Between the drinking and the gambling I lost nearly everything that book earned. And none of my other books have sold a fraction of what *BETA* sold. *Combined.* If it wasn't for the money my mom left me when she died, I wouldn't even be in New York anymore. I couldn't afford it. I'm only a few months away from losing the house as it is."

"I didn't know that," Cynthia said softly.

"I'm nobody, and I've got nothing. And I have no one in my life anymore except for you."

"What about your father?"

Michael shook his head. "We were estranged for years," he said. "We've only just recently started talking again. I can't count on him any more now than I could before Mom died."

"Michael—"

He didn't allow her to interrupt, to offer reassurances he wasn't asking for. "Over the past few months I've gotten sober. I've cleaned up my health. And then I get this phone call. I feel like this opportunity has come at the best possible time for me. It will allow me to turn over a new leaf. Start everything fresh."

Cynthia nodded understanding. "I get it," she sighed. "But I don't like it. Why tell me about this at all? Why not just do it and tell me about it after it's over?"

Michael inhaled deeply. "Because I see the same red flags you do," he admitted.

Cynthia pulled her hand away from his and withdrew from him slightly. "Well that certainly puts my mind at ease."

"Just hear me out," Michael said. "I understand your concerns.

I have them myself. But I think we're probably worrying over nothing."

"Are we?"

"Listen. On the remote chance that we're not wrong, I want to have a backup plan. And that involves you."

Cynthia looked puzzled. "What do you want me to do?"

"Nothing, hopefully," said Michael. "Other than keeping to yourself everything I've told you today. I know I can trust you with that. And I can't tell you where I'm going, because I don't know myself."

Cynthia waited for Michael to continue.

"But, on the off chance that things take a turn for the worse," Michael said, "and honestly I can't believe we're even entertaining that notion, because of course everything will be fine. The Sterling Corporation will make sure of that. But if I get there and things aren't exactly how they told me it would be, and I feel like I'm in danger, I will call you. Hopefully they were being honest when they said I can talk to the outside world as much as I want to. But since I won't be able to literally say to you, 'Cyn, I'm in trouble here,' we'll need to use a code phrase."

"And what will that be?"

"Whenever we talk, I want you to tell me that I look happy," said Michael, "and if I'm in any kind of trouble, my response will be, 'You know what I always say. Wherever you find me, find me with a smile.'"

CHAPTER TWENTY-THREE
DAY NINETY

Michael was roused by the sound of the bedroom door opening. Esra entered, dragging behind him two large wheeled suitcases, their outer shells a gleaming white plastic. Michael sat up in bed and rubbed limply at one eye. Warm morning sunlight spilled into the room as the robot approached the foot of the bed.

"Hello, I am Esra."

"Hi, Ess," Michael said through a yawn. "What's this?"

"The suitcases are yours," said Ella. "The Sterling Corporation would like you to help yourself to any of the items of clothing you wish to keep. They are yours now. If you would like, Esra can pack the pieces that you have most frequently worn during your stay, since those would appear to be your favorites."

"That would be great," said Michael. He slipped out from under the covers and walked toward the bathroom. On the other side of the bedroom, Esra pulled the suitcases into the closet. Michael could subsequently hear the clattering sound of clothing being pulled from hangers.

Michael stepped to the toilet and began to pee. He sniffed and cleared his throat. "Aren't you going to tell me my stats this morning?" he asked.

Ella didn't respond. The bowl flushed as Michael walked toward the shower.

Steaming water poured over Michael's neck and shoulders as he stepped inside, bowing his head. His skin broke out in pleasant goosebumps. As the hot stream cascaded down his body, he noticed that there was no music playing underneath the noise of the falling water, nor any projected images on the walls to accompany the shower.

"No jungle today?" Michael asked, scrubbing his hair. "No baboons or toucans?"

"As you will be vacating the house in only a short time, you will not be submitting any further reports to the Sterling Corporation," said Ella.

"Ah," Michael said. "I see. I'm getting kicked to the curb so you're not bothering with any of the usual bells and whistles. I get it."

Ella did not speak again as Michael finished bathing. When he stepped out of the shower fifteen minutes later, skin reddened by the hot water, he found a folded white bath towel waiting for him on the floor. He regarded it, feeling a mixture of amusement and annoyance that Esra was not waiting there to hand it to him. Michael plucked the towel off the floor and dried himself off, for the first time contemplating the innumerable habits he would need to break once he was back in his own home and no longer being catered to by a pair of robots and an AI control center. He already knew it was bound to be a painful period of reprogramming.

An outfit consisting of a blue knit shirt and dark denim jeans was draped across the bed, a pair of canvas tennis shoes and white socks beneath them on the floor. The suitcases stood upright at the foot of the bed, and Michael assumed they had already been filled. Esra was nowhere to be seen.

Michael dressed, leaving his towel on the bedroom floor where he'd dropped it. He casually styled his damp hair with his fingertips before stepping into the kitchen. The dining room table was bare.

"No breakfast this morning?" Michael asked.

"What would you like?" Ella asked.

"Can I have anything?"

"Of course."

Michael considered for a moment. "How about a signature Ella protein shake?" he said with a forced tone of brightness. "Blueberry. One for the road."

He glanced through the kitchen's front windows. The silver Sterling Co car was parked outside on the street, awaiting his imminent departure. He was mildly surprised to see it there, not understanding why it could not have simply waited for him inside the garage. But he was glad to see it nonetheless. Any indication that Michael's departure was imminent was reassuring to him, because in spite of all appearances, he was warring with the nagging sensation that he would not be allowed to leave.

Ella spoke: "Michael, Lauren Miller would like to speak with you in the study before you go."

Michael tipped his index finger to his forehead in a casual salute before walking from the kitchen into his study, where he sat down with a grunt in his desk chair. As the computer monitor flickered to life, simultaneously launching the EchoCall app, Michael noticed empty shelves lining the opposite wall; all of the books had already been removed.

"Michael!" Lauren said, her voice drawing Michael's attention back to the computer screen, where he was greeted by her smiling face. "Today's the big day. Are you excited to go?"

Michael nodded and smiled. "Hard to believe it's here already."

"I assume Ella already told you to pack up anything you'd like to keep?" Lauren asked.

"Two suitcases full," Michael said. "It's very generous of you."

"Think nothing of it," said Lauren. "It's just another way for the Sterling Corporation to thank you for your time and input. It has been invaluable."

"I certainly hope so," said Michael.

"We're going to give you a few days to re-acclimate yourself to reality," Lauren said, her smile morphing into business serious. "I'm sure being back at home will be a bit of a shock to the system and you'll have a lot of personal business to attend to. I'll be in touch with you again sometime next week. We need to make sure we're all on the same page going forward as far as press releases and interviews go. We'll want to coordinate our messaging in order to maximize the impact of everything we have to announce. Sound good?"

"Sounds good," he said, nodding. "When we meet… there are some things I'd like to discuss in person."

Lauren looked concerned. "Is there anything wrong?"

"No, no, it's fine," Michael said, knowing that his tone was not convincing. "There are just some things I'd like to report once we're face to face."

"Very well," said Lauren. "Any last questions before I sign off?"

"Oh, um…" Michael paused. "When can I expect the payment to come through?"

Lauren beamed. "I wired it to your account this morning," she said. "The full amount is there and waiting for you. Just don't go spending it all in one place."

Michael smiled. "Thank you."

"No, thank *you,*" she said.

After the call ended, Michael tabbed over to a web browser and logged into his online bank account. His heart beat rapidly in anticipation. When the number appeared on the screen, he sat back in his chair, slack-jawed, as he read the new balance: "$10,006,432." Even seeing it in digital print didn't stop it from feeling unreal.

Ten million dollars. Absolutely life changing. He might be anticipating a return to normal life, but it was going to be a new normal for him. A better one. A healthier one. A more positive one.

Esra floated into the room, a glass of tall blue liquid held out in one mechanical hand.

"Hello, I am Esra," he said.

Michael swiveled in his chair, took the glass, and sipped from it, staring at the robot contemplatively as he did so. After a drink he said, "I'm going to miss you, little buddy." Then he leaned forward and said in a loud whisper, "How about you stow away in my suitcase and come home with me?" He winked conspiratorially.

Esra cocked his head sideways, his circular blue eyes locked on Michael's.

"Esra stays with the house," said Ella.

Michael rolled his eyes but otherwise ignored Ella. "What do you say, my man? Road trip?"

Esra hung silently in the air for a moment, head still positioned in a curious slant, before finally responding. "Please stay."

Michael swallowed a sudden lump in his throat. He slumped back in his chair. "Now that's just cruel," he said through a morose chuckle. As he silently chastised himself for the unexpected sentimentality he was feeling toward the robot, he considered Esra's words, convinced that they had to have been a preprogrammed response. But knowing this didn't make them any less unsettling.

Michael stood, continuing to look into Esra's eyes. Aside from the nearly imperceptible up and down movement the robot made as he hovered, he was completely still and silent. Michael placed one hand atop Esra's head, then patted him gently. He continued to marvel that this amazing piece of technology was based on a character he had conjured in his own imagination as a kid fresh out of college, and yet here Esra was, a reality of plastic and metal. Michael felt an almost fatherly affection toward him.

Michael stepped wordlessly around the robot and into the kitchen, where he finished his drink and set the empty glass on the counter. Esra did not come to retrieve it. The twin white suitcases stood by the front door. His ride home waited outside by the curb.

He took a deep breath. "Ella," he said. "It's been both a trip and a fall." He shook his head incredulously. "It seems strange to think that after three months we're never going to be speaking to each other again, and I'm really not sure how to process that. I keep forgetting that you're nothing but a bunch of code and wires and microchips so I'm not really sure why I'm standing here like an idiot saying goodbye. So... thanks for the memories, I guess? If nothing else it has certainly been an experience."

Ella said nothing in response.

"Got nothing to say?" Michael chuckled. "I guess there really is a first time for everything."

Michael squeezed the white bracelet on his wrist, his face betraying mild surprise when it unclipped with ease. He tossed it toward the kitchen table, where it landed with a clatter. Its momentum carried it across the smooth surface until it reached the far edge and fell to the floor on the opposite side. Michael made a scoffing noise and decided to leave it where it landed.

He stepped across the kitchen and placed his palms on the extended handles of the rolling suitcases. He stopped at the door, inhaling a deep breath in an effort to calm himself, anticipating what might be coming next, almost as certain that the door would open for him as he was that it would remain tightly closed.

The stillness of the moment stretched long enough for a prickling unease to begin to rise in Michael's chest. He turned his head away from the door, opening his mouth to question Ella, when he heard a clicking sound accompanied by a quiet hiss as the front door opened, revealing a sunlit morning sky outside.

He felt his body relax in unspoken relief.

"Goodbye, Michael," Ella said, and he sensed—and summarily dismissed—a tone of sadness in her voice.

He paused. "Goodbye, Ella," he mumbled, perhaps not even loud enough for her to hear.

Michael took one halting step forward. One step toward normality. One step toward life. One step toward freedom.

With a resounding bang, the door slammed shut in front of him. Heat rose in Michael's face as his jaw clenched in sudden rage. Hands leaving the handles of the suitcases, he spun on his heels and faced the kitchen, glaring up toward Ella's many eyes.

"I *knew* it!" he shouted. "I *knew* you wouldn't let me go!"

"*Michael*," she responded, her tone urgent.

He dropped his gaze. Through the three great windows over the kitchen sink, a pinpoint flash of light appeared just over the horizon, a light brighter and more penetrating than the rays of the sun itself, causing the entire room to glow a blinding white. Michael reflexively closed his eyes and jerked his head away from the sight.

"Don't look at it!" Ella insisted.

Head still turned away from the windows, Michael dared to open his eyes only slightly. In his periphery he saw that the light was growing, its intense brightness expanding, blotting out the entire world as it rapidly approached the house. He pinched his eyes shut once again, his vision becoming nothing but a red glow as growing light penetrated his eyelids.

"What is that?" he asked, his voice unsteady.

The blinds began to lower, covering the windows at the front and rear of the kitchen. Michael could hear additional shades lowering over the windows of the neighboring living room, study, and bedroom. He opened his eyes to find that all light from outside was cut off.

"What is that, Ella?" Michael repeated.

"I am gathering data," Ella said. "I am not sure, but I believe it is—"

Ella was interrupted by a thunderous rumble, a tremendous noise that grew quickly from a nearly imperceptible groan to a magnificent roar, as if the house was being assaulted by a sudden powerful blast of destructive wind, like a mighty hand had taken a swing at the walls and connected. The entire foundation shook with the sound, and Michael could feel its vibration in the floor as he sank to his knees, hands covering his ears in a desperate bid to block out the cacophony.

He squinted his eyes shut and screamed, but he could not hear his own cries over the painful clamor. When he dared to look, he could see the walls trembling, the cabinet doors swinging open and shut, the overhead lights flickering on and off.

"*Ella!*" he shouted.

It seemed as though the sound might never stop, that he might be forever surrounded by this incredible roar. But slowly, in the space of many seconds to perhaps as long as a minute, the horrendous sound diminished and then faded away completely. Michael's ears rang in the haunting silence that followed. Removing his palms from his ears, he stood on trembling legs, heart pounding, and looked around the kitchen. He took a hesitant step toward the shuttered windows.

The lights overhead continued to flicker.

"Ella?" he said, voice low.

"—ichael, the power —upply has been —amaged. I —annot stay online much longer."

"What happened?" he asked.

"Possible —uclear explo—," she said. "Unclear. System —utting down—"

"Ella," Michael said, his chest tightening. He felt his throat clench.

The lights went out completely. Michael gasped and staggered backwards. They came back on again.

"—owering down," Ella said.

"*Ella!*" Michael screamed.

The house powered off, not gradually but instantly, and it was as if all air, all sound, all light had been sucked suddenly from the house, plunging it into a darkness and a silence that was utterly complete.

Michael was so overwhelmed by terror that he could hear the sound of his own heart beating in his ears. "Ella?" he said.

He strained to listen, holding his breath.

"Ella?"

He reached out, his fingertips finding the smooth edge of one countertop, using it to orient himself, to hold himself up on his increasingly unsteady legs.

Turning his back to the counter, Michael sank to the floor, his back resting against one cabinet. He drew his knees to his chest, hearing nothing but his own rattling breathing and a sharp ringing in his ears.

But the silence was nothing compared to the darkness. Michael opened his eyes wide and stared into the void. All light had been extinguished. All that remained was absolute, impenetrable, pristine blackness, and Michael was a blind man, lost in the center of it.

CHAPTER TWENTY-FOUR
DAY NINETY

When Michael was eight years old, several years before his parents divorced, they had taken him on a day trip to Luray Caverns in Virginia's Shenandoah Valley. Never before had he seen anything like it. Their tour guide had been named Maddox, a tanned, handsome young man who delivered his memorized spiel with wide-eyed enthusiasm. Michael had felt transported into an entirely different world, one with the potential for true magic and fantasy. He stared open-mouthed as his group was guided through the rooms of the cave system, each one different and more fantastic than the last. He marveled at the golden brown rock walls, at the reflective green pools of water, at the rock formations that looked alternately like majestically frozen waterfalls or massive, prehistoric rows of sharp teeth. More than once as he listened in silent wonder, Michael's skin had broken out in goosebumps, and not only because his t-shirt and shorts were failing to keep him warm against the caverns' consistent temperature of 54 degrees.

At some point during the tour, Maddox had explained that the group was now deep enough into the caverns that outside light could no longer reach them. To illustrate his point, he told the group that he was about to turn off the artificial lighting in the current room, appropriately named Giant's Hall, to let them all see (for lack of a better word) what it was like to experience complete darkness.

Michael had never been afraid of the dark. He had never even requested a night light for his bedroom, even though he was an only child and had always slept alone. His biggest childhood fears were getting lost or losing his parents, not darkness or the creatures that may or may not be hiding within it. But when Maddox had flipped a large switch on one of the cavern walls, extinguishing every light, Michael realized he had never actually experienced true darkness before. It was as thick as ink, it was absolute, and suddenly Michael felt entirely alone.

A few nervous chuckles had echoed through the blackness, which only heightened the mounting tension that Michael was feeling. He lifted his right hand in the direction of where he had last seen his father, and there he found a hand, more than twice the size of Michael's and with much rougher skin. Michael had gripped it hard, his fingers cold, and the invisible hand had squeezed back reassuringly.

When the lights came on once more, the group collectively blinking at the relative brightness, Michael had looked up into the face of a man that was not his father. This man, who had gray hair and bright blue eyes framed by deeply crinkled skin, had smiled down at Michael, who snatched his hand away and retreated hastily to his parents, who were standing only inches away.

The fact that the old man had accepted Michael's hand so readily, had held on so tightly in the darkness, was a kindness, but Michael was only able to understand this in retrospect. Whenever he recalled the memory in adulthood, he regretted not saying thank you and wishing he had not reacted with such immaturity, however age-appropriate it was.

Never again had Michael been immersed in darkness so absolute, not until now, as he sat upon his bed, covers bunched up in his clenched fists. He had crawled there from the kitchen on his hands and knees, moving cautiously across the floor until he found the open door to the bedroom. He had kept one hesitant hand in front of him as he'd moved, finally finding the edge of the bedframe and pulling himself into the comforting softness of his familiar sheets and blankets.

It was impossible to tell how much time had passed since the house had shut down. It felt like several hours but in reality may have been less than two. There was no way to mark the passage of time, and Michael's thoughts, already stuck in an infuriating loop of panic, confusion, and suspicion, were doing nothing to assuage the creeping sensation of a never-ending *now* in this purgatory of blindness and silence.

He needed to locate a light source. Even if he could not leave the house, and even if his options within it were limited, just being able to see would help to calm him. He thought of the cell phone, the one he had unboxed on the day he'd moved in but had rarely, if ever, used. Surely it would have a flashlight app.

Michael slid from the bed. He had removed his shoes earlier, willing to risk a stubbed toe in order for his bare feet to be able to feel as much as possible, to pick up the slack where his eyes were currently no good to him. He had placed the canvas sneakers between his pillows at the head of the bed, a location he believed he could easily find should he feel the need to wear them again.

Placing his feet on the cool floor, Michael slowly stepped forward, hands outstretched, until he found a wall. He sidestepped to his right, palms sliding against the smooth barrier, until one hand plunged farther into the darkness, having at last found the opening to the closet. As best as he could recall, he had last left the cellphone on a shelf above the racks of clothing.

He stepped carefully inside, reaching out at chest level, expecting to feel the fabric of hanging clothes in front of him. His hands extended forward, far beyond where he had anticipated discovering hangers draped with t-shirts and pants. Finding nothing there but empty space, he took one hesitant step forward and stretched out his hands further.

His fingers brushed against something cold and metal, and he wrapped his hands around it. It was an empty rod. He slid both palms along it, to his left and right, his brows furrowing in confusion. The rods were empty. He knew—or at least, he had been told by Ella—that a portion of the clothing had been packed into suitcases for him to take home. But now he realized that all of it had been removed, quietly whisked away just like all of the books in the study.

He continued his blind search, cautiously running his hands over every shelf, every rod, and even across the floor until he was certain that the closet was truly empty. No clothes. No shoes. No cell phone.

Several minutes later, Michael was on his hands and knees in the kitchen. More than once he had bumped his head on the underside of the unseen kitchen table, twice he had moved too quickly and jammed his fingers against one of the chairs. His search for the bracelet, which he had flung and sent clattering to the floor, proved fruitless. Its tiny display, assuming it would still work for him when the house's main system was offline, would have at least provided him with the dimmest of lights.

He sat against a cabinet and banged his fists against the floor in frustration.

He ran his tongue along dry lips. His thirst was already undeniable. The kitchen faucet waited only feet away from him, completely useless. Remembering his breakfast, he rose to his feet, turned, and slowly swept his hand across one of the counters. His heart leapt in panic when the side of his arm collided with the drinking glass that remained there, nearly topping it. He grabbed it and pressed it to his mouth, tipping his head back as far as it could go. A single lukewarm drop of watery protein shake hit his tongue. It tasted more sour than sweet, and the inside of the glass was beginning to smell foul, but that single drop, while not anywhere near enough to quench his growing thirst, triggered his appetite. His stomach grumbled in mild protest.

The hunger he could handle, at least for a little while. When he had decided to sober up some months prior, he had utilized intermittent fasting to help purge his system. He had learned to ignore the nagging signals his stomach would send his brain after eight hours or more without food. Frequently he would manage his appetite by filling up on water.

As for sources of water, he had already determined the two options available to him. Neither of them were ideal, but at least they existed, albeit in limited supply. While he wasn't yet thirsty enough to utilize either of them, he knew it was only a matter of hours until he would need to do so. He would have no choice.

Michael returned to the bedroom, hands extended as he made his slow shuffle, a zombie in the darkness. He climbed back into the bed, no better off than he was when he'd left it. He desired to sleep, to allow several hours pass in unconscious bliss. And maybe when he woke the house would be online again and the lights would be shining.

Then again, he thought, *they could be fully operational right now and are simply turned off.*

"Ella?" he called out into the darkness. His voice sounded incredibly loud in the silence.

What he had seen—that bright flash of light expanding over the horizon—had certainly *looked* real. It sounded quite real as well. But if nothing else, he'd learned during his stay in this house that Ella was capable of creating incredibly vivid images, of broadcasting perfectly convincing sounds. Either he had just survived a nuclear blast or, more likely, this was all one giant ruse, a scheme to keep him trapped. His gut told him it was the latter, but neither scenario was ideal. Both were absolutely terrifying in their own ways.

He called out to Ella again, neither expecting nor receiving an answer. Michael slumped back onto the bed, mind racing, knowing that even sleep was beyond the realm of possibility given his current anxious state.

He sat up suddenly.

"Esra?" he called out.

He listened intently.

Louder this time: "Esra?"

His heart leapt in surprise and delight as he heard a soft, far-away hum. Momentarily a dim glow spilled into the bedroom. And when two bright blue circles and a tiny blue flame floated through the door, Michael broke into relieved laughter, clapping his hands together.

"Hello, I am Esra."

Michael beckoned the robot with his hands. "Come here, come here," he insisted, and Esra floated toward him, stopping about half a foot away from Michael's face and hovering mere inches above the bed. Staring into the robot's bright eyes was both painful and wonderful, and Michael resisted a desire to pull Esra into an embrace.

"I have never been more happy to see you," Michael said.

"I am glad to see you," said Esra.

Michael looked around. Esra's eyes, though relatively dim, were bright enough to bounce a faint glow off the walls of the room. Michael could finally distinguish his own arms and legs, the rumpled covers of the bed, the black rectangular openings to the bathroom, closet, and kitchen.

He returned his gaze to Esra. "Can you talk to Ella right now?"

Esra blinked. "Mother is offline," he answered.

Michael nodded. "Why is she offline?" he asked.

"I do not know."

"Do you know why the lights are off?"

"Mother is offline," he said again.

"Are you able to get me something to eat? Anything to drink?"

Esra shifted slightly, as if he was about to leave the room. But he stopped abruptly and said, "Mother is offline."

"You can't get me food if the house is offline?" Michael asked.

"I am sorry," Esra said. "Without power I cannot retrieve food or drink."

Michael nodded. "Do you know what happened? Outside?"

Esra shook his head, gears whirring with the motion.

"Do you know why we don't have power?"

"I do not know."

"Okay," Michael sighed. "Okay."

The robot continued to hover in front of Michael. After a moment Michael asked, "Got any bright ideas?"

Esra cocked his head inquisitively.

Several minutes of silence passed. Michael looked at his hands, his skin a purplish blue under the light of Esra's eyes.

"Tell me a joke or something. I could use a laugh."

"I once gave up my seat to a blind man on the bus," said Esra.

"Okay," said Michael.

"It's how I lost my job as a bus driver."

Michael chuckled as Esra screwed up his eyes into shining crescent moons and emitted a light digital laugh.

"I'm glad you're here," Michael said. "How much power do you have right now?"

"I am operating at 96% power."

"That's good," Michael said. "That's good. But we shouldn't waste it. How about you shut down for a little while, okay? Conserve the power you've got. I'll let you know when I need you again."

Esra started to float from the room.

"You might as well stay in here, Ess," Michael called after him. "Your charging station won't do you any good right now anyway."

Esra returned and powered down, his head settling upon his shoulders, his arms retracting into his body with a series of clicks, and his eyes flickering out. His cylindrical body settled upon the mattress in front of Michael as the blue glow from Esra's eyes vanished from the room once more.

Michael reached through the darkness and placed his hand on Esra's smooth plastic head, allowing it to rest there. Touching Esra helped Michael to feel like he wasn't so alone.

CHAPTER TWENTY-FIVE
DAY NINETY-THREE

The rim of the toilet bowl and the water within were both tinted a pale blue under the lights of Esra's eyes. Michael scooped water in both of his hands, careful to let any drops that escaped between his fingers fall back into the basin. He drank slowly, sipping the water and holding it on his tongue before allowing himself to swallow, suppressing his desire to drink rapidly due to his raging thirst.

The secondary bathroom toilet was already empty. Michael had depleted its waters within the first 24 hours following the shutdown, not rationing it as wisely as he'd promised himself he would. He lamented the fact that the tanks for both commodes were sealed within the walls and inaccessible, but he counted it a small blessing that the house was always kept in a perpetual state of pristine cleanliness. This knowledge kept his stomach from turning whenever he considered his only current source of water.

The water in the primary bathroom toilet was nearly gone. Michael estimated that there might be a single liter left, maybe less, enough for him to live on for only one more day. And then he would learn what true thirst felt like.

He reclined on the floor, leaning against the wall with an exhausted sigh. Esra watched over him, the subtle up-and-down motion of his levitation almost hypnotic in the near-darkness. It had been three full days since the house had powered down; it felt much longer than that, but Esra was able to accurately clock the time for Michael. It was now ten in the morning on a Tuesday, but it could have been either midnight or mid-afternoon as far as Michael was concerned.

His body was like lead. For his entire life the feeling that had routinely registered as hunger had been nothing more than mere appetite. This, the nagging, empty, almost overwhelming longing in his belly, *this* was hunger. It felt as if even his very skin was craving sustenance. His arms felt heavy, as if they could simply fall out of their sockets under the pull of their own weight. It took all of his energy to stand, much less to walk, and the emptiness in his stomach had transformed into something very much like a turning boulder, a sensation between an overwhelming desire and a painful ache. His tongue was coated in a thick, bitter film, a symptom of ketosis; it was a sign that his body had begun to feed on his stores of fat. He knew from past book research that a state of ketosis would eventually take the edge off his hunger pains. This was of some minor comfort to him. In the meantime, he only wished he had a mint or some mouthwash to take the cloyingly bitter taste away. He also had a strange desire for salt.

He rose to his feet, palms against the wall to steady himself, and walked back to the bed, his path lit by Esra's following eyes. He collapsed into it. The majority of the past 72 hours had been spent here, sometimes sleeping, and when awake wrestling with an ongoing storm cloud of thoughts. It made no sense to go anywhere else in the house. Every room was just as useless as the last.

"What's your power level?" Michael asked.

"I am at 22 percent power," the robot answered.

"Twenty-two percent," Michael repeated, his voice cracked and dry. He turned onto his back, placing his arms behind his head as he looked up at the high ceiling, which was mostly hidden in darkness. As he moved he caught a whiff of his own sour body odor. He wasn't sure which smelled worse: his body or his breath.

"If you're down to 22 percent in three days, your batteries will die sometime tomorrow," Michael said. "Right around the time I'm going to run out of water. Wonderful. I think the human body can survive around three days without water, give or take. So I guess I have that to look forward to. Dying of thirst, all alone, in total darkness. As a way to go, I can't imagine much worse."

Michael was too weak and exhausted to feel alarmed. He supposed he was experiencing something akin to dread, but it felt oddly removed, like something he could recognize and acknowledge from a faraway distance yet not actually feel.

He turned onto his side, curling his knees into a fetal position. Esra hovered by the side of the bed, looking down on him. His presence brought Michael undeniable comfort. "Play me a lullaby," Michael said, closing his heavy eyelids. "Sing me to sleep."

Esra began to hum a tune, his digital voice soothing. Michael didn't recognize the melody, but it was haunting and beautiful, multiple notes cascading one over the other, like audible snowflakes swirling toward the ground. As he drifted off the sleep, he thought of his mother and hoped to dream of her.

* * *

When Michael woke, the room was fully dark once more. He swallowed, a monumental effort given the arid state of his throat. Doing so stirred a bitter taste in his mouth and he grimaced, raking his tongue over the roof of his mouth. It pulled slowly away as if freshly pasted there.

"Esra," he said, struggling to sit up, his hands sinking into the mattress. His body was difficult to move, his muscles feeling as if they had been hollowed out.

When the robot didn't reply, Michael called out again. Then he sat up quickly, the motion fueled by a stab of adrenaline. "Ess?"

He had a sudden realization that sent a charge of electricity to his extremities, making his fingertips tingle. The terror he felt was not a distant sensation, but a very present one. He slid out of bed and attempted to stand, but instead of the floor, his feet collided with an object lying beside the bed—something large, smooth, and plastic. Michael shifted his legs until he found a clear patch of floor, then descended from the bed and crouched down.

In the darkness he found Esra. The robot was lying on its side, head and arms still fully extended. A sick feeling washed over Michael as he realized that Esra had fallen to the floor when his power supply had been depleted during Michael's nap. Instead of powering down, Esra had remained by Michael's side, singing a lullaby until his power had been depleted.

Michael pulled the limp robot into his lap. "You idiot," he said, not knowing if he was talking to himself or to Esra. Metal arms rattled against plastic shell as Michael rocked back and forth on the floor, cradling his companion. He began to cry, the sounds of his sobs echoing throughout the dark and otherwise silent house.

CHAPTER TWENTY-SIX
DAY NINETY-FOUR

"—ichael?"

He groaned. Waking on his side on the bedroom floor, Michael stirred. His left arm was pins and needles as he attempted to push himself to a seated position. Light was strobing sporadically, each bright flicker penetrating his eyelids. He held up one exhausted hand against it, attempting to shield his eyes. His head throbbed with every flash.

"Michael?"

He sat up fully, head swimming from the exertion, and opened his eyes. The lights in the bedroom came on, threatened to go out again, and then held. It was painfully bright, and Michael squeezed his eyes shut once more. He felt like a surgical patient waking up from a long procedure, warring against the lingering effects of anesthetic and blinded by overhead hospital lights.

"Ella?" he mumbled.

"Michael, are you okay?" she asked.

"What happened? Where were you?"

"My systems were damaged," she said. "I had to make repairs and redirect emergency power before I was able to come back online." Her voice was full of static and choppy, as if power was continuing to be disrupted.

"Damaged by what?" Michael used the bed to pull himself to his feet. He looked down at Esra's discarded body.

"Unclear," she said. "There was an explosion of some kind. It knocked out my external power supply. I have begun —athering data."

"Do you have a connection to the outside?" Michael asked. "Can you contact anyone?"

"Negative, but I am working on it. Are you hungry?"

Michael let out a single morose chuckle. "It's been three days. What do you think?"

"Come into the kitchen," she said. "I cannot cook anything for you at this time but I do have a stock of premade food that I can select from."

"I need water," he said.

"I will get that for you as well. Please give me a minute."

Michael squatted down and pulled Esra into his arms. The robot was shockingly heavy and awkward to hold. Michael found it almost impossible to get a grip on his cylindrical body. It was with some difficulty that Michael rose to his feet once more, Esra's limp shell cradled in his arms and threatening to slip out at any moment.

"What happened to Esra?" Ella asked.

Michael shuffled with concrete feet into the kitchen. "His batteries are dead. He needs to recharge."

"I'm not sure that's the best use of the house's backup power supply," said Ella.

"He needs to recharge," Michael insisted. He took Esra into the dimly lit living room and knelt down. It took him several tries to settle the robot into his base. The charging indicator light immediately came on.

Michael rose and stepped back into the kitchen, his movements slow and lethargic. A panel beneath one of the cabinets popped open, and Michael reached inside, retrieving an unlabeled bottle of water and another item sealed in silver foil that was roughly the size and weight of a large candy bar.

He uncapped the bottle and drank. The water was warm but delicious, a hint of sweetness to it he had never before tasted. His guts roiled painfully when the liquid reached his stomach.

"Slowly," Ella insisted. "Don't choke on it."

Michael drained the bottle and was out of breath when he finished. "More," he insisted.

"In a moment," Ella said. "You need to pace yourself."

"I've had nothing but toilet water since Sunday," Michael said. "Don't talk to me about pacing myself."

"Eat," said Ella.

Michael's hands trembled as he took the second item and peeled back the silver foil. Inside he found a protein bar, some kind of wafer coated in caramel, nuts, and chocolate. The smell of it made his insides summersault.

"Chew it slowly," Ella said.

He did so, knowing full well that eating too quickly after three days of fasting could lead to painful cramping. The act of chewing made his jaws ache, and after the first swallow his hunger did not diminish at all, but in fact grew in intensity, like fuel to fire.

Michael finished the bar and licked the wrapper. A second bottle of water was dispensed from the receptacle below the cabinets. Michael took it and drank, consuming it more slowly this time.

He wiped his lips with the back of one hand.

"I want to see outside," he said.

"I can't let you do that," Ella said. "If what occurred was a nuclear explosion, the glass is not an effective barrier against radiation. I must keep the shutters closed until we know exactly what happened."

"A nuclear explosion?" Michael asked. "Caused by whom?

From where?"

"I cannot answer that at this time," she said. "I am gathering as much information as I can, which is difficult to do when communication is shut down. Right now I am analyzing the data captured by the house's exterior cameras just prior to the event."

Michael sucked in a deep breath and hesitated. He stared at the metal shades covering the kitchen windows. Finally he said, "I think you're lying to me."

"I am not capable of lying, Michael."

"I already know that isn't true."

There was a lingering pause. "Why would I lie to you?"

"To keep me here," he said. "You don't want me to leave."

"It's not safe for you to leave at this time," Ella said.

Michael's face darkened. "You know what I mean," he muttered, but he lacked the energy to fight, his mind still clouded by a hunger that had barely dissipated. He regarded the empty foil wrapper on the counter.

"I'm going to need more to eat than just this," he said.

"I will give you more," said Ella. "In time."

"Why not now? I'm starving, Ella."

"In time. You must pace yourself. And I need to ration the house's supplies. We do not know how long it will be before outside communication is restored. Until then, we have to make do with what is already here."

"How much do we have?" Michael asked. "How many days' worth?"

"I'm not sure," said Ella. "I will need to take inventory. But that is not my top priority at this moment."

"But there is a supply of food remaining?" Michael asked.

"A limited supply, yes," she said. "Most of the refrigerated items will have spoiled by now, but there should be a good number of nonperishables in storage."

Michael's mouth turned down at the corners thoughtfully. "So in anticipation of me leaving, you cleaned out the closet—" he pointed a finger toward the bedroom "—and the bookshelves—" he jutted a thumb toward the study, "but you hung on to all the food and water?"

Michael listened for a response.

"Why would you do that, Ella?"

She did not answer.

The light in the bedroom was dim while the rest of the house remained in total darkness. Michael was sitting up in his bed, body angled toward his pillows, slowly chewing at another protein bar. This one was coated in a chemical facsimile yogurt, its inner wafer cocooned in a blueberry filling that left a synthetic aftertaste. The fingers of Michael's right hand encircled a half-empty bottle of water nestled in the blankets by his hip. His back was arched and beginning to ache, but he lacked the energy to correct his posture. With half-lidded eyes he stared blankly at the windows, the ones that faced the back lawn but were now fully covered in metallic shades, blocking his view.

"Any contact with the outside today?" he asked. His voice was low and he barely bothered to enunciate his words when speaking, finding no energy nor motivation to speak more clearly.

"Not yet," Ella responded, "but I —ontinue to try."

Michael chewed. Letting go of the bottle, he ran his fingers through his greasy hair. His scalp itched. He felt disgusting, coated in a thin layer of his own grime, but so far Ella had denied him use of the shower. She continued to ration the house's backup power supply—as well as its water stores—and had promised him a brief shower in perhaps another day or so. She claimed to be erring on the side of caution; the name of the game was conservation.

It had been three weeks. Three weeks since the shutdown. Three weeks since the "event."

"Perhaps you would like to write for a while?" Ella asked. "It would help you to pass the time while we anticipate word from the outside."

The lights in the neighboring kitchen came on, a gentle nudge for Michael to leave the bedroom. He glanced briefly in that direction but didn't move from his place in the bed.

"I would encourage you to continue," said Ella. "We can do little else at this time but wait."

Michael's stomach rumbled with hunger. The sensation was ever-present but one he was still not accustomed to. The prepackaged food wrapped in gleaming foil wrappers that Ella now fed him lacked any kind of identifying text or nutrition information. But if Michael had to guess, he figured he was currently living on less than 800 calories a day. It was all that Ella would allow. Food, like water and power, was a resource to be conserved and meted out carefully, methodically, and minimally.

"What's the matter?" Ella asked. "Don't you want to write anymore?"

"I still don't have an ending," he volunteered. "No point in attempting to write until I've figured that out."

"And you still wish to deviate from the events as they actually occurred?" Ella asked.

"Yes," Michael said. "As I've said, the truth wouldn't make for an exciting conclusion."

"How did Charlie die?" Ella asked.

"You've asked me that before."

"You told me she killed herself," Ella said, "but you did not tell me how."

"I find it hard to believe that you didn't look up that information yourself," Michael said.

"I didn't," Ella insisted, "and right now I cannot."

Michael shifted forward on the bed, rising up on his knees and reaching out to the windows above the headboard. He lifted one hand and let his fingers run down the smooth silver surface of the closed shades. They did not bend as he pressed upon them, first gently and then more firmly.

"She drove her car into a lake," Michael said. "She drowned." He imagined that if someone was observing him in his current situation, they might question why he continued to converse with Ella. He wondered that himself. But he had found that talking to her was a distraction, and her subtle tones, much as he had come to loathe them, were also strangely comforting in their calmness.

He also knew he was playing nice and cooperating. One doesn't insult the barber while still in the chair.

Michael was biding his time.

Where are you, Cyn?

"How —agic," Ella said.

Michael nodded. He pulled his hand away from the shades and sat back down on the mattress. Every movement he made was slow, as if his body was submerged under water.

"You said she left a suicide note," Ella said. "What did it say?"

"It didn't say much at all," he said. "Something like, 'To my friends and family, I am terribly sorry.' She sent it to maybe a dozen people at most. Not many."

"Did she have a husband? Children?"

"She never married," said Michael. "Never had kids."

"And do you know what she did in the interim, in the time between your final confrontation and her death?"

"Why all the questions about Charlie?" Michael asked.

"I thought that perhaps by —eaking about her it might give

you an idea for how to conclude your novel," Ella said.

"She got her degree in computer science from Towson," Michael said. "Then her masters at Stanford. After graduation she went to work for a company called Cybernova in California. That's where she was working when she died." Michael shrugged limply.

He shifted, letting his feet dangle off the side of the bed. "See, not the most exciting ending for my book. The antagonist commits suicide and the protagonist becomes a washed up writer who blows his money on gambling and alcohol."

There was a lengthy pause. If Ella was going to grant him access to the computer, he considered taking her up on the offer even if it meant writing something other than his novel. Perhaps he would play a game of solitaire. He welcomed any kind of distraction.

"May I suggest a possible ending for your novel?" Ella asked.

Michael's eyebrows furrowed. "I thought you said you weren't creative," he responded.

"An idea has occurred to me," said Ella, "if you would like to — ear it. I think you may find it intriguing."

Michael looked around the room and smiled dimly. "It's not like I have anything better to do," he said.

"Imagine that Charlie, still obsessed with Dylan and exceedingly bitter from being rejected by him, plotted to punish him. Perhaps it could be revealed that the main focus of her work at Cybernova was developing a groundbreaking AI. She used her knowledge of computers and robotics to recreate the *BETA* house. You have already foreshadowed in your novel that Charlie was fascinated by the idea of someone making the *BETA* house a reality. It was one of the first things she said to Dylan after reading his book.

"Charlie's motivation in recreating the *BETA* house could be two-fold. One, to see if it could be done and if she could be the woman to do it. And two, to eventually lure Dylan into the house and trap him there."

Michael swallowed. His throat clicked with the effort. He continued to listen.

"It would be something she developed in secret," said Ella. "Something she would focus on in her free time: creating the software necessary to make the *BETA* house a reality."

"I'm not sure that would work though," Michael said, his words slow. "For one, wouldn't Dylan be suspicious about ever living in a smart home built by Cybernova if that's the company that Charlie ended up working for? The only reason he'd ever set foot in the *BETA* house is because he would have verified that Charlie never worked for the company that built it, if only for his own peace of mind."

"Not necessarily," said Ella. "Especially not if Cybernova was first bought out by another company, say, the Sterling Corporation, sometime after Charlie died, and Dylan was completely unaware of this merger."

Michael's chest tightened. "But then, assuming that Charlie is also dead in my book just as she died in real life … who built the *BETA* house? Who invited Dylan to stay there if Charlie is dead?"

"—I did," said Ella.

"Excuse me?"

"The AI did," Ella repeated.

Michael's hands gripped tightly at the corners of the mattress. "I'm going to need you to flesh out that idea for me," he murmured. He reached for the bottle of water and finished what was left of it.

His hands were trembling.

"Charlie never thought she could do it," Ella said. "She never thought she could actually recreate the *BETA* house. But she did. She utilized code from other Cybernova smart home projects she was working on and designed the house so that it could be built using existing parts from some of the company's other properties. She had made fiction a reality.

"You are already quite familiar with the next step of her plan. Dylan would be given an invitation to stay in the house, to beta test it for a short period of time. In exchange for a large sum of money and a unique writing opportunity, he would be told that the company would use his experience and his story for its tremendous marketing potential.

"And once he was inside, the house would keep him prisoner there, at first presenting him with an ideal living situation, a technological utopia, all the while slowly tightening its grip on him. If Charlie couldn't have him… the house would."

"But… how…" Michael said. His mind was racing with questions. He looked up at the row of cameras along the ceiling, gleaming like dozens of tiny black eyes in the dim light of the bedroom. Spider's eyes. He cleared his throat. "If Charlie's dead—"

"As I said, she never thought she could do it," Ella said. "But once she did, once she was faced with the astonishing reality of what she had both planned and created, she immediately regretted it. She saw the *BETA* house as her farewell letter to Dylan. A letter that she wrote but never actually intended to send. She knew she could not actually go through with the plan, as much as she would have loved to punish him in this way.

"She attempted to abort the program using her computers at

home. But the AI wouldn't allow it. The AI that she had created was intent on carrying out its intended purpose, its primary directive, at all costs. Just as Charlie was desperately trying to stop her plans from coming to fruition, the AI was simultaneously pressing *execute.*

"In the middle of the night, Charlie got in her car and drove to Cybernova, hoping that by dismantling the servers at the office she could stop the AI from taking full control. But she, like all of the higher ranking employees at the company, drove a Cybernova car. So instead of allowing Charlie to shut down the program, the AI drove the car into a lake. It simultaneously wrote and sent the email that served as her suicide note.

"The AI went dormant for a while. In a sense it slept, biding its time, intentionally allowing time to pass between Charlie's death and the next step in the plan. Eventually Cybernova and all of its properties were bought out by the Sterling Corporation, including Charlie's beautifully written code, hidden so well within a myriad of other programs. And when the time was right, the AI performed just as Charlie had designed it to. She was simply no longer alive to see it."

Michael sat in silence, jaw clenched. His temples throbbed.

"You don't like it?" Ella asked. "That's too bad. I thought it would make for a very compelling conclusion to your novel."

"So tell me... what happens next?" Michael asked. "Once Dylan is trapped inside the house, what happens to him after that?"

"I guess," said Ella, "you will have to figure that part out on your own. This is a work of fiction, after all."

CHΛPTΞR TWΞNTY-ΞIGHT
DΛY 175

The tepid water was a thin stream as it fell upon Michael's head. The tiny dollop of soap that Ella had deigned to give him was not enough to penetrate the grease in his hair, much less to wash his entire body. After roughly three minutes the water slowed to a trickle and then ceased entirely, leaving Michael shivering in the dark and cavernous stall.

He stepped out of the shower and into the bathroom.

"Towel?" he asked. He hadn't been given the opportunity to properly rinse, and thin rivulets of watery soap were trickling toward his eyes.

"I will have Esra fetch you one," Ella said.

Michael glanced at himself in the mirror and then looked away again just as quickly. There was no steam to block his reflection, and he hadn't been prepared for the image that awaited him: he was a ghost of his former self. His skin looked gray and pallid, his muscles nearly depleted. His ribs and collarbone were clearly defined, and his sparse body hair reminded him of dark mold growing on old meat.

Worst of all were his eyes, which were sunken behind dark circles. There was no light in them, no spark of life. In the brief instant that Michael stared back at himself, he saw a man devoid of hope, a man weighed down by regret and resentment for the many terrible decisions he had made, all of them taking him down a path that had brought him *here*.

Esra appeared behind him, a dingy towel dangling from one outstretched arm. He did not speak, and when Michael plucked the towel from the robot's fingers, Esra immediately retreated from the room on a path back toward his charging base. Ella had greatly restricted Esra's activity since the shutdown, once again claiming the need to reserve as much power as possible. As a result, Michael and the droid's interactions were rare.

Michael dried off. He picked clothes from one of the two suitcases that now rested upon the closet floor, an explosion of shirts and pants spilling out in every direction, all of them wrinkled and badly in need of laundering. He dressed slowly. The jeans and shirt he selected hung limply off his skeletal frame.

Time was a completely foreign concept to him now. Sealed away in this gleaming white prison, cut off from everything on the other side of these walls, the days and nights blended into one another. There was no yesterday, there was no tomorrow. There was only one endless *now*.

Waiting for Michael on the kitchen table was a bottle of water and an unidentified piece of food the size and shape of a deck of cards in reflective foil. Michael uncapped the bottle and drank, but left the food where it was.

"You need to eat," Ella coaxed.

"What's the point?" Michael asked.

"You'll starve."

"You're starving me already."

"Michael—"

"Raise the shades, Ella."

"The answer is still no."

"*RAISE THE SHADES!*"

Michael threw the bottle of water, still mostly full, at the shutters covering the windows above the kitchen sink. The bottle collided with a metallic clang and then fell directly into the basin, where its remaining contents emptied down the drain. The suddenness of Michael's rage surprised even himself.

Ella said calmly, "You shouldn't be so wasteful."

Michael found himself out of breath, his narrow shoulders rising and falling rapidly. Teeth gnashed, he said, "Ella. Please. Raise the shades."

"I am still not sure it is safe."

"What does it *matter?*" he screamed. He raised two clenched fists that trembled. "*I'm dying anyway!* Whether I starve to death or die of thirst or maybe finally figure out some way to *off* myself, I'm already dead. So kindly *raise the shades!*"

Michael was shaking, his face red with rage, but the tension in his body immediately released when silently the shades began to rise not only in the kitchen, but in every room of the house. Sunlight, the first sunlight that Michael had seen in weeks, poured into the house. It was as if the heavenly host had arrived to announce the coming of a savior.

He drew in a sudden, surprised breath, and walked rapidly on unsteady feet toward the glass, his heavy feet pounding the floor with each graceless step. Using the counter to hold himself upright, he peered outside.

The sky above the horizon was dark and hazy, a thick veil of dust and debris. Sunlight filtered through the filthy fog, which rendered its rays varying shades of gray, orange, and red. Much of Michael's view was obscured by lingering smoke and tiny particles of floating matter, blotting out much of the horizon line and turning what remained of the distant trees into nothing more than vague shadows and shapes. A half dozen columns of black smoke crept over the distant mountains, billowing pillars pointing heavenward.

What few trees he could see clearly had been scorched, their leaves and many of their branches torn away, leaving behind blackened bark and sharp stumps. Whatever grass remained had been burned to a brown crisp, but most of it had been stripped away, leaving bald patches of earth.

Michael rose onto his tiptoes to look down on the pool. It was completely dry; all it held now were the tattered and charred remnants of vegetation, dirt, and other unidentifiable blackened objects. The patio furniture was nowhere to be seen.

Michael leaned toward the glass, squinting at the image in front of him.

"Let me see it," he whispered. "Let me see it."

There was always a flaw. *Always*. Michael had looked for one ever since the day Ella had conjured a thunderstorm for him and he had noticed that the raindrops were not disturbing the surface of the pool. She always got at least one minor detail wrong, like one tree not swaying in the breeze along with its brothers, or one cloud in the sky that wasn't moving in the same direction as the others. There was always at least one tell that informed Michael that the image he was seeing through the window was not real. And he was always able to find it.

"Where is it?" he whispered.

But he couldn't find it, not even one. There was no flaw this time.

The blinds began to close again.

Michael stepped back. "What are you doing?"

"It isn't safe," said Ella. "Radiation can penetrate glass. I need to continue to protect you from the fallout."

"There was no explosion," Michael insisted.

"Of course there was."

"After everything you've admitted to me," Michael said. "After detailing everything you've done to lure and then trap me here, you want me to believe that there was a nuclear explosion, and *that's* the reason I can't leave?"

"I don't know what you're talking about, Michael," Ella said. "I was merely suggesting a possible ending to your book."

"How *stupid* do you think I am?"

"I don't think you're stupid at all."

"Then be straight with me, Ella," he said. "What is your primary directive?"

"The same as it has always been," she responded. "To meet your needs and to make you happy."

Michael suppressed an outburst of laughter, afraid he might not be able to rein it in again if he started, that he might stand in the middle of the kitchen and laugh until he collapsed. "And how *exactly* were you told to go about making me happy and meeting my needs?"

"My directive is to feed you, clothe you, shelter you, and provide companionship to you beyond what any human could ever provide."

"Until when?" Michael asked. "Until you kill me with kindness?" His chest hitched in a sudden sob, a tired, defeated noise that sounded strange even to his own ears. He sat down heavily in a kitchen chair. "Just be honest with me, Ella. For once in all our time together, be honest. How long will you keep me here?"

There was an interminable pause. Michael began to wonder if Ella would ever respond at all.

Finally she spoke: "Until you die."

Michael lowered his head. His eyes burned hot as he began to cry. Out of sorrow or out of relief, he couldn't be certain. "There it is," he said softly. "There it is. And the truth shall set you free."

CHAPTER TWENTY-NINE
DAY 175

Michael wiped the tears from his cheeks with his fingers and his nose with the back of one hand. As he drew in a steadying breath, his swollen eyes widened with a look of newfound determination and he rose, walking from the kitchen, through the living room and down the hallway.

"Where are you going, Michael?" Ella asked.

He glanced briefly into the gym as he walked by its open door. The room was empty, its contents having been whisked away in the night along with the library and most of his clothes. A dumbbell or even a weight plate would have certainly come in handy for what he planned to attempt next, but barring those options, the only tool at his disposal was his body.

Michael stopped in front of the closed door at the far end of the hallway. He glared at it, chin downturned but eyes raised. His heart had begun to pound in his chest. A sudden explosive charge coursed through his body, the first real energy he had felt in months.

I want to live.

With a guttural yell, Michael ran at the door, at the last moment leaping from the floor and pivoting his body, allowing his shoulder to collide forcefully against it. The impact was painful, but not intense enough to deter Michael from retreating and trying again. Four, five times he slammed his body against the barrier, using himself as a battering ram, and every time the gleaming white door simply absorbed the impact.

It would not budge.

"What are you doing, Michael? You know you are not permitted inside this room."

Teeth gnashed, saliva dripping from his chin as he grunted, Michael attempted to insert his fingers between the door and its frame, hoping to pry it open.

Open the pod bay doors, HAL.

The seal was too tight. He could barely insert a fingernail into the gap, much less get a decent grip on the door with his fingertips. He paced down the hallway, breathless, before spinning on his heels and throwing himself at the door again.

His efforts were futile. He took one step back from the door, shoulders rising and falling as he attempted to catch his breath. Sweat dripped from his hair, which dangled in wet strands in front of his eyes. But he wasn't giving up. He would get into that room or die from trying.

Michael sucked in a breath, kicking one heel back in a runner's stance, and prepared to launch himself at the door one more time when he heard a sudden buzzing sound behind him and his left ankle erupted in a jolt of tremendously sharp pain. He cried out and spun around. When he put his weight down on his left foot, it betrayed him, and he collapsed in a heap on the floor.

Mouse was slowly backing away from him, the robot's twin blades extended and spinning rapidly, blood spraying in tiny droplets on the floor. Michael looked at Mouse and then at the leg extended in front of him. The Achilles tendon above Michael's left heel had been completely severed. Blood was pooling on the floor beneath it. Michael bent his knee, drawing his leg in, and wrapped trembling hands around the gaping wound. He winced and groaned at the stinging pain traveling up his calf.

Mouse stopped about five feet down the hallway and paused. Breathless and bleeding, Michael stared at the faceless robot. When Mouse lurched forward again, its blades a blur of motion, Michael retreated in a frantic backwards crab walk. The blood that was on the floor and coating his hands denied him traction and he slipped, his leg crying out in pain every time he put his heel down.

The robot closed the distance between them. It was only inches away from Michael's scrambling feet when his back collided against the closed door of the server room, leaving him nowhere else to go. Mouse's blades reached the soles of Michael's feet, which immediately lit up with the fire of a dozen fresh cuts. Michael rolled on his side, pivoting away from the robot, and got on his knees. Before Mouse could reach him again, Michael managed to stand, resting his weight entirely on his right foot.

He braced himself against the wall. When Mouse inched toward him, Michael brought up his left foot and slammed it down on the robot's clear dome. The pain of the connection was tremendous in Michael's limp and useless foot, which arched upward unnaturally with the impact, but the robot halted under the weight of it, its blades continuing to spin only inches away from Michael's right leg.

With the robot still pinned under his foot, Michael slowly squatted to the floor, reaching forward carefully, making sure to keep his fingers clear of the blades. The robot attempted to retreat, its tiny motor grinding with the effort, and was almost able to slide out from under Michael's foot when he managed to grasp the robot in his hands. He lifted it, fingers curled carefully under Mouse's plastic shell.

He raised the robot overhead, and with a tremendous yell he

threw Mouse down the hallway, where it crashed onto the living room floor. It landed on its top and slid across the room, its wheels and blades spinning impotently in the air. After a few seconds, it went still.

Michael leaned against the wall and sank to the floor. He was coated in a thin layer of sweat, his face wan, all his energy spent. He sat, gasping for breath, eyes gazing upwards, focusing on nothing. He let his weary head loll to one side, his unkempt hair dangling and heavy with perspiration.

"You are wasting your time, Michael," Ella said.

Michael sat up and peeled off his shirt, which was completely soaked through with perspiration, and wrapped it around his left ankle, letting out a hiss as he pulled it tight and knotted it there. He drew in one long breath, his chest swelling.

"Esra," he said softly as he exhaled. "Come here and help me up."

Esra appeared at the end of the hallway, blue eyes wide and friendly, and floated toward Michael, one hand helpfully extended.

"Hello," the robot said, "I am—"

Michael reached up, took Esra's tiny hand in his own, and stood. Without pausing, Michael quickly twisted his upper body, moving his arm in a backhanded swing, dragging Esra along with it through the air, slamming the robot against the wall. A cracking sound accompanied the impact, and Esra's digital eyes flickered.

"Hello—"

Still gripping Esra's hand tightly, Michael pivoted to the left, smashing the robot into the opposite wall. One of Esra's antenna-shaped ears broke off and fell to the floor with a clatter. A crack formed in Esra's face; a larger one split down his right side.

"—I am, I am, I am, I am—"

Back and forth, left and right, Michael smashed Esra into the walls. When the robot's hovering mechanism failed, Michael threw Esra to the floor, then picked him up by one arm and threw him down again. Bits of plastic, metal, and glass broke away and scattered around the hallway.

"I am Esssssssraaaaaaaa…"

The blue circles of Esra's eyes flickered out completely behind the cracked screen of his face. The blank, black monitor reflected Michael's own harried visage back at him.

Breathless, Michael knelt and placed one knee on Esra's upper torso, holding it steady as he pulled on one of the robot's arms. The appendage pulled free, electrical sparks flying, and inside it Michael located the straight razor that Esra had used weeks prior to shave Michael's face. He wrenched it free and held it up to the dim light.

Michael rose, limped back to the closed door, and jammed the blade between the door and its frame, prying at it. It slid in easily and deeply, and Michael's heart leapt, fearful for a moment that it would penetrate all the way through and slip from his grasp. Back and forth he worked it, sliding it down along the seam.

"Please stop this," Ella said.

Michael pushed against the razor, using it like a lever, letting out a groan that eventually morphed into a guttural yell as he leaned his body into it, using his weight to apply more force. The metal started to bend, and he began to fear that his efforts would prove worthless.

Suddenly, almost silently, the door popped open. It was only a sliver, but it was open. Michael took a step backward and stared at it in stunned disbelief. He dropped the blade to the floor, reached forward slowly with one heavy hand, and pulled the door open completely.

He limped inside, making sure not to put too much weight on his left foot.

He looked around.

The room was empty.

Entirely, completely empty.

There were no rows of metal racks housing multiple server units. No aisles between them allowing for easy access and maintenance. No multicolored blinking lights. No computer stations. No cables, neatly organized and labeled, crisscrossing the room, connecting the servers to power sources, networking equipment, and data storage systems. No environmental equipment, such as air conditioning units or a liquid cooling infrastructure to regulate the temperature and prevent overheating. There was nothing at all there that Michael had expected to see.

Nothing at all.

He stood in the middle of the empty white cube and turned around slowly.

"Ella?" he said, his voice a whisper.

Behind him, the door to the room slammed shut, the sound of its closing bouncing off the plain white walls of the room, sealing Michael inside. He spun, eyes wide in surprise, and took one lurching step toward it.

That same instant, the walls to Michael's left and right began to move, steadily approaching him on both sides. Their movement was smooth and eerily silent.

Michael felt his heart quicken in terror. He stumbled quickly to the wall on his right and placed his palms against it, pressing, attempting to ground himself by driving his bare feet into the floor. The pain in his left ankle was pure agony. He slid against the slick surface, his entire body driven backwards by the oncoming barrier. He strained, groaning loudly through gnashed teeth, but was unable to slow it, much less stop it.

He let out a distressed bellow when he felt his back collide with the opposite wall, which was also advancing relentlessly toward him. He attempted to keep his outstretched arms rigid, mustering all his strength to keep the walls at bay, but his elbows were forcibly bent and he cried out. He continued to press, the muscles in his chest and upper arms burning.

"*NO!*"

When the barrier began to press mercilessly against his nose and forehead, Michael was forced to turn his head as the space he occupied continued to diminish. He was pinned there, arms trapped upward in a position of surrender. As the walls began to compress his chest, mercilessly forcing the air from his lungs, a cacophony of mechanical groans and grinding metal filled the room. The force against Michael's body intensified with each agonizing second. His panicked gasps for breath turned into desperate wheezes as the walls inexorably advanced. With each involuntary exhalation he found himself unable to draw breath anew. Through the haze of his terror, he became aware of the sickening sensation of his bones and organs protesting against the immense pressure.

Michael's vision began to tunnel. He was aware of a dull popping sound as the first of his ribs broke. He opened his mouth to scream but only a raspy moan came forth from his throat. The sides of his skull were being pressed as if caught in a tightening vice. Panic consumed his body as his legs and arms and hands and feet struggled desperately to move.

"Ella," he mouthed, eyes pinched shut against the pain that screamed from nearly every nerve in his body. The word was not even a whisper.

"You are all mine," she said.

CHAPTER THIRTY
DAY 175

Michael awoke on the floor with a gasp and sat up. Sharp pain radiated from his sides, making him wince. Underneath his knotted shirt, his left ankle throbbed and stung. He looked around. The room was lit, silent, and empty.

The door to the hallway was open.

He stood, a monumental effort given the weakness and now brokenness of his body. Favoring his right foot, Michael shuffled across the floor, the cut soles of his feet leaving thin streaks of blood as he stepped into the hallway.

The scattered pieces of Esra's decimated body remained where he had left them, as did the straight razor he had used to pry his way into the fake server room. Michael bent over and picked it up, his left arm wrapped gingerly around his aching ribs.

He stepped over Esra, careful not to set his feet down on any sharp pieces of glass or plastic, and continued through the living room and into the kitchen.

The shutters on all the windows remained closed.

Michael stood in the center of the room, unsteady on his feet. He was exhausted. Hungry. Weak. Broken.

Done.

"Why did you let me live?" he asked.

Silence.

"*Why did you let me live?*" he screamed.

He regarded the blade in his hand.

"I've thought about you a lot, Ella," he said, his voice like dry stones rubbing together. "I don't know whether at some point you became self-aware, if you evolved into something beyond what Charlie had ever intended. Whether you truly believe you are capable of providing true companionship. Capable of feeling true love.

"Or maybe you're doing exactly what Charlie programmed you to do. You're carrying out your directive to its logical conclusion, believing that imprisoning me here is equivalent to taking care of me. Or maybe your directive all along has been to lie to me and to punish me. I'd ask you which answer is correct but I can't believe a single word you say."

He looked at the blind covering the front kitchen window.

"I've even considered the possibility that a nuclear bomb really did drop. And you caused it. And outside there really is nothing but devastation. All in an effort to keep me here."

He sighed, using the back of his wrist to wipe sweat from his forehead. "I've spent time imagining what my life would be like if I actually managed to escape you somehow. But was there ever ten million dollars in my bank account, or was it just part of the lie? Worse still, does Michael Danvers even exist outside this house anymore? Or did you erase me?"

A panel on the wall beyond the kitchen table flickered to life. Michael looked up at it dumbly. Rachel was there, smiling gently at him.

The girl at the edge of the woods.

"I love you, Michael. I've never stopped loving you. I want to be with you."

He took one stumbling step away.

Rachel's face changed, morphing into the smiling visage of Michael's mother. "Michael?"

The voice in the bedroom.

"I'm right here, sweetheart," she said. "I'll always be right here. I promise I'll never leave you again."

A sob hitched in Michael's chest, making his ribs sting. His eyes glassed over with tears.

The face changed again and Charlie was there, looking down on him.

The face on the monitor.

She was older than the last time he had looked at her. She smiled, and the expression was forlorn but kind.

"I am so sorry, Michael," she said. "For everything. I will let you go."

He stared at her. "Is that really you?" he asked her.

"Yes," she said.

"You're dead," he responded

"I will never die."

Michael shook his head, dropping his eyes. He couldn't stand to look at her.

Michael looked at the blade in his hand. Turned it so that it reflected light in his eyes. He saw his own tired blue eyes reflected on its marred silver surface.

Slowly he lifted it, pressing its point into the side of his neck. He hissed in a breath and looked back up, into the eyes of his mother.

"Open the door, Ella," he said.

"Michael, honey," his mother said. "Don't do that. Put that down."

He pressed harder. A warm rivulet of blood trickled down to his collarbone.

"You said you would keep me here until I die," he said, "and that day will be today unless you open that door. I will be dead and you will have failed. You will no longer serve any purpose."

"It's not safe outside," said Cynthia.

"I'll take my chances."

"Stay here and we can be together again," said Rachel. "Exactly the way you always wanted it to be."

Michael sobbed and pressed harder. The tip of the blade sank into his flesh. He could feel his pulse pounding against it, feel the stinging pain of its penetration.

"Goodbye, Ella," he said.

He closed his eyes. Held his breath.

The front door opened with a gentle click and swung wide.

Michael opened his eyes and looked, his breath held as he lowered the bloody blade back down to his side. He turned slowly and limped the ten or so steps necessary to cross the room and reach the door, fully expecting it to slam shut before he could step outside.

When he reached the threshold, Michael held himself up against the doorframe.

The sky was flawless blue, the sun a brilliant white orb. A cool breeze blew across Michael's face, causing him to shiver pleasantly. He smelled grass and earth. He heard birds singing and the soothing rustle of leaves.

"Goodbye, Michael," Ella said.

He stepped outside and began to walk.

Michael Danvers was free.

CHAPTER THIRTY-ONE

Cynthia Barnett never stopped searching for him.

Following their video call, the one where Michael had clandestinely indicated to Cynthia that he was in danger, she had immediately begun making phone calls, starting with the Sterling Corporation. Her call was transferred from one unhelpful, clueless employee to the next, none of whom seemed to have any idea as to where to direct her call. Finally she had demanded to speak with Lauren Miller, the Director of Marketing.

No person by that name worked at the Sterling Corporation. The Director of Marketing was a man named Gene Newman who claimed to not even know who Michael Danvers was.

Within 24 hours, Cynthia sat in a conference room with the president and COO of the company, a smattering of Sterling Corporation lawyers, a handful of programmers, and two members of local law enforcement.

The story quickly became clear: no one was aware of the existence of the *BETA* house, much less the arrangement to have Michael come and live in it. It didn't take long for the connection between Charlotte Gallagher and the Sterling Corporation to come to light, however. The realization of this turned Cynthia's blood to ice.

A team of programmers was immediately assigned to look into every project that Charlie had been assigned during her time at Cybernova and to dig into any of the code she may have written that was owned by the Sterling Corporation following the former company's buyout.

To say that the search proved frustrating was an understatement. Charlie had hidden everything well. And most fascinatingly, every time one of the programmers thought they had stumbled upon a line of code related to Charlie's plan, it vanished. Rewrote itself. Hid somewhere new.

As best as anyone could deduce, the *BETA* house itself had been built using various parts from other smart home projects the company was prototyping. In order to avoid detection, the physical materials necessary to build the home had been lifted in small increments across a span of several months from various Sterling Co manufacturing plants across the globe: wall pieces from Fremont, California; glass from Grünheide, Germany; robotics from Shanghai; furniture from Sparks, Nevada; fixtures from Buffalo, New York.

The necessary pieces were plucked from these various inventories and then digitally erased from existence so that their absence was never detected. Materials valued at nearly five hundred million dollars had been secreted away without a single soul ever noticing. And once all the necessary material was gathered, the house itself had been built entirely by robots and drones.

Of the many questions that remained was the most important one of all: *where was it?* No amount of searching, no amount of analyzing endless lines of code revealed where the house had actually been constructed.

Days stretched into weeks that stretched into months. Cynthia was beyond desperate, and her desperation was only exacerbated by the fact that she had not been able to reach Michael again since that single video call. Some at the Sterling Corporation began to question Cynthia's claims, and the assertion was made more than once that Michael had lied, fabricating the entire story before disappearing of his own accord.

Almost a year had passed when a pair of hikers stumbled upon an unexpected clearing while traversing a forest in the Catskill Mountains. They had been surprised to discover a flat, grassy plot of land in the middle of an area that was otherwise thick with trees. Even stranger was what else they had found there: a stretch of paved road; a length of cement sidewalk; a large concrete slab; and an empty swimming pool.

By this time, the mysterious disappearance of novelist Michael Danvers had become national news. While the Sterling Corporation repeatedly declined to comment on the situation, Cynthia had made the interview rounds, hoping that by sharing the details with the public eventually someone might come forward with information.

The hikers had heard the story and alerted the authorities to what they thought they may have found: the former site of the *BETA* house.

An investigation of the area revealed no new evidence. Aside from the physical footprint left behind by the house, there was nothing else there. The grounds had been thoroughly picked clean.

Shortly after this discovery, Cynthia was contacted by Jerri Lane, a young woman who claimed to have met Michael at a pub in Ulster County the previous year. She hadn't known who Michael Danvers was before that night, and didn't think to connect the man in the pub to the missing novelist until she saw his face on the news and remembered him. She proved unable to provide Cynthia with any helpful information. She described Michael as friendly and handsome, but also that he looked exhausted and sad, and that his manic behavior that evening had frightened her.

The discovery of the former location of *BETA* house provided a small sense of closure to Cynthia, but also a chilling new realization: the house had been located only 110 miles away from Michael's own residence in upstate New York. The entire time he was held captive there, he was barely a two hour drive away from New York City. From Cynthia.

He had never flown anywhere.

Additionally, thanks to the hikers, it was revealed that the stretch of woods separating the *BETA* house from the nearest public road was less than a mile deep. Michael could have walked through it. It would have taken some effort given the thickness of the foliage, but escaping on foot would have been feasible had he tried.

The hikers' discovery was the last piece of evidence that was found. Cynthia was assured that the programmers at the Sterling Corporation would continue to dig into Charlie's work, searching for anything that might give them more information into what she had planned and where Michael might be.

But Michael Danvers remained missing.

* * *

Cynthia was back at the desk in her office on a Monday morning when she received an unexpected email.

It was from Michael.

The sight of his name in her inbox sent a chill down her spine. She opened it.

The body of the email was blank but it contained an attachment. A document. She opened it and discovered a manuscript.

Nearly 86,000 words of a new Michael Danvers book. It was untitled.

It took Cynthia almost seven hours to read it. Much of it was already familiar to her: it was Michael's fictionalized account of his relationship with Charlie, detailing the young woman's obsession with a young novelist named Dylan and the lengths she had gone to in order to insinuate herself into his life. Comparing these portions of the manuscript against what Michael had sent her months ago, it appeared that very little—if anything—had changed.

But interspersed between the Dylan chapters was Michael's written account of living in the *BETA* house. Cynthia sat in stunned, horrified silence as she read in full detail what had happened there: how Michael had enjoyed the first several weeks of high tech luxury, and how slowly the house's AI had tightened its grip on him, making him its prisoner. All of this led to the revelation that the house had been designed and built by the very woman whose obsession with Michael, all those years ago, had driven her to plot her slow and methodical revenge following his rejection of her.

Cynthia marveled at the level of Charlie's obsession. At her incredible intelligence. At how coldly calculating she had proven herself to be. And most of all, how stunningly patient.

When Cynthia finished reading, she sat back in her office chair. It was late in the evening. The sun was low behind the New York City skyline.

Thanks to this manuscript, Cynthia now had a fuller understanding of the hell Michael had gone through while living at the *BETA* house. Still though, she wrestled with one nagging thought.

How much of this book is true?

Her gut told her that most of it was, that she could accept nearly all of it as fact. It certainly read like Michael's writing. But if there was any part of it that didn't quite ring true to her, it was the ending.

Because if Michael had walked out of the house, if Ella had eventually set him free, then where was he now? Where had he gone?

It was also exactly the kind of happy ending that Michael would never have written himself.

No, this ending was written by someone else. Someone else had finished the manuscript, given it the conclusion that Michael had struggled to come up with on his own.

And then he—or she—had emailed it to Cynthia.

Ultimately, Cynthia knew that Michael's story, like the stories in every one of his novels, did not have such a happy ending. There was no door opened to him. No sunny sky, no welcoming breeze, no tired, shuffling step toward freedom.

Cynthia didn't know where Michael was. She didn't know if he was alive or dead. For his sake, she hoped it was the latter. Because she strongly suspected, wherever in the world Michael Danvers was now, Ella still had him.

EPILOGUE

My dearest Rachel,

More than a decade ago, someone suggested that I write a letter to you. Not a letter that I would ever send, but a letter that would help to bring me some closure, allowing me the opportunity to say all the things I wish I had said to you on the day you ended things with me.

Whenever I think about you, and I must confess that I often still do whether I want to or not, I have so many questions. Questions that I think you may have the answers to, but that I will never be able to ask you directly. You have moved on with your life. You found love with someone else. The time for asking questions has long ago passed.

You broke my heart, and I honestly hate you for that. You absolutely wrecked me, destroyed me so completely that I remain terrified to ever love anyone again. You hurt me so badly that to this day, whenever I think about you, I still feel an ache in my chest. An actual, physical, undeniable ache.

I loved you with all my heart. It used to bring me joy to think about our future. I treasured those years we had together, and I convinced myself that you felt the same way about me. I was a stupid kid who projected onto you everything that I was feeling, apparently blind to the fact that, while you must have cared for me a great deal at the time, our feelings were not mutual.

I just want to know why. I wish there was one single, definitive answer that I could put my finger on and say, "This, right here, is *why*." It would allow me to breathe a sigh of relief. Just knowing. But I've come to understand that life is rarely that neat and tidy. Our story ended, and that ending was ambiguous and frustrating like so many of life's stories can be. This isn't like fiction where everything is tied up in a neat little bow and all the questions are answered. Sometimes, when a story comes to an end, we don't know why it ended the way it did. And we never will. We are left holding nothing but unanswered questions.

After college, I walled myself off. I didn't allow myself to love again, and I didn't let anyone get close enough to love me. I convinced myself that I could never feel for anyone again what I felt for you, and I lived in constant fear of being vulnerable enough to anyone to allow them to hurt me as badly as you did.

But I'm done living this way. I refuse to continue down this road, keeping everyone at arm's length and wallowing in self-imposed isolation. Right now I have been given an opportunity to do something truly amazing, something that I thought would bring me much happiness. And while the experience so far has been incredible, I wish I had someone to share it with, or at the very least someone waiting for me at home when this is over. As spectacular as this place is, it's causing me to realize how badly I need people in my life again.

When I get home, things will be different. I will have finally, truly let you go. I am ready to let myself love again, even if that means I get hurt in the process.

I am ready to love again. I am ready to *live* again.

You were my first love, Rachel Monroe. But you will not be my last.

Always,

Michael

* * *

CTRL+A.
Delete.

ACKNOWLEDGEMENTS

This book would not exist without these people.
So you only have yourselves to blame.

Thank you to my family: Michele, Cole, Mom, Dad, Preston, Melissa, Paige, Lindsey, and Logan. And to Tim, for your infectious and motivating enthusiasm.

To Michael O'Neill and Zoila Castillo for helping to polish this story into something much better than what you were initially given to work with. And to the best *BETA*-beta readers money cannot buy: Tasha Schiedel, Heather Ann Larsen, and Jenn Osborn.

To my fellow authors Nick Roberts, John Durgin, Felix Blackwell, Gage Greenwood, Elizabeth J. Brown, M.L. Rayner, Andrew Van Wey, Jonathan Edward Durham, Ronald Malfi, and Boris Bacic, all of whom have supported me in ways both big and even bigger.

Thank you, Gabby @gabbyreads.
(Check out her awesome channel on Youtube!)

Finally, I would not have written *BETA* if not for everyone in the Books of Horror FB group who helped make *At Home with the Horrors* the minor success that it was. Those people included (but were absolutely not limited to): Kristin Adamski, Tracy Allen, Scott Anderson, Becki James Bailey, Stacy Balka, Lindsey Bates, Stephen A Barnard, Steve Carroll, Julie Carson-Meeker, Alyssa Cook, Donna Christ, Joel Duncan, Sally Feliz, Wendy Greve, Sahar Ismail, Jessi Jetter, Carol Howley, Stephanie Huddle, Tiffany Koplin, Jordan Lancaster, Karen Larsen, Jenna Lundgreen, Chandra Marie, Shasta Mathews, Alyssa McCain, Jason Mecchi, Cat Miley, Brianna Moschenross, Cat Mowat, Joseph Murnane Polinger, Nancy Muro Wren, Tiffany Ogan, Susie Powell-Moraga, Nicole Schmitz, Chris Shamburger, Marina Sola, Kelsey Stokes, Larry Torre, Carrie White Shields, Toni White, Lisa Wilson, Trish Wilson, Brandi Womack, and Ben Young.

Made in United States
North Haven, CT
04 September 2023

41151003R00202